PRAISE FOR ROSE M. JONES

"Rose Jones is truly anointed for such a time as this, to pen such an amazing story of the circle of life involving love, loss, triumph, defeat, victory and ... back to love. I enjoyed following the journey while the story navigated through some of the hardest issues facing our families today. This was truly inspiring.

I suggest that all parents and their children, school administrators, teachers, and other staff members, District Attorneys and their staff, Judges and the judicial staff members, Law enforcement, counselors, and anyone who has been entrusted with the lives of children, read this story together and make ia required reading for training. There is some of all of us in this wonderful work of art! Congratulations to Rose for her job that is exquisitely done."

—Angela Woodard Faison, Minister

""I thoroughly enjoyed reading *Mildred the Bird Lady*. I could not put it down after the first chapter. Ms. Jones wrote with clever surprises that kept me reading late into the night. Not wanting to miss the next bombshell. It also enabled me to talk to my granddaughter."

—Virginia, retired business manager

"I love Ms. Jones's style of writing. She is truly talented and brilliant. Someone to watch for future books."

—Jim Burris, Author, Artist, Illustrato

After reading *Mildred the Bird Lady*, I was so caught up in it I felt as if I was sitting on the park bench watching the story unfold. Ms. Jones's narrative of the characters and emotions was refreshing. *Mildred's Legacy* is the rest of the story."

—Sue Y., entrepreneur

Mildred's
Legacy

Second Chance Kids

Mildred's Legacy

Second Chance Kids

ROSE M. JONES

 Torchflame Books

Durham, NC

Published 2022, by Torchflame Books
an Imprint of Light Messages
www.lightmessages.com
Durham, NC 27713 USA
SAN: 920-9298

Paperback ISBN: 978-1-61153-480-1
E-book ISBN: 978-1-61153-481-8
Library of Congress Control Number: 2022919403

Dedicated to all the kids
trying to change their lives,
whether from addiction, crime,
or other circumstances.

Change must come from within.

VIII

AUTHOR'S NOTE

MILDRED'S LEGACY: SECOND CHANCE KIDS, was inspired by the first novel in the series, *Mildred the Bird Lady,* written and published in August of 2021. After completing that novel, I felt that the story wasn't finished. Many of my readers pleaded for more, not wanting the story to end. With every twist and turn of the first novel, an idea was created for the continuum into the second novel.

I am in recovery from alcohol addiction. Through many years of trials and failures, I finally embraced sobriety. While writing this novel, I achieved nineteen years of sobriety. In early recovery, I worked with teens in high-risk family environments. They, too, were addicted to drugs or alcohol. I saw teens struggle with peer pressure to do drugs and alcohol to fit in with the crowd. They would eventually end up in juvenile detention centers or worse. I have also seen parents torn with grief over a child who died from an overdose. Heartbreak was in every phone call I received from the kids begging for help. They were all asking for a second chance. The system was failing them.

Although I did not personally have any dealings with the judicial system, I felt the need to combine the legal system with the kids left behind. The kids in today's world are dealing with more temptation from peers than kids of decades past. Some kids commit illegal acts to stay alive. I have been an advocate for teens before they are plagued with the horrible life of addiction or living the uncertainty of the system. Teens look for guidance, love, and acceptance. I have found that I can connect with teens and parents in my writings.

Mildred's Legacy: Second Chance Kids is influenced by my personal and business concepts. My husband and I have a business where we assist both male and female adults with drug and alcohol addiction to find a better path in life. I hope that writing about change will help create change.

Although Mildred was primarily featured in the first novel, *Mildred the Bird Lady*, her principles, teachings, and life lessons continue through the pages of *Mildred's Legacy: Second Chance Kids*. The main character, Mary, takes the life lessons learned from Mildred and continues her legacy, her dash in life. Mary deals with peer pressure. I hope that this story will open doors for parents to talk to their teens. The subjects such as peer pressure, drugs and alcohol, teen dating, and sex are all addressed. Parents can have conversations to talk about healthy decisions and teens can speak to their parents about life.

This second novel is about Mary providing space for people to talk about life and change their lives. While we all have that dash between our birth date and the date of our death, this novel follows the lives of eight teens struggling with the judicial system. They learn to navigate through anger, temper tantrums, vandalism, truancy, and belonging to find healthy love. These teens learn what real love and sacrifice are. Mary sacrifices a part of herself with each child she encounters. Each child realizes that there is much more to life than jail time. Through the spiritual guidance from Mildred, Mary fulfills her dash just a bit more with each passing day. Through this, Mildred's dash continues to make a difference, even after her passing. This is her life, her legacy.

Through this novel, I can make my dash more significant. When I'm gone from this earth, I hope someone reads my book and gives their dreams a second chance. This will make my dash so much more meaningful.

CHAPTER 1

IT'S EARLY APRIL; the sun is high in the sky, warming the earth. I can't help but want to take the time to sit in the garden. I like listening to the birds as they fly around the feeders I have placed for them. Since it is early spring, only the first flowers are peeking their heads out of the ground, telling everyone, "I'm here!" It is a much-welcomed sight after a Chicago winter. Even though the sun is at its fullest, the air is still crisp. Remnants of snow piles are still dotting the grounds, trying so hard to keep their grasp on the winter they love so much. The struggle between the seasons is all around.

Opening the back door off the hall from the kitchen area, I find the inviting garden in which I used to sit for hours with Mildred. I head on out to the table and chairs, usually covered with beautiful vines and flowers of every color imaginable. I'm met with a blustery gust of springtime air, but I don't allow this to discourage me from venturing out. I know that I'm not appropriately dressed to be out in the cold, but the sun's rays lure me out to play. Making my way out to the garden, I carefully navigate the walkway still plagued with ice, waiting to hurt me. It doesn't stop me. I'm determined to make my way.

On my way out through the walkway, I notice that Antoinette has placed a warm blanket on a chair for me. I guess she knew I was going to come outside today. The blanket is comforting in the fight against the brisk spring air. With the sun caressing the earth, the garden is coming to life after a hard winter's slumber. I perch myself on the chair and pull the blanket around me. I desperately try to find any sign of green peeking out from the brown grass. Just a hint, that's all I need.

Early spring is like a symphony with the sun as the conductor. Each flower waits to be told the stage is now theirs. I'm eager for the flowers to begin their play on the stage of life. Each flower has its purpose. Oh, how I yearn for the bold colors of reds and yellows softened by the pinks and purples as they dance. Anticipation of the show is hard to ignore, but it is so worth the wait.

I'm facing away from the manor, but I feel the presence of someone behind me. I hear a soft voice from a young girl. Her voice sounds cautious and frail, almost afraid to speak.

"Here is your coffee ma'am." The young lady comes around and stands before me with a tray of coffee and pastries. She must be a new staff member. I like to feel that the staff is like family more than just here to serve. She sets down a tray on the table before me. Oh, someone must have told her what I like in the morning. It is strange to be waited upon, but I became accustomed to it with Mildred. I now know precisely what Mildred was talking about when she mentioned years ago that, to some, it appeared that she had many friends. In truth, she paid people to be there at the manor.

"Oh, thank you, my dear," I respond with proper gratitude.

No one is a servant; they simply serve. I don't believe in people serving me as a duty. Even though Mildred, in her passing, set the entire staff up for many years of income, I still feel a bit uneasy asking for things that I could do for myself.

"My pleasure, ma'am," she says with a warm and meek smile.

"Oh dear, please call me Mary, or Ms. Mary, as most do. No need for that ma'am stuff." I try to ease the tension. Antoinette must have just hired her because I do not recall seeing her around the manor before.

"Yes, ma'am." She notices that she has made the same mistake as before. Her face begins to redden, either from the embarrassment it causes her or from the cold. It's hard to tell which is the true cause. She quickly corrects herself, "Yes, Ms.

Mary." We both giggle at the error; it was not meant in harm.

I turn back to the table where my piping hot coffee is sitting along with the pastry and reach for the coffee. The young lady reaches for my cup and saucer to reposition them.

"Honey, I can handle that. You don't need to do everything for me," I say with a little snap.

"Yes, ma'am," she says, obviously upset at her misdoings. She forgot and called me ma'am again.

"I'm sorry, dear." My voice is much calmer. "I did not mean to snap so harshly. I can do things. Sometimes I need to take care of things myself." I try to explain, but somehow, I think I make things worse.

The young lady backs up a step or two, then folds her hands against her apron. She is noticeably chilled from the air and looks almost like a scolded puppy.

"I guess I just need my morning coffee." I chuckle to lighten the tense atmosphere.

Like every morning, I wake up with a love affair in my coffee cup. I reach for my cup and saucer once more. Ah yes, Antoinette must have set up the tray because it has my creamer on it. The love affair can begin.

I put hazelnut creamer in my dark roasted coffee and watch the dance begin. The rich hazelnut creamer pierces the dark abyss and begins to resemble the arms of a lover. The arms reach for their partner so that they can hold each other on the dance floor. The dance is for young lovers. The cup must be disturbed to start the dance but not too much. The coffee and creamer cannot become one, not yet.

The music in my head is romantic to match the young lovers' tango across the dance floor in my cup. The creamer swirls hold their partner close while the black coffee fights for its very existence. The deep blackness of the abyss succumbs to the match made in heaven. The black roasted coffee soon becomes a masterpiece of golden-brown coffee with an aroma fit for a queen.

The elixir warms my soul this brisk morning—a much-welcomed feeling. Before this meek young lady notices, I must pull myself back into reality. I put the coffee cup to my lips and drink in the essence of the dance before me. My heart is warm as I feel the young lovers dance down to the pit of my stomach. Ah, my senses are in overload. The brisk cool wind brushes my skin, causing goose pimples. However, the inside of my body is bursting with flavor and warmth from the dance of lovers.

Putting the coffee cup carefully back upon its saucer, I casually turn to speak to the young lady as she stands before me, waiting for direction. I quickly change the topic of discussion to prevent her from knowing about the dance that has just taken place. But what shall I talk about? It would be crazy to talk about the weather. We all know it's still cold outside, even with the sun beaming above. Not to mention the poor young lady is beginning to shiver. It's not like Antoinette, with whom I can talk about anything. Hmm, oh, I got it!

"Is Charlie in the kitchen by chance?" I ask. He must be. My husband loves nothing more than to create delicious food.

She looks puzzled before attempting to answer. "I'm not sure who that is, ma'am, I mean Ms. Mary." Looking a bit upset at trying to remember my name, she backs up a few steps.

"Oh, dear, it's okay," I reassure her, showing that no harm is done. "I haven't seen you here before." I reposition myself in my seat. "What is your name?"

"Mia," she says under her breath. She's cautious, like I'm going to yell at her.

"I'm sorry, dear, I didn't hear you," I say to prompt another answer and turn my head to better hear her soft voice.

"My name is Mia." Her eyes begin to lighten as she responds. Mia appears to be in her teens, even though I know that is far from the truth. Everyone looks young to me. I must have seemed very young to Mildred when she first met me.

Nonetheless, once broken out of her shell, Mia is bright-eyed and stands up straight. I know she is on her best behavior in my presence. I can see that her mother has given her excellent guidance, much as Mildred did for me.

"But," she pauses, unsure if she should speak.

"What is it, dear?" I must know what she wants to say. It drives me nuts when people don't finish their sentences. I guess I get that from my mother.

"My real name is Amelia," she says as she looks to the barren floor. "But," her eyes raise to meet mine, "everyone calls me Mia." She stops once more. "Except my Momma. She calls me Amelia." I can tell that she loves her mother with all her heart. Her eyes soften as well as her voice. The bond between a mother and daughter is far too strong to break.

"That is a beautiful name." I look up into the clouds as if to hear angels. "Amelia." I try to reassure her just how beautiful her name is. "Don't let anyone take your name away from you. It is a gift from your mother."

Amelia smiles. "I never looked at it like that."

"Well," I pause to reach for my coffee cup. "Amelia, if I may call you that, I know you do not know me yet, but I'm Mary or Ms. Mary. Charlie is my husband, and he runs the coffee shop while popping in and out of the kitchen with the staff. He is also a teacher at the school. You'll meet him soon enough, but please, dear," I take her by the hand, "please relax. You are in a very special place here."

Antoinette comes around the corner into the gardens with a hurried look.

"Oh, Amelia, there you are," Antoinette says with relief as if she has been looking for her for quite some time. Amelia's smile brightens. Her eyes meet mine in a silent conversation shared for only a split second between us. An understanding of her importance in this world fills her heart.

"I see you have met Ms. Mary," Antoinette says with a half-smile. She is standing with purpose, every bit the boss because she is Amelia's new boss. Even though we are like a family here at the manor, we still need accountability for each job performed. Antoinette is my right-hand man, if I may say. She runs the manor. I just live here; well, I own it. Amelia's face turns from warm joy to a young girl again, as if she is in trouble when actually, she is far from it.

When Amelia isn't looking, Antoinette gives a little smirk and a wink to tell me that it was all an act.

"Yes ma'am, I have." Amelia's posture is more rigid in Antoinette's presence.

"Ms. Mary, is there anything else Amelia can get for you this morning?" Antoinette asks.

"No, I don't believe so," I respond. I flash a smile of approval in both directions, they have both done their jobs well.

Antoinette turns her attention to Amelia and instructs, "Amelia, you are needed in the kitchen for silverware."

"Yes, ma'am," Amelia says. As she turns to leave the garden, I feel the need to reach out for her hand once more.

"It was nice to meet you," I pause with a warm smile, "my dear Amelia." I make sure we make eye contact so I can tell her that she is valued here at the manor.

"Yes ma'am, I mean," and she pauses with an embarrassed smile, "I mean, Ms. Mary. It was nice to meet you as well." She walks away with a skip in her step.

A few more steps and Amelia becomes a memory.

Antoinette walks over. "May I?" She gestures to the chair across from mine.

"Antoinette, you know you don't have to ask permission for anything from me." A giggle fills me.

Antoinette turns around to look at the doorway to make sure Amelia is gone, "I know, but I need to make it look good." We both have a good laugh before Antoinette returns to business.

She pulls out the adjacent chair and sighs deeply. She does so much, she must be exhausted.

"You really need to take time for yourself, you know," I mention to Antoinette with a concerned voice, pulling my blanket closer to me. I remember her tireless days with Mildred. She was at her beck and call for her when she was so ill. Antoinette kept the manor running and in tip-top shape while Mildred was ill, and no one really knew just how ill she was.

"I know," she says as she takes another deep breath in, and, while letting it out, she rolls her eyes as if I have said this a thousand times.

"You know?" I question as I sit up more in my chair.

Antoinette fidgets. Sitting still is not in her nature.

"You and Alfred are the very backbone of this manor, not to mention to everyone here as well," I remind her. "Eventually you will need to pass the torch, much like Mildred did."

"Are you saying retire? Me?" her hand grasps her chest, "Me, retire?" She looks at me as if I have three heads.

"No, not really retire. You live here," I assure her. "I mean delegate. Give projects to others so you have more time to enjoy life."

"Hmm." She is beginning to understand what I'm talking about. She had been so caught up assisting Mildred, and now assisting me, with the manor's daily activities that she let life get away from her. "Maybe a vacation would be nice."

"So," I giggle under my breath. I lean over to her and whisper close to her as if we were planning a secret get-away. " Where are we going?"

We both give a big chuckle that comes deep from our bellies.

When she finally catches her breath, she says, "Oh, it feels so good to laugh."

"Yes, Antoinette, it sure does."

We are both so caught up in the moment and that we don't realize Amelia is standing back in the doorway. Antoinette quickly gathers herself and becomes Amelia's boss once more. Being caught having fun and being a boss do not look good together., At least not yet. Not until Amelia gets through her first week of work.

"Yes?" Antoinette directs her attention to Amelia.

"They told me to come talk to you. I finished rolling silverware for the coffee shop." Amelia rubs her arms. The brisk wind has made its presence known.

"Go ahead and go back into the kitchen and I will be there shortly," Antoinette instructs.

"Yes ma'am." Amelia turns and starts back.

"Boy, you sure do play that part well," I say with a smirk and little giggle.

"Yeah," Antoinette stands with a small grunt and then a smile. "I do, don't I?"

She pushes her hands down her dress to smooth out any wrinkles. It is far too cold to be ironing out any wrinkles with just your hands. We both have another laugh as she goes through the door.

Laughing with Antoinette reminds me so much of my times with Mildred in the garden and all the laughs we shared. Oh, how I miss Mildred and our laughs in the garden. Sitting in the garden, drinking my coffee, and eating the pastries that Amelia brought out to me makes me remember my dear friend. Mildred enjoyed tea more than coffee. We had some of the most extraordinary conversations about life at this very table. Even though our friendship began in the park so many years prior, this table will always be special to me.

All types of flowers are beginning to come to life around me. Early April is still cool up here in Chicago and quite frankly, it could still snow. But today the sun is high in the sky and it is heating the air around me, much to my delight.

Mildred's gardens are normally filled with such color. She made sure the gardens would bloom constantly with different variations of flowers and foliage, although it was hard to have winter flowers. When all the flowers bloom it brings in the honeybees. I personally take care to stay away from the honeybees, though I do understand their importance in the world of biology. Along with the foliage of spring color and the bees who've come to pollinate them, comes the sweet songs from the many different varieties of birds. I begin to take a special interest in the birds and think of all my friends down at the park bench. I must go feed them today.

While gazing off into the wild outdoors, I feel someone approach behind me. Not paying too much attention to them, I ask, "Have you ever seen so many birds come to visit here? They seem early this year."

Waiting for an answer, I keep watching, wide-eyed and curious. Then, a warm, loving hand slowly surrounds my shoulder. This hand is not one of the many men or women working in the kitchen; they would not hold me so. This hand is warm, large enough to be able to wrap the fingers around my shoulder and partly down my arm. It feels like safety, security. Alfred.

"Sometimes, I need to stop and look at nature just as you are doing Ms. Mary."

His voice is low, rough and manly, but also protective. It sounds like it is wrapped in a deep caramel or silk. I know this sweltering voice all too well. I place my hand lovingly on top of his. Because of the safety and security that his hand bestows upon me, I cannot help but tilt my head on top of his warm hand. Then, my head lifts to see the person who spoke.

"Mildred sure would love this time of year," I say, turning to look at him, holding back the many emotions surrounding me. I feel the love from Alfred's presence. He was always by Mildred's side making sure everything was taken care of. I honestly don't believe this man ever sits down. He is always pulling weeds, planting new flowers, painting, or working on a screen door, but always with a smile on his face.

"Ms. Mildred would sit out here for hours. I think she would have sat here and watched the seasons change if she could. She didn't mind how cold or warm it was." His voice turns to a jovial chuckle.

"I bet she would," I agree.

A few minutes pass. We are both mesmerized by the moment. He speaks first.

"Ms. Mary, it is quite cold out here for you. Is there anything I can get or do for you while I'm here?"

I have to think for a moment. I usually respond with a subtle, "No, everything is fine," or something along those lines, but today is a bit different. "Why, yes, there is," I mention.

"Yes Ms. Mary?" His smile is large and bright. I don't know if I've ever seen him without that smile, waiting for instruction. His eyes are slanted with joy. His skin, although dark in nature, has been kissed by the sun, even though the year is young. It looks tough from all the years of working outside with no regard for the sun's damage.

"You work so tirelessly here. Don't you ever just sit down and enjoy life?" I gesture for him to sit next to me in the garden.

Alfred settles into the chair across from me. I notice his grunt as he sits. "Oh, Ms. Mary, my body isn't quite what it used to be." We both chuckle. "This cold air plays hard with my bones."

We sit in silence for a few moments, taking in the beauty of the world behind the walls of the manor. We are so close to the city, but there is safety behind these walls.

Within these walls is an entirely different world, our world. The big iron gates at the entrance protect our peace and tranquility. I remember gazing at the very gates that stand so tall and proud at the entrance as a child. I was always warned that the old lady that lived behind them was mean and hated children, a reputation seemingly confirmed by all the toilet paper that graced the ornate iron gates each and every Halloween. But, once I got to know the woman in hiding, I soon realized that everyone was wrong. Mildred was a kind soul. I still feel a twinge of guilt about the toilet paper.

Each section of the grounds has its own purpose. The museum is in the front with many steps to get up to the front entrance. The entrance is grand with tall cement pillars that stretch as far as the eye can see. To a child, the pillars are giants. The museum is open for all to come and see the world through an artist's perspective. Hopefully it will inspire them to be artists themselves. That is where the School of Art comes in.

The School of Art is connected to the museum itself and is also encapsulated by the walls, though the manor is very spread out. The School of Art is a school where kids come to learn not just the fundamentals of education, but also the beauty of art. It is a special school primarily for wealthy children and artistic children honing their crafts. Students come to learn the arts of dance, drawing, music, and painting. This is where students come to learn the finer elements of life. They don't believe it, but this school teaches them to be a gentleman or a lady.

My old friend Sandra came here when we were young to learn piano. I watched her play in the auditorium. She played in front of hundreds of people. The music I heard from her was astonishing. I had no idea she was that good. Even though she went to public school with me, she attended this school to learn piano.

Then there is the art of dance. Mildred herself was a dancer. She told me how her husband helped her fulfill her passion for dance. They opened the Art Museum as well as the School of Art together in hopes of helping the community. This way, Mildred could pass on her life's wealth of culture to those wanting to learn as well.

I also have a hall dedicated to my artwork, in which I have brought my favorite subjects to life through my drawings. Mildred and her birds are living in each drawing displayed down that hallway. When I go down the hallway, I'm always compelled to stop at each drawing carefully displayed behind glass in preservation of each memory of her. The hallway was her gift to me. It has been much too long since I have been there. I must visit soon.

Oh, my mind is wandering again. I turn my attention back to Alfred.

"You know, Alfred," I say while I'm watching the birds fly to and fro, "there is something that you can do."

"Yes Ms. Mary, anything." Alfred waits for instruction patiently.

"You know," and I can't help but pause and think of the task that I am about to ask of him, "you know Mildred loved this beautiful garden." I can feel the warmth of the sun upon my face, as well as the cool spring breeze blowing, as if it just did not want to give winter away quite yet. I close my eyes and take it all in.

Alfred takes a deep breath and lets it out slowly as his face softens with the mere mention of our dear ol' friend.

"Yes, she sure did indeed." Alfred's tone is somber in reflection. "How can I help you, Ms. Mary?"

"Well," I take a moment to gather my thoughts. I guess I'm much like Mildred in that way. "The flowers are more stunning with each passing day and season."

"Uh-huh." Alfred interrupts my thoughts. His attention is taken by the mere aroma of the flowers coming up to greet us.

"And the flowers need the bees to pollinate them, so they thrive with each passing year." I speak like I'm a teacher. I gaze out over the gardens.

"Uh-huh." Alfred is still waiting for the instruction like the much-awaited punch line to a joke. Anticipation is killing him.

"The birds come and go, then come and go once more," I say. My hand gestures over the flowers and then to the bright blue sky, dotted with cotton candy white clouds above. The sky is very deceiving. In appearance, it looks like a warm summer day, but instead, it is a brisk spring day.

"Well, Ms. Mary, I do see all kinds of birds come to visit this beautiful garden each and every day as well."

"Yes, well." I turn to him to catch his full attention. A warmth comes from within my heart and my face radiates with joy. "Where do they go?" I ask. I feel something almost like the deep sadness of losing an old friend.

"Well, if I were a bird," and the jovial chuckle comes from his belly beneath his work overalls, "I think I could answer that. But, as you see Ms. Mary," Alfred sticks his thumbs in the straps of his overalls and gives a quirky smile, "I'm not a bird."

This thought sends us both into a fit of laughter.

"I would like to see bird houses in the garden." I point over to the right side of the garden. "Maybe one over there." I search for other perfect spaces for a bird house to be placed. "And maybe one over there." I point to a different location.

"I believe Mildred would have loved that." Alfred's voice becomes somber once more.

"Then we might have babies and hopefully the garden will be full of not only beautiful flowers, but also songs of all different types of birds."

Sirens from the city steal our attention. They are quite a contrast from the quiet trickle of the water fountain in the nearby pond. But, living in Chicago, sirens are common. This time they are unnerving and quite distracting. I turn back to Alfred to regain his attention.

"But, if you can, please figure out what type of birdhouses would best suit birds here in Chicago, so we make sure they come to stay," I instruct him.

"Yes, ma'am," Alfred says.

I purse my lips. "You remember," I look into his eyes to see my friend and not just a caretaker. "It's Ms. Mary."

Alfred's face lights up with the warmth of a child.

"I remember, Ms. Mary." He takes a moment to compose himself. "When you took over for Ms. Mildred, I thought of you as Mildred's special child and have ever since." Alfred is quite a bit older than I am, and it's strange to see him running the manor instead of sitting here with Mildred. "I will try not to say ma'am. But if it's alright with you," he bends over next to me as he begins to stand, "I need to do the same thing that Antoinette is doing, if that is okay. Mildred would appreciate it." Alfred gives a little wink as he looks at the doorway.

Ah, I got it. Alfred and Antoinette are both showing the other employees—especially the new ones—they need to respect me. I get that, but I'm also their friend. I nod and give a little wink back.

Once again, distant sirens take our attention, but this time they are getting louder. Before we know it, more sirens join in with the other ones to form a symphony of screaming tones piercing our ears. The symphony of sirens is not one for applause. The off-pitch screams are also met with the airhorns that add a sense of urgency. These sirens give me an eerie feeling. The feeling is quite different from the others evoked by the pleasant morning.

"Alfred, that sounds close to the manor," I say, fear building inside of me.

"Yes, it does, but I haven't heard of anything going on." He takes a quick glance back at the door. Everything seems to be in order.

As quickly as the sirens came, they change pitch as they pass the manor. The sound that was being pushed toward us is now being pulled away, changing pitch again. With this change, our anxieties calm, only, once those sirens pass, more fill the void. These sirens are different, different in tone and different in the horrible song they are attempting to sing. Something must be happening.

"I hope nothing bad..." I stand and reach for the table to steady my balance. I am distracted by the sirens and unable to finish my sentence.

"Me too, Ms. Mary," Alfred says as he takes his hat off his head with his right hand and then wipes the dirt from his forehead with his left. He swats his hat against his leg to clean off the dirt from the planting he did earlier in the garden and carefully places it back upon his head. "Me too." He looks a bit uneasy and worried, but in Chicago, anything is possible.

I turn to gather my cup and plate. Amelia has entered the doorway to come into the garden to check on me. Her pace is hurried and quite distracted.

"Oh, Ms. Mary," she says as she rushes to the table. She has to jockey around the chairs that we displaced. "Please, let me get that for you." Her voice seems much different than earlier. Her head is lower, shielding her face from me. She almost seems like a different person her demeanor is so changed.

"Come, dear." I get her attention to stop her work so I that can see what is wrong.

"I'm okay. Please allow me to get your dishes." She refuses to look up. Her refusal makes me a bit angry. I feel myself begin to scold her like a child.

"Amelia, please, stop!" I reach out to touch her arm. I remember my mother grabbing me like that as a child. The reaction I received from Amelia is the same reaction I gave my mother. The sheer shock and horror upon her face are enough to remind me to love her, not to scold her. My chest tightens from the anxiety filling the air.

Amelia stops dead in her tracks, and she reveals her face. I see tears forming in her eyes. Her face is distorted in an effort to fight back the flooding emotions, reddening with each passing moment.

"What's the matter?" My voice is calm, trying to soothe her pain. Although my insides are twisting with fear, I do not dare allow it to be seen.

"Have you heard what's going on?" she asks. Her eyes are full of tears. Instead of grasping for the dirty dishes, she put her hands up over her face to try and hide them, to no avail. The tears break through, and her body pulses with each sob. This is beginning to look like one of those ugly cries.

"No dear, I've been out here with Alfred talking about the bird feeders. What happened?" I'm deeply concerned. I'm not sure if something happened inside the school or if it had something to do with the sirens piercing the brisk air.

"The school." Amelia's face is fighting back fear. She is trying so hard to calm herself and be professional in front of me. Her breathing becomes labored, and she is unable to compose herself. With her hands covering her face, it's difficult to understand her between sobs.

I have to ask once more, "What do you mean?"

She pulls her hand down from her face in order to speak to me. I'm obviously confused from the response.

"The sirens?" She tries to get me to understand. "The sirens," she has to stop to breathe, "went to the school." She cannot hold herself together enough to breathe.

"What do you mean?" I'm caught off guard by her tears and broken words due to her labored breathing. The school—our school? It can't be our school here. The sirens were off in the distance, not here. A wave of horror rushes over me like a tidal wave in a hurricane.

"Do you mean," I'm so afraid to ask, "the city school?"

All Amelia can do is nod. Her blubbering sobs render her speechless.

"Oh dear," I say, trying to comfort not only her, but myself as well.

She composes herself enough to get a few words out.

"The school is on fire. My daughter, she's there!" The severity of the situation sinks in. The concern is all over her face. This young meek girl is not a girl at all. She is a mother. You know, you see people, but when you look at them, you don't really see them. This young lady fears for her daughter's safety. I would have never thought she was even old enough to have a child. She appears to be a child herself.

"Honey, what are you still doing here?"

"I can't leave. I'm working," she says as if I did not realize. She's trying so hard to be an adult, but she is a child herself and in complete chaos.

"Amelia, please leave!" I give her the order with a loud, stern voice. "Go to your daughter!" I grab her shoulder and attempt to turn her away.

Amelia grabs the dishes carefully so as to not break any of them and runs toward the door to the manor. She slips on a small patch of ice but regains her gait. She makes a quick turn to the right which leads to the kitchen. She is trying to fulfill her responsibilities despite the chaos in her life. It shows great character, but I think she was trying to impress me, as well as Antoinette.

I make my way up the sidewalk out of the garden. I'm careful not to find that patch of ice that Amelia found earlier. I make my way into the manor where I run into Antoinette. Even though Antoinette looks quite preoccupied, I must stop her.

"Did you know the school is on fire?" I question.

"Yes, I did. I'm allowing the ones with children in the school to leave so they can be with their families," Antoinette informs me. Even though she knew that I would approve she looks at my face to see that she did the right thing. How could I not approve?

I sigh with relief. "I'm glad you took care of that."

Antoinette, with clipboard in hand, is taking note of everyone leaving, running to take care of their children. I plan on asking who all needed to leave so I can check on them afterward.

Just then, Amelia comes running around the corner with a jacket and purse in hand. In a hurried voice, she calls, "I will let you know what is going on, and I will be back today if I can."

"Honey, go!" I point my hand to the door. "Go! Take care of your daughter."

"Thank you, Ms. Mary!" Amelia turns and sprints down the hallway that leads to the employee parking lot. A few more are close behind her, leaving to do the same. It is beginning to look as if our manor was on fire with everyone heading for the doors.

"Antoinette," I say as I turn to her, "let's turn on the TV to see if anything is on the news."

"Good idea." Antoinette has my daughter, Millie, in her arms as we go into the other room where the TV is. She sets Millie down and pulls up the breaking news report. Millie sits on the floor playing, undisturbed by and unaware of all the commotion.

Almost every station has the news report on. The school is indeed on fire, but blessedly there are no reports of people or children being hurt or trapped. The video reports show flames billowing out of the top. The cameras pan to show the children being escorted out of the school. Some are in tears holding each other while others are laughing, cheering on the flames. The cameras are pointed at the firetrucks and firemen, all working hard to save the school. It looks quite hopeless to me, but I'm not a firefighter to know one way or the other.

"Oh, look how horrible that is!" I can't help but feel the pain of the building. This school is the very one I went to as a child. The footage makes me squirm.

I can't watch this. It feels like a horror movie, and I'm watching with one eye covered. I lean back in my chair and hear Mildred's chastising voice in my mind. Leaning back in any chair was not acceptable to Mildred. I was always taught to be proper around her, ladylike. However, this feels different. I feel out of control. I need to find a way to help.

My mind is taken over by the thoughts of yesteryear. I remember back when I was going to this school. I was in art class. The kids made fun of me because I was a friend of Mildred, or, as they all called her, the Bird Lady. My mother did not allow me to talk to Mildred. When I was on school trips to the park, I always made a point to speak to her. She later became my dearest friend.

Then I remember back in English class where I thought I found my first true love, Jake. I was so happy just to be asked to the homecoming dance at school. I felt warm and loved. I was so wrong. Anger flares within me as I remember how he raped me after he gave me that awful drink. I still do not know what was in it. It must have been drugged. I was just so happy to finally have a boyfriend. I felt like I finally belonged. I was in the "in" crowd with him and Angel.

I used to run to the park just to talk to Mildred. I remember when I told Mildred just how ecstatic I was that Jake asked me to the dance. She taught me how to act like a lady, to cross my legs at the ankles and not my knees. I remember when she told me to walk in front of her. I felt my heart lift a bit. It was strange. It was like I was in a fashion show walking across the stage for her. She told me that I walked like a boy. Mildred's southern drawl made it feel much worse. I knew I didn't walk like everyone else, but a boy? I never thought I looked like a boy.

She taught me how to sit correctly in in a chair with my back up straight and off the back of the chair. To elongate my neck but not look like a snob. She said that a lady always used a coverup over her knees.   A coverup? How could anyone actually look at my dress when I was sitting down in a chair? I didn't understand that then, but I do now.

All of this seemed weird, but Mildred taught me to be a lady, not a grown-up, but a real lady. She also taught me about real love, not lust. That homecoming dance was when Jake raped me. It was very difficult to tell Mildred, but she was the only one I could tell. Mildred taught me that mixing alcohol and going on dates so young is not a good combination. She taught me about peer pressure, taught me to be my own person. My own mother didn't tell me anything about this.

Then I thought of Sandra. She was my best friend in school and cared for me no matter what. So many kids made fun of her big, thick glasses and freckles. I got into a lot of trouble that day I got into a fight for her, but it was well worth it.

I had wanted to be invisible in school, but I couldn't be invisible and stand up for myself or Sandra at the same time. Mildred taught me that I needed to stand up for myself to be respected. Demand respect to be respected. I got into a fight because the girls in the school were not respecting Sandra. I remember being in the bathroom crying so hard that I wanted to die. Sandra talked to me and assured me that everything was going to be okay. Looking back now it was funny. After I stopped crying, I remember laughing because we both had freckles.

The memories keep flooding in, and I find myself drifting off inside my head. I can't stop the memories both good and bad from flooding my mind. Even the TV can't drown them out.

Once, while on a field trip to the park, I had an assignment to draw a picture for my final. I couldn't help but draw Mildred. She was the main subject in almost all my drawings. On this particular field trip, we were lining up to board the bus and head back to school from the park. All of a sudden, I heard one of the guys making fun of me for talking to Mildred, or, as everyone called her, the Bird Lady.

He grabbed my sketch pad and saw the picture of her that I had just drawn. He held it up for everyone to see. I wanted to die, to become invisible. Why was I always the butt of their jokes? Was it because of Mildred?

"Look at the Bird Lady!" he yelled to the other students. Laughter erupted and it was all pointed at me. I got on the bus. The teacher heard all the yelling and joking. He had seen what was happening. He told them to be quiet. They didn't listen. Instead, one of the guys began to chirp like a bird. The next thing I knew, more kids were chirping as well. They were all making fun of me and my new friend the Bird Lady, Mildred to me. My sketchpad was ripped from my hands, and suddenly it was being passed around the bus. I tried desperately to get it back.

My sketchpad was mine, the manifestation of personal visions in my mind. The drawings were how I saw life. My drawings were not of the normal things that other kids drew in class like a tree or a dog playing in the park. No, my drawings were more intricate. I had never really liked drawing big things. I would rather draw the finer details of life. To take my sketchpad was almost the same as taking someone's diary and reading it aloud. It was a violation of my inner world.

The memory seems like it was yesterday. The anger, the embarrassment was as overwhelming then as it was now.

"Stop it!" I had yelled.

I can hear the other kids in my mind making fun of me and saying, "Stop what? Chirp chirp!?"

I reach for my sketchpad to pull it close to me to keep it safe.

Everyone is making fun of me.

I yell once more but this time, it feels much louder.

"I said stop it!" I demand.

They didn't stop, so I take a deep breath and yell as hard as I can.

"Stop it!"

"Ms. Mary," Antoinette calls my name to bring me back. I hear Antoinette's voice, but nothing is registering. I can't respond. My body and mind are back in school when I was a child. I hear Antoinette but not really.

Antoinette asks once more, "Are you okay?"

I feel like a hand is reaching for me from a distant world. I find myself slumped in my chair. Wait, something feels off. I find myself shaken from what felt like a dream—or was it a nightmare? It feels like both.

I'm disoriented and at a loss for words. "Yes." I sit up in my chair instead of slouching. This is no way for a lady to be seated, and trust me, I hear Mildred's voice resonating in my head.

Still feeling disoriented, I say "I was just remembering times in school."

Just then Antoinette bursts out in laughter. Why? Why would she laugh like that watching the TV with all the fire stuff? I don't understand.

"What on earth is so funny?" I ask with a bit of anger. I don't find anything funny at all.

"Ms. Mary," Antoinette says, still giggling. Oh, now I'm beginning to be visibly angry. "Ms. Mary. You were sound asleep. You don't remember yelling to 'stop it'?"

"Umm, no," I say, almost embarrassed. Was I really asleep? Trying to compose myself, I say, "I was thinking of the school kids making fun of me for talking to Mildred." My voice trails off. I add, "I guess I was yelling at the kids to stop it."

"Mildred told me all about that stuff." Antoinette is trying to comfort me. It isn't working though. My stomach still feels queasy like it was just yesterday. "Are you sure you're okay?"

"Yes," I say as I pull myself upright in the chair. "Yes, I was just remembering all the times I had in that school. Now, they are going," I pause, "up in flames." My voice has a horrible sadness to it.

Our attention is back to the TV. The sight before my eyes is haunting. So many children running for safety as their home-away-from home is torn away.

I feel so bad for them. I get up, wanting to leave the room without saying anything else on the subject. It is still a horror movie I can't turn away from. My heart is in too much turmoil. Antoinette seems glued to the TV as well, where reporters are trying to give the latest news. She appears to be in as much shock as I am.

"Oh, those poor children," Antoinette says under her breath. She shakes her head in disbelief.

The TV station is showing some kids laughing and pointing to the flames. My stomach, oh my stomach. I feel a sickness brewing deep within me. My heart is hurting so much that I want to cry and yell at the same time. Why? Why are you kids so happy that the school is burning? Don't you even care? I rub my stomach with my right hand over and over like a pregnant woman does to comfort her baby. I guess I'm the baby, and I'm comforting myself, or at least, I'm trying to. I find the need to look away from the TV to check on Millie once more. She is still just as content as ever, still playing.

An eerie feeling comes over me in memory of what time of year it is.

"If I remember right," I say as I look up in the air for answers, "their prom and graduation is coming up. It is always in the gymnasium."

Watching the newscast, it appears that the fire is most prevalent in the gymnasium area of the school. Flames are still billowing out of what use to be the roof. The exposed raw steel frame structure is standing its ground, unwavering beams that hold not only the burned roofline, but also all those precious memories of yesteryear.

"Well, not anymore," Antoinette says as she points to the TV.

My voice softens. Ironically, it sounds like Marilyn Monroe, a deep disbelief, "No, I guess not."

We both stare at the TV in complete shock. It is disheartening to see the children's reactions as their school burns right before their eyes.

Seeing the ones that are cheering the fire on brings back some of the worst memories. I drift back in time to when I was a child in art class at that very school. Sure, I may appear to be watching the TV intensely, but that is far from the truth. My stomach is in my throat waiting to be expelled. I feel physically sick, not just at the images on the TV but also at the images being recalled in my mind. I can't take any more. I turn and leave. I know I should have said something, but I don't have it in me.

CHAPTER 2

I WANDER THE MANOR IN DISMAY. I wander to where Alfred is working, and he stands to greet me.

"Ms. Mary, are you okay?" Alfred asks.

"Not really." I must have a distressed look.

"Is there anything I can do for you?" Alfred asks with great concern. He put his hand of security upon my shoulder, but it still isn't enough to comfort my internal pain.

"The fire," I think about what I want to say, "the fire has me upset."

"Ms. Mary, I think it has a lot of us upset as well," he says, trying to console me. He pulls me close like a father would his child after a bad breakup with a boyfriend. He holds me, but only for a moment. I find the strength to pull back and get a second wind.

"I want to go there." It feels like a good idea. Sadly, Alfred doesn't feel quite the same. The look upon his face is that of true disapproval, but that does not stop me.

"Now, Ms. Mary, that sounds like a place you really shouldn't be while all this is going on." Alfred tries to change my mind, but it doesn't work.

"But," I take a moment to breathe before I get upset, "you don't understand. My heart hurts to see the building burning."

"Well, if you are so determined to go see it, let me drive you." Alfred sets down everything that he is carrying. "Just let me get the keys, and I will meet you out front." Next thing I know, Alfred is off and gone to get the keys to take me to the fire.

I peek in on Millie and Antoinette to ensure I'm okay to leave. I find it hard to voice any words, but Antoinette knows what my face is saying to her. She waves her arm as if to give me permission to leave, so I do.

I gather my coat and my purse and meet Alfred out front as he requested. He is the perfect gentleman as always, holding the door open, awaiting my arrival. After I swing my legs into the car, Alfred ensures I'm all clear before he closes the door. He seems a bit hurried as he scurries around the front of the car to the driver's side. I guess my anxiety rubbed off on him. With my coat on and purse in hand, Alfred drives me to the fire.

As we get closer to the school, the smell of burnt wood permeates the air. The symphony of sirens still continues from all directions. Many other fire departments are arriving at the scene. We are met by police officers blocking the roads so on-lookers can't get close. Sad, but I guess I'm an on-looker.

"Ms. Mary," Alfred says to get my attention. His face is plastered to the front window trying to see through the thick smoke. "I can't get us any closer to the school."

I have my head close to the window like a schoolgirl in complete awe trying to get a closer look. I sit back in my seat.

"I know," I say, sounding like a dejected child. I feel like I'm pouting.

Just then, Alfred pulls into the parking lot of a nearby store next to some TV station trucks and says, "Here, no one will see us park here." He pulls between two news vans and turns the car off. He looks at me like a parent.

"Now, Ms. Mary." Oh, boy. His voice sounds like a father figure. Ironically, he is old enough to be my father. And quite frankly, when I went to see Mildred, he was sort of a protector and a father, so I don't really mind. I need the comfort and security anyway.

I turn to look at Alfred in a childish manner.

"Ms. Mary, I can't tell you what to do, but," his face turns toward the fire across the street, "I will be here when you get back."

Did he just say that? It sounded like he just gave me permission to leave the car and go check on the children.

"Are you sure?" I have to ask, the childish schoolgirl close at hand.

"Now Ms. Mary." He looks at me with his face turned down but his eyes still meet mine with a little smirk.

I can't help it. I fling the car door open and burst out like my father just told me I could go out for the night.

"I promise I won't get too close," I reassure him.

As I get out of the car, I look around to see if anyone sees me. I feel like a secret agent going on a mission. I can hear the song from *Mission Impossible* playing in my head. Oh, what am I doing? This isn't a joke! I'm sneaking around like I'm breaking the law.

I make it as far as in front of the TV station vans. I was too afraid to get any closer. Besides, the heat from the flames is so hot that it burns the air around me. My heart is melting from the heat as well. I feel my mouth open wide, ready to catch flies as my mom would say. I cover my mouth with both hands. Plumes of smoke billow from the building like a tribal dance. Ashes from the building fall all around. The longer I'm out of thecar, the more I feel the intense heat, even though it is far away. With every breath, I can taste the ash as if I'm licking the bottom of an ashtray. I experience the fire in all four dimensions, an experience I wish to forget, but I am sure I will never be able to.

The sheer vision before me is enough to break me. I feel my tears attempt to wash the ash off my face, but how could they? They just make horrible streaks, confirming the burning before me. I can't stop them. My school. That is my school!

I notice a group of people standing off to my right. I don't pay them any mind. I'm in shock and don't care who sees it. I feel the group of people get closer and then closer. I pull my eyes away from the horrible sight to see a camera in the midst of the chaos. They are filming the horror show. They are filming me. Then I hear a faint voice attempting to capture my attention over the screaming firetruck symphony.

"Miss?"

I hear it but I really don't care.

"Ma'am?"

There it is again. But this time, I hear a word that I must admit is unnerving to me. I turn to see who it is.

Upon turning to my right, I see a man holding a TV camera on his shoulder and aiming it right at me. There is also a young girl, all dolled up, attempting to report for the local news team. She looks perfect and has a bubbly voice to match. How is this possible? This young, twenty-something reporter dressed to the nines with her perfect hair, perfect dress, and high heels that should only be on a hooker, is cramming a microphone in my face and calling me "ma'am". She has a napkin, probably from McDonald's, up against her face, shielding the smoke from infiltrating her virgin lungs. She probably smokes but doesn't make the connection that this smoke is just as bad. How can I be judging her at a time like this?

I hear the bubbly voice once more. "Ma'am". The heat from the building is now in the depths of my soul. My anger builds. I want to throw up. I want to scream at this young girl.

Pull yourself together. I can hear Mildred's voice deep within my mind.

I carefully turn in the reporter's direction, so she now understands I'm listening to her. Here it comes again.

"Ma'am, can you tell me why you are so upset at the school being on fire?" she asks as she thrusts the microphone back in my face. Really? A tragic moment like this and she is going to ask me why I'm so upset? Why isn't *she* upset? Not a tear can be seen in her eyes. How can she just stand there and watch this neighborhood school burn while the kids are dancing in the streets? I now see her as a puppet. She is being what everyone wants her to be. She is a sickening TV personality that doesn't have a personality of her own. Does she not have a heart? I find myself speechless.

I try to talk to her. I can't find the words. I look at her with a blank stare.

"Do you have kids in this school?" There is that awful childish voice again.

"No, I don't," I reply.

"Then, why are you so upset?" she asks again.

I feel the anger burn so hot that I can't help it anymore. I envision myself picking her up and throwing her like I threw Angel when she hurt Sandra in school, but I don't dare resort to that. It is a comforting thought.

"I went to school here." I turn to watch the school in flames. "I graduated from here." I slowly turn back, realizing that I'm being interviewed for live TV. I find the need to be on my best behavior, even though my thoughts are anything but ladylike.

"So why are you so upset?" she asks stupidly.

"These children," and I turn toward the school once more, "have no idea what they are losing." I have to compose myself. "This school has been in this great city for many years." I am referring to Chicago of course. "This school is a safe haven to many." Gathering my thoughts, I add, "and many memories are going up in flames."

I notice that the cameraman is beginning to feel the wrath of my words. He is no longer intent on his job. He must have attended the school and realizes now what I'm talking about. His face turns a nice shade of red while he attempts to hold back his own tears. He holds the camera as best as he can.

Not missing a beat, the young reporter asks, "Do you have memories from here?" Seriously? I just said that I graduated from here and these kids are having their memories burn before their eyes. I know that she is trying to do her job, but come on. Asking childish questions just makes her look even more childish herself.

I guess the look I give her is priceless because the cameraman rolls his eyes. Then, he notices that I saw him. We have our own little understanding that this young reporter is too green to understand the importance of community.

"Yes, many." My response is short and poignant. Here it goes, I can't hold it back. Before even realizing that I'm responding, I ask, "How about you? Do you?"

Her childish antics are quite unprofessional. To be a good reporter, she should have empathy and at least attempt to relate to the public. Instead, she is relating to the children dancing in the street in complete abandon of their old friend. For all I know, if this school was on fire and she was a student here, she too would be dancing and yelling for the school to burn.

The cameraman is quite surprised that I turned the tables. He pans the camera over to the reporter. I guess this is unheard of. She looks like a deer in the headlights. Part of me is glad to see her squirm. She looks at the cameraman in a way that resembles a goat getting scared. They just fall over dead in their tracks. She quickly composes herself as best as she can.

"Um, no, I grew up on the west coast, you know like L.A.," she says, sounding very Valley Girl just then. Her voice changes along with her accent. I actually wait to hear, 'as if', but it never comes. That would have been great to catch on national live TV.

"Oh, I'm sorry," I respond with a twinge of quirkiness. I feel I have overstayed my welcome. I turn to head back to the car where Alfred was waiting but I see that he has been standing off in the distance and saw the whole thing. I know he doesn't approve of my attitude toward the reporter, but deep down, I think he knows I had to get the last word in.

As I'm leaving, I feel a dainty hand on my shoulder.

"Wait." It is the reporter.

"Yes?" I say as I turn to her with the manners I was raised to have—manners she should have learned as well. I see a dainty hand with freshly manicured long nails against her white skin.

"I need to know who you are for the newscast." She has a notebook with her, and I can see that it is a press release granting them permission to use the interview.

"But you said it was a live broadcast," I say.

"Well, it kinda is," she says with a childish giggle. "You know, like I still need to edit it and it will run on the next breaking news story." Oh, there it is. The words of L.A. fall into place.

"So, it wasn't live then?" I asked.

"Not technically," she says with yet another nervous giggle. Oh, how that is aggravating. Those giggles show me just howyoung and naive she really is. I see it now.

"My name is Mary Parker." I keep my maiden name for my art. "My husband and I took over the Art Museum and the School of Art just down the way."

"Oh, you are the one that took over for Mildred," she adds. How does she even know about Mildred? This reporter looks to be about twelve.

"Yes, I did." I really don't want to talk about it, so I leave to meet up with Alfred.

Walking around the news van, I see Alfred peering around the side.

"All ready, Ms. Mary?" he asks. My getaway driver is ready to roll.

"Yes, I think so," I say with a great sigh. "Did you see that young girl interview me?" I ask, like I'm not totally sure that it really happened.

"Yes, I surely did." He says with a smirk-turned-into-belly laugh. He adjusts his hat.

"Why are you laughing?" I ask as I sit in the passenger seat. Alfred closes the door behind me and gets into the driver's side. He is still giggling.

"Alfred, why are you laughing?" I need to know if I missed something.

"Oh, Ms. Mary." The giggles turn into a full-on laugh. "You handed that young girl the interview that only a professional could have done. She is going to wonder who was interviewing who." He pulls out of the parking lot and continues, "I know the cameraman sure got a kick out of it."

"He did?" I ask. I wasn't really positive about what just transpired. It happened so quickly that I can hardly remember.

"He surely did. Oh, Ms. Mary," Alfred pauses. "When I watched you over there, I couldn't help but see Ms. Mildred. You are such an inspiration for this community."

"Why do you say that?"

"You handled yourself with poise and redirected the reporter to see the community and not the building on fire. Mildred would be so proud of you." There is admiration on his face that only a child could miss.

"Mildred would have been proud of me?" I ask in a sheepish voice. Oh, I wish she were here with me. You know, I did feel her with me. It was like she was giving me the strength to turn the report around. I needed to show the importance of the school and what it means to the community. I take a slow breath in and close my eyes, cherishing the mere thought of Mildred being by my side. I didn't expect to come to the fire, but now I do feel a bit better.

"You did good, kid," Alfred says with a warm glow upon his cheeks.

"Yeah?"

"Yeah."

"Thank you for taking me." Our eyes meet only for a moment as he drives away from the scene.

"My pleasure Ms. Mary. My pleasure."

We drive back to the manor with memories of that moment dancing around in both of our minds. We don't say anything else the whole ride back. The big iron gates welcome us back, providing a sense of protection from the outside world of uncertainty as they open wide for our arrival. As we drive through them, I feel my heart ease just a bit. Just knowing that Mildred would be proud is enough for me.

While Alfred is dropping me off at the front grand entrance, Antoinette is coming down the stairway to meet me. Alfred leaves with the car to take it around back, and I meet with Antoinette.

"You okay?" she asks cautiously.

"Sure, I was even interviewed," I say as I make my way up the stairway.

"Oh, yeah, we all saw it."

"Already?" I say, confused. I thought the young girl was going to edit it and chop it all up to make me sound like an idiot.

"No, it was a live broadcast," she says.

"Live?" I thought she had to…

"Oh yes, and I particularly liked the part about her being from L.A." Antoinette bursts out into laughter. "I don't think she realized that it was live, or that she made herself look stupid."

We both can't help but laugh so hard that it is hard to believe that our city just experienced a great tragedy. As we walk up the stairway to the grand porch, Antoinette remembers and stops dead in her tracks. "Ms. Mary, Charlie is here, and he is looking for you to eat dinner with him instead of at the manor tonight."

"Mm, sounds like he has something good cooking." I love his cooking. Being married to a chef has its advantages.

The rest of the afternoon passes quickly, and later that evening, I find Charlie hard at work, slaving over the cutting board and chopping his little heart away. He looks so good in his apron and tight jeans. He looks just as good as he did when I met him in the café. I wrap my arms around him from behind so as not to disturb his chopping. Secretly, I want to distract him.

"Hey baby," I say, with a muffled voice because my face is buried in his back.

"I heard you had quite a day." He stops chopping and turns around to give me a big hug.

With my arms around him and his around me, the safety of his love is enough to make any girl melt. My eyes lift to his. His dark curly hair is draped down to his nose and probably quite honestly needs to be trimmed, but I love it like this. His dark Italian skin makes his eyes stand out like no other. Oh, am I honestly lusting over my husband? I can't help it. He bends down to kiss me so gently. I feel like a schoolgirl once again. My heart isn't racing but rather calm, loving. I take a deep breath and regain my composure.

"I missed you today." My voice is calm.

"I bet you did." Another kiss follows his words of silk.

He turns and pulls me over to the table. "I made dinner for us." He motions me to sit. "Please allow me to finish."

"Where's Mildred?" I expect our little bundle of joy to be eating with us tonight.

"She is in bed already," he says.

"Bed already?"

"Yes, well it is late for her," he reminds me.

"I was hoping to make it back before she went to bed, but that's okay."

Charlie has made a beautiful dinner for us. Looking down at the masterpiece before us, I notice a thick piece of lasagna with many layers of meat, sauce, and different varieties of cheese all melted to perfection.

After serving the lasagna, Charlie puts the finishing touches on the bowl of bright multicolored greens with carrots, cucumber, bacon bits, and other veggies. It is stunning because he didn't just make a salad, he created a salad. His carrots are cut to perfection like flowers, and the bacon bits are not store-bought. Everything from the croutons to the bacon bits are handmade and hand-cooked. He cooks his bacon bits and seasons them just as he cuts his croutons after seasoning them and baking them to perfection. He is, in fact, my own personal chef that I have the pleasure to be married to. I chuckle at the thought.

"What is so funny, my love?" He questions me as he reaches for the carafe of Italian dressing he just mixed. He drizzles the dressing over our salads and then tops it with fresh cracked pepper.

Charlie moves over to his chair to tell me that the show is over and that we can eat. Oh, the aroma of the smooth, melted cheese, warmed garlic, and tomato sauce that is layered between each layer of noodles. He doesn't cook like this often because we are simply too busy with the manor. He also runs Mildred's Tea Room—part of the Art Museum—along with cooking classes. He is living his passion. His mother taught him how to cook as a young child, and now he is teaching children the art of cooking.

Dinner is so incredibly delicious. Carefully blotting my lips, I can't help but look at my husband. It seems like such a long time since I've been able to just sit here and look at him. He doesn't notice me watching, but I think of the first time I saw his black curly hair draped over his nose. He was finishing his creation.

Cooking is an art. He puts his heart and soul into his dishes just as he did on our date at his restaurant.

Just then he springs to his feet and runs to the door, "Oh, I almost forgot!"

Charlie runs into the kitchen, and all of a sudden, I hear pans clanging. I try not to ruin his evening; I just stay at the table and wait.

Next thing, Charlie comes around the corner carrying two plates of molten chocolate cake with powdered sugar on top. He comes around me and carefully places the warm plate of chocolate delight in front of me. The smooth aroma permeates the air as if we were in the middle of a chocolate factory. He puts his plate down at his seat and then smiles a heartwarming smile.

"Now just one moment my love." He instructs me not to touch the masterpiece before me. He disappears into the kitchen once more. I gaze longingly at the chocolate molten cake. It is as if it is calling my name.

Next, a cup and saucer are placed beside my dessert. He has a coffee carafe, and he pours each of us a nice cup of hot coffee.

"Now honey, you know I can't forget the creamer." He pulls a bottle of creamer out of the pocket in his chef apron.

"May I?" he asks as if we are on our first date.

I blush from sheer love and admiration. My heart is melting all over again.

"By all means." And I raise my hand above the cup.

He opens the creamer and pours just the right amount into my cup. Then he hands me a teaspoon.

"You can do the honors, my dear." I grasp the teaspoon to begin the dance of lovers. I gently tap my teaspoon into my coffee. It disrupts the black coffee with hazelnut creamer. The dance of lovers begins once again. Oh, twice in one day, how delightful. I watch as two young lovers twirl on the dance floor inside my coffee cup. I could watch this dance all night long, but not tonight. Charlie is the focus of my attention tonight. I'm just wondering why the fanfare with the dinner.

Charlie sits at his chair and pours his coffee as well. He likes his black and strong. I'm much the opposite. I love the sweet aroma of hazelnut creamer that tickles my taste buds.

After dinner and our delicious dessert, we sit and talk over the dinner dishes. It's something we started again on our date at Charlie's Café, and it's still one of our favorite pastimes.

"Now back to you my dear." Charlie takes a deep breath and sits back in his chair to loosen his waistband's hold upon his full stomach. His physique is still quite manly, but we both have gained a couple of pounds. Well, Charlie maybe one or two. I, on the other hand, have found the rest of the few.

I feel like a bus just hit me after such a wonderful dinner. My feelings that I have been stuffing deep down are forced to surface again. If I'm going to talk to anyone, it has to be Charlie. He is my best friend, well, along with Lilly.

"I watched my old school go up in flames today." I sit back as well. "It was hard." I want to cry but I can't. "All the memories came flooding in as I was watching the flames shoot out of the roof." My stomach flips with that big lasagna I have just eaten. I lift my eyes to meet his. "You know what I mean?" The conversation has turned serious. No more romance, no more dance in my coffee cup, just pure adult conversation between us.

Charlie smiles sympathetically. I know he's trying to show that he knows what I feel, but how could he? His school, dreams, and memories didn't just burn up before him. I know he can't understand, but I accept that I still need to talk.

"I went to that school as a child. I had childish dreams. Childish memories both good and, well, some not so good." I give way to a brief silence. "Memories of art class, Mildred in the park, Sandra my first real friend..." I find myself hiding inside myself. I lift my eyes to meet his attentiveness.

"You know, things like that..." I trail off.

"You know, I saw you on TV," he says with a half-smile. He appears almost afraid to tell me.

"You didn't!" I'm almost too embarrassed to say.

"Yep, and let me tell you, you really gave that reporter a run for her money." A chuckle follows each word.

"Well, she didn't understand the importance of the school to the neighborhood. And she won't either, she's not from here." I have to stop. The anger is creeping up once more.

Laughter bursts from Charlie, "Yeah, L.A."

I feel a half-smirk come. I really needed that laugh. Charlie knows how to make me smile when I'm down.

A few moments pass. Not an awkward silence by any means, just a reflective silence for both of us.

"You know," Charlie breaks the silence, "you have some time so you can go see your Aunt Jackie if you want."

"Yeah," I say with a tone that isn't very convincing.

I really do want to see Aunt Jackie, but I'm not sure about Cousin Travis and certainly not his thing with all the welfare cases. Oh, I shouldn't be so harsh, but seeing Travis throw his life away to be with his child's mother is upsetting. Not to mention Aunt Jackie has to basically raise all of them. Travis sure hasn't grown up. The kids are a few years older now but still under Aunt Jackie's roof. To me, that isn't grown-up behavior at all. Seeing Travis party as much as he did when my mom died was enough for me. I don't think I could ever forgive him. Well, I guess I can forgive, but I will never forget.

"Maybe I will go see Lilly," I say as I reach for the dirty dishes.

"No, I will do the dishes," Charlie insists.

I've had a rough day, so I take him up on his offer. Besides, the dishwasher basically runs all day anyway with the classes and the restaurant.

"I'm going to call Lilly and see if I can come for a few days."

Charlie clears the table.

"Are you sure?" I ask.

"Absolutely. Go enjoy some time away for a few days." Charlie has his hands full getting ready to go into the kitchen. "I've got this," he reassures me.

"Okay," I lean over to kiss him. "I will see you later dear."

As I turn to leave the room, excitement grows in me. I have not seen Lilly for quite a while. She and her husband have been just as busy as we have been with the original Charlie's Café. It will be nice to get away.

CHAPTER 3

THE MORNING COMES quicker than I want. I arrived at Lilly's quite late last night, and we went straight to bed. I can hear the stirring of breakfast downstairs, so I venture out.

"Ah, there she is," Lilly says as she flips another pancake.

Lilly isn't domestic in any capacity at all. When I met Charlie, who owns Charlie's Café, she wanted to date him. I was a shy, timid office worker that basically lived in my little cubical right next to Lilly. While I was the quiet play-by-the-rules girl, she was the life of the party. The room changed as Lilly walked in. I was always a bit jealous of that, but I realized that she hadn't met the right person to settle her down. All that changed when she started spending more time with me at Charlie's Café and was introduced to Charlie's head pastry chef, Michael.

After Lilly met Michael, her whole world changed. She was no longer the fly-by-night, go-from-one-guy-to-the-next, girl. She actually changed when he was in the room, having a similar effect to Mildred teaching me manners. It was almost like Mildred taught her proper manners, but we all know that didn't happen.

Lilly has always been beautiful, tall, and thin, with dark-complexioned skin and wicked tiny, thin braids hanging past her waist. They flow with her every move. They are mesmerizing. I used to want to be like her, the life of the party, the one everyone turns to see as she walks into the room. She is classy, educated, and, I must say, drop-dead beautiful.

Mildred taught me that I'm special in my own way. It took me a while to be happy with that.

"Did you sleep well?" she asks with her head in the refrigerator.

"Oh gosh, yes." I'm so pleased to have a change of scenery even though the manor is a life of pure luxury. Change is good, but never permanent.

Lilly twirls around to pour a glass of orange juice for one of the kids and doesn't miss a beat.

"The kids didn't keep you up, did they?" Her eyes make contact with mine. I had forgotten how deep and dark her eyes really were. Her eyebrows are perfectly manicured, and they accentuate her features even more. She is truly beautiful, and she literally just crawled out of bed. Ugh, jealousy twinges my stomach.

"Oh no, not at all," I reassure her. I search for a seat. The kids are everywhere.

"Good, because they had a slumber party last night and, well," she, chuckles "sometimes slumber parties can get a bit loud at times."

"No, actually I didn't realize they were all here." I feel so stupid. How could I not have realized the downstairs was full of kids? I guess Lilly's house is a bit bigger than I thought. The manor can be the same in that way. It is so spread out with two levels that I never really know what's going on unless Antoinette or Alfred tells me. Now that I think about it, that's a sad thought.

Lilly doesn't miss a beat. She has pancakes flying around the room and onto plates like a pro. I have never seen her like this. She must be learning a few things around the kitchen with Michael. She seems a totally different person, domesticated. Oddly enough, I think I like this version of her a bit more, although, the wild Lilly is still lurking in the distance somewhere. I know it.

As we spoke, my little Millie popped her head around the corner. "Millie!" Lilly smiles. "Honey, are you hungry?"

Lilly reaches down and swoops Millie up in her arms and kisses every inch of her face. Millie laughs and laughs. Millie is such a happy little girl. Lilly sits her in a chair with a booster on it. I smiled, too. Millie looks like a young lady, all prim and proper. She looks up at me, and I can't contain my melting heart.

People say she looks like me when I was young, but I'm not sure I could ever look that good. Lilly places a plastic plate in front of Millie with her very own pancake. Her eyes light up like a Christmas tree. Oh boy, I see a bath in our future with all that syrup.

Kids are eating all over the kitchen. Some at the table, some sitting up at the bar, some just shoving pancakes in while standing up. It doesn't seem to matter where they are eating, just so long as they get their fair share. Finally, with all of them eating, it is quiet for a few moments.

Suddenly, one throws her hands up in the air and yells, "I'm done!"

Millie mimics this with her right hand high in the air, yells, "I'm done!" and shoves another pancake in her mouth. I know she doesn't really understand that they are in a race, but she wants to be part of the room.

It just occurred to me that when kids eat, it is a race. No one savors their food at all. I shake my head in dismay.

Another one yells and then another. I smile as I gaze around the kitchen at all the young girls stuffing their faces. They truly are enjoying the game.

Then all at once, they all just get up and leave. I can't help but sit there with my mouth wide open in shock as I see the dishes, silverware, glasses—some half full of orange juice—sitting there with no regard for cleaning or helping. It's like being at my Aunt Jackie's house. Travis would do the same thing, and Aunt Jackie would allow it. She never yelled at him. Sometimes I think she wanted him away from her and out of the room.

Lilly just digs right in and grabs a handful of dishes. I get up to help.

"I'm really happy you were able to come see me," she says as she loads the dishwasher.

"Yeah, me too. I needed some time away." I want to really talk to her, but she is so busy.

Before we know it, the dishwasher is loaded and running. The kids are all packing up their things to go back to their own homes. Normality is just around the corner, whatever that is.

Lilly bends down to talk to Millie on her level with her hands perched upon her hips.

"Now, how about you, young lady?" she questions.

Millie looks up with her mouth slammed full of pancakes and syrup running down her chin. Her poor little face is trying to smile with her chipmunk cheeks. She settles for a head nod.

Lilly reaches for her plate and begins to clean off the table in front of her.

Lilly asks if I want another cup of coffee or juice. I graciously decline. It is strange seeing her like this, waiting on me and Millie. We go into the den to sit in some peace and quiet.

After getting settled on the couches, I notice Lilly pulling her legs up underneath her like she used to when we were sitting together at each other's apartments. Now this is the Lilly I'm used to.

"Michael is already at the bakery. As a matter of fact, he's been there since about 3 o'clock."

"Wow, that's early." I had completely forgotten how early Charlie used to get up to run the coffee shop. He used to bake all the fresh pastries early every morning—a task that was not for the lazy. Once, when we were younger, I remember being on a date, and him saying that he needed to go home. He left early because he was working the next morning. To me, it was actually later that night that he was baking.

Watching Lilly pull her braids out of her hair tie, I'm once again drawn to her beauty. Her braids cascade over her shoulders like a dark river of chocolate. She has a nervous habit of picking at her braids, examining the ends to see if she had split ends. That is her real hair. I have no idea how long it took her to grow it that long, but I'm lost in her locks of hair.

"Millie, you doing okay?" Lilly begins with small talk.

"Yup!" Millie responds with a smile of grandeur.

We watch as Millie plays with a book. She acts as if she is

reading it. Her finger traces the words on the page and her mouth moves like she is reading the pages to someone. Page after page, she sounds like a pro. Suddenly, I turn to Lilly to break the silence. She speaks before I can.

"Did you see that fire?" she asks with a childlike burst of energy.

"Yeah, I did." I rearrange the pillows behind me so I can be more comfortable.

"Wasn't that the school you graduated from?" she questions with a concerned look on her face.

"Yeah, high school," I remind her. It hurts desperately to admit that, but my emotions are still running high. I know the night's sleep did some good, but when I woke up, the memories came flooding in once more.

"Yeah, not college, I knew that," she teases. Still carefully examining her hair, she takes another sip of her coffee.

"Did you see the interview on TV?" I hope she didn't see it. I hate being the center of attention. I'd been forced in front of the camera.

"No, I haven't seen much TV. I've been running so hard I never get a chance to watch TV much. Besides, with the kids here, they watch what they want to. You know, cartoons and all."

How could I forget the house full of chaos?

"I was interviewed by a young reporter that acted like the school burning wasn't a big deal. I think she would have been one of them cheering it on to burn down completely," I say with distress.

"Well, that's pretty unprofessional."

How ironic. Back when we worked in insurance, Lilly was the most unprofessional person I knew.

"It makes me angry. She couldn't understand why I was so upset with it burning." I sit back in my oversized chair. I feel like I can relax around Lilly.

"So, you went down there?" Lilly leans in to get a better understanding.

"Yeah, I did," I say as I bite my bottom lip.

"I knew it wasn't far from the manor, but how did you get close?"

"I didn't. Alfred drove and parked the car between some news vans. We weren't supposed to be there, but we were," I say with a little smirk. I had felt like a spy.

"So, what did you see? I just heard about it," she asks with a concerned voice.

"It was awful." I rub my eyes, still swollen from all my crying yesterday. "Flames were billowing out of the gymnasium. Kids were being escorted out of the school. Some were crying and some were actually cheering watching the school burn." Anger filled my voice.

"I don't know, Mar. I think I would have cheered if my school was on fire." She has a smug look on her face.

"Well, I had a lot of memories burn up in front of me." I sound wimpy, even to my own ears.

"But Mary, they didn't burn up in front of you. Memories are etched in your mind." Her smile is comforting. I miss seeing that smile from our time together. "You take your memories with you." Now she sounds like Mildred.

I feel a bit foolish looking at it now. I got so upset that a building, a pile of bricks, steel, and everything else inside was on fire. I glance down at Millie to contain my thoughts. She's right. It wasn't my memories that were on fire. It was just a building. My memories are safely locked inside my mind, where they belong.

"You know, they were going to have their prom and graduation next month in the gymnasium," I say.

"Well," she looks around the room for answers while scratching her temple, "that's kinda hard now."

"I wish I could do something. I feel so bad." My voice trails off.

"Bad? Bad how?" Lilly can't grasp my uneasiness about the whole situation.

"Now they can't have their prom or graduation at the school."

"And..." She waves her hand for me to go on.

"I wonder..." I get a mischievous feeling about myself.

"Oh crap, Mar, what are you going to do?" Lilly knows that when I get an idea I usually get in way over my head. This is one of those times. Besides, I'm trying to fix something.

"What if I open the School of Art and allow the public school to have their prom and graduation at my school?" Looking for approval, I can't help but roll my lips inward and open my eyes wide open. It looks a bit strange, I know, but when I get nervous, I tend to do stupid things like that.

"Actually," Lilly smirks, "I think Mildred would love that idea." I can see the wheels spin in Lilly's mind. She holds her hand up while pointing a finger outward.

"You do?" I give her a weird look with my lips wrinkled and my eyes bugging. "You really think this is a good idea?" I am actually shocked that Lilly is agreeing with this.

"Well, yeah." Lilly sits up, excited. on her legs now instead of wrapping them beside her. Her posture is one of excitement. "It's a school of art, right?"

"Yes." Oh boy, what is she thinking? Now *I'm* nervous.

"Well," she looks at the ceiling and gestures widely, waving her arms like she is parting the clouds above, "you can have your students decorate with their talents and make it a prom they will never forget."

"Hmmm." This may be a good idea. I can see it now. Artwork adorns the gymnasium like an enchanted forest or the deep blue sea full of various creatures. My mind is bursting with ideas, and images of kids from both schools working together as a community instead of being so separate. I know the kids that go to my School of Art are, well, a bit more affluent. Most kids are in private lessons for arts such as piano, dance, or singing. The kids in the public school usually don't care about art or the arts. I must admit, the problem kids are in the public school, too. Maybe by doing this, the problem kids can see what art is all about, and they may want to change. My mind is wandering so fast that it is hard to control.

"So, whatcha think?" Lilly is always good at making the best of a horrible situation. No wonder so many people like her.

"I'm going to go to the principal of the school and tell him the good news. I'm opening the doors of the School of Art to the public school. What could go wrong, right?" I can think of many things, but I don't want to dwell on them.

"Right! I think it is a great idea," Lilly adds. "You would be helping the community just like Mildred has taught you, well, us."

"You are right." Firm in my decision, I want to make plans right away. But today is Saturday. It's hard to talk to the school on a Saturday.

Feeling much better, we talk about other stuff. It feels like old times with my best friend again. Oh, how I've missed her. I must visit her more often.

"Hey, you want to go to the coffee shop?" Lilly jumps to her feet.

"Sure." It is like old times. After the kids are picked up, Lilly and I drive down to Charlie's Café. Lilly's husband Michael is now the business partner that runs the entire operation. Charlie kept his name on it to keep it local. As we drive, Millie sits quietly in the back seat watching out the window.

Walking through the door, I hear familiar bell chimes as we enter. I remember that bell so distinctly from many years ago. The décor has changed a bit, but for the most part, it is still a quaint pastry and coffee shop. Lilly and I used to come here for lunch while we worked at the high-rise selling insurance. It's busier on Saturday, so a hostess seats us because of the crowds just begging to come in.

As we sit at a table, I look at the walls of yesteryear. There are remnants of things that were here when I came here every day to see Charlie, such as the chair in the corner where his mother used to sit and wait ever so patiently for her loving son to finish working. Charlie took such good care of his mother before she passed.

Above the chair is the drawing I did of his mother. Lilly and Michael left it up in honor of Charlie and her. His mother is dressed in her finest Azalea Bell dress and hat. Her facial features are frail, but if you gaze into her eyes, you can see the life she once held. It is weird seeing it here. It was at her funeral. However, the recipes for the pastries mostly came from her. It is only fitting to have it up as a memorial.

The layout of the café is as if it had never changed hands. The chairs have been reupholstered, but the tables are the same. The lighting is still as quaint and elegant. And then I see it!

"Lilly!"

She jumps and looks around with concern. Millie jumps as well.

"It is still here! You kept it!" A smile spreads across my face.

"What are you talking about?"

I think Lilly really doesn't know what I am talking about, but, you know, playing dumb is okay with me. I lift my arm and stick out my pointer finger with its unkept fingernail polish over in the direction of the wall. "Look!"

Lilly turns around like an owl perched on a branch looking for its meal.

"My picture is still in a frame on the wall!" I'm so excited that I get out of my seat to get a better look at my first piece of artwork.

As I get closer, I see that my old friend the coffee cup is very well preserved under the protection of the glass. It is protected by the very frame Charlie put it in. I carefully lift it off the wall, my old friend, and hold it close to see the detail in the cup, the handle, and the cracks in the cup that reveal the life that was once there. Then I notice the mark on the bottom, the very mark that Mildred taught me I needed to put on each and every piece of artwork to show the world that it is one of a kind. The piece belongs to me, the artist. A sense of accomplishment flows through me.

The day I drew this , I had come to the café looking for peace and quiet. It was my first time at the café, and when I met Charlie, the owner.

Charlie was quite smitten and a really handsome man. His charm and personality won every girl over as he filled their coffee cup or took their order. Charlie ran this business like it was his own kitchen. He felt that his customers were visiting him at his home, and he made sure his customers felt it, too.

When Charlie saw me drawing the coffee cup with his name on it, he asked if he could have it to hang on his wall. I never really believed him. But, when Lilly and I came into the coffee shop a couple of weeks later, we saw it. My picture hung with pride for all to see. It was my first art exhibit, even though it was only one sketch of a cracked coffee cup. It was mine.

"Hey everyone," Lilly attempts to get everyone's attention. "If you look over there, you will see the artist that drew the coffee cup that has been on display. Her name is Mary Parker."

The room roars with cheers and clapping.

My face burns with embarrassment. I turn to face the group of people eating in this quaint café that once was run by Charlie himself. I must say, Lilly and Michael have done a wonderful job keeping the old-time elegance but also incorporating upcoming pastry ideas through serving new sandwiches for lunch. I'm very pleased to see Lilly so happy. She deserves it.

Lilly raises her voice again to inform them that I'm also the artist behind the portrait of Charlie's mother. Again, the room fills with praise.

"Mommy, you draweded dem?" Millie asks.

"Yes, honey I did. Do you like them?" I ask.

"Pretty," Millie says while peering into my eyes. Such a young lady in such a toddler body. She seems far older than she is.

After a few moments, I turn to carefully place my artwork back on the wall and say a quiet goodbye to an old friend. My heart is warm with accomplishment and peace. The picture that Charlie wanted so badly to hang on his wall was the beginning of my success. I had to overcome my insecurity and my fears of not being good enough. My art teachers all said I was a natural artist. I guess they were right. Had any of my teachers seen my wing in the Museum of Art? I'd love to know what they think of me now.

Heading back to the table, I see Michael sitting down with Lilly. He is covered with dough and powdered sugar, just like

Charlie always was. Oh, he smells so good.

We exchange hugs and quick hellos, and he is off behind the wall to stay. Lilly and I have a wonderful day reminiscing about the old days. But most of all, we talk about how wonderful our lives are today and how they will only get better in the future. We sure aren't selling insurance anymore.

CHAPTER 4

THE WEEKEND WAS MUCH NEEDED, but too short. Sunday night, Millie and I were back home. Come Monday, I want to go to the school to talk to the administration about helping with their prom and graduation, but first, I need to inform everyone of my decision.

Early Monday morning, I head to the kitchen where the staff is preparing the day's pastries and baked goods for the café. Charlie is hard at work teaching his students and yes, they work early as well, if they want to learn the real cooking experience. Now is just as good a time as ever, despite the nerves making a home in my stomach. I'm about to embark on a huge endeavor. I want them to accept it.

Even though I'm extremely nervous, I can't show it on the outside. My insides are rumbling like I just ate a really spicy meal. Oh, here it goes. I just need to get started and hopefully, everything will go okay. Why wouldn't it? I have an awesome support system here. What could go wrong?

I take a deep breath and gather everyone, urging them to take a seat or at least stand around the huge center island in the middle of the kitchen. Charlie, Alfred, and Antoinette are my front line while there are countless others that fall in behind them. I need to talk to them first before I do anything else.

My hands are sweating. My nerves are coming out to the surface. Charlie notices and diverts their attention for just a few more minutes so I can pull myself together.

"Does anyone want coffee and a pastry that just came out of

the oven for our meeting?" Charlie asks.

One of his students opens the oven doors and reaches in for one of the huge cookie sheets of the golden-brown pastries that they just learned to make. The aroma is so inviting and welcomes us closer. Carefully, using both hands as instructed, he places the large cookie sheet on the cooling rack and looks at Charlie for instruction.

Charlie looks at me and asks, "Do I have a moment to finish this lesson?"

I smile at his leadership. "Of course."

Charlie holds a shiny spatula and turns to the class, asking them to watch him as he demonstrates the correct way to remove the pastry off the steaming hot cookie sheet.

Charlie holds his tool firmly in his right hand while using his left hand to hold the cookie sheet with a towel, not a hot pad. He slides the stainless-steel spatula quickly under the pastry while he describes the delicate nature of the dough and filling. Then he describes how to slide the spatula under the pastry as well as how to slide the pastry onto the cooling rack or plate for service.

One of the students tries it, and, unfortunately, smashes the pastry, pushing all the wonderful gooey filling onto the pan. Embarrassed, the student holds his hands over his face.

Charlie takes hold of the stainless spatula and cleans off the gooey mess. "When I was learning how to do this from my mother, she told me to take ownership of the action." Charlie ensures the student is paying attention by looking at his face and then back down at the cookie sheet. "See?" He glances up once again. "She told me to slip the spatula under the pastry quickly."

He does exactly what he is describing to the students. After he has the pastry on the spatula, he lifts it up for all the students to see the placement, wanting to show that disturbing the pastry even when still hot can be done without destroying the beautiful creation.

"May I have a plate?" Charlie turns and asks the class.

One of the other students puts a small plate in front of Charlie as requested.

Charlie grabs a shaker with powdered sugar in it and sprinkles some on the empty plate. Then he carefully puts the pastry down in the center of the plate so as not to disturb the filling or the fine pastry shell. With a spoonful of raspberry puree, Charlie drizzles the pastry with bright red juice. He reaches over to a bowl full of berries including raspberries and cut strawberries and puts a few on top of the pastry.

"Now to make it pretty." Charlie gives a wink in my direction because he knows I love to watch him teach. He takes great care in everything he does, and teaching kids to do the same makes him so happy. Charlie then sprinkles a bit more powdered sugar on the creation, but it still isn't finished. He tears off a sprig of mint and places it next to the pastry, then picks up the plate to examine it. He lifts it up to eye level, turning it round and round. He then places the plate down for the whole class to see. He stands upright and smiles.

"And there ya go!" He waves his hand over the plate like a TV host showing the board on a game show.

The kids all clap with approval. Antoinette and Alfred clap as well. I'm so full of joy that my face begins to hurt from smiling so big. This was a huge help with taking the pressure off the real reason I called this meeting.

"Now it is your turn," Charlie turns the job over to the class. "Your taste testers will be waiting for you when you are finished. Please serve with a cup of coffee," he requests.

The class gasps.

"I'm just kidding. I have that covered. You focus on how to make the plate look pretty. Presentation is a major part of the experience. If it looks messy, why would someone want to order it? When it is beautiful, people remember it," Charlie says.

"Let's go into the other side of the kitchen so the class can practice. We can't move the ovens, but we can move to another location," I request.

As we move to the other side of the room, I meet up with Charlie and tap him on the elbow. He turns and those black curls flop on top of the bridge of his nose. He rolls his eyes and attempts to tame the curls into submission. Oh, I wish he wouldn't. I love his curls, his style, him.

"You are such a great teacher."

A warm smile shines out from the depths of Charlie's soul. "You just like to eat my cooking." He bends down and kisses my forehead. My heart is warm. I feel butterflies in my chest. I can't help it. I'm still in love with him after all these years.

After we settle at another table, the students bring our pastries. Charlie examines each plate.

"Nicely done," Charlie says with a smile. "It looks pretty, and the presentation is good. The pastries are fluffy. Puff pastries are hard to handle, and you hit this one out of the park! Very well executed!" Charlie is extremely happy with the attention to detail each plate displays. A pastry chef's job isn't just about cooking sweets, it is also about the presentation of the dessert. It has to look as good as it tastes.

We all sit with our pastries and a cup of coffee. I have hazelnut creamer in front of my plate. We all settle in for our meeting.

After eating our pastries and talking small talk about the students' achievements, I have to change the subject. I need them to understand why I wanted everyone to take time out of their precious day to attend. I'm still nervous. I have to begin.

"I know you all are busy, but we need to talk about something important." I stop and take a deep breath, then take another sip of my coffee in preparation.

Setting my cup carefully on the saucer next to my empty plate, I look up at the group before me. They are not just employees of the manor. They are, in a sense, my family. So why am I so nervous? Closing my eyes, I take a deep breath.

"Ever since the fire in the city school the other day," I gather my thoughts and begin again. "The fire has," I find myself pausing for a moment, "it has me really upset." I can see everyone completely understands my emotions as I pause to collect my thoughts once more.

"It's a crying shame," Alfred speaks in a broken voice. He is shaking his head while looking down at the table. "We saw it firsthand."

"Yes, it is," Antoinette says. I look at Antoinette and nod my head in agreement. It seems we all came to the same understanding that this is very tragic.

"I brought you here to talk to you about how I am feeling." I am feeling a bit more at ease speaking about how I feel and what I plan on doing, but I am still uneasy.

"Are you okay?" Antoinette asks.

"Not really, but I think I have a solution," I say.

"A solution? How?" Alfred asks because he doesn't see a problem for me to fix.

"Well, most of the school is still in operation, except the side where the gymnasium was," I inform them.

"It is April. Their prom and graduation are next month." My voice is filled with concern.

"So..." With a confused tone Alfred asks, "What do you need us to do?" He looks confused. I suppose I haven't gotten to my idea yet.

"I want to open our school to the public school and help them with their prom and graduation." I look at each one, in turn, to see how each of them reacts.

Alfred was a bit concerned for a moment. Then I see his face change. "Okay," Alfred gives approval.

"You know you need to sell this to the teachers over at the school," Antoinette says.

"Yeah, I know, but think about it," I say. "We are an art school. We can make this special for them by using our students' art and turning our gymnasium into something like an enchanted forest." I want them to see what I see. I know that is hard because I see the world very differently than most. It isn't black and white. I am able to see between the lines that are between the lines. This is my gift. I see detail. I want to bring joy to those children. They just went through a horrible tragedy, and I so badly want the people here to agree with me.

"It will be a huge undertaking." Alfred seems suddenly weighed down by the sheer number of kids in that school. The numbers are much larger than in the School of Art. "We already have our own prom and graduation to do."

"Yes, it will be. But, they have nowhere to have their prom, not to mention their graduation ceremony festivities. I think if we open our doors and help them, it may bridge the gap between the kids in the neighborhood." All of a sudden, their eyes open with enlightenment and fear.

Charlie smirks and winks in my direction. Even though my idea may be crazy, he believes in me.

"You know," Alfred starts, "Mary has a good point." He rubs his eyes. "It is going to be tough, but it may be good for the community. You know, to bring them together."

"I think it would be good." Antoinette agrees, though I can see she is still skeptical.

Alfred chuckles and looks up at the ceiling.

"What's so funny?" I ask.

"Oh, you know, Mildred would be so proud of you right now." The room lightens.

"Mildred? Really?"

"Yeah, Mildred." Alfred shakes his head. "She believed in you and now I can see why."

"Well, thank you, Alfred." I feel like I want to cry. I dream of living up to Mildred's expectations for me. Looking at everyone at the table, I ask, "So, do we all agree?"

"Absolutely," Antoinette votes.

"Honey, you know I support anything you do. I think it will be good for the community as well," Charlie says.

"Well, you know how I feel about it. Mildred would be proud of you. So yes, I'm for this," Alfred adds.

"Okay!" Renewed hope builds in me. I begin to bark orders like a cheerleader leading the team to victory. "So, Antoinette, can you please talk to the teachers to get them on board? I will go to the city school system to talk to the principal. We need to act fast to get this going. It will be the best prom they have ever seen."

My pep talk works. I felt the need to do something, and thanks to Lilly, I now know what that something is. I'm just happy they see it as I do. Now to get the rest of the community on board.

Seeing that it is just 10:30, it's a good time to head to the school to talk to the principal. Alfred volunteers to drive me, but this is something I need to do on my own. Millie is going to stay with Antoinette, as she normally does anyway.

The drive is somewhat surreal. Maybe I should have let Alfred drive me, if only to not be so alone. I know that he wanted to drive me like he usually does, and I suddenly feel all alone and want him with me. I have to pull myself together and do what I need to do.

Pulling into the school brings a rough sight: my old friend bruised, burned, and roped off like a crime scene. This is a hard sight, but it is the reason I am here. I take a moment to steady myself and head to the front doors.

Parking in the visitor parking area close to the school still feels weird for me. It's been years, and I know I'm not a student anymore, but it feels odd to be a visitor. Getting out of the car, I make sure my dress is hanging straight and I look professional, fixing myself in my reflection from the car window.

"Well, Here I go. Mildred?" I take a deep breath. I can't turn back now.

Walking up to the front door, I see this is not the same school I attended many years ago. They've changed things around. I reach for a door and tug it open, but it doesn't move. Locked. Why? I move to the next door handle; it is locked as well. I reach for another door. It too is locked. School is in session, but the doors are locked? Through the glass I notice a security guard walking closer. He meets me at the next door down.

"May I help you?" The security guard is young and wearing a regular uniform: white shirt, black pants, and badge all displayed properly. His badge states 'School Resource Officer.' What is that? I'm a bit confused. Maybe it's because of the fire?

"Yes sir," I say. "I would like to see the principal, please."

"And your name is?" He seems courteous and respectful.

"Mary Parker from the School of Art," I pause for him to

recollect, "the one next to the Museum of Art?"

"Yes ma'am." Oh, that term. I can't stand people calling me ma'am! "How can I help you?"

"I would like to speak to the principal about the fire," I state.

"What about the fire? Do you know anything?" His interest piques like an investigator.

I feel a bit unnerved. I don't want to talk to him. I want to talk to the principal.

"No, I don't. But I want to help." I feel like he doesn't want me to talk to the principal, so I ask again.

"May I speak to your principal?" This time my voice is a bit firmer.

"Follow me." He opens the door for me. The sight inside is extremely different from what I knew as a student. So much so that I know my face is showing dismay.

He leads me to an entryway that looks much like an airport security corridor. This was not here when I was a student. When we came to school, it was inviting and fun. This school looks cold, prison-like.

"Please step through here, ma'am." He directs me to walk through the metal detector. "And please, place your purse on the conveyor belt." I do as he asks. My purse disappears into an x-ray machine. It pops out the other side. I proceed into the security device.

"Is this really all necessary?"

"Ma'am, you have no idea." He reaches for my purse and hands it to me. "Did you go to school here? Or do you have a student here?" He is calming down, and that puts me at ease a bit.

"I went to school here," I say as I gain composure by putting my purse back on my shoulder.

"Oh, I recognize you." The officer gives a little smile. "You're the one they interviewed on live TV." His finger is wagging at me. Quite rude.

"Yes." I purse my lips, waiting for whatever he is going to throw at me.

"You really gave that reporter what she deserved." The officer breaks into a smile. "You went here?" he says as he looks down the hallway. I sense he, too, has fond memories of the old school, not this cold, prison-like building.

I peer around and see whatever remains of the school I knew. It is quite different now. The floors are dingy, and the walls are covered with posters advising against drugs and violence.

As we walk the hall, it feels strange. The halls feel smaller than I remember them. As a child, everything was grand. The people were giants. The school fit us. Now I feel like I'm in a different world. I live so close to that world and am yet disconnected from it and what these kids are really going through. I feel even more compelled to complete my mission.

"Right here, ma'am." The security officer points toward an office not far down the hall, marked with a sign.

"Thank you so much for your kindness." I smile to show my appreciation and enter the hallway.

"Oh, ma'am?" he stops me. "Thank you for being so nice to me." I can see that his heart is hurting. "I get so many parents and kids that treat me like I'm their enemy." He looks down at the floor. "I'm just here to keep them safe, you know?" He looks up. "I'm not the enemy just because I wear this uniform."

"I know." I smile. "Thank you for keeping the kids safe."

I continue down the hallway and turn at the sign reading "Principal." I enter and see a receptionist.

She moves her phone from her ear to her chest and looks up at me. "May I help you?" I feel as if I'm interrupting her.

"My name is Mary Parker. I'm from the School of Art. I would like to speak to your principal." I don't want her to think I'm a parent here to fight about my son or daughter doing something stupid. I actually need to talk to him.

She puts her call on hold and pushes another button to call the office right behind her. This seems lazy, but if this is how it's done, then so be it.

I hear a few utterances of "Uh-huh" and "Okay." Then she hangs up the phone. "You may enter." She instructs me to go into the room where the principal is. Again, I find this very unprofessional. He should have come out to meet me and then guided me to his office. Oh well, I guess I'm putting my expectations on their way of doing business.

The principal is sitting behind his desk. Without any instruction, I sit in the chair in front of his desk, feeling like I am a student being scolded. I don't care for this at all.

He shuffles this mountain of paperwork out of the way and looks up at me. "What may I do for you miss...?" He's trying to be cordial, but his manners seem a bit off.

"Mary Parker. My name is Mary Parker. I'm from the School of Art." It seems I'm more of a nuisance here than I'd wanted. It seems to take much too much effort to look up at me. He does so with reservation. Well, at least that is what his face is telling me.

"Yes, Ms. Parker. How may I help you?" His voice is quite condescending. He appears to have an authority complex, or is it just protectiveness of his school? I can't tell.

"I went to school here many years ago." I readjust myself. "I'm quite upset due to the fire."

"The fire?"

Now I'm questioning why I'm wasting my time here.

"Yes sir. I know that your school's prom and graduation are next month, and the part of the building where you hold these is terribly burned." I'm not sure if he can hear that yes, I'm educated, and yes, I care about my old school.

"Hm, yeah, that's a problem I have not yet thought through." He puts his head down knowing that he does indeed have an issue at hand. He takes off his glasses and rubs his forehead while attempting to think.

"I want to help."

"How can you help us?" He finally seems to see me as an equal and not some fly-by-night woman from the street.

"I want to offer my gymnasium for your prom and graduation." I sit up in my chair. "My students will do their art projects in correspondence with decorating for your prom. I was hoping for an enchanted forest or something along those lines." I try to sell my ideas once more.

"Hm, I had not decided how we were going to have a prom. I even thought of canceling it." He sits back in his chair and places his glasses firmly back on his face. He then notices that they are smudged. He removes them once more and cleans them with his dress shirt.

"Oh no, you can't cancel it!" My voice of disapproval is not met with an eager and open mind.

"So, let me get this right." Here comes the smart aleck once again. "You want my school to come to your school to have our prom and graduation with no strings?" Did he really say strings? What does that even mean? He puts his freshly cleaned glasses back on his face. Oh, those dang glasses are getting me upset. He is more concerned with them than he is with speaking to me.

"Why yes, is something wrong with that? I want to help the kids. They have gone through a rough time, seeing their school on fire."

He immediately stops me. "Rough time? These kids?" His anger builds with each word. "Some of them cheered as the flames billowed out the roof! They actually wanted the school to burn down!"

"I did notice that," I admit.

"So why would I reward them with a prom and graduation?" He asks a serious question, seemingly wondering why he even tries with the students.

"Not all students feel that way. What I witnessed standing by the fire was kids crying. The only place they felt safe was on fire. I felt the same. I grew up here and went to this school. My fondest memories come from this very school. It is for them that I'm reaching out to help give them the prom of their life and the graduation they deserve." My persistence and the reasons I provided somehow turn his attitude around. I think I finally have broken into his hard shell.

"I want to bring our community together, and I think this is the way to do it," I add, putting the icing on the cake.

"Together?" he says with an attitude. "If you look at these kids, they are dead inside."

Did he just say that?

"Wake up! Have you noticed the school is nothing like it was when you went here? We have metal detectors and security systems to keep out the gangs and drugs. Teen pregnancy is also rampant. The kids couldn't care less about what we are trying to do for them. They don't even want to be here. We are losing the war." His defeated demeanor is hard to bear.

"Yes, together! Somehow this community needs to heal. And I think this is the first step." One last-ditch effort, and then I'm leaving.

The principal sits back in his chair and rocks a few times, contemplating the possibility that this could be a good thing for the community. When he stops rocking, he appears defeated.

"Okay. Let's try to make this work."

I stand and reach out for a handshake. He stares at it for a moment, but then reaches out. I should have read the resistance, but I did not. Our hands meet and we shake in unison. A compromise or mission accomplished? It doesn't matter. It is time to get to work on making this event a memory these kids will keep forever. I must return back to Antoinette and Alfred so we can get started.

On the way out, I'm met by the same security guard.

"Well?" he questions.

"The prom and graduation will be held at my school, the School of Art," I say with a bounce in my step.

"Whew, I hope you know what you are getting yourself into," he says under his breath.

"It is just a school with a different name and different kids. Things will be just fine." I'm not sure if I'm assuring him or myself. I need to do this not only for me but for the community. What could go wrong?

CHAPTER 5

SINCE THE MEETING YESTERDAY, I can't contain myself I'm so excited. I need to check how the progress is coming on the prom. It is literally two weeks away, and the excitement is killing me.

"Have you seen Antoinette?" I ask one of the kitchen staff.

He shakes his head no. Mildred's advice floats through my mind: when asked a question, you should always be courteous enough to provide an answer. I'm much too excited and anxious to correct him, though. I move on to the next person in my path.

"Has anyone seen Antoinette?" I ask a group of servers.

Their answer seems to be all in unison and rehearsed. "No."

Just then Alfred comes walking around the corner near the kitchen. If anyone knows where Antoinette is, it's him.

"Have you seen Antoinette?" I ask for what seems to be the millionth time.

"I believe she is in the sunroom," he says graciously.

"Thank you so much," I say. Without missing a beat, I head to the sunroom.

As I enter, I run my fingers along the edge of the grand piano and look over toward the huge fireplace, and the portrait of Mildred hanging above the mantel. Antoinette is standing with her back to me, bending over a table set for what looks to be the command bunker of operation High School Prom. Antoinette is handing out pieces of paper and instructing students she has picked to work on projects. It seems a bit odd to have the students here in the manor, but I'm sure she has her reasons.

To my left, there is a white board with writing, arrows, and what seems to be chicken scratch on it. It is unclear if Antoinette is planning a prom or acting as captain to a football team. I'm sure Antoinette and the others understand what is on it, so I just take a seat next to her in an attempt to get in on the action.

To my right, Millie has a bunch of magazines all around her, as if she is searching for the perfect photo, whatever that may be. She has the kid safety scissors next to her. I know that Antoinette will keep her safe, so I don't dare disturb the artist at hand.

"Ah, Ms. Mary," Antoinette says with a smile. "I'm so glad you are here." She glances back at the few students in the room and then back to me.

Oh boy, what does that mean? Now I'm a bit nervous, but I'm open to what the plan is.

"Thank you, Antoinette. I'm really happy you have taken on the task of helping the students get organized to hold the prom for the other school."

"She has this all under control Ms. P.," one of the girls says in the back.

"She does?" A sense of relief fills me.

"Yes, she does. And this prom is going to be the coolest prom they will ever go to," says a young lady next to her.

"Cool, huh?" I'm glad to hear that. I was beginning to worry the kids from the other school will think we are putting on a snob prom just because the kids in our school pay to come here. Our school is for the cultured students. It enables them to hone their passion while also getting an education in all the other subjects. I know that most kids think that our kids must be rich to be here. To some degree, I guess they are, but I try to see all the kids as just kids.

Just then, one of the girls runs over and brings me a paper with a diagram for me.

"Look Ms. P.!" She is so excited she can hardly contain herself. She pushes the paper in my face. I almost get a papercut on my nose. Boy, that would be a bit weird.

I take the paper and examine the details. I see where the stage, drink station, and food station are. There are several squares on the paper to show how the tables are arranged, and then there is the dance floor. It looks great! She puts another paper in front of the one I'm looking at.

"Take a look at this one."

And so I do, attempting to match her enthusiasm. I stare at the diagram, trying to make heads or tails of what everything is. I see what looks to be paths but am not sure.

"Oh, goodness."

"See?" She points out different parts of the paper. "This is called the Enchanted Prom where everything is from the enchanted forest."

Everything looks amazing on paper, but I'm getting lost in how much work is still needed to get it all done.

I glance down once more at Millie. She is busy talking to herself and attempting to work the scissors right. But hey, she needs to learn.

"Do you like it Ms. P.?" she asks.

The children are working so hard and are asking if I like it each step of the way. I'm so pleased they are willing to open their hearts to the other students. I know there can be bad blood between the schools, each one thinking the other school is cooler than they are. I remember what that feels like, to be set apart from the cool kids. But are the other kids really cool? Or are the kids that go here the cool ones?

"Why yes, I surely do." I touch her arm gently to show my appreciation and approval. "This is going to be the coolest," I giggle, "the coolest prom ever!"

I turn to Antoinette with a bit of concern.

"Are you sure the students will be able to get this done in a couple of weeks? It sure is a lot of work." I have to ask because, quite frankly, I just can't see it being possible.

"Sure they will!" Antoinette exclaims. "I have the teachers forming teams in accordance with the artwork that needs to be completed." She smiles to assure me. "Everything will be perfect."

I nod, feeling a bit reassured. For now, I need to go back over to the city school to let them know how it is going and that we can be ready for them.

Going back to the school is still an eerie feeling. The caution tape is still up because of all the work going on. It doesn't look to me like they've accomplished much. Everything still resembles a crime scene, or at least, still feels like a crime scene to me.

Making my way to the front door, I'm met by the same security guard or resource officer as they would like them to be called. He is still dressed in his finest uniform, trying to look the part.

"Hello again," he says as he directs me to the only unlocked door. His voice is inviting.

"Hello to you as well." I smile. Realizing I must have sounded a bit snobbish, I quickly correct my grammar.

With my coat and purse already in hand, he rushes ahead to grab the door for me.

"Let me get that for you." Well, that is a change from how we met before. He is actually kind and not condescending.

"Thank you so much," I say as I walk through the entrance. Ugh, I forgot about that airline security zone that I have to traverse. I head to the table and the machine to check in.

I put my purse on the conveyor belt. Off it goes into the machine that x-rays all my personal belongings. I guess if it keeps them safe or makes them believe they are safer then I'm all for it. I head over to the metal detector.

"Ready for me to go through?" I ask, hoping my voice can stay as bright and cheery as I mean it to be.

"I sure am." The guard motions for me to walk through.

I do so. A sharp blast of alarms goes off and a big red light begins to flash. Startled, I stop dead in my tracks.

"What happened?" I ask the guard assisting me.

"Umm, do you have any weapons on you?" Immediately his demeanor changes into police mode instead of school resource officer.

"Good grief, no," I respond. As if I would actually have a weapon to begin with.

I am starting to notice more and more students coming out of their prospective classrooms. They are all checking out the alarm to see who has a weapon, like a pride of lions checking out their feeding grounds, waiting to pounce on their prey. Except *I'm* the prey. Even though my attention is on the mass of students, I still have to comply with the officer's requests.

"Can you please step over this way?" He directs me to another table next to the one that ate my purse. By this time, another security officer is coming right toward me. He looks a bit angrier than he did the first time I met him.

"Ma'am, can you please lift your arms up?" His voice is stern and very demanding.

"My arms? Umm, yes, I guess I can." I feel a bit nervous. I have never been in any kind of trouble before. Mildred taught me to mind my own business and do what I'm told. Because of this, I got really good grades and was never in trouble.

I lift my arms as instructed. Then my nicely tucked-in blouse is pulled right out and upward. I'm not sure if my stomach is showing, but the brush of wind sure makes it feel as if I'm on full display. Then it happens. His hands are on my body! He starts at my armpits. He begins pushing upward with his hands to ensure I have nothing in my arms.

The students are all gawking at the train wreck unfolding. Some are laughing, and some are in such shock that their mouths hang wide open. A couple of students are holding their phones, and it looks like I'm on camera. Oh, this is not going to be good. I can just see it, my face plastered all over the internet with the officer's hands all over my body. I'm not a student. I'm a grown woman being felt up by the security police. After the officer pushes upwards in my armpits checking for weapons, his hands move to the front of my arms, then down the back. I'm really not sure what I could be hiding in my blouse. The buttons on my blouse are stretched as far as they can hold. I feel them pop open the farther he reaches. The students seem entertained. I feel like a freak show.

As if that wasn't bad enough, the officer then runs his hands down both sides of my torso. Feeling a bit violated, I feel my face becoming far redder than it was a few moments prior. This is not how a person should be touched when I don't even know who this is.

I can't help but question him while he is feeling me up, or down, or whatever he is doing.

"Is this really necessary?" I ask with a wavering voice, obviously shaken a bit by the nonsense.

"Ma'am, when the alarms go off, I need to make sure you are not bringing anything into our school," he tries to reassure me. Let me tell you, I am not reassured by anything.

"Can you please turn around?" he asks, or demands, as I feel it. He puffs his chest out to show authority and that he was in control. It only makes me feel more uneasy.

"Um, yes sir." I turn around. Now I find myself facing my jury made up of children from this school. The kids are still staring. The officer's hands continue all over my body. Oh no! Stop that! I am feeling so embarrassed, and I can't stop it. My face flushes red. No place on my body is untouched. He feels all around my bra, pushing up and around. This is completely disrespectful. I feel a few more buttons pop open. Why am I here? Why is this happening? My bra is exposed to all the kids that were there for the show watching. I am the center of attention in this show. I want to scream, but I can't. How is this allowed? He is groping me!

I look over at the kids. Some have their mouths wide open in shock seeing me, an adult, being treated like this. I must have shown how distressed I was because then I saw the principal coming to my rescue.

"Officer Daniels," I hear a man yell down the hallway. I cannot see him because of all the kids standing around and laughing. "Officer Daniels, you can stop the inspection with her." My knight in shining armor has come to my rescue.

As he is making his way down to the security area, he motions to the students to get back into their classrooms. He does this by waving his arms in both directions like he is working on an airport runway. I don't hear his voice over the kids, but I'm sure he isn't sweetly instructing them to disperse.

"This is Mrs. Parker from the School of Art." As if that actually means anything to either officer. The one I met before knew me, but I think the other one, Officer Daniels, might be his boss. He sure didn't stop him from all the touching, groping, and asking questions, and he knew who I was.

"I'm sorry Ms. Parker. We can't be too careful with school violence and all," says the principal, attempting to explain all the commotion.

Grabbing my coat and my purse, I feel like I want to scream. I feel so violated. I don't realize just how many buttons are open until I look down. I try to close my blouse as fast as I can. Even though he is an officer, his hands were all over my body like I was a criminal. I'm so far from a criminal, he wouldn't know one if he saw one. I'm dressed appropriately. I act and speak appropriately. How could he even think that I'm going to do harm to this school? I'm here to help this school. I gather myself both physically and emotionally so I can get on with my visit. If I acted as I felt inside, it would not be pretty. I feel like I need to call the police to report a crime.

"Shall we?" The principal begins to lead the way to his office. He leaves the security area like this is a common event. He doesn't say "I'm sorry" or "stop that." He says nothing! No apologies, nothing!

I glance back at both security officers. I want their names for reference. It is not right to treat another professional as they just treated me. Trying not to be too noticeable, I glance at their badges. Ah yes, Daniels is the officer who violated me. Officer Harnette is the one that I met before. Harnette seems harmless now, but Officer Daniels is one to look out for. Making a mental note, I proceed down the hallway, feeling like I'm walking the hall of shame. The students have mostly dispersed, but I know they'll be whispering about me for weeks.

This day is quite different than the other day that I was here. Off to the right, I notice two young men still standing together and watching my every move. They do not appear to be doing anything wrong, but they look a bit rough around the edges. They look far too old for school here. They must have failed a few grades.

Groups of students are congregating, all trying to get a glimpse of who is in trouble. Each student stretches their neck to get a good look before heading back to class.

"Get to class!" the principal yells as we pass them. "Now!"

No one really cares. They all just stand there.

I look back at the two as we pass by. One boy rubs his nose in an odd way like he has a runny nose. He then gives me an evil look and squints his eyes. Then I see it: his hand looks like a gun. He is doing this to intimidate me or scare me. I guess it's just to get a reaction, but I find myself clutching my purse closer to my body. Why do I react that way? Do I really think or feel like they are going to rob me? His evil stare is what gets to me. I quickly break eye contact. I don't want him to see any type of fear. I lift my head up and keep on walking.

"I said get to class!" the principal yells once more. "Now!"

The two boys separate and leave the hallway, but not before the one boy turns around to get another look at me. We continue to the office.

After entering the office, I notice a young girl sitting in a chair in the reception office, waiting for the principal. He looks at her and I am in total shock at what happens next.

The principal points his finger at the girl and berates her right in front of me. She is dressed in all black, which feels fitting for this school.

"Why are you in my office again?" he asks in a stern voice. "I will deal with you after I talk to her." He points to me. He just called me "her"! I feel like he just put me on the same level as an unruly student that needs a talking to, a true lack of respect in all forms.

This is a different world. I'm not accustomed to such yelling, such disrespect of others. My school is open to suggestions, welcomes new ideas, helps others, and most of all, respects those around us. This school is just the opposite. I want to run, but I need help.

Sitting down in front of the principal, I suddenly feel as if I'm the one being disciplined.

"What did she do, if I may ask?" I have to know why she is being treated so roughly.

"She was smoking in the bathroom again," he says as he sits in his big leather chair. "This is the fourth time this week we've caught her skipping class to smoke." I can see his displeasure and hear the disappointment in his voice.

I look at him with unasked questions.

"I keep seeing these kids throw their lives away to drugs, smoking, sex, and gangs. It makes me so angry. I feel like I'm fighting a battle that just can't be..." and he stops midsentence. I think I have finally found the human side of him, but only for a moment.

I don't dare tell him that my school is much calmer, civilized even. What if he sends some of the violence to my school?

I change the subject. "I came to report that everything is on schedule for the prom. Everyone is working hard for it to be the best prom your students will ever attend." I'm gloating and I know I shouldn't be. I need to rein myself in.

"The best?" He laughs. I think I struck a nerve

"My students are working very hard on the design and props."

He stops me again. "Props? Design?" His face says it all. He thinks I'm wasting my time.

"Yes, it is the Enchanted Prom," I say with a small chip on my shoulder.

"Enchanted you say." Now he's mocking me.

I feel like a child being made fun of all over again like I was in school. After my internal combustion, I lift my head to regain my status. As I look up, I notice him shaking his head and holding back his laughter. Am I in over my head? I'm beginning to understand why his students have such horrible attitudes. Their principal has the worst attitude of all, and it's reinforcing their bad behavior. I see nothing positive, no positive role models. I need to keep my cool. Oh, this is harder than I could have ever imagined.

"Yes, enchanted," I remind him once again. "Why? Do you have another idea?" If he has any input, I'd like to hear it now.

"Do you have any idea what you're getting into?" His questions are condescending. "We don't have anything like an Enchanted Forest or whatever you want to call it. We just have music and tables with chairs. We supply punch and maybe cookies. We don't put much work into it because it always seems to be broken afterward. It's a true waste of time if you ask me. So, are you really up for this?"

"Yes." However, I'm beginning to question what I'm really getting involved in. "Why do you ask?" I feel like a fish out of water. I just don't understand how my beautiful school could turn so, oh, I can't say it, bad, trashed, hopeless. Well, I asked for it.

"Have you looked around? Do you not understand the caliber of students in this school?" He looks at me like I'm stupid.

An angry warmth grows deep in my stomach and climbs to the back of my throat. Trying to fight the urge to scream, I collect myself to respond. "I do."

"When was the last time you watched TV? Do you watch the news? Do you even live in this neighborhood?" The look on his face makes me want to hit him. He looks so much like my own school bullies, Susan and Angel.

It takes conscious effort, but I wrangle my frustration. "Yes, I do, Mr.," I glance down at the pretty, shiny plaque on his desk, "Mr. Johnson." I stiffen. "I went to school here, then on to college, then I moved back to Chicago where I took over the School of Art and the Museum of Art." I run down my credentials to combat his arrogance. Why am I explaining myself to this jerk? He doesn't deserve my explanation. Oh wait, I'm feeling the same thing the students here feel: ungrateful.

He sits up a little taller. I think he understands I'm not backing down.

"I felt bad about the fire. The kids need a place for their prom, and I wanted to help. Now if you do not want my help, then..." I'm tired of dealing with this man.

His face softens.

"I'm just saying," his demeanor is more somber, "the kids here are usually from broken homes, behind in their education, and struggling in everything, both life and school." He calmly explains his point. "They come from gangs and violence, and are often drugged up, you know? They're dangerous for," he stops, afraid to finish, "dangerous for your kind of school."

"My kind of school?" I understand what he means because of what I just went through, but it still rubs me the wrong way. "I know the school is broken, just as the kids." I look into his eyes with empathy. "Isn't that why they deserve the best prom that I can provide for them at my school?"

He looks defeated. He is not used to being wrong. He smiles.

"I plan on giving them what they deserve. I'm also having my students do projects to earn credits while helping your students." I think I'm getting the upper hand in this conversation. However, my stomach is killing me. I feel like I'm going to throw up. I fight through it anyway. "So, do you have any other ideas?"

"No, I think your ideas sound good. I just hope you're able to keep things under control. Do you need security?"

"Security?" I ask, thinking of the security I just went through where the officer subjects kids to pat downs.

"Yes, security. You know, metal detectors, officers."

My sinking feeling now feels like I'm on the Titanic with a slow, eminent drowning approaching. What should I say? If he thinks I really need security, do I? Attempting not to show just how rattled I'm, I cautiously rise to my feet. It pains me to think of groping students as they walk into the prom.

"I will get back to you on that." I pick up my purse and jacket and head to the doorway. "I must get back to finalize details." As I'm heading out the door, I realize that I did not properly thank him. I pause and turn back. "Thank you for your time."

While walking out of the school, I'm more cautious of my surroundings. How can these children feel this way every day in school? Being in a state of fear or constant hyper-preparation is not a good learning environment. With each passing hallway, I glance down to see if oncoming traffic or danger is coming. Once back at security, I find only Officer Harnette.

"Can I ask you a question?" I stop.

"Sure, you can." He is very polite this time.

"Is this school always on high alert?" I'm afraid to ask, but if anyone knows, it will be him.

"Unfortunately, yes. Since school shootings, drug busts, and gang related crime rates have been rising, we need to be on our toes. We never really know what each day will bring. I can't tell you everything, but some days, I don't know how these kids come to school. I'm glad they can come, though, since some come just to get out of their own homes. I see it. I see everything." There's a sadness to his voice. I understand that. I feel it, too.

I set my purse and coat down so I can listen to him. I feel a sadness in his words.

"These kids are important to me. I'm here to protect them. That's why when the alarms go off, our team goes into action."

"Yeah … about that," I have to interrupt him.

He meets my eyes. He knows what I'm going to say.

"Never mind. I understand." I want to tell him so badly that I felt violated. The other officer had no right to put his hands all over my body. I'm not a criminal. I can't help it if my watch sets off the alarm.

"I'm sorry about that. He is my boss. I wanted to tell him who you were, but I couldn't show him that I was backing down from an alarm. I need to be on full alert at all times." He tries to explain himself to me, and I really do understand. His job was on the line. I get it.

"It's okay. Things are very different at my school," I say. "I can hardly believe how different things are from back when I was a student here."

"Times sure are a-changing," he says with an ironic chuckle.

"They sure are," I say as I grab my belongings and head out the only open door. That seems like a fire hazard, but if it is the only way to keep the kids safe, then so be it.

CHAPTER 6

BEFORE I KNOW IT, THE BIG DAY IS HERE. Operation Enchanted Prom is in full swing.

I want to make sure everything is perfect, so I head to the gym to check everything out. Immediately after I open the door, I feel as though I have stepped into a different world.

The door opens to a moss-covered brick walkway. In the dim lighting, I see what appears to be a lush forest. It appears to be right out of a fairy tale. I know the normal gym floor has been covered to protect it, but you can't tell through all the beautiful props.

The brick walkway leads to an arch made of cardboard and paper-mâché, also painted to look authentic, like it has been there for many years. Through the arch, the scene opens up to a grand, forest-like ballroom. My students have really stepped up to the plate when I needed them to.

Trees on each side of the ballroom are in full bloom. Moss hangs haphazardly from each branch, giving the enchanted forest it's signature, magical feel. The lighting from the drama department makes the forest feel mysterious and eerie, and as I look closer at the props, I notice little animals between the trees. Their bodies are put together, so they appear almost to true form. It is like fairy-tail visions of grandeur. The birds are tropical and brightly colored, and I hear a couple of speakers playing forest sounds with animals in the background. The fog machine puts the icing on the cake. I know I'm looking at props, cardboard, and paint, but my mind is tricked into believing the forest is real, complete with all its mystical creatures.

The ballroom has spaces for students to sit on the sidelines or dance in the middle. The stage is flashing in blues and greens with moss draped off the stage and all the props. The DJ is getting ready behind the makeshift stone wall, also made of cardboard, hiding his audio equipment. He has set his lights to match the music blaring from the bank of speakers, and he seems well prepared to take the room to a new realm of dance and energy.

The whole thing is magical. My prom days were nothing like this. Seeing the set up, I know this event *will* be perfect for the other school. They deserve it.

I make my way off the dancefloor and toward the seating, where white oversized tablecloths give an illusion of furniture covered for years just begging to be seen again. The centerpieces on the tables are tall glass vases with vines and moss-like plants draping down across the table. Brightly colored flowers mix perfectly with the deep greens and mosses, and the tables are fully set with actual place settings to give a sense of elegance for the kids.

The culinary department has set up a buffet of food. The kids can go through the line and choose exactly what they want: salad, entre, and side dishes all made to perfection. The food table is also decorated with flowers and moss. It is so incredible seeing my students stand behind the food table in black pants and white shirts, prepared to serve the other kids without any reservation. The drink table is set up in the same manner. They have a choice of punch, water, or lemonade. Two more of my students man the drink area, refilling ice and drinks. It looks catered, but I know my students learned how to serve the food specifically for the prom. The fact that it gave them a way to earn grades was a bonus.

We're all set. I'm feeling good with my decision to help the other school. This gives my students a real opportunity to cook, decorate, and display their work. Their effort made this all possible, and I can see their pride emulating at each turn.

Taking one last glance around the enchanted forest, I take a deep breath. Oh, I'm so nervous. But why? This is absolutely perfect. I give the okay to open the doors. Oh Mildred, am I really ready for this? *I wish you were here.* Here we go.

Seeing the children's eyes light up as they walk into the room is priceless. A feeling of calm emulates from within me. I know this was a lot of money for our school to invest, but it's all worth it when I see their mouths drop open in awe. Girls in gowns and guys in tuxes make this a picturesque moment never to be forgotten. I feel like a cruise director sending the students to the food stations, drink stations, and some to the photo section so they can get their pictures taken with their dates. Electric energy fills the air, music pounding with each beat. Students keep coming and coming. I didn't realize just how big the school really was. I know we're fine with the capacity of the gymnasium, but it's still overwhelming. Soon the room is so full of dancing teens that I can't see the opposite side.

The teachers, Alfred, and Antoinette have this under control. I need to step back and allow my students to shine while the students from the city school enjoy their special evening. I retreat to the manor. After all, the music isn't something I'm used to.

A couple hours pass, and I think I may have been asleep on the couch. A burst of energy flings the door open and screams my name.

"Mrs. P. Quick, we need you!" It takes a moment for my startled brain to put two and two together, but I recognize her from the drama department.

"What? What's wrong?"

"Please come back to the gym, Alfred needs you." She grabs my arm and starts pulling me toward the door.

"Alfred?"

We run the short distance to the gym to see what's happening. Loud yelling turns to screaming, and horror fills my stomach.

I open the door behind the DJ and take it all in. The gym has broken out into a riot. Girls in ballgowns are crying with blackened faces that were once made up to perfection, makeup streaming down their faces. Their mascara smears as they wipe their faces. Food, decorations, hairpieces, everything you could think of is flying in the room. Even the beautiful glass centerpieces are smashed onto the floor. With each turn of my head, my stomach feels closer to my throat. With each step I take, glass crunches under my shoes.

In the chaos, I notice a girl in platform shoes and a mini dress completely inappropriate for a high school prom. She is holding a streamer torn from a prop, waving it in the air like she's dancing at Woodstock, oddly content in her own little world. If I'm not mistaken, she looks a bit high, but who am I to judge? There is too much going on for me to focus on one young lady. I grab the streamer out of her hand, and she stops mid bounce.

"Hey. That's mine," she says with a giggle. She is *definitely* in her own world.

"Young lady, you need to leave," I say very quietly but sternly, attempting to be diplomatic while poking her in the chest with my fingernail. She doesn't care what I say. Instead, she picks up another piece of streamer and continues twirling around. She trips in her platform shoes, and I want to laugh, but I do not dare. Nothing fazes her. She just gets back up, giggles, and continues her solitary dance.

Behind me, I hear a crash that forces me to turn back to the DJ table. Two girls are pushing each other and pulling each other's hair. The walls around the DJ booth soon fall, exposing his equipment to the mayhem. His face turns a horrible shade of white while he watches his equipment fall. Somehow the music is still playing.

Someone is able to turn the main lights on. With the situation lit up, I'm in shock at the disaster in front of me. All my kids' hard work is trashed. I run back to the DJ booth and find the plug feeding the horrible, thumping speakers. Without taking a moment, I yank the plug out of the wall the music stops abruptly. Now I'm in control, or so I think.

"Stop this right now!" My voice strains to yell over the unruly mob. I try again, "I said STOP!" This time a couple of kids take the time to look at me.

Our students that once appeared to be professional servers

are all in tears. Their pristine, white button-down shirts are painted pink from the punch. I see one young lady trying to salvage some of the food, but it is no use.

I look past the mob to find Alfred in the middle of several guys. A few have pulled their bow ties off and unbuttoned their shirts, exposing their childlike bare chests, acting like drug lords or gangsters. They have their hands on their hips. Panic grips me as I remember those metal detectors at the school. Did any of them bring a weapon? They could have hidden them under their tuxedo coats.

Before I can do anything more, police rush in, fully dressed in riot gear. I shake my head. This is a sight for the city school system, not here.

I have to stop something before it begins. I run to Alfred's side because I am afraid for him. This type of behavior is not tolerated in our school. The closer I get to Alfred, the more I understand the severity of the situation. If they have guns, this could become a mass school shooting. Worse, it would be at *MY* school.

"Come over here and say that!" a young man says as he puffs up his chest toward Alfred.

"It is time for you to leave. This was a nice prom until you and your friends decided to disrespect that young lady over there." Alfred points over to a group of young ladies who were dressed to the nines. Now their dresses are torn, hair is down, but they are still trying to look tough, standing in a gang-like semi-circle. They are huddled around one girl in particular. It looks like they are protecting one of their own, one of their pack.

The boys continue to taunt Alfred. I can see it in Alfred's face: he wants to strike.

"Whatcha goin' to do 'bout it old man?" The boy pushes Alfred in the chest. Alfred stands his ground, his hands firmly on his hips in an attempt to keep from hitting the young boy. I have never seen Alfred like this.

"I said it is time for you to leave." Somehow, Alfred stays calm so as not to set the boys off any more than they already are. His hands are still on his sides but kept close by for emergencies.

Alfred appears calm, even though he seems to be struggling with his composure. It seems to be taking every ounce of energy for him not to engage with their childish antics. I am so proud of Alfred because he understands the childish nature of the kids and does not react inappropriately.

"Whatcha gunna to do 'bout it ni....?" Oh, this was the wrong thing to say to Alfred. Alfred is pushed to the edge of his nerves. This just went way past dangerous.

Thankfully, the police get between them and begin manhandling the boys out of the gym. One by one, they are taken out and put into police cars. How could this have gone so wrong?

I've never seen Alfred singled out for being black. I actually forgot he was black. Or better yet, I never really saw him as being black, to begin with. He's my dearest friend. The kid was taunting him to react to the slur. Alfred did not react. He kept his cool and attempted to de-escalate the situation. I saw Alfred's face become distorted forcing the emotions deep within his body. Now that the danger has been resolved, I move to his side. His bottom lip quivers and his eyes burn in anger. His body is tense. The pressure cooker is about to blow. The police presence seems to bring him back to earth. With the dangerous situation under control, I ask what happened. I need to hear what Alfred has to say.

"Alfred," I pause, waiting for his attention. "What happened?" My voice is very stern and demanding. "What on earth?" I force him to look around the gym with me. He is still on high alert, much like a soldier.

"Mrs. Mary," his head goes down, and his eyes are visibly hurt. His breathing is very fast for a man of his age. He appears beaten up internally. He tries to speak once again. "That young lady," he points to the group of young ladies, "is pregnant."

I follow his hand. Her face is black from mascara, just like the other girls I saw at the first entrance. Her hair is no longer up on her head in curls held in place by hairspray but down in sections, hanging on by bobby pins. She appears much like an assault victim. The other girls don't look much better.

"She is pregnant by one of those," he cuts himself off, clearly wanting to say something against to his nature. Instead, he bites his lip. "She came with another young man that is obviously not the father. When they saw each other," Alfred shook his head in unbelief, "let me tell you, Mrs. Mary, it was on!"

"Oh no," I say, trying to imagine the moments before the fight.

"Two boys, the father of her baby and her date, began fighting. One of them saw her with the other guy. He pushed her and that started the fistfight. I tried to step in when she got pushed, trying to protect her. She began fighting, too. Next thing I noticed was that she had a bloody nose, and then everything broke loose. Their friends starting fighting and then their girlfriends started swinging and pulling hair, and before I knew it, everyone was fighting each other. I don't think they realize why they started fighting to begin with." Alfred rubs his head again, trying to figure out just how it got so bad so fast.

I'm speechless. Unsure what else to do, I place a gentle hand on his arm.

"Mary, I really tried to stop it all," he says with a defeated voice. "I really did. I think they might be in two rival gangs."

As the kids are being escorted out by the police, the rest of the lights are being turned back on. The damage is unimaginable. All the hard work that our kids did for them is smashed, torn apart, and stomped on. It looked like a war zone. Our Enchanted Prom turned out to be the Prom from Hell.

The DJ attempts to put his equipment back into cases but is slowed by the tears streaming from his eyes. A lot of his equipment is broken beyond repair. Food from the tables covers the floor and the walls. How did that happen, a food fight? I can only think of the hard work the kids did learning new food dishes and plating them just right for their grades.

The floor is slippery from the punch bowl being knocked over. The glass vases are in millions of pieces. It looks like everything was just trashed and thrown across the gym floor. The beautifully decorated cupcakes are smeared all over the place. The nicely painted decor is now stained a bright red color from the punch.

In the midst of everything, I see Principal Johnson with his hands on his hips shaking his head in disbelief. Or is this exactly what he expected? Our eyes meet, and it's almost like he is begging for forgiveness. We both know this behavior is unforgivable.

Then, Principal Johnson mouths across the room, "Metal detectors." Anger fills me. How could he still have such an "I told you so" attitude? And after what I'd seen at his school, how could I not have listened?

I look around the gym again, trying to figure out if any of it is salvageable. It's not. Some of our kids have begun cleaning up the wreckage, but the weight of this lands on them, too. One picks up a tree branch, looks at it, and bursts into tears. Cleanup is going to take several hours, even if we band together.

Principal Johnson is still standing in the doorway. He doesn't offer to help. I'm pretty sure he needs to go down to the police station and notify the students' parents. Honestly, I don't want to see him. After all, he did ask me if I wanted security. I just want to hide and lick my wounds. I'm sure my students feel the same.

CHAPTER 7

THE PEACE OF THE MORNING is a welcome shift from the chaos of the night. I know my students are still noticeably upset, and rightfully so. I am so happy the police were able to react so quickly and handle the students that were making such a problem for Alfred. They put in a lot of effort to make it beautiful. And then there was Alfred. I will need to check on him today.

It takes a bit to find him, but eventually, I do. He is sitting in the gym taking note of all the damage from the night before. All the decorations are gone and in the trash as if they never existed. The janitor is sweeping the floor, and slowly, it is beginning to resemble a gym once more.

I take a seat calmly beside Alfred. I think we both feel a bit like wounded dogs that lost a champion fight.

After a few moments, I put my arm around Alfred. I feel his body relax. His eyes lift.

"You know, Mrs. Mary," he pauses as he glances up to the right, then down at me, "you know, Mildred would have been proud of this." He motions around the gym.

"I sure made a huge mistake, didn't I?" I hang my head in shame.

"No, actually you didn't," he says as he turns to look into my face.

"How could you even say that? This was a complete disaster! My great idea turned into a complete riot." I feel horrible.

"You have a heart like none other." His smile resonates from his otherwise somber face.

"But," I want him to stop. This is all my fault.

"No buts. You opened your heart, and you opened the doors of the school to another school in need. Those students are very different from ours here," he reminds me.

"I noticed that while I was at the school talking to the principal. I was worried I couldn't pull it off."

"You pulled it off, and the kids pulled it off beautifully." He nods decisively. He, at least, is convinced I did the right thing and did it well. "Mildred would still be proud of you for trying to make a difference."

"You keep saying that." I can't believe him as I scan the gymnasium, seeing the damage burned into my memory even though it's mostly clean by now.

"I'm sure that some of the kids appreciated it beyond what you know, but then a few of them had to ruin it for the entire school." Alfred sounds sad again.

"I really tried." Tears threaten me again. I feel so defeated.

"In this day and age, things are different than we remember them. Gangs and street violence are in the news every night. We are so fortunate to have the kids we have in our school. Not that I'm saying that the drugs, gangs, and violence are only at that school." He stops to gather his thoughts. "I'm not saying that at all."

I give more attention to the conversation.

"Those kids are faced with violence every day, not only on the streets, or at home, but also in their school where they are supposed to feel safe." Now Alfred is saying everything I'm feeling. "Just for a moment, they were given the gift of safety, visions of splendor, and the chance to be just kids again."

This is exactly why I wanted to give the kids a night to remember. Now it's a Saturday that will never be forgotten.

"With all said and done, the school didn't take any damage. The DJ should be paid by the principal from the other school since it was his students that smashed his system." Alfred looks to see if I agree, but he seems satisfied.

"I agree." I find myself remembering just how distraught the

DJ looked as his equipment was being smashed.

"All we lost were a lot of cardboard props, some food, and dishes." He smiles. "That is not a financial loss for you, but it is an emotional loss for our students."

"I know." I can't help but put my head down in sorrow. "I'm giving each of them an A for their talented work, but I know that isn't enough and I don't know what else to do."

"I'm sure you will come up with something." That grand Alfred smile comes to light up the room once more. "You always do, kid."

Alfred gets up slowly and proceeds to the doors. I stop him.

"Alfred?"

He turns, and I take a moment to look at Alfred's features. He stands with a slump, and it seems that today his hunch is a bit more pronounced.

"I'm so sorry about them treating you differently," I add cautiously.

"Different?"

"Yeah, the racial stuff." It feels strange talking about race with him. I just didn't see him in that way and haven't noticed our differences in years.

"Mrs. Mary, that stuff just doesn't bother me anymore. I understand it's a way they talk to each other or try to start a fight." He pauses, "I will admit, it was mighty tough standing my ground when those thugs came at me. I felt like I needed to fight back to defend my heritage. But I don't know why they were acting like that, being black as well. I hope they will learn to respect each other and lift up their black heritage instead of putting others down."

"I'm glad you didn't react," I say.

He chuckles. "I'm too old for that nonsense." He turns to leave the room once again.

I look around the room and shake my head. "I tried Mildred," I whisper. Wallowing in self-pity won't do much good, so I leave to get some lunch.

While eating in the sunroom, Antoinette and Alfred both

grace my presence once more.

"Mrs. Mary, I got a phone call this morning from the police department," Antoinette says.

"I thought everything was taken care of last night. Why on earth are they calling me?" I say.

"Oh, no one told you." Antoinette fidgets with her skirt. She is a bit sheepish and seems not to want to divulge the information, but it is important for me to know.

"What happened?"

"Seems we had some vandalizing last night after all," Antoinette informs me.

"Vandalizing? Where?" Nothing is out of place at the manor that I know of. Alfred did not let me know of any wrongdoings, but last night was rough and I guess this is to be expected.

"It's better if I show you." She leads the way to the side of the gymnasium. This gymnasium is quite large and all painted white, or, used to be painted white.

Alfred points to the wall. It is covered with spray paint, all colors imaginable.

"Oh heavens." The prom from hell just doesn't seem to end. "I have the police on the way," Alfred says.

I sigh, "Again?"

Antoinette just rolls her eyes and goes back into the manor, not wanting to be involved.

Examining the vandalism, I can't help but notice the artwork in the crime. It's actually quite nice. Out of habit, I check the lower right corner and smile. Mildred taught me that no matter what kind of art I did, I had to put my mark on it to prove ownership. Our vandal did the same.

The police arrive around the corner of the building. If I'm not mistaken, I think a few of the officers were here last night.

They examine the graffiti, talk quietly together, and then one of the officers comes over to where we are standing.

"Is this your building Miss?"

"Yes, it is." Then I add, "It's the back of the gymnasium for the School of Art."

"Well, I have seen this before." And the officer points to the right-hand corner.

"You know who this is? You know who did this?" I ask.

The officer drops his head, and with a feigned heavy heart, he says, "Yes ma'am. He just got out of jail from your little party last night." The officer has a condescending demeanor.

"My party?" I give him a little attitude back. "It was the prom for the other school since their school burnt down! It was not a party!"

"Yeah, okay." He flips his notebook closed as he smirks.

"I will bring him by with a can of paint so he can repaint the wall." He and his partner disappear back around the corner, I'm assuming to their police car.

I look to Alfred in dismay. At least they are taking care of it.

The officers are long gone, but for some reason, I can't get myself to leave the vandalism. I take a step back from the wall so I can get a better look.

"Are you okay Mrs. Mary?" Alfred asks with great concern.

My gaze at the wall is turning into somewhat of a trance. Even with Alfred talking to me, I just can't turn away. The wall holds my attention. "Mrs. Mary?" Alfred asks once more.

"Oh goodness, I'm sorry, Alfred." I find myself apologizing for ignoring his questions. "Yes, I am."

Alfred turns to go into the manor, sees I'm not following, and asks, "Mrs. Mary, are you coming?"

My eyes follow each line as it changes color, blending to perfection. The paint is meticulously placed for shading and contrast to form depth in the picture. As I step back even further, I see the forms taking shape. I'm in complete awe of the sheer magnitude of the piece. How on earth did he get the paint so high up the wall? How long did this take? After looking at the details, I notice that the picture he spray-painted is a mural of a street corner, but it doesn't keep scale, which is why it was hard to decipher. The longer I look, the more I'm certain I know what it is. It is a street corner downtown. I recognize the shops, awnings, doorways, even the bricks. Such detail, but it seems as if I'm the only one who really sees it. Everyone else sees paint sprayed on a pristine white wall with no rhyme or reason, just vandalism. Oh no, not to me. This is art in its rawest form.

I can't help but look down in the corner to see if the mark is there. You know the one. The mark that an artist puts to show that this work belongs to the artist and no one else. I look everywhere and I can't find it. Oh wait, there it is! Next to a doorway near the flowerpot is the distinctive mark of the artist, like mine. I look at the signature again. This mark isn't a name. That would be far too obvious and probably too dangerous for this artist. This art is, at its nature, illegal, so it makes sense he wouldn't put his full name like I do. This mark is very subtle, inconspicuous, almost secretive. I see it, and the police officers noticed it, too.

Alfred is still there, watching me. I need to answer him.

"I'm mesmerized by this." I gaze over the piece in its entirety again before I can find the words to finish. "This," I take a slow breath, "artwork." There, I said it. I did not see this as vandalism at all. "You know perception is reality only to the perceiver."

I know what I mean, but I think Alfred is a bit taken aback by my statement. However, after a few moments, Alfred completely understands my vision and my response to this vandalism. He knows that Mildred taught me not only to see what is in front of me but to "look between the lines" as they say. My drawings are done in great detail, but not on a grand scale like this. I appreciate it. .

Alfred and I go back into the manor to wait for the police to return. It's not long before we return to the crime scene. The police return with a young man in tow. He seems to be about fifteen or so. His head hangs low, and his arms are secured behind his back by metal handcuffs. So young to be in this type of trouble.

The other officer comes around the corner with two more kids that appear the same. However, one of the teen boys is not ashamed at all. He has a smug look on his face. He becomes quite combative when he sees us all standing by the vandalism. The officer grabs his arm and pulls him close.

"Boy, straighten up." He gives a stern order while shaking his arm.

All I can remember is the day my own mother grabbed me like that and shook me in front of all of those people in the park. I was crying so loud and hard. She was embarrassed of my actions. I only wanted to talk to the Bird Lady, but she did not want anything of the sort. She shook me so hard that I felt every word reverberate through my bones. She meant business. Much like this officer.

I can't keep my mouth shut. Oh, I wish I could, but I can't.

"Officer, is this really necessary?" I ask while walking over to the young boy.

"Ma'am, he did a crime, and he is here to clean it up," the officer says as if he is taking out the daily trash. This is not a young teen in his eyes. This young man is tomorrow's criminal. He begins to turn him around to gain access to the shackles. This forces the young man to face me.

"Son, what is your name?" I ask.

The young boy just looks at me, unsure if he should speak or not. After all, the officer still has his arms tied by the metal handcuffs. The officer once again shakes his arms from behind. This upsets me, but I don't show it.

"Bud, you speak when spoken to," the officer demands. "Now tell her your name."

The young boy is obviously embarrassed now.

"Luke," he says under his breath.

The officer shakes him once more. "Tell her your name boy."

The young boy looks up at me with childlike eyes, "Luke Peterson."

"Luke Peterson what?" the officer prods for him to finish.

I'm a bit taken back by the treatment that the officer is giving him, but I'm seeing results, so I leave it be.

"Luke Peterson, ma'am," he responds.

"Better," the officer says, and the metal bracelets come off.

"Well Mr. Peterson, I see that you painted my wall along with the other gentlemen here," I mention as I wave my hand around to the other youngsters before us.

"Yes, but..." Once again, the officer grabs his arm and gives him a little shake into submission.

"Yes sir?" I ask.

"I only helped with the ladder." The young boy almost looks upset that it is not his creation we all were admiring in silence.

"The ladder?" I question.

"Yes, ma'am." And he points over to the ladder in the bushes.

I hear a deep quick sigh from Alfred. "Mrs. Mary, that is my ladder. I was cleaning the gutters and must have left it out here."

"Alfred, this is not your fault, but thank you for letting me know." I wait for Luke to fill in the blanks.

I quickly turn back to Luke for more explanation.

"Umm..." the young child is now refusing to answer. The officer, who is still holding his arm, shakes him once more.

"When you are asked a question, you must answer," he demands.

"Ma'am, I only held the ladder while he sprayed the wall." Luke is now pointing to the first boy that arrived with the other officer. He just ratted him out. Yeah, this is not something that is highly looked upon when dealing with street kids. But now I have to ask him why he did this.

While turning to talk to the other young man, I notice that the third officer arriving on the scene is bringing paint cans, rollers, and tarps. This enables me to speak to the child.

"So, what is your name?" I ask.

"A.P.," he responds.

"No son, your real name, not your street name," I demand.

Acting as if I'm making him give up a secret, he looks at me as if to plead me not to ask once more.

"It's A.P., ma'am," he insists.

The officer walks over and grabs his arm as well. "Your name."

His face turns white. "It's..." and he is afraid to finish.

"What is your name young man?" I ask.

"It's Avery Pollics." His eyes are glued to the grass.

The other two boys burst out in laughter.

"His name is Aaa-Vreee!"

The laughter is annoying and quite uncalled for.

"Luke, how is that funny?" I ask.

Between the laughter he answers, "No one has ever heard his name before. Aaa-Vreee." And the chuckles continue. "We all just call him A.P., not Aaa-Vreee."

"How is that funny?" I ask again.

"Um, it just sounds funny," he says, trying to make me understand.

"Well, Luke, I don't think it's funny at all." I turn to the third young man. "And you?"

"Christian, or Chris Gill." He wants to make sure that his response is not made fun of. Chris seems to understand the severity of the situation.

I think I have them figured out. Luke is the troublemaker whereas Chris is a follower trying to fit in. Chris keeps looking toward Luke as if looking for directions for how to act. Someday, him following Luke's direction is going to cost him a great deal. Much like today, he is acting all tough but only when Luke is throwing cues to be so. Chris kid could be a good kid if he has someone else to follow, a positive role model.

Now Avery, on the other hand, is quite different. He appears to be the oldest of the three. He is the real leader. He leads in a quiet, reserved way, and I don't think he means any harm. But, if Luke held the ladder, what other rolls did Chris and Avery play in this criminal act?

"So, I'm curious." I see all the young men now standing side-by-side as instructed by the officer. "Who did what here?"

Luke is quick to answer. "I held the ladder, as I said."

"And?" I prod for answers.

"Well," Chris begins to speak. "I did help with the paints, but," he stops mid-sentence, and his eyes dart to Avery, silently apologizing. "A.P., I mean, Avery, did most of the painting."

Avery's body shrinks with a deep breath outward. He is caught red handed. No way to get out of this.

I turn to the wall and point out the mark next to the corner on the spray painting.

"So, this is your mark?" I ask Avery.

His eyes lift as if asking how I know what a mark was.

His demeanor is quiet but firm. He really doesn't want to speak, but the officer will probably shake him again. "Yes ma'am."

I give a little smile of approval, hoping the officers don't notice.

I have to control my excitement. "Did you come up with the idea?" I ask Avery.

"Well, kinda," he says under his breath.

"Kinda?" I ask.

"It's our street corner." He doesn't really want to confess this, but I know this corner.

Just then, one of the officers with the paint rollers pushes the roller at his chest and says with a stern voice, "Get to work!" He commands the three kids to paint over the crime scene.

There is distinct disappointment on Avery's face as he is told to erase his masterpiece. His eyes lift to meet mine as if begging me to stop them, but I can't stop it. What they did was vandalism, and against the law.

With each stroke of the paint roller, the mural disappears. The thoughtfulness of the artistry being erased from the once again white wall, until all that is left is the bottom corner.

Avery, painting that corner, gets to his mark and stops. The roller just can't go any further. It is as if someone is holding the roller and keeping it from going over his mark. The more he tries to paint over it, the more the opposing forces are stopping it. He turns to me, and tears are rolling down his face. He is destroying the one thing left of him, I mean the artwork, his artwork. I can feel the pain throbbing through his veins. It would have killed me to take my mark off my works of art. It is hurting him so badly that the young teen is actually crying.

"Look Aaa-vreeee is crying like a ba-bee!" Luke yells.

Avery wipes the tears from his face with his sleeve. "I got paint splattered in my eyes." He tries to cover it up, but I know better.

Then it happens. The mark of a masterpiece is just a memory, erased. It is replaced with the bland white, just as if it never was there to begin with.

With the wall painted white again, the young men are all instructed to apologize to me and Alfred. Alfred stands there with his arms folded throughout the entire paint job. He knows that the boys were being reprimanded. He has to stay out of the jobs of the police officers. Avery is the last boy to apologize to me. He looks into my eyes, and I see something amazing. He is truly sorry. His words are meaningful and honest, unlike the apologies of the other two who said sorry because they were told to. They are not sorry at all.

The officers take the boys back to their police cars in handcuffs.

"What will happen now?" I ask one of the officers.

"They will probably be released to their parents but have to report for their court dates."

"Court dates?" I ask. Really, court dates? They are children.

"Yes ma'am. You will be notified since the crime scene is on your property," he says as he closes the door behind Luke who is now safely in the back of the cruiser. "This sort of stuff happens all the time with these bad teens now a days. We just try to clean up the mess and make them pay for their mistakes. Stop them now before they commit really bad crimes."

The officer seems cold and distant from the entire situation. It is such a norm in his world that this is just another day on the job.

I look over at the other cruiser and see Avery with a long-drawn face and red eyes of shame.

"Would you like to attend the court dates?" the officer asks me. His questioning makes me realize that most don't attend.

"Yes, officer, I would," I add.

After the police cars drive away, I stand and stare at the now-blank wall. I feel ill. What just happened? This feels wrong. I don't know why, but it feels wrong. After a while, Alfred puts his arm around my shoulders and guides me inside.

The court date is set for that Friday.

CHAPTER 8

THE COURTROOM IS FULL OF TEENAGERS, a fact that surprises me more than I'd like. What could they possibly have done to warrant this many of them having a court date? Each teen sits beside a parent, if not two. Each child is called before the judge. The parent stands behind while the child pleads their case. One after another. Time drags on. I am hearing cases of Petty theft, car vandalism, trespassing, the normal kid stuff. I glance at the clock on the wall. We are running out of time, and there are still teens who have not been heard.

When the end of day finally arrives, the bailiff announces that the cases not heard today will be heard first thing on Monday. The judge leaves the bench and those in the room stand. I glance around, and notice that all three teens from the graffiti at the School of Art are still in the room. In particular, I look for Avery. When I see him, he is heading right for me with, most likely, his mother.

"Mom." He stops in front of me. "This is the lady whose wall I spray painted."

His mom doesn't seem quite sure how to react to him introducing us, and cautiously holds her hand out for me to shake.

"Well, I'm sure you know my son Avery." She purses her lips as she looks at her son in disappointment.

"Yes, I have met him," I say while shaking her hand.

"I'm Mrs. Edwards, his mother." She seems a bit formal, odd.

Their last names are different from each other. "My name is Mary Parker." There's no need to stir up more trouble.

As I look at her, I get the strange feeling that I have met her before; I just can't figure out from where. She looks like she wants to talk more, but the movement of the crowd leaving the court room sweeps us up like a tidal wave and pushes us out the doors. We get separated in the crowd, but I know I will see her again on Monday.

Later that evening, Charlie and I sit down for dinner over another of his fine creations—savory pork chops with an apple drizzle along with stuffing seasoned to perfection.

"How do you like this one?" he asks.

"Charlie, you know I absolutely love *all* of your cooking." He looks like a cat who ate a canary. "Did you teach this one to your students?"

"Sure did." Charlie's face brightens as he smiles.

"Perfection." I shovel another spoonful into my mouth.

"Kids, can you come out please?"

Confused, I look around to see who's lurking in the distance. Four of Charlie's students come out from the kitchen all dressed in white smocks, like chefs, with napkins draped over their hands.

Charlie looks up at them from his seat at our table. "Can you please tell us what we're eating for dinner tonight?" Charlie speaks as if he is the host of a TV show.

"Yes sir," one of the kids speaks up. "You have a center cut of pork loin cooked in an apple cranberry sauce with finely chopped apples and pecans for texture. The apple is the sweet whereas the cranberry is the tart bringing the flavor together. The drizzle is then accompanied by a side of roasted stuffing complimented by," and the student stops as if he has forgotten what he is supposed to say.

Another student speaks up, "The roasted stuffing is complimented by chopped apples to add texture and flavor." She smiles as she finishes the main course menu.

"And for dessert?" Charlie asks.

"We have dessert too?" I get excited.

"For dessert, we are continuing with the apple flavor, and we have a baked apple cobbler topped off with vanilla ice cream and a drizzle of caramel," the third student finishes off the menu.

"Perfection!" I say. "Absolutely perfect!"

"Okay class, you may go back to the kitchen." They all return to the kitchen. "Well done, well done."

I gaze into Charlie's eyes, "I'm so proud of you. I know your mother would be so proud as well."

"I'm finally doing what I've always wanted to do." His smile seems to radiate from deep within him. "I'm teaching what my mother taught me."

"They are going to be fine chefs when they graduate."

"Thank you."

I take another delightful bite. By this time the four chefs are long gone, and now it is just the two of us in the dining room.

"Has Millie eaten?"

"Yes, she is eating with Alfred and his family tonight. I wanted to make this experience as much like a real restaurant as possible for them to learn."

"It was perfect." I lean over and kiss him.

One of his students comes out with our cobbler.

"How was your day in court?"

"They didn't get to see the judge." As I begin to swipe my lap for the crumbs.

"Why not?" Charlie sits back in his chair.

"There were too many kids there, and the court didn't have enough time for all of them." I feel a great sigh. I try not to allow it to escape, but it is too great to suppress.

"Wow, there are that many kids in trouble?" He seems surprised.

"Yeah, I thought the same thing." I take a bite of my apple cobbler.

"Something," and I stop mid-sentence. "I don't know. Something feels off." I put my fork down and take a breath. "I don't feel right about this."

"This?"

"Yeah. Taking kids to court and punishing them because

their parents don't provide them a good life at home. They're acting out for attention."

"Well, not all of them," he says.

"No, not all of them." I pause. "But, think about it." I feel like a lawyer pleading my case. Here I am, the one whose property was vandalized, but I'm defending the kids? What is wrong here? Everything about this feels strange.

"The kids I saw today did things to get attention from their parents or teachers."

"How do you know?" Charlie really wants to know what I saw.

"Well look at Avery for one. He wants to be an artist, that's pretty obvious. He doesn't have anywhere to do his art so he found the one place that he could. Unfortunately, it was my wall at the school. But I saw his face when they forced him to paint over it. He was crushed. And I think I know why. It was vandalism in their eyes, but it was art in his."

"Yeah, but what he did is against the law," Charlie reminds me.

"I know, but—"

"No buts Mar. He broke the law." The prosecution has spoken.

"If he had proper instruction and proper rules to follow, I think this kid could actually make something of himself. He's got talent!"

"I saw it. It was good, but again—"

I cut him off before he can finish the sentence. "It's against the law."

"Is he the only one?" Charlie asks.

"No, there were a few in trouble for stealing from a store."

"Stealing?" Charlie attempts to show me just how crazy I sound. He is taken aback, and I can't blame him. I'm sticking up for the criminals when I should be charging them for the crime.

"Yes, stealing." My voice wavers. I just want him to understand where I'm coming from.

Charlie seems afraid to ask. "Stealing what?"

"They stole candy."

"Hm, candy," he repeats, walking the line between condescending and thoughtful.

"If you ask me, they could have a part-time job to buy candy instead. They looked old enough."

Charlie is a bit confused.

"Another girl was stealing baby supplies from a store," I say, and my outrage slips into my voice. She shouldn't need it yet, and even more, she shouldn't have to steal it.

"Baby supplies?" Now Charlie knows I'm upset.

"I wanted to ask if she had a baby and needed the stuff for her own child, but I couldn't."

"I see your point now." He seems more thoughtful now. "What else did you see today?"

"One young girl was there for breaking and entering."

"That sounds pretty serious," Charlie says.

"Not really." Sadness overcomes me. "She was breaking and entering into her own home while her mother was at the store. Her mother locked her out of her house while she went shopping."

"Shopping?" Charlie asks.

"How do you know that?"

"Her mother had to be there, not only for her child but also for the victim side like me." I sit up straighter to help my food settle. "She told the judge in front of everyone."

"Everyone?" Charlie asks, as if he doesn't really understand how this court works.

"She said she didn't want her 'little brat' inside alone."

"She actually called her own daughter a little brat?" I can hear the disbelief in his voice.

"Yeah, and you know it was raining this morning?" I shake my head. "To keep your kid locked outside in the rain. No wonder she broke into her own house." I found myself justifying why the kids were doing what they were doing.

Charlie leans back, lost in the silence with me. We're both a little stunned at how bad things could be out past the walls of the manor.

I break the silence first. "There has to be something missing in today's kids that is causing all of this crime. Maybe," I say, grabbing for an answer. "They are kids! Kids acting out," I plead my case. "They're looking for guidance, instruction, protection, or something to live for. Or maybe they just want attention from their parents!" I feel like I found the problem, but what's the solution? I feel stuck, not knowing how to make this situation better.

"Well, Mildred always told you 'to see change, you have to be the change'," Charlie reminds me.

"Yeah, but how?"

"You know those kids are nothing like your kids here."

I nod. He's right.

"These kids come from loving homes, well most of them. They have talent and that's why they are in this school, to learn, not to cause trouble. Those kids carry guns and knives. They deal drugs, take drugs, steal for drugs. Look at the young girl that was pregnant at the prom that started the riot between the gangs. Remember the riot we just had? They come from dangerous backgrounds and dangerous neighborhoods. You know the ones." I know Charlie is trying to talk me out of whatever I'm thinking of. He knows how dangerous the prom became.

I begin to see the social and economic differences, not to mention their mannerisms of behavior and treatment of other students, but this seems to drive me more, not deter me.

"They need positive role models, loving environments," I respond.

Charlie interrupts me, "And you think you can just go into each of these kids houses and make their parents start to care about their kids? Most of those parents are kids themselves. They probably didn't even want to have kids to begin with. Mar, you can't change the world."

"Yeah, you're right, but—"

"You have such a huge heart, and that is why you have this

school to begin with. This is a hard city. You know that. You grew up here, too."

"Yeah, but I'm not a bad person." My voice comes out shrill and defensive.

"You're right. But you had a loving mother that kept you safe from all of that. You have always told me she wouldn't even allow you to go to the park by yourself to see Mildred."

"Right, but—" I try to cut in.

"Not to mention she tried to keep you from talking to Mildred because she thought she was homeless and going to hurt you, didn't she?" His words are coming like a machine gun.

"Yeah, but—" I try again.

"You're the person you are today because she was so protective."

"But Mildred wasn't going to hurt me." I finally get my words out.

"Your mom didn't know that." He's calmer now. His point has been made, and he doesn't want to fight about it.

I feel it coming and can't stop it. My stomach turns with my emotions, and I swallow around the lump in my throat. I don't want to cry. Not tonight, please God, not now.

"I went against my mom. That's how I met Mildred in the first place! Mildred was more of a mother to me than my own mom was. She raised me, sure, but Mildred taught me things, listened to me." I stop. My tears are getting in the way.

"I know, Mar. That's the point. You had people that cared about you growing up. They don't." He takes a breath. "That's why they're doing what they're doing. They're breaking laws to get attention, even if it's bad attention."

"There has to be a better way than what I saw in that courtroom." I want to fix this, but I'm not sure I can.

"I love who you are Mary. You are the most selfless person I know. You are more concerned with the young man—"

"Avery?" I correct him.

"Yes, Avery," he continues, "than you are with the vandalism to the gymnasium wall." A warm smile from the depths of Charlie's heart spreads across his face.

"Thank you, Charlie, I love you, too."

Charlie gets up from his chair and I realize how late it is. I love our nights like this. We live such busy lives that our late-night conversations have become a good relaxing ritual. Charlie offers me his hand. When I take it, he gently pulls it to his lips. That gentle kiss reminds me of the first time I met him. He is still such a gentleman.

"I'll meet you upstairs after I prepare the kitchen for tomorrow's class. It doesn't look good for the teacher to allow the kitchen to remain a mess overnight."

Charlie grabs the dishes and disappears through the kitchen doors.

Much of the manor is quiet, so I go upstairs and check on Millie. She is sleeping quietly in her crib, though she hardly fits anymore. She'll be ready for a grown-up bed soon. I wish she could stay small forever. I want to protect her every move. I'm getting tired, so I head to our room and prepare for the night. But first, I call Lilly. I need to hear her voice.

The phone rings and rings but she doesn't answer. I leave a message for my dear friend and tell her to call after court. She'll want to know what happens. I wish I could talk to her about this.

CHAPTER 9

MONDAY COMES QUICKER than I expected. I know that time is always the same pace, but it just seems like it is here before I realize it. Going to court is not high on my to-do list, but it is something I have to do. Putting on clothes appropriate for court, I take a glance in the mirror. Well, here we go again.

Court opens as usual with teens sitting with their parents in the audience. The court reporter announces that the judge will continue the cases left from Friday first.

"All rise." The court comes to order and the judge enters.

There are only a few teens called up to be heard. With each case, I become more and more restless. I'm trying so hard not to interfere, but I think even the judge has noticed by now.

Case after case, I get more fidgety and squirmier in my seat. I keep feeling this horrible poke in my back like I'm being prodded to stand. I turn around and no one is there. Besides, I'm on a wooden bench that makes a horrible squeaking sound each time I move. No one could possibly be poking me. So, where is this feeling coming from?

Out of nowhere, the pain runs through my back forcing me to stand. All at once the room's attention turns to me.

"Can I help you?" the judge says in a low, stern voice.

I turn around, hoping to see someone behind me. Maybe the judge is talking to them. I'm not so lucky. It's just me standing here like an idiot.

"Ma'am, can I help you?" the judge asks once more.

An officer whispers to the judge, and then he looks up at me once again.

"Your name is Mary Parker, correct?" His voice is low like a smoker's. My heart lurches in my chest, but I'm not sure why.

"Yes, your Honor," I say, hoping I sound as respectful as I'm trying to be.

The room becomes loud with talk.

"Quiet!" the bailiff yells. Everyone stops talking instantly.

"Ms. Parker, you are the plaintiff in the case regarding the three teen boys that vandalized your property. Is this correct?"

Once again, "Yes your Honor." My answers are short and to the point. I feel like I'm the one on trial with everyone drilling holes into me with their eyes. I look around the room, trying to avoid their judgement.

"May I help you with something Ms. Parker?" he asks once more.

"Yes, your honor." Oh, crap, did I say yes? I meant no. Or ... did I? I can't stop it now. What is wrong with me? Why am I standing here like I have some sort of power over this court?

The judge glances at his watch and calls for a short recess.

I'm directed back into the judge's chambers, which isn't much more than an office with a beautiful desk and many law books. The judge sits behind the desk and offers for me to sit as well.

"Well, Ms. Parker, I'm only taking the time to talk to you because I know you are a valuable asset to this community with the Museum of Art and the School of Art. However, I cannot stay in my chamber for too long. So, how can I help you?"

I'm quite impressed that he would take the time to hear what I need and want to say. I hadn't really expected to get this far.

"May I ask questions? I mean, can I speak freely, your Honor?"

"Sure, you can." The judge sits back in his oversized office chair, getting ready for whatever I say.

"I see these teens being brought to this court for various reasons such as trespassing, breaking and entering, vandalism and many other charges." I want to make sure he has all the information I have.

"Yes, ma'am."

"There has to be a better way."

"How do you mean?" He seems a bit put off by my questions.

"The young lady that was in court on Friday, the one who stole baby supplies from the store. Has anyone asked her *why* she was stealing baby items? If that young lady has a child of her own and she cannot take care of it," I pause to collect myself. "Has anyone taught her how to take care of her baby? If she is a child as well, how will she know how to take care of her baby if she is not educated to do so? Maybe all she knows is stealing. And if that's true, can't we find a better solution than to lock her up away from her child? Shouldn't we instead teach her how to be a better mother?"

The judge listens quietly.

"Another case, the one where the child broke into her own home when it was raining. Her mother didn't want her there while she was out shopping, right?"

"Yes."

"What about charging the mother with not taking responsibility for her children and keeping them locked out of the house in adverse weather?"

The judge crosses his arms.

"In the case of the vandalism to my property, I'm not charging the young boys. The police department took the charges for me. I see these young boys as needing guidance in life from positive role models."

The judge seems put off. Perhaps I overstepped my bounds. I am putting him on the bench, as you would say, to provide alternative punishments instead of just remanding them to the juvenile hall for a certain amount of time like jail.

"Ms. Parker, each of these kids has done this time and again. We've tried community service. We've tried fines. We've tried probation. It's a joke to them. This is all we have left."

I shake my head. "There has to be something else we haven't tried yet."

"Fine. What would you have in mind, Ms. Parker?" He doesn't seem to think I'll have anything better to suggest.

I take a deep breath. What am I doing? I can't stop myself

once I've started, though. "What about an alternative program at my school?" Did I just say that? Did I just ask to put these young teens in trouble in my school and offer my help to them? What am I doing?

"Like an afterschool program that is part of their sentence?" he clarifies.

"Well, I am offering classes at my school. When they complete my school and graduate, the charges will be taken off their records. Then they can start fresh in life." Where in the heck is all this coming from?

"Let me get this straight. You want these kids, these kids known for stirring up trouble, to attend your school instead of the city school. When they graduate, you want them to start with a fresh record, free from any wrongdoings. Is this right?" he asks.

"Yes. These kids need guidance, and they also need a passion to work toward."

"What do you mean, passion?" His anger has faded and he seems more willing to hear me out.

"Well, take Avery. He is an artist, but he doesn't know where to paint. I can teach him the correct places to paint that aren't going to get him into trouble. He can be inspired to paint instead of punished."

"Hmmm, like a school for second chances?" He rubs his chin.

"Yes, your Honor. I'm sure there are other students out there that have talents that are misdirected. If they qualify for the program, they can come to my school at no charge. As long as they are in the program, they have to abide by all rules. If they mess up once, then you can go ahead and sentence them. But, if they graduate, they will have life skills and hopefully a passion to drive them to succeed." I try to hide my uncertainty. This program doesn't even exist. What am I doing?

He nods slowly. "A school for second chances, I like it. We can test it out. But Ms. Parker, I can't wipe their records. They will be sealed when they turn eighteen as the law dictates." The judge has a renewed plan to help troubled teens change their ways. "Hopefully this plan means they won't be in the system again, which means that record will never have reason to be unsealed, allowing them to be productive members of society. I will get with the city schools and probation department to put this program together."

The judge stands and refastens his robe. "I need to get back to court." He motions to the door. "Shall we?"

As he heads back to the bench, I return to my seat in the audience to observe. I still have no idea what poked me and forced me to stand. Maybe it was Mildred forcing me to make a change happen. I just hope I can do this. I should have all summer to get the school ready for this program to begin in the fall. What did I just do?

After the hearings, I head to the park bench to watch the birds fly in. I feel that they're coming to say hello.

"I'm sorry, I've been gone for much too long. I need to come visit you more often."

Reaching in for a handful of birdseed, I notice a bird standing in front of me, looking at me. It turns and I see it has a broken leg. It can't be! I know this bird. My long-lost friend has come back.

"Where have you been?" I say as I throw another handful down.

Another group of birds flies in and pushes my little friend out of the way. Oh no, this can't be. I move my legs to disturb the birds, and they seem to get the hint that I'm trying to feed my friend. I feel so overwhelmed. I wish Mildred was here to talk to. I need her guidance so badly. Or maybe I just need a hug.

Taking a deep breath in, I close my eyes and imagine that Mildred is here. I want to cry. Watching the birds does calm me but not as much as Mildred did. I look toward the water. The sun is reflecting off the ripples from the wind. It begins to sparkle, dancing on the water, and before I notice, the sparkles take over my mind and I'm no longer looking at the water. They are so beautiful. My heart calms even more.

I close my eyes once again.

"Thank you, Mildred," I mumble. "I miss you so much."

The birds are fed and have flown off. I must be heading home.

When I get there, even though I'm tired from the day's activities, I find Millie. She is in the sunroom with Antoinette. Millie is sitting on the floor having a little tea party with her teddy bears. I plop down hard on the chair beside Antoinette.

"Ugh, what a day," I mumble.

I stare at Millie, seeing how wonderful it is to be young again. She looks so beautiful. Her red curls are much like mine when I was young. Her hair is a bit darker than mine was, though. I can see some of Charlie's color in there as well.

Millie has her teddy bears in a circle with pillows holding them up, giving the illusion that they are sitting up on their own. She holds a teacup in her hand with grace and elegance. Her pinky is up and everything. I just wish the teacup wasn't invisible. I would love to see her with it. She grabs for the teapot and holds it up, as if she were pouring it far away from each cup. She begins with one teddy bear and continues to the next, then onto the next. Then she pours tea for a bear that isn't there.

"Are we missing a teddy bear?" I whisper to Antoinette.

"Um, no," Antoinette mumbles.

"Who is she pouring tea for?"

"That," Antoinette pauses, not sure if she should reveal the secret, "that is Millie's secret friend. You know," she says.

"A secret friend?"

"Yes, like an invisible friend?" Antoinette speaks quietly so she won't disturb Millie.

"Has this," and I'm not quite sure how to ask, "has this invisible friend been here a lot?" I ask.

"Well, usually around teatime." Antoinette giggles.

I turn to watch the tea party once more. Her elegance is illuminated.

"Oh Mrs. Mary, haven't you ever had an invisible friend?" Antoinette asks with even more giggles.

"Not that I can remember."

"I had one," Antoinette speaks up.

"You did?"

She looks at Millie and smiles. "Sure did." Antoinette winks at Millie.

I think for sure she is pulling my leg, showing Millie that having an imaginary friend is totally fine.

"She will grow out of it," Antoinette reassures me. "Besides, I think she likes having a friend to play with."

Later, upstairs in the main bedroom, I take a moment to catch my breath and ponder about today. I look down at my nails. They look quite rough. Reaching over to my nightstand, I look for a nail file. But as my hand searches, I find an envelope. Oh my, my heart races. I forgot I had this. I haven't seen this envelope in a really long time. I pull it out.

I carefully open the envelope and get a wave of emotion. This letter was written to me by Mildred when she was on her death bed. I still remember the day I read it for the first time.

The letter is folded three times to fit in a legal-size envelope. Opening it is surreal. The letter starts in the worst possible way.

> Dear Mary,
>
> I'm sorry that you are reading this letter, but I have been writing it for quite some time. No one knows of this letter except you and my lawyer. He has the only copy.

Reading this brings back memories I pushed far away. I feel like crying, but I have to keep reading.

> My Child, when I met you, you were such a little, naïve, beautiful girl. I sat upon the park bench in such terrible pain, talking to God, pleading for my husband to come back to me. He was my only friend. Sure, everyone at the manor is a friend, but I pay them to be. Alfred may be close to me, but you are so different. I asked God that if I could not have my dear husband back, then send me an angel. And then, you were there.

I have seen you grow up and develop the most
extravagant qualities. You have become a person
whom I deeply admire. When all was against
you in school, I saw you persevere. So many
classmates were against you talking to me. They
mocked you and called you names. They did
horrible things to you when you tried to be a
friend to me. You stood your ground. You became
brave.

Regarding your mother, when we first met,
she saw me as many others saw me. I was a
disheveled lady feeding the birds in the park.
Therefore, I must have lived in the park, making
me homeless. I never tried to correct you
mother's thoughts of me. I saw you overcome
someone else's thoughts and wrongdoings to find
the truth. And this you did. For this, you gained
integrity, truth, and justice.

I have seen you grow from being a small,
headstrong child to a beautiful young lady full of
life. You learned from me things that I wanted
to teach my own daughter. As time passed, I
thought of you as my daughter. I gave you a
locket just as my husband gave me to ensure your
return. Over time, you have returned, still with
the locket placed securely around your neck for
safekeeping. It is just as if you were guarding my
heart. With this, you displayed honesty.

Oh, the locket. Where is my locket? I spring to my feet and
run to my jewelry box. Where is it? It has to be here!

I rummage through the items that I have acquired through
the years, including some of my mother's jewelry and a few pieces
from Charlie. I keep digging. Where is it? Panic sets in. Where is
it?

Digging once again, I find the locket down at the bottom, as if it was put there so it would be the safest. Pulling the locket out, I polish the front of the locket where the large M is with my finger, until the M is bright and beautiful just as the first day I saw it. Now for the inside.

Carefully placing my fingernail in the latch, I pop it open. I'm so afraid of hurting this heirloom. The hinge is rough but still working. I open the locket to reveal the two photos, one of Mildred and the other of her husband. She told me her husband gave her this locket to remind her that he would come back to her after being drafted for the war. The photo on his side of the locket shows a scared young man, far too young to be in battle.

I feel compelled to read on, so I close the locket and slip it over my head, putting the locket inside my shirt where it belongs, close to my heart.

> When your mother died, you didn't see me, but I was there with you. When you were hurt in school, you didn't see me, but I was there with you. When you walk down the aisle on your wedding day, you won't see me, but I'm there for you. When you have your first child, you won't see me, but I will be there for you. All you need to do is hold the locket close to your heart, and I will be there, just as you were there when I buried my husband, and for many years after.
>
> You taught me that life is still worth living. Dreams can still be achieved. My dash has been fulfilled. My child, you were the last and final part of my dash, and my dash has been completed. I have seen your dash become ever more meaningful with each passing day.

I miss her so much that I can't stand it. Mildred, Millie, was named after Mildred. I promised her that. I hold the letter close to my chest and fight back tears.

Now the meaning of this letter is twofold. One, so you know just how much of an angel you have become to me over the years. And two, to act as a letter of instruction to be completed by my lawyer once you read this letter.

The manor has been turned over to you, my child. The staff comes with the manor for its upkeep and maintenance. Their salaries have been covered for at least ten years. I know Antoinette is not really needed as a nurse. However, she is excellent at keeping the daily functions in order. Alfred is wonderful at maintaining the land, as well as the manor. He understands what is needed for daily functions.

I take a deep breath, as if I was reading this for the first time.

The Art Museum has been donated to the city. It is still under the control of the corporation, which the lawyer can assist you with. Classes must be maintained in categories. However, you have one entire wing that has been dedicated solely to your artwork. I expect your pictures to be displayed in frames under glass, to fulfil a dream of yours.

I do have one last request: I want the halls to be filled with the laughter of children. The children of our lives are the future of existence. Assist them in finding their dreams and achieving their passion in life. Maybe even one or two of those children may be yours. I entrust everything I have to you, my Child.

With Love,

Mildred, The Bird Lady.

This letter makes me realize that I'm doing the right thing. I know this program is going to be tough, but Mildred expects me to be the change to allow these children to realize their dreams. I can do this.

I wish Millie could have met Mildred. I wish I had an elevator to take her up to Mildred to find the penthouse of peace and understanding. I know that no elevator exists like that, but I can still dream.

I carefully fold the letter and place it back into the envelope. My heart is warmed with love. My dream is to become half the woman Mildred was. I will be the best mother to Millie as I possibly can be. I will be the wife Charlie deserves. It is what Mildred would want.

After placing the envelope back in its drawer, I lay back on my bed. The locket is safe, right where it belongs: next to my heart.

CHAPTER 10

AUGUST COMES QUICKLY. Today, I have a meeting with the teachers before they set up their classrooms for the first day. I'm nervous, and I feel sick to my stomach. Taking a deep breath, I look upward and whisper, "Mildred, please help me get through this."

Entering the school today feels different. The vibe is a bit off. I need to get this meeting going.

Once in the main office, I reach for the microphone to make the announcement.

"Good morning, everyone. Welcome back. If everyone could please come to the gymnasium for a quick meeting, I would really appreciate it. I have coffee and pastries from Charlie. The meeting will begin in twenty minutes. Thank you."

Well, the first step to this huge endeavor has begun. I'm not sure what to say to everyone. They look to me for guidance, and I'm just as much in the dark as they are. I need to appear confident, ready, excited. I take a deep breath. This is going to take some work to pull off.

While getting set up in the gymnasium, a few teachers enter. This is a teacher in-service day. We are all ensuring the school is ready for our first day, moving desks, checking lightbulbs, ensuring the plumbing is running correctly.

Teachers file in one by one, and then in groups or departments. Our school is not large by any means, but I do have a healthy staff. They take their seats in groups. I'm glad to know the teachers are bonding together through this endeavor.

Once everyone has arrived, I walk to the front. I have already set up a table for myself to stand beside if I need. When I get nervous, I tend to pace, and I hope the table will keep me centered.

"Everyone, please get your coffee and find a seat," I say, struggling to be heard over the roar of the crowd.

Looking over the teaching and faculty staff, it is nice to see everyone in more casual clothing. On days like today, they can come in shorts, jeans, tennis shoes, or whatever is most comfortable for them. Even I'm in jeans and a T-shirt today.

As I stand in front, the room calms to a quiet without another word from me. I love this school environment. We are much like a family here, and that is how I want it to stay. I'm just afraid that after today our little family may change.

I take a breath to gather my thoughts and look the room over to ensure everyone is ready to begin. Everyone but me, I think. I'm just as nervous as they are.

"Thank you all for being here." Oh, what a stupid thing to say. They *have* to be here. Attempting to regain my composure, I continue. "I hope all of you had a wonderful summer. As you all know, we are starting this year a bit differently."

The noise builds to a mild roar as everyone talks to each other. They quickly refocus their attention on me. "This school was founded by Mildred and her husband Harold, with her passion to pass on the gift of dreams, goals, and cultivating dashes. As you know, our school went through some rough times with the prom last year. We all felt horrible when the city school had its fire. We did try to help. Unfortunately, it did not turn out quite like we wanted it to. Some of those students were forever changed by seeing how a real prom is instead of a get-together called a prom. I wish all of you could have seen their faces as they walked into our prom. I know some of you were there."

Some of the teachers shake their heads, while others look worried.

"As you may also remember, we had an incident of vandalism as a result of the prom."

The teachers and staff murmur again, and for the first time, I need to quiet them.

"I went to court representing our school against the vandals. What I saw there, as some of you know, was a horrible problem within our city. The children in Teen Court are just being reprimanded for their crimes. Those children have no guidance, no goals to shoot for, no way to even begin achieving their dreams. Their dreams are overshadowed by drug addictions, absent parents, and no real role models to look up to. This is where the new pilot program, the Second Chance Program, comes in. We are going to be the pilot test site for this new program to help our next generation."

Some of the teachers are becoming aggravated. Everyone was informed of this long ago, but some seem very nervous and rightfully so. I'm nervous as well.

"I know this is all new for us. This program will enable the participants to put their lives back on track."

"What about the violence from the other schools spilling over to our school?" a teacher in the back asks. The room comes to life. Many teachers are speaking to each other, making the room echo. I raise my hand to restore order. The gym eventually returns to silence.

Taking my place, I speak again. My fists are clinched and dripping in sweat. Oh, please don't see my fear. I pray for the words, and they fall from my mouth. "These kids have to qualify for the program. There are stiff penalties if they do not comply with the rules." I'm trying so hard to show them that I have this under control, but do I really?

"We are only taking a small number of kids as we test out this new program." I make eye contact with a few of the teachers to see if they are getting on board with the idea. "I will be carefully monitoring the program, so I will be in the school every day this year. You will not be in this alone. I need you to come to me for anything and everything. If you have an issue, come to me. If you have a problem, come to me."

"What if they bring drugs into our school?" another teacher asks.

"What if we have gang violence in our school like the other schools do? I don't want any school shootings or violence here." The teacher looks around at the others, trying to gauge their reactions to his concerns.

I feel his fear. I felt his fear just in that one day I went to the school and was felt up by the security guards. The kids were all like wolves watching their prey, me, waiting to pounce. I cannot show any of that fear here. I have to suck it up and be the strong leader. I have to keep them calm and on board.

"Their probation officers will be in the program monitoring progress as well. Kids with violent crimes do not qualify. Only the kids with smaller, less-offensive crimes qualify." I try once more to sell the program to them.

I feel the room's mood lighten. I'm making progress. They are coming on board. This may actually work.

I rub my fingers together, grasping for my next word. Oh, please help me. I need to make this work. I need to let the teachers know that it will work.

"Mildred always told us," I stop and look around at the teachers. It seems that as soon as they hear Mildred's name, they all want to hear what is next.

"Mildred always told us that in order to see a change, we have to be the change. This is exactly what our school is doing."

I can almost see the glimmers of hope beginning to bond the teachers together.

"We are going to show these students that there really is a better life out there other than committing crimes. We are going to give them opportunities that life otherwise hasn't provided." I feel like a cheerleader doing a pep-rally for our team.

"We will show the students that when their own parents don't believe in them, we do." A warm smile emulates from within me.

"This will not be easy, by any means. We have two days to get our school ready for classes to begin. Again, if you need anything, please let me know so we can address it."

The room begins to stir. Everyone welcomes other teachers back for yet another year. Chairs squeak as everyone stands. Oh, I miss the quiet at the manor already. I don't know if I'm ready for this either, but I will not allow any of the teachers to see that I'm nervous or doubting my decision to do this.

After our meeting is over and some of the teachers have returned to their classrooms to set up, I hear a loud ruckus coming from the front of the school. Alfred, who is busy helping one of the teachers with a ladder from the storage room, says, "Mrs. Mary, I will see what that is." He quickly puts the ladder aside and heads to the door leading to the front of the school. At the same time, officers come around the corner with large boxes on carts.

"What on earth is all of this?" I'm quite taken aback by the way the officers are just bursting into the building and making so much noise. The judge is close behind. This is a strange sight.

The judge, out of his chambers, is dressed very differently. Sure, he is in a suit, but it is still more casual than the black robe he wears to court.

"I have your delivery to be set up," one of the officers says as he sets down the dolly. A huge thud rings throughout the school, and then another thud as another crate is removed from the dolly.

"Wait, what is all of this?" As if I didn't have enough stress today, now this?

"These crates are for your Second Chance Program." The judge speaks with authority.

"Ok, but," I glance around at the crates, trying to figure out what they could be. "What are they?"

"Well, since you are going to be dealing with teens with records in the criminal justice system, I ordered metal detectors for the front entrance to your school." The judge seems quite proud of himself.

"You ordered what!" I can't hide my shock.

Images of being felt up by the officers at the other school when I was just trying to talk to the principal rush into my mind. Oh, not in my school! I will not subject my students to treatment like what I went through.

"No." I'm angered at the mere thought. "No. No!" I can't say it enough.

The officers look to the judge for direction. The judge seems surprised that I am refusing such a gesture.

"Is this part of what you thought I needed?" I'm not being very cordial.

"Other schools depend on this. It keeps the guns and knives out of the schools, so no violence enters."

"But we don't have that problem here in our school!" I'm quite angry. Am I doing the right thing? It is far too late to back out now. If I back out, the kids enrolled into our pilot program will not be able to attend and will probably have to go back to Juvenile Hall.

Then I see a box labeled "Cameras." Metal detectors and cameras, in my school? What have I done? I feel the blood rush from my face.

I close my eyes for an instant and take a deep breath to calm myself, so I don't say anything rash. Oh, trust me, I want to scream at them all. That would not be good nor ladylike.

"I will make a deal with you." I put on my bargaining face. "I will take your monitoring system so you can watch the kids' progress," I point to the camera system first, "but I will not accept having metal detectors here at all." I point to the metal detector crates. I want them to know I'm serious about this.

The officers seem like deer in headlights, just standing there, unsure what to do.

"I will not subject my students to going through metal detectors and have officers manhandle them, waiting to pounce on their every ding or siren with flashing lights. My school is a school of safety and freedom, freedom of expression. Having this over their heads," I put my hands on the crate closest to me, "this creates a bad feeling as soon as they walk through the doors. I will not have this in my school!"

The judge rubs his head.

"Have I ever had any instance where the police were here because of a gun or knife?" I ask everyone.

"Not that I'm aware of," one of the officers says.

I turn to Alfred, begging for support, "Have you?"

"No, Mrs. Mary." He adds, "Our students respect our school and want to be here."

"If you put those things here, this school will become no different than the city schools!" I straighten up to stand my ground. "Those," I point to the camera system, "but not those." I tap my finger on the crate I'm standing next to. "If we don't believe in these kids, why will they believe in us?" I stop for a moment to see if it is sinking in. "If we don't trust these students, why will they trust us?"

The slight shuffle of feet behind me grabs my attention. I turn around and see that all the teachers have come to see what the commotion is about. This is justifying their fears. I was trying so hard to calm them and now this!

I start barking orders. "I suspect the cameras connect to Wi-Fi?"

"Yes," one of the officers pipes up.

"Good, then I will not see any wiring." My voice is getting a bit rough.

"No ma'am." He looks a bit scared. He's just here to do the installation and I've thrown his day into chaos.

"Okay. Entrances and maybe the cafeteria and maybe some common areas *only*," I instruct.

"Yes ma'am," he replies once more.

"I want those out of my school." I point to the crates.

"Yes ma'am." The officers move the crates to the door.

"One more thing," I request. "I want the password to the program for monitoring the system. I want to see what you see so everything is above board." I hear nothing. "Will that be a problem?"

"That isn't going to be a problem," he adds.

"Good, this is my pilot program, my school, my kids, and I'm responsible for their involvement." I turn to face the teachers. "This is a school where the kids are free to learn and free to be artistic. I do not want it changed in any way."

The teachers begin to smile, and I think they can see how much I'm trying to support them as my administrators while also supporting my students. I feel powerful. My fears are subsiding. I *do* have this under control. At least for the moment.

The judge and probation officers leave. The installers get to work putting the cameras up. It goes quickly. They are gone as fast as they came. The cameras are small and almost unnoticeable. I'm okay with this.

Thursday and Friday end up being nerve-racking, but we get through it. Everything seems set. The teachers are ready for the new school year. Now the anticipation for Monday. I hope I get through this weekend.

Taking a much-needed moment to regain my sanity, I walk out in the garden where I scan through the flower beds and see the beautiful multitude of colors on display. Charlie comes out holding Millie and my day is suddenly perfect.

"Hey there little one." I reach out for my cute little girl.

"How was your day?" Charlie hands Millie over.

"Well," I want to cry, but I do not dare. I have Millie in my arms. I do not want to upset her. "The officers came along with the judge and brought in these big metal detectors to install them."

"Metal detectors? You mean like an airport or a federal building?"

"Yeah, well they have one in the city school that I had to go through." I find myself quickly stopping my words because I do not want him to know what I went through at the other school. He would definitely have stopped me from doing this program.

"But, why?"

"To keep weapons out of their school." Oh no, I think I opened up a door that I did not want to open.

I see Charlie's face change. He is worried, probably running through scenarios in his mind of guns and school violence.

"Mar, are you sure this is a good idea?" Charlie is noticeably uneasy.

"Well, I was worried, but our school here is different," I try to reassure him. Actually, I think I'm trying to reassure myself.

Millie gets fussy, so I let her down. She begins to play with a nearby flower, looks up at me and says, "Pretty."

I smile. "Yes, honey, just like you."

Charlie slips his arm around me, "Let's go inside and get something for dinner."

One of his creations does sound perfect right about now. I reach down and pick up Millie once more. She begins to cry and reach outward toward the flowers. I know how she feels.

CHAPTER 11

BEFORE THE FIRST DAY OF SCHOOL, Charlie and I take some time to sit in the garden. Millie is at the table with us, but she is occupied with her coloring book.

"The birdhouses are doing well, I see." Charlie points out a new family of birds entering the big, blue house near the pond.

"Oh, yes, I have been so busy that I haven't noticed." Feeling guilty, I examine our garden a bit closer.

Antoinette comes out and heads over to where Millie is concentrating so hard on her coloring.

"Look Anti!" Antoinette is too big of a mouthful for her, so she gave her a nickname. She lifts her picture up for her to see.

"Oh, how beautiful." Antoinette is bursting with joy. "Come inside now and let's get your breakfast."

Antoinette lifts Millie out of her chair, and they head inside the manor.

"Are you ready for today?" Charlie asks over coffee.

I sigh. "I hope so."

Today is the first day of the Second Chance Program through the juvenile court system. I will say, I am extremely nervous. After seeing the students in the city school, I know I'm getting in way over my head, but I have to do something. I examine my dress to ensure I look good enough for today. I know there aren't any wrinkles, but that doesn't stop me from trying to press them out with my hands. I'm so nervous; I feel a mess.

"I have been planning all summer for this program. I have the list of participating kids, what the crimes are—no violent ones—what they want from this program, and where they are academically. I have classes already in order and yeah," I nod my head, "I'm ready."

"It's going to be a big day." Charlie gives me a hug and we head inside. He heads off to teach his own classes and I make my way to the school.

My eye is drawn to the parking lot, already full of police cars. What did I get myself into? As I reach for the door to the school, there is a horrible rumble in my stomach, as if something is telling me not to go in. But, if I don't go in, the first day will be a disaster. I can't have that. How can I support the teachers and staff if I feel so scared about starting this program? I can already feel the difference in the atmosphere, and this is exactly what I didn't want to happen. Is this feeling just in my head or do the others feel it, too? At least my school doors aren't locked.

Walking down the hallway, I check the time. I'm running later than I usually would. I need to go directly to my office. I walk carefully since I have not worn a dress and heels in quite a while. I don't want to make a fool of myself already.

As I turn into the office, I notice there is an unusual number of people. I'm met with a few officers. The Second Chance Program participants sit on the chairs outside the office door. This whole thing feels strange. I make my way inside. My stomach feels stuck in my throat. I feel sick. What did I get myself, I mean, our school, into? Here we go.

"Please come into my office and let's get the paperwork started for these kids." I motion for the officer in charge to come in ahead of me. He stands before me with a multitude of folders in his arms.

He looks very intimidating. With his belt fully equipped with his gun, handcuffs, and other pouches, it is hard to look at him and not his belt. I'm not even in trouble, and I'm frightened by his presence.

"Where should we start?" I take my seat behind my desk.

He throws the pile of files right in front of me, and they make a thud as they hit the desk. This is not a good way to start here, but I give him the benefit of the doubt.

"Well, that's how we are going to start the day?" I did not mean for that to come out, but oh well, I said it. I roll my eyes but quickly gather my civility. "Which file is first?"

The officer looks at me like I'm a juvenile delinquent as well. This is not professional at all. His mindset is already made up.

"Why are you even bothering with these kids?" he asks in a condescending tone.

"Why?" My attitude quickly matches his.

"Well, yeah." He sits down in the chair in front of my desk. Having the big belt on his uniform, sitting in the chair is a bit cumbersome. "Why even care about these kids? They break laws and now we are allowing them to go to your swanky school?" His voice is loud enough to carry into the office on the other side of my doorway. The kids can hear him.

"Hmmm." I stop before I say something that will get me in trouble.

"Do you think that sending them to this school is really going to make a difference? Do you?" The officer's face is distorted with an attitude to match.

Okay, that's it. I cannot believe what I'm hearing. This is an officer of the law, and he is obviously involved with the Second Chance Program with the court system. So why the attitude? How can these kids listen to this officer and honestly believe that they have a chance to make it? The more he speaks, the angrier I become. I'm trying to hold my anger in, but the longer I try to hold it, the more my blood begins to boil. I take a deep breath and put my hands under my desk, folding them in my lap so he doesn't see my nervousness or anger. I need to answer, but I don't want to. How can he be so cruel? My words spill out of my mouth at a hundred miles an hour. I'm a speeding freight train heading for derailment. Either way, I can't stop it.

"Yes, I do! These kids need a chance to change their path. Sure, they have committed crimes and yes, they are in trouble for their actions. But if no one steps up to the plate and shows them the correct way to treat others, the correct way to dress for success, the correct way to make it in this world," my anger is beginning to boil uncontrollably. "If no one takes the time to help these kids! WHO WILL?"

I stand and slam my hands on my own desk. I'm so angry and by trying to keep it in and be professional, I feel like my internal organs are going to melt. My anger is spilling over like a pressure cooker vent.

"Each of these kids deserves a chance to change their lives! They deserve a chance to become productive people. They need to find their path in life, their passions, their God-given talents." I can hardly take a breath. "Coming here they have a chance to alter their dash!"

"Talents?" the officer yells, "Dash? Really?" He attempts to calm himself, but it doesn't take long for him to raise his voice once again. "You talk about finding their way in life. They've found it! It's a life behind bars *where they belong*!"

"And that is your solution?" I find myself boiling with anger. "You would just throw these kids away?"

The officer is in shock. I'm shocked myself. I feel so outraged that I just can't help it, even if I can't remember the last time I screamed at someone like this.

"Is everything okay Mrs. Parker?" the secretary yells as she enters the office door. I raise my hand to stop her in the doorway.

"Yes, thank you." I take a breath and calm my temper. "We are just getting the paperwork completed so these children can attend our school." I get ahold of myself, not only for me, but for the entire situation.

After sitting back down and regaining my composure I say, "So, where are we?"

The officer begins to understand that I mean business, so one by one, we go through the files. Each file has a photo of the student and their arrest record attached to the front page. On the next page is the transcript with their prior school records. After that is a letter written from the student stating why they wanted to be in the Second Chance Program. It has all the 'I'm sorry' and 'I don't want to be in Juvenile Hall' stuff. I do not want to read their letters because I need to *see* just how sorry they are for the crimes they committed by their actions. One by one, we get each student set up. Then it is time for me to meet the students.

I walk out into the room where the Second Change Program participants are sitting. They are all restless. If I were them and had just listened to how the officer feels about me, I would want to run. However, if they ran, they would certainly be bound for a life behind bars. First, I want to show them why they're here. I adjust my attitude so I'm more upbeat and positive. The show must begin. Is it really a show? I want these kids to be something better than this.

"Okay boys and girls," I say with an encouraging tone, "I would like all of you to follow me."

They all stand, but not without hesitation and griping about it. Now, I know for a fact those grunts and groans are not because of age or exhaustion, achy muscles or bones. They are made in protest. I need to keep the momentum high for this program to work—let alone get started.

"Follow me." I head to the doorway. The police officers look at me with confusion. "You may come with us," I add.

We walk from the School of Art over to the Museum of Art. It is a short walk but a few of the kids drag behind like I'm dragging a dog with a new leash. I feel like all four of their paws are stretched out and I'm dragging them on the floor.

We enter the museum through a side door and make our way to the foyer of the museum, close to the ticket booth.

"Are we going in there?" one of the students asks.

"Yes, we are," I say, keeping the mood positive.

"But I thought we were going to school over there," he says.

"Yes, you are, but you all need to see something and understand where this program came from." I head down one of the hallways. "Right this way."

Entering the hallway, we come upon a plaque, and I make everyone stop. It is the plaque of dedication to the beloved Mildred from her loving husband, Harold.

They slip into silence as they read the plaque. One of the

young men asks, "Who is Mildred?"

"She is the reason why this program exists. Her dream was to help kids and teach them the finer things in life," I explain.

"How do the finer things in life help us get charges dropped? I don't see me as a finer kinda thing girl. I'm a felon kinda girl," one young lady asks.

"If all you are worried about is getting your charges dropped, well then, maybe this program is not for you." The participants look at each other. I think they suddenly know that I mean business. This is definitely different for them.

I turn to the plaque once more and continue. "Mildred and her husband dreamt of having this School of Art. It was built off the Museum of Art, the building you are in now. She instilled in everyone she met that in order to see a change, you must be the change." I feel pride radiate from within me. This is abruptly extinguished.

"Why does that have anything to do with me?" the young man interrupts once more.

"Come this way and I will show you." I lead the mass farther down the hallway.

"Look," one of the kids points out, "Is that a picture of Mildred?" He points up at the portrait. "Oh, another one," he informs us once more.

I smile. "As a matter of fact, this whole wing is dedicated to Mildred and her birds."

"Birds?" I hear from the back.

I turn to another plaque, the wing dedication plaque. "I'm Mary Parker, the artist that drew all of these."

He doesn't seem to believe me. "You drew all of these?"

"Sure did." I'm proud but also very humble seeing my dear friend encapsulated in time.

"Why did you draw so many pictures of her?"

"Hmm, you know, I'm honestly not sure. She was a lady I met in the park with her birds. I saw her several times over the years. We became beautiful friends over time. If you look at the pictures, you can see her age in some." I run my finger over the nearest picture, in which she is feeding one of her birds.

"So why did you draw this one?"

I look over. Another of them is pointing at one of my drawings.

"Mildred had birds that she took care of, and well, I needed to draw one for class." I smile.

"Class? You mean like school?"

"Yes, I had to turn these in to my teacher for grading. Mildred wanted me to display them here in the museum." I'm getting off track. I want to talk about Mildred so badly, but that is not going to get them into their classrooms.

I turn to go down another hallway. They all follow.

"These are classrooms where kids learn to dance ballet. They dance down there in the auditorium." I point down the hallway.

Some of the kids seem to see the importance of the pictures. A couple still could not care less. They have their phones in their faces. It is time to get back to the school and do the paperwork for classes. I lead the way back.

The prospective students for the Second Chance Program are escorted into the conference room. The students are getting restless. Moving them to another room was a good thing to break the monotony. I hope the little field trip between the school and the museum helped, but I'm not so sure.

Once the students are seated in the conference room, I enter with the file folders in hand. The officers are in the room, and this puts a damper on the mood. It is like they are still in jail. This is not jail. I can tell that their attitudes are off after hearing the officer questioning the program. This is a learning environment, and I want to keep it that way.

Looking at all the students, I remind myself that they wanted to be in this program. It makes me feel a bit better. Avery is sitting in one corner. I give him a little smile, but I do not dare point him out.

"I would like to first thank each of you for joining us in our School of Art. I know that each of you has different reasons for why or how you got here, but I want each of you to know that you are a regular student here. However, because of the program, you have different parameters."

One of the young men sets his papers down. I'm not sure, but it looks like he was chewing on them and making spitballs. That is so gross. "What does that mean?" he asks.

"What is your name sir?"

"Nicholas," he says, a little taken aback that I even asked.

"Your last name?"

"Thatcher. Nicholas Thatcher." He seems to be well-spoken but very preoccupied.

I respond with an answer none of them want to hear. "Parameters mean that you guys have different rules to follow."

"Yeah, I knew it," Nicholas mutters. He goes back to his little fortress of spitballs like he is going into battle.

"But they aren't any different from other students here," I try to reassure him.

"How do you mean they aren't different?" A young lady asks.

"And what is your name dear?"

"Alice Gardner," she says as she stands. I'm not sure whom she is putting on a show for or if she really thinks that she is so special that she needs to stand when saying her name. Quite amusing. Even though her clothes say money and her hair is styled to perfection, I can see her face says something quite different.

"Well Alice, same as the other students, you must come to school every day and on time. You must participate in classes. You must get good grades or at least try to get good grades. You must want to change everything." I'm interrupted once more.

"What do you mean change everything?"

Avery asked this question. I have to keep things the same, so I ask, "What is your name young man?"

He gives a little smile and responds, "A..." He stops, realizing that he was going to give his street name. He corrects himself. "Avery, Ma'am." I smile. He heard me when I told him I wanted his real name and not his street name.

"Okay, well Avery, changing everything means your friends,

the people you hang out with, the way you dress, the way you act toward people. Treat others with respect. Change places that get you into trouble. Things that get you into trouble. You know, basically everything in your life. You need to want to change to become a better person. Study to get good grades instead of dealing drugs on a street corner, things like that." Avery's face sinks like the Titanic.

"What's wrong Avery?" I ask.

"Ma'am,"

I have to stop him. "Now first, I'm Mrs. Parker or Mrs. P. Not ma'am."

"Okay Mrs. P., that seems hard. How do you expect us to change all that and learn here, too? You even know where I live. My homies on my street corner think this place is a joke. How do you expect me to get new homies?"

"Once you start going to school here, you'll understand what I'm saying, and it will happen on its own," I try to reassure the students. They all look worried as well. I hear a sigh of relief from the students, but a few groan because they are not sure what they are getting into. "Let's get started. I have your class schedules here and a map of the school. Please come up one by one."

One of the young ladies is dressed in all black with long scraggly hair draped down one side of her face. She has on black combat boots with black pants that have a lot of chains hanging from them. It is strange that when she moves, it sounds like a wind chime. This is definitely a fashion statement; I'm just not sure what she is trying to say. She has her own style, and it is okay.

"May I ask your name?" I look at her, but she is not looking at me. I try to get her attention once more. "What is your name?"

The young men burst out in laughter. Then one blurts out, "That's Goth Girl."

"Goth Girl?" I ask with great concern. "I don't think that's her real name." I direct my attention to the young lady. "Now what is your name dear?"

She keeps her head down, like she is ashamed of something. I'm not sure yet what it is, but I will figure it out.

"And your name is?" I ask once more.

"You heard them. Goth Girl," she says under her breath.

"Honey, please pull your hoodie down. You are not outside." She pulls her hoodie down to reveal her hair.   It is long and actually quite pretty. I notice that either she is very shy or trying to hide something. Her hair is literally over her face on one side. Oh, I get it. I saw a rock star do this. Anyway, it could use some brushing and maybe styling. "I know that's not your name. Shall we try again?" I ask.

"Rain. Well, it is actually Rainelle." She is quite negative when she speaks. She speaks in snappy answers, short and to the point. "Rainelle Hensley, okay?"

"Well, Rainelle," I rustle through my papers to find her folder, "I have your class schedule here." And I give her the schedule. She takes a look.

"I don't do art," she says, pointing to the art class.

"Well, if the class isn't fitting for you, we can change it later. But until then."

Rainelle gives a huff and then leaves the conference room to head to her class.

"And how about you?" I turn to the young man that was sitting next to Rainelle.

"Yes ma'am." He puts his phone down and comes up to the front where I am.

"What is your name, son?" I ask as he makes his way around the chairs that have been pushed around since Rainelle has already left the room.

"Sam Beckette."

"Ah yes. Here you are." His file is right on top. Pulling his paperwork out of the folder, I see the charges the police department has down for him: computer fraud. Really? This young man is a computer hacker? I'm trying not to judge him right off the bat, but I'm going to have to watch him. However, he is here in my new program so it can help him with his future.

Sam reaches for his schedule and looks it over, going through it class by class.

"I don't see any computer classes here," he inquires as he

seems to be testing me.

"That's because there aren't." I feel informing him of this is almost a deal breaker.

"But I know how to use computers and can basically do anything with them." I hear a bit of a whine in his voice.

"I have been instructed not to allow you to have access to computers until you have completed the program requirements."

"Requirements?" he questions.

"Yes, let's just get through the first part of this and we can revisit your computer classes. Deal?" I feel I am negotiating with a criminal about when he can be a criminal again. Oh no, I can't think like that. It is so hard not to judge. He doesn't look like a criminal at all. Sam has blond curly hair, blue eyes, and he is quite small. He looks quite childlike. I guess you just never know.

"I can live with that." Sam heads out the door to locate his classes.

"Oh yes, Alice you are next." I look up at her, and the young lady that showed off for us a few minutes earlier is now acting rough and tough. What a change right before our eyes.

She comes up to the front where I'm sitting, and I hand the schedule to her. She has an odd smell. I have not smelled any type of perfume like this before. She looks into my eyes, and I see an empty shell.

She leaves the room without a thank-you or anything. She just walks out. How can a young girl be so damaged that she completely shuts off the world around her at the drop of a hat? I'm going to keep my eye on her as well.

One of the officers comes in through the doorway with a young man in tow. He has another file in his hands.

"Here is another one for you," the officer says with a smirk on his face. Oh, this begins to make me angry again, but I keep my cool. "His mother dropped him off late."

"Thank you," I say with an inviting voice while holding out my hand to grasp the file from the officer.

"What is your name son?" I ask.

I get no answer. Feeling as if I'm being ignored, I ask again. "What is your name?"

I look at his file and I see his name. His name is Hunter. With Hunter standing in front of me, I begin to glance over his file. I look up at him again, and I notice he isn't speaking after asking him his name a few times. Looking a bit further into his file, I notice he has a mental illness. That's no big deal. I think we all have some mental illness somewhere. Hunter is diagnosed as Autistic. Well, after looking at his file, I can understand the diagnosis. His grades are top of his class. There are notes that he does not speak much, but he does speak. He is more of a thinker and a doer. So then why is he here?

Hunter stands next to the officer and observes everything. He is sizing up the others in the room. His swaying back and forth is subtle but still noticeable. His eyes are ever moving, taking it all in.

Looking at the police arrest page, I see a photo of a young boy up against the wall in tears. He appears to be in complete terror. This is a bit different than the other files I have. The other kids look almost proud to have their mugshots taken, like it's a rite of passage for them. Not for Hunter. His arrest was much more traumatic.

It seems that Hunter was arrested for vandalism as well. I see a lot of this charge. Hunter draws on the walls of the school, bathrooms in stores, walls at his own home with his parents. He just can't keep his hands off the walls. Well, this one may be a challenge, but again, he is here for a reason. I see I need to put him in the drawing class. Hopefully, I can hone in on his skills and funnel his attention to the correct place to draw.

"Well, Hunter Ashford," I begin, attempting to make a connection with him, "welcome to the program." My smile is inviting, and I must say, I'm trying to hide the concern. I don't want my school to become a canvas.

I turn to the door and call in the office administrator to make Hunter a schedule for his classes. I instruct her to put him in advanced classes but also in a drawing class.

"Hunter, can you go with her to the front office so she can make you a class schedule?" Still no response. I do, however, see a tiny bit of a smile. I hope it's because I'll be challenging his intellect while allowing him to draw.

"Can I test him to see where he falls in the class roster? I see you want him in advanced classes but how advanced and which ones?" she asks.

"Yes, that is a good idea. His testing will show just how far ahead he is," I agree with her.

As he is leaving the room, he turns back to me, "Thank you." He spoke! He actually talked to me! Renewed hope fills my heart. It's only been ten minutes, but this feels like a minor breakthrough.

Okay, who is next? Looking at the files I see Azza.

"Azza? Asia?" I say as I look around the room.

A young lady with a rough attitude stands. She looks like she does not want to be here at all. Oh boy, this one is going to be tough to handle. I can see it already.

"My name is Ah-Zha Syed. It's not Asia." She is quick to correct me. But if someone butchered my name, I guess I would feel the same way. Her name is unique and special to her.

Glancing at her file folder, oh brother, another one. Vandalism seems to be the norm for this program. It appears that Azza has temper tantrums as well and tends to destroy what is front of her. Great! I need to give this young lady something that will calm her down, enable her to concentrate and focus. I'm thinking pottery class. This will be a huge challenge, but hopefully she will be able to calm down enough to make something.

I call in the secretary once more. I instruct her to make a general class schedule but add pottery to the schedule.

Just then Azza bursts out, "Pottery? Really?"

The officer stirs and stands up straighter. Azza notices that he is ready for the kill. She immediately puts herself back in her box to contain herself. Not a good first impression on the first day of the Second Chance Program.

"Okay, I guess I'll try it. I don't want to go back to Juvenile Hall," she says with a defeated tone. Her posture is calm along with her words. Maybe she will actually try, maybe not.

Azza heads out to get her schedule from the secretary. I don't get any other response from her. This young lady is going to be a tough case but that's why I'm here. She deserves a second chance just as much as anyone else.

I look up at the next one in the program, a young man sitting in the back corner with his head down like he is concentrating on something.

"Young man, it looks like you are next." I attempt to get the student's attention, but I need to go to him, he's so preoccupied.

As I get closer to the young man, I see he has a knife in his hand. He is gripping it with a tight fist. The knife is scraping and gouging into the desk. What? He is carving something in my beautiful conference table!

"Stop!" I yell.

An officer comes busting in the doorway.

"Stop it!" I yell once more.

The officer notices just what is happening and that he has a knife. The officer then sprints over to the area where this young man is digging into my table. He grabs the knife out the young man's hands, and it catches him off guard. The young man has headphones. He has no idea what we have been talking about. He didn't even hear me ask for him. He was just sitting here in his own little world digging, carving, digging, carving. My beautiful table has horrible scars in it.

"Hey," he comes to his senses.

The officer throws him to the ground like he's a threat. He has a knife on school property.

"Stop!" I yell at the officer this time. He is holding the young man down on the floor with his face buried in the carpet.

"Is this really necessary?" I have to stop what is happening, even though I'm horribly scared because of the knife. I'm beyond livid because of the damage to my beautiful conference table. I have to understand why we are here.

I plead with the officer to let him up. While begging the officer to allow the child to sit back in the chair, the knife is handed off to another officer who quickly takes it into the other room.

"See! This is exactly what I was talking about!" the officer yells. "This is why you need metal detectors. If you would have let us install them in the beginning, this would not have happened."

"I see that." My attitude is coming back since we have already had words earlier.

"Why are you even giving this thug a second chance when this is what he does?" he asks.

"Please allow him to sit down," I beg.

The officer plops the young man in the chair in front of the damage. I don't think we can repair it.

"Son, what is your name?" I ask, trying to get the young man to engage in the program.

"Joseph," he mumbles. His eyes roll in his head condescendingly. Then he looks up at me.

The officer grabs the young man and pushes him back against the seat. I look at the officer, unable to contain my frustration.

"Officer, I can handle this. Please, allow me."

I turn to the young man and ask once more. "Son, I didn't hear you. What is your name?"

"My name is Joseph Ogden." He lifts his head, and his hair is so long that his eyes are barely visible. He swipes his right hand across his forehead to push his unruly hair aside. Now I can see his face. He has anger in eyes. I can see that he really does not want to be here, but this may be his last chance before prison. I look at his file again. He is almost eighteen.

"Do you want to be here Joseph?"

He rolls his head in an attempt to tame his hair again. "Not really." His attitude is not something I'm accustomed to dealing with. My students love school. My students want to be in school to learn. He clearly does not want any of this.

"So why are you here then?" I want him to answer me. I'm confused.

"The judge," he says as he looks up at me. "The judge made me come here."

"Well Joseph, 1 want you to understand, since you were not listening in the beginning, that you have rules here. If you break the rules, you will go back to Juvenile Detention. However, if you graduate from here your charges will be gone. You will have a fresh start."

"What kind of rules?" His attitude is still very apparent.

"Oh, you know." My attitude is beginning to match his. 1 find myself sounding like I'm from the street as well. "Come to school every day. Get good grades. Participate in programs." I'm afraid to continue, "and," here it goes, "you have to stop doing drugs, stay off the street, and submit to drug tests and stuff while you're here."

Joseph sits back in the chair and looks up at the ceiling like he is thinking about it. Really? He has to think about that?

He gives a deep sigh. He doesn't any other options. "Oh, 1 guess." He says this like it is a chore to be here. Well, it may be, but 1 have him now.

"And no more knives or guns on school property!" 1 add.

He looks up at the officer. "Okay," he says because 1 think being thrown to the ground wasn't on his plans today.

1 look for his schedule and something feels off. After looking at his classes 1 realize that he needs something more. 1 write on his schedule, and 1 put him in shop class. Since he likes carving wood, well then, let him.

1 hand the schedule to him, and he looks it over. 1 see a glimpse of a smile. Did 1 just make a breakthrough?

"Shop class?" he asks.

"Sure, you obviously like carving wood. Why not carve wood and make art with it?"

"But 1 need to use wood carving tools. *Like knives*."

"Yes, you do," 1 acknowledge. "The tools need to stay in the classroom. Is that going to be a problem for you?"

He thinks for a moment. "No. 1 guess 1 can do that." He seems a bit happier now. This just might work for him. 1 do hope that he becomes a better man than the one 1 met today.

I look up and see Avery is the last in the room. He has been listening to all the other participants in the program.

When Avery comes up to the front, he is very different than when I first met him. He is no longer the quiet mastermind that he portrayed himself to be. He is a bit more vocal. Talking is a far cry from what I saw last time.

"I have not told anyone that we have met before. You are just another student here," I say.

"Thank you for that. You know I'm really—"

I stop him midsentence. "I know, but here you don't have to apologize. Here you need to change and make something of yourself. That is how you can repay me."

He put his head down, "Yes ma'am."

Avery reaches out to take the schedule from me. He looks at it. I haven't finished his classes.

"My classes are missing." He turns the schedule to me.

"Yes, I know, I need to talk to you about this." I motion for him to sit next to me. He does.

"I know you have great talent with paint, particularly spray paint." I look in his eyes.

"Yes Ma'am." He gives a snicker.

"Well, first, I'm Mrs. Parker or Mrs. P. here."

"Yes Ma'am, I mean Mrs. P.," he quickly changes his response.

"Anyway, I think I want to start a new program or class with you if you agree to it?"

"What do you mean, me agree to it?"

Now I have his attention. "I want you to start a new class here painting murals with spray paint." I smile from ear to ear.

"Me? You want me to teach a class on spray painting murals?" His surprise is more than he can handle. "But that's what I got arrested for."

"Yeah, and thank you for reminding me." I giggle. "You won't be the actual teacher. But you will help teach how to spray-paint with techniques, form, and how to blend like you did on my wall."

"It is easy to do." He begins to open up with light in his eyes.

"The spray paint has to be sprayed certain ways to make it do special things."

I understand what he is trying to say. "When I draw, it isn't the actual picture that is the art. The art is how the pencil is held and how much pressure is used, the direction of the stroke, the thickness of the lines. Painting is the same, but I don't know how to spray-paint." He doesn't know how to draw with a pencil.

"You understand the mechanics of the sprayer. You understand the motion of the sprayer. Everything about it. That is why I want you to teach this." I look at him. "Is this something that you want to try?"

He sits back in the chair as if he is thinking about the rare opportunity I offered him. I can see the wheels turning in his mind. A smile, a worry, a look of accomplishment, and, "Yes, I would love to teach this."

"Good, now let's get your class schedule finished in the other room." I get up from my chair. "This doesn't mean you can skip the other classes. You still need to participate in other classes and graduate."

"I understand." He throws his arms around me, and I'm in total shock. He hugs me, and then, I'm not sure, but I think he starts to cry. Oh no, not him. It would not be cool for a student like him to cry. He pushes me away.

"I can't thank you enough." An honest smile of gratitude radiates from his face.

Now I know I'm making progress, and it's only the first day.

With everyone in their assigned classes and the officers finally satisfied enough to leave the school, I take a moment in my office. I take a deep breath of relief. I made it through. I actually made it through the first part of the program.

Pulling my list of participants out, I go over it once more. Avery, Sam, Joseph, Azza, Nicholas, Hunter, Alice, and Rainelle. This is a good start for this program. Not too many to over-take the school, but just enough to make a difference.

Taking a breather, I need to think about what the heck I

got myself into. I know that I'm doing the right thing, but can I handle it? Sitting back in my chair I stretch my legs out under my desk. Oh, it feels so good to relax. Closing my eyes for a moment, I try to clear my mind.

"Mrs. Parker?" a faint voice comes from the doorway.

I look up and see the secretary. "Yes?"

"I was afraid I was interrupting you," she says as she comes into the room.

"I just needed a moment," I say with a great sigh. "Just feeling a bit overwhelmed." I begin to rub my feet under my desk. What I wouldn't give for a massage from Charlie right about now.

"I can understand. Hunter should be finished with his tests soon." I nod and she leaves.

Only a few minutes later, I'm interrupted by one of the officers bursting into the conference room with Alice in tow, dragging her around like a rag doll. What in the world is going on already? I slip my shoes back on, so he doesn't see that I was rubbing my arches.

"Well, Mrs. Parker, I told you so." The officer says with a smug look on his face and an attitude to match.

I look up to see Alice, and she is no longer rough and tough but extremely sluggish. Her shoulders are droopy, her face is elongated. She is attempting to be alert but to no avail; her eyes keep rolling around in her eye sockets. The more I look at her, the more I see her eyes in a pinball tournament going back and forth. The officer is to the point of holding her upright.

"This one is high already," the officer adds.

"What a shame, young lady." I point my finger at her. "You didn't even make it one day."

The officer turns her around and her arms follow like she is a stuffed rag doll. Before I know it, the handcuffs are on, and they are out the door. I don't honestly believe he needed to put the handcuffs on. She didn't look like she had the strength to leave the room even if she tried.

I pick up the folders and pull out Alice's file. One down and it's the first day. Did I make a mistake trying to do this program?

CHAPTER 12

NOT MUCH LATER, a teacher knocks on my door. *As if this day could get any worse.* I close my eyes and slowly take a breath. I need strength. What else could be wrong?

I ask the teacher to come in and sit down. He closes the door. and I immediately begin to worry that whatever it is, it must be bad.

"You know the young man, Nicholas, who is now in my class?"

I feel sick. I just can't handle much more.

"Yes, Nicholas." I pull out the files, thinking I'll have to send another student back to Juvenile Hall.

"Do you know he has a horribly disgusting habit?" He wrinkles his nose.

"A habit already?" How can this be? It's the first day of school.

"He eats paper." The teacher makes a horrible noise.

"What do you mean, he eats paper?" I'm afraid to ask.

"He tears off little pieces of paper and then puts them in his mouth. I'm not sure what he is doing with it. I haven't seen any spit balls flying in the room, so my guess is that he swallows it." Again, the look of disgust.

Reluctantly and under my breath, I say, "Let's go talk to him." I don't dare allow him to see my anxiety. This young man does not deserve my reluctancy to help him. Besides, the teachers all need to know that I have their backs no matter what.

We head down to his classroom. When we arrive, we watch through the window in the door. Nicholas has no idea we are there. Sure enough, he tears a piece off his notebook and puts it in his mouth. The teacher reaches for the doorknob. I grab his hand to stop him.

"Wait, let's watch him and see what he does with it." I'm curious.

Nicholas chews and chews and then spits it out in his hand. Then he forms the wet paper into shapes. I'm quite surprised at this. Strange as it may be, he's creating sculptures, just really tiny ones. I take a step back. I can't believe how strange this first day has been. I'm afraid to even think of what could happen next.

We open the door and motion for Nicholas to come out of the room. We do not need to embarrass him in front of all his new classmates. I just need to understand what he was doing.

Nicholas comes out, and I can see that he is thinking that his time is over at this school. It is far from the truth.

"Can I take him down to my office for a few minutes?" I ask the teacher.

"Sure," the teacher rubs his head and rolls his eyes while he heads back into the classroom. He's had a rough day as well. I close the door as we leave.

Walking down to my office once more, I try to bring up small talk with Nicholas so he doesn't know why I want to talk to him. We get to my office, and he sits down without asking.

"Nicholas, do you know why you are in my office with me?" I ask.

"No." His head is low. Seeing the tough nature of this young man, I proceed with caution.

"You aren't in trouble," I reiterate.

Nicholas is looking at the floor holding onto his book bag. I can see his breathing grow more intense as if he is going into a fight-or-flight mode. He is very closed off. I need to break the ice. I need to get inside this young man's mind and show him that I'm not a threat.

"Can I ask you a question?"

"Yeah, I guess so." He is very hesitant to answer.

"Why do you chew on paper?" It is very hard to ask, but I have to.

"You know." He lifts only his eyes to me, which feels a bit strange. He's like a scared animal sizing up a threat. "To make it wet," he says as if I should know.

"Then what?" I try to keep my voice calm and inviting, asking open-ended questions so I get more than a yes or no. I want him to open up to me.

"I make things with it." He turns to his book bag and pulls it up to the desk. As he opens his book bag, he pulls out a clear box. The box is full of things, but I can't tell what they are.

I lean in to show interest while keeping a slight distance for safety. I'm nervous, but I don't want him to see that.

"Wanna see?" he asks. I think I see a tiny smile emerging from his face.

"Sure." Do I really? I mean these are spit balls, full of spit.

Nicholas pulls open the plastic latch and then begins pulling little figurines out and putting them on the desk side by side. I'm in shock at the talent this young man has. As he is placing them out for display, I can see his pride in his work. I may be the first person to ever really want to see what he was making. I can only imagine how much other kids made fun him for chewing the paper, without really knowing what he was doing. I wouldn't dare make fun of him. I just don't understand him, yet.

"I like to make these guys here. I paint them and then I can," he stops mid-sentence, scared to keep going. "I play... with them like army men." He shows me each person one by one. His eyes are lightening, and the anger is subsiding. I think I'm getting through to him. He seems more vulnerable, open, like a kid again. I'm still cautious.

"How impressive."

I reach down and pick up a flower, and then another one. It's gross to think he was chewing on the paper to make these beautiful flowers, but I'm so intrigued. "You like making flowers too?" I ask.

He smiles. "Yeah, I make them for my mom," he adds.

As I look at his sculptures, I get an idea. "Would you like to make flowers out of other stuff like, sugar?"

"Sugar?" He sounds confused.

"You can make flowers out of sugar. I know the teacher, well chef, that can teach you all about pastries and teach you how to master making flowers for wedding cakes and all. I have an idea. Will you meet me at the end of class?"

He begins to pack up his figurines and heads back to class. I'm just beginning to figure out how I'll tell Charlie my idea when I look up and my secretary is standing in my doorway with a strange look on her face. I can see that she wants to talk, but nothing is coming out. I guess the day really can get worse.

"What's wrong?" I'm afraid to ask. My face feels flushed. Do I really want her to answer?

"It's Hunter," she mumbles.

Oh great! Another student in the program. Why did I start this program? Oh yeah, to help them. But in the meantime, I'm going to have a heart attack.

"What do you mean Hunter?"

"You need to take a look at this."

Reluctantly, I rise from my comfy chair and head out the door with her. She took Hunter to a classroom that was not in use for him to take his testing. We walk down the hall and enter the classroom where Hunter was. He is not sitting at a desk taking the test. Instead, he has already covered our school walls with his impressions.

I enter the classroom expecting to need Alfred to set up the room to be repainted. However, that is not the case. Not the case at all. Instead, I see something extraordinary. There are three six-foot whiteboards side-by-side at the front of the classroom. He is standing in front of them with a marker. My breath catches. What if that's not dry erase? But as I get farther into the room, I turn around to take it all in.

Hunter is hard at work drawing on not just one whiteboard, but all three of them. I step back even further to get a better view of the picture on the whiteboards. Hunter is still hard at work. I don't think he realizes I'm there, his concentration is so intense.

"Wow!" I say out of sheer amazement.

Hunter has drawn a complete city skyline. High-rise after high-rise, windows, doors, bricks, they are all perfect! Hunter's drawings are the exact opposite of mine.

Hunter's drawings are of a macro view of the world. My drawings are the micro view of objects. His drawings are full of grandeur. The architecture in his drawings is utterly beautiful. So, this is what everyone has been talking about. This is not vandalism at all. At least, I don't see it that way. This is pure art. He just doesn't know how to express his art. In this classroom, he had the huge canvas to work on, the three white boards.

"Hunter?" I ask.

He becomes startled. He turns around, realizing that I have been standing there. He suddenly becomes very shy and withdrawn, and he starts rocking from one foot to the other. His autism is very apparent because he is rocking back and forth with anxiety.

"Honey, I'm not mad about you drawing this," I try to reassure.

"You aren't?" His voice is timid.

"No, honey, can you come back here with me for a moment?" I request.

Hunter puts down his marker and begins to walk back to where I'm standing. He appears to be waiting for his punishment.

"Hunter, turn around and face the front with me."

Hunter very reluctantly turns around, and this makes him very nervous. He steps back to be in line with me so I'm no longer standing behind him. I see his eyes go over his drawing. He appears to still be drawing in his mind.

"Where did you learn to draw like this?" I ask in a calm tone.

Hunter just stands there gazing at the whiteboard. I need him to talk to me. Oh, please talk to me. I take a chance and put my hand quietly on his shoulder. I bend slightly to be on the same level as him. Well, that wasn't far to go. Most of the students here are taller than I'm anyway.

"Hunter?" I turn to him and ask once more.

"I like this," he mumbles. "But," he stops, cocks his head to the side to get a better view, "it's not finished."

"Who taught you to draw like this?"

"Nobody," he answers, still examining his work.

"Is this what you see in your mind?" I ask, begging to get inside his head.

"I guess," he says with a nonchalant tone.

"Did you know I like to draw too?" I want to show him that we are more alike than he realizes. I draw too, therefore, I cannot judge his drawings.

He looks at me with a little smile. I think we make a connection in that moment.

"You know, when you draw, you connect to people in a way that only you can understand," I say, putting my arm around him. Taking a chance, I begin talking again. "That connection is what makes you special." My smile is warm and inviting.

"I am?" He looks at me with childlike eyes.

"Sure, you are. You're the only one I've ever seen who draws like this."

"You draw?" he adds.

"Yes, but nothing like this. I draw very small details of life." I hold my right hand out with my finger and thumb showing just how tiny my drawings are. Even if it is way off scale.

Hunter looks at me, confused.

"Small things, details like a leaf on a tree." I wave my hand up like I'm trying to touch the tree branch. "Or a hand on an old woman." I hold out my hand and then touch it gently with my other hand. Wow, I just said I have the hands of an old woman. I'm trying to show him that even though we both draw, we do so in very different ways.

"Hmm," he says under his breath, trying to put things into perspective.

Glancing back at the boards, "Now I understand why you got in so much trouble for drawing," I add.

Hunter hangs his head in shame. "Am I in trouble?" he mumbles.

"Nope! This is a school for you to express your talents. Don't let anyone put you in a box or define you with your diagnosis. We're all unique in our own ways. You just happen to be autistic. I *want* you to keep drawing these beautiful cityscapes." I pause to make sure I still have his attention. He seems to be wandering off. "I want you to keep drawing, but I have rules for you."

He turns back to look at me. "Rules?"

"Well, I guess more like guidelines to follow." I try to soften the blow. Rules seem pretty harsh, and I don't want him to run.

Hunter looks at me, afraid of the rules.

"Do not ever draw on any walls, desks, floors, or whatever is school property. I want you to draw on things like this," and I point to the whiteboard, "the whiteboard. I want you to use only dry-erase markers to draw on the whiteboard. Later we will get you a bigger board to draw on. Because you need lots of space." And I wave my arms in the air to show just how big of a space he needs.

Hunter laughs. Oh, that laughter is music to my ears. This young boy is not afraid to talk. He was just looking for the right person to talk to. The right person to understand his words and to admire his work. I'm that person.

I turn and see the secretary standing in complete awe at the magnitude of his drawing. It is huge and perfect. Oh right, he was supposed to be taking a test. How did I get so sidetracked?

"Hunter, I thought you were taking a test," I remind him.

"I did," he responds.

He hands me the papers off the desk and shows me that they are all done. He did the tests and drew this wonderful drawing on the whiteboard, all in that one hour.

"Impressive," I muse.

Even after a cursory glance, I can already see he got all the questions right. Every single one. This kid is learning at a college level, and we need to keep his interest in school by teaching at a college level.

"School is boring," he says as he turns to the whiteboard. "That's one reason why I draw. I take the tests and I'm finished way before the other students. I just sit there."

"Makes total sense to me." I can't help but glow with admiration for this young boy.

I look up at the secretary. "We'll need to enroll him in college classes as well as classes here so he can still be part of the Second Chance Program."

"I'll get right on it." The secretary leaves the classroom.

"Hunter, I must say, I'm really impressed by your learning ability and your artistic ability as well."

"You are?" I don't think he has ever heard anyone praise him. They all see his drawings as vandalism.

"Yes, I am. Let's head down to the office and get your schedule squared away. First, can I take a photo of your masterpiece?"

"What about the whiteboard?" he asks.

"Just leave it. I really like it," I say with a smile.

Hunter is smiling, but he still seems nervous to talk to me. He rocks back and forth again. It's okay; he needs to channel that energy, but for right now, he needs to rock. I drop him off with my secretary and then return to my office to wait for Nicholas.

I am waiting for Nicholas to come back to my office. While I wait, I ask Charlie to meet me in the kitchen classroom. Charlie is confused, but I think he may like this.

Just then Nicholas comes around the corner.

"Ah Nicholas, great, you are here!" I say.

Nicholas seems confused about why I asked him back to my office, but I have a surprise for him.

"Get your book bag and come with me," I instruct.

"Where?" he asks, and his voice wavers a little.

"I want you to meet someone," I say gently, hoping to reassure him.

We walk to Charlie's kitchen classroom a large room with four full kitchens and many tables for learning. The tables have a butcherblock top on each of them.

Arriving in the kitchen, I see Charlie. His face lights up as soon as I come into the room. I guess he was having a rough day too.

"Charlie, this is Nicholas. Nicholas, this is Charlie." They shake hands.

I ask Charlie to get some fondant out of the cooler. He does but he still looks confused as to why I'm asking.

Charlie puts the fondant out on one of the butcherblock tables. He unrolls it and takes the paper off. It is quite cold. He looks to me for what to do next. I'm usually not the one in charge in his kitchen, but this time I'm calling the shots.

"Ok, now, Nicholas, wash your hands and then can you please come over to the table?" Nicholas does so, standing with me. Charlie looks between the two of us, waiting for this to make sense.

"Nicholas, will you make a flower like you do for your mom?"

"With that?" he questions. He has never seen anything like this.

"Yep."

"I don't know what that is." He's very cautious.

Charlie picks a corner off the roll and hands it to Nicholas. Nicholas holds the cold fondant with his two fingers.

"It looks like playdough." Nicholas laughs.

"Eat it," Charlie instructs, a glimmer of understanding in his eyes.

Nicholas puts the fondant in his mouth and his eyes light up as he looks at me. "It tastes like sugar." Nicholas has a grin on his face.

"Now take some more and make a flower, like you do for your mom," I instruct once more.

Nicholas begins to reach for the fondant. Charlie stops him.

"Here." Charlie hands him a pizza cutter. "Use this to cut out however much you need." Charlie rolls the cutter around the fondant and cuts out a section. "See, like this."

He hands him the roller and Nicholas holds it carefully. He then decides just how much fondant he wants and begins to cut it out.

"Now, this is kind of like sugar so you need to work a bit faster with it or it could melt from the heat of your hands."

145

"Really?" Nicholas asks, giggling.

"Yep." Charlie reaches down for the rest of the roll and begins to roll it up. "I'm going to put the rest of this in the refrigerator until we need it again."

When Charlie gets back to the table, Nicholas is molding a perfect flower, much like the ones he molds for his mother. Charlie's eyes reveal just how impressed he is. The flower is small but beautiful.

"Can you make the stem and leaves for it?" Charlie asks.

Charlie hands Nicholas some more fondant. This time the fondant is green. The green color is soon molded into a beautiful stem with two leaves on each side of it. Nicholas puts it down on the table next to the flower and pinches them together. When he looks at me, his face is full of so much joy that he can hardly contain it. Then he looks at Charlie. Charlie is obviously very impressed.

"How did you learn this?" Charlie asks Nicholas.

"I dunno. I make them with paper," he responds.

"Paper?" Charlie asks curiously.

I squinch my nose and look at Charlie. It's gross, and I'm sure he really doesn't want to know the answer.

"Yea, I chew the paper to make it wet and then I can mold it into anything I want. I make my mom flowers." Nicholas is so excited that he gets his book bag and pulls out the figurines and flowers he makes for his mom. "See?"

Charlie is afraid to touch them since Nicholas just told him that he chews them up first, but Charlie is able to see the detail in each flower and figurine presented before him.

"Is this what you wanted me to see?" Charlie asks me.

"Yes, it is." I'm trying to hold back the excitement. "When I saw this, I thought you might teach him the art of cake decorating with fondant. At least this stuff he won't have to chew first." I have a hard time containing my laughter.

"How would you like to be in my cooking class, well, baking class?" Charlie asks Nicholas.

"Sure, but how do I change my schedule if I'm already in classes? Doesn't my probation officer need to know?"

"Probation officer?" Charlie is now a bit taken aback.

"He is in the Second Chance Program," I say.

"Oh, yeah," Charlie is obviously concerned, but his admiration for Nicholas' talent with the fondant puts his fears on the back burner. "Kid, you have some real talent there," Charlie says as he put his arm around Nicholas.

"So, what do you think? Want to learn to bake?" Charlie asks one more time.

"Hmm, my mom would like that, but I have never cooked before."

He's trying to talk himself out of this already. "That's why you are here, to learn," I say.

He looks down at the fondant flower for a moment, thinking.

"Are you game?" I bite my lip, hoping for a good response.

"Sure, I will learn how to cook for my mom." A little smile shows on his face.

"Great! I will make your schedule corrections so you can take cooking classes with Charlie."

"Charlie?" he asks.

"Uh, yeah," realizing I called him by his first name. I fix it, "Chef Charlie to you." I have to remember that we are still in school here, and I need to keep things professional to some degree.

"Oh, yes, Chef, got it."

"Go back to your classroom for the end of the day, and then back to my office later for your new class schedule, okay?"

"Yes, Ma'am."

Nicholas puts his box back into his bookbag and heads out the door. I have a really good feeling about this young man.

Once he's gone, I turn to Charlie. He looks just as conflicted as I feel. He glances at his watch. "I have to go, see you later?"

I nod. He heads back off to the restaurant.

CHAPTER 13

TODAY FELT LIKE IT WOULD NEVER END, so when it finally does, I decide to take time for myself. I need to sit by myself outside to get my head together. Once out in the garden, watching the flowers and birds, I finally let my emotions out. After a day of holding myself together, it feels good to cry a bit. Lost in my own world, I don't hear the door open.

Charlie has Millie in his arms, and they have come to make sure I'm okay.

"Mommy?" Millie asks.

I quickly try to hide my tears of exhaustion and frustration. I'm not sure why I'm crying. This program is going to be a success. I can feel it. I just don't understand why it feels so hard. Millie's arms wrap around me.

Charlie sits in the chair beside us, allowing Millie to comfort me.

"Mommy? You okay?" She's grown up so much in the last few months, it's scary.

"Yes, honey." I wipe the tears away so she doesn't see them. I'm not sure why, because I'm sure she already noticed. I know Charlie did.

"Honey?" Charlie asks quietly.

"It's just been a long day." I pull my jacket up over my shoulders as if to trying to hide.

"You know Millie, I have been at the school all day." I stop because I'm not sure just how much I should tell her.

Millie sits on my lap and looks up at me, hanging onto every word I say.

"I'm helping teenagers who have gotten into trouble."

"Twouble?" she asks.

I giggle. She's so cute. "Yes dear, trouble," I correct her.

"Honey, I tried to tell you this was not going to be easy. These kids are very different from the ones you are used to in your school," Charlie says.

"I know."

Charlie can hear the distress in my voice. I just can't hide it.

I turn to Millie once more. "Millie?"

"Uh huh." She perks up.

"These teenagers have done bad things, and those things got them into trouble," I try to explain.

"They be bad?" she asks.

"Yes, but I'm trying to help them not be bad." I try so desperately to break it down into terms that she can understand at her age.

"Have you heard of me talking about the dash? You know the one that I speak about when I talk about the lady that you were named after?"

"Um, kinda?"

"Kinda? Hm," I'll have to tell her about Mildred again. "Right now, lots of teenagers are being bad, going down bad paths in life."

"Okay."

I think she is following. "I invited some of them to our school, so they have a chance to change and be better. Changing their path of life again." I know I'm losing her, but I have to keep going.

"So many mommies and daddies don't talk to their children about what is right in life and what is wrong. Some kids don't have mommies or daddies to talk to about anything."

I look at Charlie to ensure he is on board with this unplanned talk with Mildred so early in life.

"Going to school is very important. Learning what you love to do is also important."

"Dancing!" Millie gets very excited.

"You like dancing, kiddo?" Charlie asks.

Millie nods her head hard with a grand smile on her face.

I look at Charlie. "Hm," I say, not really surprised, almost expecting it.

"That's nice dear, dancing it is. But this is different." I try to keep her focused, a task all its own with this little girl.

Millie jumps down and begins to dance around as if she was cued. She tries to reach her arms up high and stumbles.

"Honey, sit down for a minute." She does.

"The lady you were named after always taught me special things like doing what I love to do, you know, like dancing." I reach out and touch Millie's shoulder.

She giggles, "I'm Balbina!"

"Also, important stuff like being a good person, treating other people the way I would want them to treat me." I sit back a bit and touch my chest.

Charlie can see that I'm struggling, so he gives a little smirk.

"Honey," Charlie tries to get Millie's attention. "She also taught Mommy that is it good to help other people when they need things."

"You mean like...," and she is totally lost for words. "Like, if Mommy is foldin' lu'ndry?"

Charlie and I both laugh.

"Well, yeah, that is one thing," Charlie giggles.

"Everything you do is important. You need to make everything special," I add.

"Special?" Her eyes open wide to match her mouth.

"Yes, honey, everything you do makes you who you are." I keep trying to make her understand what I'm trying to say. She will not understand learning about the dash yet, and I think this may be a conversation for much later.

Just then, Millie jumps up and begins dancing around again. "I'm special, I'm special." She twirls around, holding her hands up over her head like a ballerina. Then she holds her hand out and it seems like she grabs onto something. "Come on, balbina, I'm special." One last twirl and she is off around the garden.

Charlie and I watch her for a moment, wondering what on earth happened.

"I tried."

Charlie sends a warm smile in my direction. "I know, honey. She'll be just fine." He stops with a smirk. "After all, she's special."

We both laugh. The day comes to a perfect ending.

CHAPTER 14

AFTER A COUPLE OF WEEKS, things seem to be going well. However, I still think I need to check in with the teachers to see how they're doing and offer my support. After all, these kids need to do better than just *attending* classes. They need to pass. After getting reports from their teachers, most of them are on track. But some of them seem to be struggling.

I notice Avery had a rough start. His grades were below average, but since he has gotten into school and a routine, his grades have started going up. Giving him the chance to show his skills to other students that want to learn spray painting seems to be helping with his morale, which has helped in his schoolwork for other classes as well.

Nicholas is average. He seems to be invisible. He is on the sidelines doing his thing and not really making any waves. I don't see any issues with his grades either.

Alice, well she never made it, so I can take her off my list. Pulling her paperwork out of the folder feels strange, but she did disqualify herself.

Rainelle is a hard one to read. She dresses in all black, also trying to be invisible. I hope she will come out of her shell. Her grades are within the parameters of the judge. So far so good.

Then I have Sam. Sam is a computer whiz, and he is great at math. His grades are above average. I have no problems with Sam in his grades or character.

Joseph's attendance is good, but his math skills are low. The judge will not allow Joseph to pass with those grades. So far, all his other classes are good, but I may need to find a math tutor for him.

Hunter is in an entirely different world. He is working at an academic level way into college while being in school here. His case intrigues me. He's a genius, and I can't understand how he could get into so much trouble as such a smart kid. He has a hard time expressing himself because of his autism, but I'm just so impressed by his learning ability. He will pass with the judge as well.

Azza's grades are low. I'm going to give her some time to see if she can settle down enough to learn. Her grades are not critically low, but they could be. I'll have to watch her.

Overall, they're doing quite well. I do need to find a tutor for Joseph. Maybe Hunter or Sam would like to help? That would look good for the judge as well. I'll revisit this in a couple of weeks again to ensure that we are still on track.

A couple of weeks later, everything seems good. I walk down the school hallway to check in on things. It has been so quiet lately I mean, no outburst in a while. This alternative art program is off to a great start. Hopefully, we are beginning to make a difference in these children's lives. At least it's better than the alternative. I know I wouldn't want to be in juvenile detention or worse, jail. It *was* hard at first. The judge's warning plays through my mind. *It's going to be a learning experience for you, Mrs. Parker* said the judge. Boy, was he right! These kids have no guidance from their parents or even a good peer to follow. That is why I wanted to do this. I wanted to take kids that were lost and help them find their way in life. You know, find their passion, give them something to live for. But, as we've all settled in, I think it's working.

As I make my way past a few classroom doors, I can hear each classroom and what they are working on. Some are quietly drawing, some are loudly playing instruments, and others are right in the middle. Most of the classrooms are calm and controlled, but as I pass the next door, one of the students becomes loud and disruptive. It is so disruptive that other students come out of their classes to see what's going on. Then I hear a crash. I need to investigate.

As I turn around, a desk flies out the doorway. Well, that isn't something you see every day. More yells, crashes, and furniture being rearranged forcefully draws me into the room.

A group of kids is gathered on one side of the room, and on the other, one young girl stands alone. The desks are strewn about the room as if a tornado just burst into existence. I guess it kind of did. Papers drift slowly to the ground as if in slow motion, almost resembling feathers falling in slow motion. What the heck! My school is a mess, just like the prom.

The young girl stands there like a deer in headlights, unsure where to run. She has long, stringy, unkept black hair that is purposely pulled over one side of her face. On the other side of her face, I notice a wide eye that is covered in black paint. Oh, it isn't paint. She has intentionally blackened her eyes with makeup. Rainelle. I'm unclear as to why.

"What on earth is going on here?" I ask in a stern voice. The division of the room is uneven. I haven't heard of any problems from the teachers with Rainelle's behavior until now.

One young boy steps forward. He is quite obnoxious, but since he is forthcoming, I'm willing to listen.

"Oh, don't pay any attention to Goth Girl." He sticks his finger out in her direction.

"Yeah, Goth Girl has these temper tantrums. She's the one that threw the desk," says a girl with blonde hair in a tight ponytail. She is a cheerleader type and much too eager to get Rainelle in trouble. This young girl has on a miniskirt and a red shirt with bright white letters on it reading "Try Me". I'm not really sure what that is supposed to mean, but I certainly am not going to ask. Tensions have been high enough since this program started.

I turn my attention back to Rainelle.

"Where's your teacher?" I look about the room. Why can't I find the teacher for this classroom? Why is this happening?

Another young man speaks up. "Ms. Jones went to get

supplies." He is dressed a bit preppy. Sam. Our local computer hacker. It seems as if he is trying to dress the part of a white-collar criminal.

Turning to speak to Sam, I feel a bit relieved. I take a deep breath, so I do not overreact because, quite frankly, I'm a bit nervous with the commotion. I'm not sure just how to calm things down. I can't show fear. I'm the new headmaster.

"Mrs. P, the teacher," Sam explains. "She's been gone for a while." He then comes closer to me and adds, "She's been gone for a long time. I'm not sure if she quit or is just not coming back."

Quit? Did Sam just say Ms. Jones quit? I knew this program was going to be tough on the teachers, but for a teacher to just walk off the job and quit? Not my teachers.

"So, what really happened here?" I'm afraid to ask.

After asking Sam for info, I realized I just turned him into something everyone hates, a snitch. The room begins to roar even louder with commotion. I hear the kids start chanting, "Goth Girl, Goth Girl," over and over.

I feel like I'm on the bus again like when I was young and everyone was chanting to me, "Bird Lady, Bird Lady!" What a horrible feeling! I can imagine just how bad Rainelle feels. No wonder she has her hair pulled down over her face. She is shielding herself from the shame.

"Shut up!" Sam screams to the other kids.

With Sam screaming, it opens up the door for me to take him and Rainelle out of the room. This way I can get some answers away from the other chanting kids.

I point at both kids. "You two, please leave the room and go to my office." I point in the direction of the door and as I was doing so, Ms. Jones comes bursting in.

"Is that my class making all this noise?" Ms. Jones is noticeably upset, which is made worse by my presence here.

"Yes, it is," I say as I look in her direction with great concern.

Ms. Jones grows worried. She knows she lost control of her students. I'm obviously upset, but I have to deal with the students first. Then I can deal with Ms. Jones.

"Kids!" Ms. Jones says in a stern voice. "Sit back in your seats." Ms. Jones makes her way back to the front of the room with her arms full of sketchpads, pencils, and other art supplies. She slams the supplies onto the desk. "Sit down!"

Sam picks up his sketchpad and follows behind Rainelle. They soon turn out of the room and make their way down the hall.

The room begins to settle, but the screeching of desks and chairs being put back into their prospective places is deafening and rakes my already pained nerves even more.

Ms. Jones makes her way back to me after she slams her supplies down. Her demeanor has softened, and with me, she seems nervous. "Mrs. Parker, I'm so sorry."

I motion her out of the room just shy of the doorway. We both exit the room but are still able to be seen.

"It's quite alright. We all knew this was going to be a tough road," I say with a reassuring tone.

Ms. Jones's head hangs in defeat. I know this is very hard on her. I feel her pain. I just pray that the other teachers are holding up. I make an attempt to inspire her to keep going.

"These kids have no one to teach them right from wrong," I explain.

"Yeah," Ms. Jones's voice is soft.

"We all took on this battle." I place my hand on her shoulder. "We all took this on together."

"Uh-huh," she says. I'm not sure if she is trying to convince me or herself that she understands just how much of our school has been broken by the new program.

"They need a role model." I lift my hand from her shoulder and point my finger at her, "and that role model is you." I just put a huge burden on her shoulders to be tougher than all those new kids in the program. "We all need to be more of a role model, not just you, all of us, really." I straighten up to take ownership, inviting her to do the same.

The classroom, once quiet, is now coming back to life.

"Now, you need to get back in there while I take care of the two down in my office."

She nods.

I turn to leave, feeling a little successful in my quest.. I notice a change in Ms. Jones. It is like I just empowered her. She has a renewed power to be able to change the world, one child at a time. She looks back through the doorway and decides to jump into the lion's den once again.

"Mrs. Parker?"

"Yes?" I stop to give her my attention.

"Thank you. I needed that." She smiles and steps back into the lion's den.

I smile as I walk down the hallway. I need to get a hold of my emotions to deal with the other two kids. I can't let them see me uneasy.

When I reach my office, both kids are sitting next to each other in silence. I'm not sure if the silence is just because I'm there, or if they really weren't talking to each other. I get a look at both kids. They are as opposite as two can get.

When I reach them, I take Sam first to get his side of the story. Besides, he seems like a talker, and well, Rainelle doesn't seem too talkative at the moment.

As Sam and I go into my office, Rainelle pulls out her sketchpad. At least she will keep herself busy while I interrogate well, not really, Sam. .

I motion for Sam to sit in the chair in front of my desk. I hate sitting behind a desk, but that is what is expected, me being the headmaster.

After we both get somewhat comfortable, I take out a notebook so I can write down notes. Sam gazes around the room, looking at all the photos of Millie playing with her daddy and me. He looks at some pottery on my shelf and then his eyes pass over a picture I drew in pencil many years ago—a flower I drew when I was four.

He rises from his seat to get a better look at it. "Was this done by your daughter?"

I giggle, releasing the rest of the tension from the room. "No." I sit back in my chair.

Sam keeps looking at it. I think he is confused.

"I drew that many years ago. I think I was four," I say nonchalantly, though I know exactly when and where I drew that masterpiece. It is a masterpiece. It is my masterpiece, my first. My Aunt Jackie said it was.

"Hmm, it looks like your daughter drew it," he says strangely. I know he doesn't mean any harm, but to say it looks like a child drew it kind of hits me wrong. I don't know why though. I *was* a child when I drew it.

"No, I drew it. I think it was my first actual drawing," I say.

"Interesting," he says strangely once again. The picture is quite out of scale and yes, it does look childlike, but I did draw it. I drew it while on a picnic with my mom and Aunt Jackie. My Aunt Jackie was so happy with my drawing that she made my mom slow down and actually look at it. It wasn't just a child's scribbling. It was a picture of a flower, well, weed, but nonetheless a flower from a four-year-old's perspective.

"And you framed it?" he asks, as if it isn't good enough for a frame. His voice isn't questioning, but his face is a bit distorted. I must admit, now I'm a bit angered by his tone. How could he question the worthiness of the picture for the frame?

"I didn't," I say kind of abruptly. "My Aunt Jackie framed it for me." I bring my anger back into perspective of the situation. "She thought of it as a masterpiece. Then she gave it to my mom for Christmas, from me."

"Oh, that was nice," he says, trying to save face.

"Yeah." I pause. He does not deserve to know the thoughts coming into my head. "That was actually the beginning of my passion for drawing."

"What do you mean?" he returns to his chair and sits slowly.

"You know, passion for drawing," I say, trying to get him to understand.

"Um, not really."

"Passion for drawing means that I can't think of anything else I would want to do."

Sam still looks confused by the word passion. I'm sure that when most kids nowadays hear passion, all they can think of is sex. Passion has nothing to do with sex. But how can I help him understand that?

"Let me try this." I sit up on my chair. "Why are you in that class?"

"I like to draw, I guess." He smirks.

"Okay. What do you like to draw?"

"Cartoon characters or superheroes." He grabs his sketchpad from the class and turns to pages showing superheroes with swords and masks. They are really good.

"Why don't you draw something like flowers?" I ask, though I know the answer.

"Because I don't like them." He then points to a superhero he drew carefully. "I like this." He rubs his finger over his drawing.

"And why do you like them?" I keep prying answers out of him in hopes that he will understand what I'm trying to get at.

He runs his finger over the fine lines of the sword and then down the jawline of the character. "I dunno. I just do." His voice becomes meek like I'm beginning to get into a part of his heart that he does not want anyone to know.

"It looks like you took a lot of time drawing his face and sword to make them perfect."

"You really like it?" His demeanor brightens, and his eyes sparkle.

"Yes, I do," I reassure him. "Do you draw often or just in class?"

"No, I like to draw all the time, but it makes my mom mad." He closes his sketchpad and puts it back into his book bag.

"Why?"

"Because sometimes I like to draw instead of doing my other homework." Ah, the truth comes out. "I draw my characters and then I bring them to life with the computer. I make computer games and then sell them. Ha, at least I'm not hacking into the Federal Trade Center."

"Do you realize what you just told me?"

"Umm, that I don't do all my homework?" Guilt flashes in his eyes. "That I actually broke into the Federal Trade Center?" His face flushes red from shame.

"Well, besides that point," I chuckle. "You just told me that drawing superheroes and cartoons is your passion." I smile.

Sam's eyes get big. "*This* is my passion?"

"Yep! Now that you know your passion, you need to practice, practice, and practice so you can get even better. But since it *is* your passion, practicing won't feel like practice. It will be enjoyable."

A sense of accomplishment comes over his face. He becomes proud.

"Did you know I have a wing in the museum with my drawings, my passion?" I ask.

"No, I don't go over there," he says.

"Why not?" How can you be a student in my art school and not even set foot in the art museum? I started to get angry at the teaching staff. Is this how it is with all the teachers? They are only in their classrooms, teaching? And then I realized that I'm talking to one of the students in the Second Chance Program. He didn't have access to the Art Museum in the other school.

"I didn't think I could go over there."

"Sam," I rise from my chair and move next to him. "You are an art student here. There is an art museum in the other part of the building. You belong there, just as everyone else."

"And you have art there too?" he asks skeptically.

"Yes, I do. Please go check it out sometime, but," and I stop, realizing that we are way off subject. "We need to talk about what happened in the classroom today."

Sam fidgets in his chair. I knew this wasn't going to be easy. Sam takes a deep breath and then talks.

"That girl, Rainelle?" he looks at me to make sure I know whom he is talking about.

"You mean the one in all black, right?" Like duh, I know, but I nod. I have to show I'm listening.

"Yeah, she dresses that way for a reason," he says as he adjusts his legs.

"What do you mean?" Now I have to know what he is talking about.

"She dresses like that so she doesn't get talked to or sat with at lunch."

"Why?"

"I know why, but I can't tell. Something about her parents." He wants to tell me, but it would be snitching on her.

"All the other kids tease her and call her Goth Girl, and I know it hurts her feelings." I can see the concern on his face, and I can hear it in his voice.

"Hm, that's not nice," I add.

"No, it's not. She is in another class with me and I," he stops mid-sentence like he is afraid to talk.

"And what?"

He lifts his head and looks around to see if anyone can hear him. Content that we are in a closed room, he spills his heart.

"I kinda like her." His voice cracks under the pressure of telling the truth.

"You do?"

"Yeah, I sit by her, and she's nice to me." He is obviously relieved to tell me.

"So why are all the other kids mean to her?" I just can't put the pieces of the puzzle together yet.

"They all think..." the pain of telling me the truth is obviously very difficult. He continues, "They think she killed her parents," he says with a whisper.

What! My hand goes over my mouth so no unintentional words can spill out of my mouth like a waterfall. My stomach jumps up into my throat. I can't decide if I'm going to barf or what. I'm in shock. Did this young girl actually kill her parents? I know I have kids from the juvenile justice program, but I was not told of any murderers. I have to shrug it off, not feed into the rumor, if it is a rumor. Oh God! I hope it is a rumor. Gathering my thoughts as well as my composure, I continue the conversation unemotionally.

"Is that why they all call her Goth Girl? To hurt her feelings?"

"Yeah, I think they are really afraid of her."

Do I need to be afraid of her? Oh, my thoughts are running rampant again. How do I stop this!?

"What happens when they chant?"

"She gets hurt and tries to run out of the room, but if a chair or table is in her way, it has to move for her to run." He explains her actions and how the chairs went flying in the room, causing all the commotion.

"So that's what happened." I prod for more information, if there is any.

"Yeah, she was just upset."

He isn't done talking. I see something on his face that puzzles me. "I want to protect her from all of them, but if I do, they'll make fun of me, too." Sam gets sheepish. He doesn't seem like the protector tough guy at all. He is more of a tough guy in his mind, like his superheroes. Maybe he hopes a superhero will come in and rescue Rainelle or maybe he wishes that *he* was the superhero. That would be a sight.

I get up from behind my desk, standing to signal he's free to go. After all, he did tell me a lot more than what I was expecting. Turning my pad of paper over, I head toward the door.

"Let's go see the young lady. You can go back to class now," I instruct.

As I open the door to allow Sam to leave, I look around to call Rainelle. She isn't on the bench where I left her. I take a deep breath before I get upset.

"Ms. Morris," I call out to the reception desk.

"Yes, Mrs. Parker. What can I do for you?" she answers in a pleasant but hurried voice. Her job can be quite demanding. It's probably become more demanding since I started this program.

I look around the room to see if I could see where she went. "Where did the young lady dressed in all black get to?" I ask, still scanning.

"The one sitting on the bench a while ago?" Ms. Morris reminds me just how long Rainelle was waiting for me to finish with Sam.

"Yes," I say with a bit of an attitude.

"I had her go in that office and sit so she could draw." Ms. Morris points to the adjacent office used for guidance counselors. It isn't being used at the moment, so it has a big round table in it with a few chairs.

"Ah, thank you," I say, letting a smile change my attitude.

I keep hearing someone nearby humming. Since this is a school of art, singing and dancing are an everyday occurrence and quite normal. However, this humming sounds like an angel. The song is quite angelic, almost liquid in nature. As I listen more closely, I recognize that comforting song. It is from the school play they are auditioning for. Shrugging it off, I go find Rainelle.

She sits at the big round table with her hoodie pulled up over her head, blocking off her sight. She has no idea I'm here. She is hard at work drawing in her sketchpad, with her head cocked to the left as she draws with her right hand. Then I hear it, that beautiful humming, I hear that angelic song resonating even louder in this room. It can't be! A young lady dressed in goth attire should not sound like an angel. She's lost in the melody. I nearly am, too.

I slowly walk into the room so I don't disturb her. I'm comforted by the humming reverberating from beneath the layers of black clothing. I don't really want to interrupt her, but I have to. Should I touch her?

"Hello?" I ask to get her attention, but to no avail.

I try once more, but this time a bit louder.

"Hello?" Still nothing.

I have to get her attention some other way. I can't really maneuver around the table to another chair because the table fills the room. I'm out of options. I have to touch her.

Carefully, I reach for her shoulder and gently tap her. She jumps almost clear out of the chair. Startled, she pulls her hoodie off her head, and her hair is still draped over her face. The sketchpad is flung off the table and onto the floor beside her. Then she pulls out her headphones. Ah, that makes sense why she could not hear me. I hate those things. Mildred always told me I could not wear them because I was missing out on life around me if my head was only filled with music from the internet. She wanted me to listen to the trees, the traffic, the people speaking, and the birds talking to each other, not to mention the sound made when the birds' wings flap really hard to take flight. She didn't want me to miss out on life. Life is full of music if you listen.

"Hi, sorry. I couldn't get your attention," I cautiously back up from any flailing limbs.

She bends over for her sketchpad. "It's okay." She tucks her sketch pad into her bag and turns her music off. Then she readjusts her hood on her head and tucks the headphones inside, out of sight. I hate hoodies. I honestly do.

We both walk into my office, and I instruct her to sit right where Sam sat before her. She plops down unceremoniously, and I'm not sure why I would expect anything different.

I close the door behind me and walk behind my desk. I think, honestly, I feel safer with a desk between us. I'm not sure if any more outbursts are going to come my way.

"I don't believe we have met yet." I try to break the ice, even though we *have* met—on the first day when the participants were brought to the school.

She just sits in the chair with her hoodie now pulled so low that it covers the half of her face that isn't already covered by her hair.

"Can you please pull your hoodie down?" Ugh, I sound like a principal getting ready to reprimand her. I can't sound like that! I soften my voice. "Can you please," and I pause to soften even more, "pull your hoodie back down?"

Out of opposition, she reaches up to her hoodie and pulls it down. Now her hair covers her face entirely. I reach over the desk as if I'm going to help her with her hair, and she quickly jerks away. Why is this young girl so cautious of being touched? Has no one even taken the time to love this beautiful young lady beneath this cloak of black camouflage? Or did someone hurt her so deeply that this is the only way for her to hide from life?

"Hey!" she says. Her voice is loud. I think she wants to scream but honestly, I'm not sure.

"I'm sorry." I didn't mean to violate her space. "I'm sorry." I remind myself that all of these students come from horrible backgrounds and upbringings. Having someone take the time to listen to them is normally met with expectations.

She pushes her hair back but only on one side, leaving the right side of her face still covered by her jet-black hair. It looks pretty messy, but it is still clean and shiny. I wonder what could cause such a thing that a young lady would hide her face so much that only her left side of her face shows? The right is always covered by her long scraggly hair.

"Are you okay?" I ask.

"Yeah," she mutters.

"As I was saying…" I'm nervous to continue, but I'm definitely staying in my lane. "I have not met you yet. I know almost everyone here, and since I started this program, I'm trying to get to know everyone who's new. So far it has been a challenge, I must admit." I look down at my desk and shuffle the papers there as something to do with my hands. They don't need to be arranged, they're already in perfect order.

Rainelle finally meets my eyes.

"What is your name dear?" I ask with my pen in hand, waiting to write on my pad of paper.

"You already know what it is," she says with great attitude. "I met you already."

Oh, this is going to be a tough one. I'm careful not to set her off. I know nothing about this young lady. I have not even read her file. I usually like to get to know each student, not what their file states. They are usually far off from each other.

"No, I don't. Not yet," I say in a voice to remind her of who is boss. It's not her.

"Yes, you do! It's Goth Girl!" she shouts.

Well, it looks like I need to get tough here.

"Well, Goth Girl, what is your real name?" My voice is now stern with authority like it was earlier. I cannot allow her to get the upper hand in this conversation. "I would much rather call you by your name instead of Goth Girl. I don't think you actually *like* being called Goth Girl. Am I wrong?"

I can see that she wants to open up to me, but that thick skin and attitude won't allow her. Not yet.

"Honey, what is your real name?" I soften my attitude again. I have to show her I'm not a threat. In order to show that I am not a threat, I have to be non-threatening. "So?" I question once more while I sit back in my chair to appear non-threatening.

She rolls her eyes."Rain," she answers."

"Are your parents Native American?" I know full well this is not the case. I know her name, but I need her to communicate with me and this is the first way to start that. "Honey, what is your full name?" I ask again. I wish students would just answer me the first time.

"Rain." She sighs heavily, signaling defeat. "It's Rainelle Nicholson." Her voice is very different, more subdued.

"Well, Rainelle, it is very nice to meet you." I smile.

"I take it you are that Mrs. Mary lady? Or Mrs. Parker?" she asks, a touch of attitude trying to reappear.

"Yes, I am. I'm Mrs. Parker. Ironically, I'm a lady as well," I say as I sit up proudly while tilting my head back and pushing my chin out. I let out a laugh as I do. Just then, Rainelle lets out a laugh but tries hard not to let me hear it.

"Oh my, did you just laugh? Did I really hear that?" I ask her. "I know I just heard you laugh." Maybe light teasing will help ease the tension in the room.

Rainelle can't hold it in any longer. She gives a big smirk and rolls her eyes.

"I heard you were nice, but you know how it is," she says with a relaxed voice.

" Uh-huh," I say in agreement.

"I just got out of jail and everything. I ended up getting into trouble again. My probation officer thought I would be good for this program here," Rainelle says. She begins to look around the room.

"Well, if he thought it would be good, then it will be." I meet her with a similar smirk.

Rainelle sits back in her chair, her eyes landing on the pictures just as Sam did.

"Is that your baby?" she asks.

"Yes, it is. Her name is Mildred."

Her nose begins to wrinkle. "Why did you name your kid Mildred? Don't you know she'll be made fun of?"

"Well, I'll tell you about her namesake someday. She was my very best friend, and, I guess, mom." I look down, taken once more by my emotions. I don't want her to see me cry.

She scans the room again and notices a stuffed dog on the shelf beside her.

"Is this Mildred's?" she asks.

"No, that actually is mine for my office," I say.

"You have a stuffed animal?" She looks confused. Little does she know, I have a really good reason for it. "Does it have a name?"

"No, not yet," I admit.

"I had a dog once." Her face lights up.

"You did?"

"Yeah."

"What was his name?"

"I think it was Buddy, but I had to leave him at the last foster family." Her voice becomes distant.

Attempting not to open any wounds, I ask, "If this were your dog, what would you name it?"

She thinks for a moment. "Is it a boy or girl?" Her face is starting to lighten up.

"I honestly don't know." I've never thought of it before now. I knew I got it for my office, but I never thought this would come into conversation, at least not yet. "You tell me. Does it look like a girl or a boy?"

Rainelle picks up the dog and holds it up to get a better look. While holding it with her left hand, she pushes back the scruffy hair to get a look at its eyes, then turns it around to get a good look from all angles. The brown fur is quite long like a Shih Tzu, so she begins to groom the dog. Watching her, I could almost see her heart release her anger. Her eyes and voice both soften. She holds the dog up close, offering it love that only an owner can display.

"Have you thought of a name?"

"Um, I got it!" She gets so excited that she forgets her hair and pushes it out of her face, revealing either a deep burn mark or a deep red birthmark that covers the right side of her face.

"I think his name is D.O.G. You know, Dee O Gee, D.O.G." Her smile radiates from within.

"That is perfect!" I exclaim.

"It can be a boy or girl, but I think it is a boy dog," she says in a childlike manor.

Just then she notices that her guard is down too far and way too fast. Fear rushes in like a tidal wave, and she grabs her hair, forcing it across her face once more. With this fearful action, the stuffed dog falls to the floor, losing her interest so she can keep her secret.

"Honey, it is okay," I try to reassure her.

"No! It's not!" Her anger is brewing once more. Her shield of protection is broken, and I see her naked with shame.

"It's a birthmark, right?"

"Yes, but everyone..." And she stops, paralyzed in fear once more.

"But, what?" I ask.

"Everyone thinks it is a burn. Since I'm in foster care, they all think." She stops talking again, and I see a tear.

"Honey, it is okay with me." I get up out of my chair and sit down next to her as I did with Sam. I'm no longer afraid of this young girl. She is obviously in pain and needs me.

"They all think I killed my parents in a fire." And the tears fall.

I put my arm around her. At first, she pulls away, unaccustomed to being touched. But her pulling away is met with a greater force from her aching heart. The need to be held and loved is much more appealing than throwing a chair and running away. This time she wants to stay. She leans into me, begging for attention. I hold her much like Ms. Mildred held me when I was lost. I knew how important her hugs were, not only to me when she hugged me, but also to her. She needed to be loved, too.

"Your birthmark makes you special. It is one of a kind. That makes you unique. Having a special unique birthmark isn't something to be ashamed of. It is something to be cherished. Your mother gave you that mark when she gave birth to you."

"But," Rainelle backs up so we can look at each other, "I don't know my mother." The tears began to show. "She didn't want me. She threw me away." The pain in this young lady's face is excruciating. I'm angry and hurt all at the same time. I think she feels the same. I don't know how to fix this.

"It's this stupid mark on my face. She threw me away because I look like a monster!" Her eyes, oh, those eyes are so full of pain.

"You are *not* a monster." I try to comfort her.

"Then why?" she pleads.

"Do you know anything about your mom?" I wipe away a tear from her face.

"No." She turns her head away. "She was young."

"That's probably it," I try once more to reassure her. "She must have been just a child herself, not really sure how to take care of you. Maybe," Oh boy, I'm really stepping on glass here. "Maybe, she gave you away so someone could take care of you the way you needed to be taken care of."

The anger is surfacing once more. I think I opened a door that I should have kept shut.

"Look at me! I'm still in foster care! No one wants me!" she claims.

I have no answers, no solutions. I can only love her on her terms, and I'm not sure what that is yet. Feeling a hollow pit in my stomach, I bent down to pick up D.O.G. and hand it to her.

"Here, you take him home. He needs a good home instead of hanging around me in this office." I offer D.O.G. to her.

At first, she is excited and relieved to have the dog, but then the bull headed requirement for her to be strong and tough comes through. If she were to be seen with a stuffed dog? Oh boy, that would not be good at all.

"Nah, he needs to stay here. Maybe someday I will take him home but not today." She hands him back to me to put safely on the shelf for her to come back yet again to hold him.

"You know, when they make fun of you again or call you names, you can come in and hold D.O.G. anytime. Would that be okay?" I stroke her long black hair out of her face. "You are absolutely beautiful." I smile.

She lifts her hand to pull her hair down once more. The pain of being seen is too hard to face.

"I understand the outburst in the classroom today, but please promise me that you won't do that again."

"I promise." She lowers her head.

"No seriously, no more, please," I ask once more to ensure that we are clear.

"I promise." This rough and tough girl all dressed in black seems more like a child with bright eyes now. I can feel that she is opening up to me. Maybe not trusting yet, but I'm sure that will come.

"Rainelle?" I need to change the subject before she leaves my office, "where did you learn to sing like that?"

"I dunno." She shrugs.

"You have a beautiful voice. You should be singing in the show. You know they are having auditions. You should go for it," I prod her.

"No, I don't want anyone to see me." Her childlike manner is now closing off again.

"See your voice?"

"No, I dress like this to hide from people. People don't want to talk to me dressed like this. It's easier. If I don't have friends, then it doesn't hurt as bad when I have to leave for another foster home. Plus, dressing like this, people expect me to be dark and mean. Makes it easier to hide my birthmark," she explains.

"I never thought of it like that. But I'm telling you, your birthmark is special. You don't need to hide it," I assure her.

"If I sang, I would have to wear costumes, and they wouldn't let me look like this," she says, defeated.

"But," I soften my voice again, "you are beautiful, and you sing beautifully." I touch her arm ever so slightly. "Please think about it." I feel as if I'm pleading with her.

I notice another smile from under the locks of hair, "I will," and a big sigh, "think about it."

"Good!" I reach over to give her a big, loving hug once more. Her arms hold me close. She needed the hug, too.

"You better get back to class," I say, noticing the time.

"Um," she stops.

"What's wrong?"

She put her hands in her pockets as she stood to her feet. "I need an excuse for the class that I missed for my probation officer. It is the only way I can stay in the program and not get into trouble. If I get into trouble, I have to leave." I'm so proud of the progress she has made just in the few minutes in my office.

"I've got you covered," I say.

"Thank you, and you know," she smiles, "everyone says you are really nice." Her face softens. "And they're right."

"Thank you, dear. Now get to class!" I instruct.

"Yes, ma'am." As she grabs her bag and heads out the door, she reaches for her hoodie to pull it over her head again. Well, at least we made progress if only for a few minutes. It's still progress. She just needs to believe in herself. It will happen, but it will take time. I'll be here waiting to see it.

With all the commotion today and checking on Sam and Rainelle, I feel I should check in with the other participants. But first, I want to pull out Rainelle's folder and see just what she was talking about. How bad could this be? I'm sure she's just overexaggerating, stretching the truth to make it sound better, typical teen stuff. However, what I see is far from that.

Her folder starts out just like all the others. The first page is a photo, and yep, she is all in black in it as well. No surprise there.

On the adjacent page is her arrest record. Nothing drastic but nonetheless, still an arrest record. I flip the page over to see her academics.

Her school files are scarce. I see several different schools here. Grades are lower than I expect, but the school years are really broken up. I go to the next page, her demographics.

This is where I see the horrible sight. Rainelle has been transferred from one foster home to the next. She never really had any parental guidance. There are police reports and handwritten reports. These are sickening! One report reads:

> Rainelle was removed from this address due to being abused by a boy in the same foster care. She had multiple bruises and noticeable mental abuse. Several complaints were filed at the same residence about other foster children.

Other pages show documented accounts of several run-aways from several locations, rapes, abuse, severe mental illness, bipolar events, lists and lists of medications. Oh, I can't read anymore. My stomach feels so sick I might throw up. How can this young lady endure such a traumatic childhood and still be a shy little girl playing with D.O.G? I look up at it, sitting on my shelf. Now I understand why she melted when she held it. I understand her need to be hugged. If I were her, I would want to hide, too. I can't read anymore.

I didn't want to read any of these files. I wanted to take every participant on an even playing field. Knowing their background wasn't fair. I wanted everyone to be treated equally, to be accepted equally, and to be given the same opportunities, equally.

Before closing the file, I look at one more page, the page for this program. Turning to the Second Chance Program, I notice a couple of things that stand out to me. I do see the qualification page, arrest record attached, truancy, and lower grades. All of this is typical for a child acting out. Then I saw the paragraph that was handwritten by her for her entrance.

While reading her entrance paragraph I see into Rainelle's

world. She wants to graduate from this program so she can go on to college. She didn't think she could ever dream of going to college. Being in foster care, she had no stable parents to support her, and she longs for support, and guidance. She also said something that melts my heart into tears. Rainelle just wants to feel like she belongs and that she is loved. She doesn't want to be hurt anymore.

Seeing that in writing, her handwriting, etches it in stone in my mind. It is from her heart. She is tired of being the underdog. This young lady has fought homelessness, sexual abuse, mental abuse, and emotional abuse. Doctors have pumped her full of medications, trying to fix the problem. Doctor after doctorstatedg that she was defiant to the point that she was completely unruly and unfit for regular classroom environments, saying she needed to be in an institution until of legal age. No wonder she wasn't adopted by a loving family. They sealed her fate with the swipe of a pen. I would have been scared of her if I was looking to adopt from a foster program and was only able to read her file. She is so much more than just a file. She is so much more than words written in pen.

What the heck does that even mean? Did they even see Rainelle? It sounds like these doctors just wrote down something and then gave her another pill to try to fix her. This poor girl.

Closing her file is hard, but it is something I have to do. That does it. Every child deserves to be loved. Oh my, I want to cry. No, I can't. I feel my face tighten up, and the fight from a tear wins. I can't stop them. I'm crying. I can't have anyone see this! Not in school!

Pulling myself together and putting the participant folders back in the drawer, I take a deep breath. I need to calm myself down before I head out of the safety of my office.

Getting up from my desk, I decide to look in on the other students. Opening the door from my office is like opening a doorway into the unknown. I can't help but wonder about the other students. What are they going through? How is their home life? How did they get into this program? I can't open any more files. I need to check for myself. With each step down the hallway, I feel my heart struggling with my outward emotions. Stop it! I have to get control here. I can do this.

I go down to our new spray-painting class and stop in the doorway to watch. Avery is holding a can of spray paint in his right hand and using a simple piece of cardboard with his left. His back is to me as he demonstrates different techniques by holding the cardboard at different angles and spraying from different distances. I'm impressed by his technique. He is able to make hard lines and faded lines. He shows how to blend colors, shade, and add depth to objects. He then instructs students to try for themselves one at a time.

His eyes catch me standing in the doorway. He stops, runs over to me, and gives me a huge smile that he just cannot contain. He now has self-worth. He is teaching. All of his students are eager to learn. From what I can see, his teaching techniques are those of an actual teacher. Hm, do I see a future teacher in my midst? He may have found his calling, his passion.

Pleased by what I see, I go on to Joseph. He is in the classroom down the hallway. Arriving in the classroom with Joseph, I notice he is hard at work on an assignment. The teacher is grading papers while all the students are working quietly at their workstations. Joseph looks up and sees me. He can't help himself, and he jumps to his feet.

"Mrs. Parker!" he exclaims as he runs over to me. I'm taken back by the sheer magnitude of his gratefulness for just seeing me. He throws his arms around me and thanks me over and over again for the new life I have provided for him with the Second Chance program.

"Well, hello Joseph." I'm happy to see his response. Trying not to fall over from the sheer magnitude of his hugs, I steady myself.

"Come over here and look at what I learned to do." Joseph pulls me to the display cabinet near the window as if he is a five-year-old showing his mother a good grade.

As I approach the cabinet, I see many figurines, each quite

different from the others. Then I see it. It is a sculpture of an eagle.

"Is this yours?"

"Yep." His radiant smile is blinding. This young man is not a reserved young man at all. He is a giddy child showing his schoolwork to me. It is an awesome feeling to see such an expression of achievement.

The eagle is done to perfection. Even though the eagle is quite small in size, the details make up for it. Each wing is meticulously carved to show each feather. The artwork is defined, each quill magnificent in detail. I'm so impressed I get closer to have a better look. The eagle's eye is elegantly defined. The talons are extended out to land on the branch it's close to. His wings are stretched out to steady himself upon landing, almost like a picture.

I'm so glad I saw him carving my desk. Suddenly, the destruction of the desk is so insignificant to the carvings that this young man now has control of. Yesterday's criminal, now today's artist capable of creating works of art that could and should be sold for a fortune.

"I'm so proud of you!" I give him another hug. He not only feels accomplished, but I do as well. Looking at him makes this program feel right. I feel a great sense of comfort and calm beginning to soothe my anxieties. It's coming together.

"Thank you." He heads back to his workstation and finishes the assignment. I must leave the classroom, so I don't disturb them anymore.

Closing the door behind me gently, I feel a great warmth within. This program is really working.

CHAPTER 15

THE NEXT MORNING BEFORE SCHOOL, I make my way to the living room where Antoinette and Mildred are sitting. Antoinette is working on the daily crossword puzzle in the paper while Millie is playing with her stuffed animals.

"How are things going over there?" Antoinette asks cautiously.

"Actually, really well." I'm so thankful she didn't ask me in the beginning.

Millie gets up and begins dancing to the commercial tune on the TV. I see her stretching out her hand and standing on her tippy toes. I gasp for a moment. Moving my eyes in Antoinette's direction while being careful not to move my head, I find myself in awe of what we are seeing.

"How long has she?" and I stop, afraid to finish.

"Well, I'm not real sure." I notice Antoinette is just as stumped as I am.

I imagine how Ms. Mildred may have looked at Millie's age. I wonder if she attempted to dance like my cute little girl.

As we watch, Millie speaks to someone as if she were in a class. It is so cute that she is playing pretend.

Millie is trying to twirl gracefully, but she trips over her own tangled legs and tumbles hard onto the floor. Her curls bounce and land as if they are in slow motion. I look over at Antoinette and we both try to hold back our laughter. When Millie bursts out into laughter we both are allowed to laugh along with her.

"You know," I look deep within for answers, "I think she wants to be a dancer like Ms. Mildred." I bite my lip.

"Hm." Antoinette's face is full of joy. "Another ballerina in the family?"

"Well, she is named after her." I lift my eyebrows almost in defeat. "A ballerina we will have then."

Antoinette returns to her crossword.

"I'm going to set her up with classes, if she wants to learn now," and I stop, checking the time. I need to go. Oh, how I cherish these moments with Millie.

I jump to my feet with a renewed sense of energy for the day. Now off to school after a quick kiss on Millie's forehead.

I'm getting excited about how this program is going. As I walk down the hall, I notice how well the students are getting along. I don't hear any yelling, threats, or even sirens from a metal detector, like in the other school. I'm so glad I didn't bow down to having those installed in my school. This may actually be working.

As I walk a bit further down the hallway, I see the bulletin board has a new flier about the Christmas spectacular coming up later this year. The artists each have specific displays; art, music, vocals, sculptures, you name it. All of the classes are participating. I'm so excited.

Just then the class bell rings, and the students change classes. Students come out into the hall from all directions like a tidal wave. I step aside and allow the waves to slide on by.

I notice Rainelle coming down the hallway toward me. She looks a bit off today. Her smile isn't there, and the light in her eyes has been extinguished. I want to go talk to her, but she seems quite anxious to get to her next class.

"Hey, Rainelle." I push by a couple of students to get to her. Her head lowers. Her hoodie is pulled up over her head, but this time it is not quite right. She seems more withdrawn.

"Oh. Hi."

Her response is quite short. It seems like her response is that of not seeing me to begin with. Did she think she could get by me in this hallway without me noticing her? Maybe she didn't see me. She looks excited to see me but also afraid. But afraid of what?

I reach for her and end up grabbing her shoulder. She screams in pain, dropping her books on the floor. The wave in the hallway stops dead. All of the talking succumbs to a complete, haunting silence. Everyone looks at me with daggers in their eyes, like I'm the one who hurt her.

"Rainelle? What happened?" I just touched her. Why did she scream? Everyone is still looking at me.

Rainelle tries to get away from me, obviously scared to talk to me. I can see that her shoulder is still hurting. She is babying her shoulder while trying to pick up her books. When the other students realize that Rainelle isn't going to have another temper tantrum, they form the wave once more.

"I can get it." Her tone is sharp. I can read between the lines. She wants me to go away. But I can't go away. I have to know what is wrong with her shoulder.

"Rainelle, stop," I demand as I reach for her books. She grabs them out of my hands. This is not what I'm accustomed to. No "thank you", nothing of the sort. She literally grabs the books very roughly out of my hands.

After she gets her books, she stops dead in her tracks. She wants to run, but I can see that she wants to talk to me. She looks petrified. Her fight-or-flight is in full effect. She is so used to running, but her need to talk to me is overcoming her natural reaction.

She turns around and looks up at me. From what I can see under her hoodie, her face is distorted, turning red. She is trying not to cry.

"Honey, please come with me and see D.O.G." She knows what that means. It has become our little code for help.

I'm able to get her away from the other students and into my office. From the corner of my eye, I see Sam following along like a little puppy. He looks really concerned, like he knew what was going on and was afraid that I was going to find out. I have to tell him to leave and go back to his class.

Rainelle sits hard in the seat in front of my desk. Her book bag slips off her knees and lands on the floor beside her. She looks up at D.O.G. Next thing I know, she is jumping up to grab him. She plops down hard again on the chair, but this time she is hugging D.O.G. Her legs are pulled up underneath her so that her knees are touching her chin. Tears are forming even though she is pushing them back. It is no use. She is safe in my office. She can cry and no one will make fun of her, especially me. I would never make fun of her.

"Honey," I start to ask, but I'm so cautious.

Her tears just keep coming. She is trying to fight them.

"Rainelle, what happened?" I find that she is so closed off that I need to get up and go over to the chair she's sitting in. I bend down on my knees, ugh, that hurts, to get on her level and I want to get on her level to show I am equal to her, not an authority figure. I speak to her with as soft of a voice as I can. "Honey, can you tell me what happened?" I gently touch her arm, but it isn't the arm that hurts. It is the other one. "How did you hurt your arm?"

"Um," she starts.

"Can you tell me?" I plead with her.

I see the ice breaking or maybe even melting. I see a young girl so afraid to speak that she can't get her mouth to form the words. I see her pain, and I'm feeling it too. Unaware, she pushes her hair behind her ear, leaving her birthmark in full view. She isn't afraid of me. I reach up on my desk and pull out a tissue. I hand it to her, and she reaches over with her arm that isn't hurt, all the while holding on tight to the stuffed animal. And then I see it.

With her hair pulled back behind her ear, which is very uncommon for her, I see not only her birthmark but, oh it can't be. Is that what I think it is? No! I want to scream but I can't. If I do, she will run for sure. The anger that was a slow boil is now blowing full force like a pressure cooker screaming to tell me it is finished.

"I can't help you if you don't tell me what you need." I push her hair back behind her ear. She allows me to touch her, and now I can see just how bad the bruises are. She also has a small cut on her lower lip.

"Um..." She wants to tell me. It looks like it is too painful to talk.

The anger is taking hold so firmly that I feel my face turning red. Since I have freckles, it is very hard to hide this. Somehow, I need to calm down. Slow down Mary, slow down. I pay attention to my breathing. Yeah, this sure is hard, trying to keep it from being seen. But I have to. I calm my heartbeat and my breathing. I think I can talk now.

"It's okay. I'm here," I try to reassure her. I run my finger through her thick black hair and trace the hair behind her ear. I hope she understands that I see what happened and that I don't have to say it. Then she speaks.

"I have to move again, but I can't!" she yells.

Rainelle is trying so desperately not to cry any harder. Holding D.O.G closer than ever, she repeats what she just said. Her voice becomes faint, desperate. "I can't move again!"

Confused, I have to ask for more. "Why? Move where?"

"I can't move because," and she stops. I know too much already.

"Because of?" I prod her with an open-ended question.

"This school! I can't move because of this school!" Her pain is now being matched with anger. I don't know if she is going to bolt out the door or stay and cry. Oh, please don't bolt and leave, please stay.

"So why do you feel that you need to move?" I ask cautiously.

Her face contorts again. More tears. Something is really wrong.

"Rain, I need to know." I'm trying so hard to stay calm.

"It's my foster dad. He," she stops midsentence, her face filled with fear, "he got mad at me." She stops to compose herself. "He grabbed me." She stops to catch her breath. "I ... I fell. I'll be fine." It is noticeably difficult to speak when you can't breathe from crying so hard.

Like I'm going to believe that. I'm not sure who she is trying to convince, me or her.

"Is this normal? Does he do this often?" I'm afraid to keep asking, but I have to know.

She tries to continue, but it hurts. "He hurts me every night."

"Hurts?" I need to ask, but I'm so afraid of the answers.

"It's just like all the other foster homes." Tears keep coming in waves.

Oh God, I was so afraid of this. "How?"

She is getting tired of my prodding questions. She has been down this road several times and is not willing to travel it again. Here comes the anger again.

"I tried to fight him off," she cries even harder. "I really did." She stops to catch her breath. "I said no, I don't want it anymore."

"What happened?"

"I woke up this morning and well," she pulls her arms close to herself, shielding herself from her words, "he was, you know." She stops. I can see her mind racing, wondering if she can really talk to me and tell me the truth. "My foster mom was gone. He was home."

I find it hard to breathe. I have to stay professional, but I want to hold onto this young lady and tell her not to worry.

She continues, "I was in the shower and," her voice disappears. "He was there...again."

Oh, hell no! How can the foster system be so messed up to the point where this young lady keeps getting hurt over and over again? I just don't understand it.

"I'm guessing you did not talk to your foster mom." I look down at the floor. I think I know the answer to that.

She sits up, wipes her face off, and poof, she becomes that hard street kid once more.

"You know, it isn't a big deal. I can handle myself. I've done it before. Like I said. I'll be fine." Her demeanor is now of a tough girl that doesn't need D.O.G. anymore. She puts D.O.G. on my desk and sits back in her chair, her arms folded against her chest like a little kid that isn't getting any candy, almost pouting. Once again, she is like a completely different kid. The mood swings are quite difficult to keep up with.

"Is that why you need to move?"

I know she is ready to spill the beans, but I'm so scared of what she is going to say. I mean, I can read between the lines, but come on.

"If I told someone, I would be moved to another foster home."

"Sounds like you need to move immediately." My voice becomes more of a protector than a school official.

"I don't know of anywhere I can go. They all want young kids. Look at me." She gets up and begins to model her finest all-black outfit, complete with dangling chains. I know what she is talking about. The outfit is fit for, well, a goth. "Who would want a teenager like me to come into their home, looking like me? They think I'm going to steal everything. One foster home thought I was going to hurt their dog because I look like this. I was only there for two days."

"What do you mean, looking like you?"

"You know, Goth Girl!" Her defense mechanisms are back up in full force now. All the progress we made is being erased in a matter of ten minutes. How can this be?

"But—"

She abruptly interrupts me, "There are no buts. If I have to move again, I'm taken out of this program, and I like it here." She is back to being a scared little girl again.

"Why would they make you leave this school?" I'm a bit confused about how this whole foster process works. I believed there were many loving families hoping to help kids like her. Why would another family take her out of a program that is working?

"I can't be in the program if I'm in a...a...a...," she is grasping for words, "another school district." She is so upset that she begins to stutter.

"How do you know that?"

"I've been in all the school districts. That's why I can't tell anyone." Rainelle suddenly gets worried. "You can't tell anyone."

I get a twinge of worry deep in my gut. I have to tell someone. It is my duty to protect her. I legally cannot keep this a secret.

"But he hurts you," I remind her of the reality.

"But you can't tell anyone! I like it here. I mean," and she stops crying long enough to get her words out, "I like you." She stops again to finally breathe. "You believe in me. You are the only one who ever has taken the time to talk to me. Well, except Sam." She lets out a little giggle.

"Yeah, I know Sam likes you."

Her face flushes. "How do you know?"

I shake my head. "That isn't important right now. We need to figure out what to do about your situation."

I pick up the phone, and Rainelle immediately becomes very agitated. "Oh yeah, call the cops! That's exactly what I need." She grabs her bookbag, ready to bolt out of the room.

"No, I'm not calling the police." I have to keep her here.

The phone is answered on the other end.

"I'm sending down a student, Rainelle." An awkward pause. "Can you please check her shoulder and her cheek for me?" Another pause. " Uh-huh, yes, okay, I will tell her. Thank you. Bye." I hang up the phone.

Rainelle is still ready to bolt, but I think she is torn by the love I have for her. She wants to trust me, but she's so afraid to.

"The school nurse is coming to take you to get checked out. She will tell me just how bad your shoulder is and if you need to see a real doctor. Until then, I need to figure out what do to with this."

Rainelle picks up her bookbag and turns to leave with the nurse. She doesn't turn with hostility. She looks defeated. She is asking for help but knows the outcome won't be what she wants. Before leaving my office, she pulls her hoodie over her head and turns in my direction.

"I know you have to tell them. Thank you for at least taking the time to listen to me. Most teachers would have just called the police. I would have been hauled off in handcuffs"

"Handcuffs?" Why in handcuffs? I can't hide the shock.

"They assume I'm the one at fault." She rolls her eyes.

"I would never treat you like that," I reassure her. "Now go get checked out, okay?"

"Yeah, I will."

Rainelle leaves my office. Despair settles on me. I have to report this. It is my responsibility to report this. But what if they take her out of my school? Out of my program? She will end up going back to juvenile detention for the crime she committed. This program will have been a waste of time. She is halfway through the school year. I have to figure out what to do. I can't let her go back to that foster house. I can't allow her to be hurt again.

I find myself holding the phone, trying to talk myself out of calling her probation officer. I have to call. I have a responsibility to call. If I don't call, then I may lose the entire program. The phone is getting heavier and heavier the longer I hold it. Oh, I don't want to make this call.

I find her file and get her information. Her probation officer number is on the page with the arrest record. Oh Lord, please don't make me call.

My trembling fingers touch the keypad. Each number is harder to press than the last. As I listen to the ringing, I beg them not to pick up. Please don't pick up. I can leave a message, and that will buy me some time to sort this out. With each passing ring, I long for the answering service to come on.

It doesn't.

Her probation officer answers. My heart feels like it is in my throat. I have to do this, even though I don't want to.

Thankfully, her probation officer is empathetic to the situation at hand. He's afraid there aren't any other foster families for her to go to. She may have to be taken back to juvenile hall until she ages out. Was Rainelle right? This can't be. How can a child be put in such a situation where she does not have a family to live with or even a stable environment to learn from? If she is taken to juvenile hall, then she *will* have to leave our school. Everything Rainelle was saying is coming true. What did I do? How can I stop this?

Just then my door bursts open. Sam is standing there in tears.

"Mrs. P, you need to come quick." His voice is out of breath and hard to understand. He is almost panting like a dog.

I still have the probation officer on the phone. I can't leave this phone call.

"Mrs. P!" Sam yells.

I pull the phone down from my ear.

"Sam, I'm on the phone." I try to whisper to him but in a tone that he will understand.

"But Mrs. P," he yells once more. "It's Rainelle!"

I calmly tell the probation officer that I need to tend to Rainelle in the nurse's office. He tells me that he will be down to the school directly. I hang the phone up and it is almost a relief that I don't have to talk to him anymore. But now the panic sets in.

I jump to my feet and grab whatever paperwork I have on Rainelle. As I'm running out of the office, I can hear the commotion down the hall toward the nurse's office. As I get closer to the office, I hear the yelling and screaming, papers flying, and office furniture being turned over. It's just like before. Oh, this can't be good. She promised me.

Turning into the room I saw something that hit me like a truck, no, a train. When the train finally passes, I realize just what is happening. Two police officers are holding Rainelle down on her stomach while trying to handcuff her. She turns her head and looks right at me.

"I thought I could trust you!" she yells.

My stomach feels like a knife has been just thrust in over and over. With each word, another thrust is felt. She thinks I am the one that called the police on her. After looking around the room, I do see why the police were called. She had another temper tantrum. This one looks far worse than the other one.

One police officer is actually sitting on her back while he holds Rainelle's hair, forcing her face into the carpet. The other officer is holding her feet. I feel a huge eruption of anger come from the depth of my soul. It just comes out of nowhere.

"Stop!" I have never screamed that loud, ever.

The police officers are quite confused. They both look at me like I'm crazy for yelling at them when they are trying to arrest and contain Rainelle. Then the officer sitting on top of her gets up and pulls Rainelle to her feet. This is not humane at all. He pulls her up by the shackles behind her back, hurting her shoulder even more. She screams in pain and tries to pull away. This makes the officer manhandle her even more. I can't take this.

I reach over to the officer manhandling Rainelle and grab his arm.

"Stop it!" I yell once more. "Stop! You are hurting her!"

The officer looks at me with eyes opened wide and then looks down at my hands clinched onto his arm. Oh no, this can't be good. Did I just assault a police officer? But I don't stop there.

"Why are you treating her like this?" I can't contain my anger anymore.

"Mrs. Parker," the nurse speaks. "I had to call the police." She sounds like a scared little girl. "She got up and started throwing things when I told her that I needed to call the police to report the abuse."

Rainelle is squirming in the grip of the officer. He is holding on tight since she was arrested for being a runaway before.

"Is this any way to treat this young lady?" I direct my questions to the officers. My questions are poignant and direct.

"Ma'am," one officer speaks. "When we came to the office for the report, she was extremely unruly and throwing items. I had to handcuff her for everyone's safety."

I'm not sure if he is trying to convince me or himself.

"Rainelle came to me for help. I sent her to the nurse's office for examination. We were going to make a report of this but not like this!" I look around the room and realize just how hurt Rainelle is. Tears are flowing down her face. Are the tears from the pain of her shoulder and blackened eye? Could the tears be that she is being taken away?

"Ma'am, we need to arrest her for vandalism to the room."

The officer begins to leave with her.

"No wait!" I stop him. I look around the room even though it is torn to pieces. "I don't see any vandalism here."

"Ma'am, you know she vandalized this room. Just look at it." The officer waves his hand around like he is on *Price is Right*, putting items on display for bidding.

I look around the room once more.

"Sam, do you see any vandalism?" I ask Sam.

His eyes get really wide, looking for what answer I'm looking for. I tilt my head so he hopefully gets the message.

Sam clears his throat, "No Mrs. P. I don't see any vandalism here at all." His chest is puffed out like he is a winner of the prize.

A few other students that are curious about the commotion are standing there with us. With each student's answer of no vandalism, the officers are puzzled.

"Well, officers, since there is no vandalism here, why is she still in handcuffs?" I ask with a smug look upon my face. Knowing I have the upper hand, I hope Rainelle sees what is happening.

"We had a call for a police report of abuse, and we came," the officer states.

"Okay, so let's take the handcuffs off this young lady and do the report," I say with a demanding nature.

The officer turns Rainelle around, forcing her shoulder to twist more. She squeals in pain.

"Now darn it, be easy with the girl. Her shoulder is injured," I remind the officer.

The handcuffs come off, and Rainelle takes a deep breath of relief. She begins rubbing her shoulder while pulling her hair over her face again.

"Please come into the office area so we can make a formal report for her." I motion for the officers, nurse, and Rainelle to go into the waiting room part of the nurse's office. We all sit down at the round table as if we are at a summit to come to a diplomatic resolution. It's a strange feeling for all of us.

I turn to Sam, and without anyone else noticing, I look up at the ceiling and take a breath before speaking.

"Sam, can you please pick up the room a bit?" I look at Sam as if to telepathically tell him to clean up the evidence.

"Yes Mrs. P." Sam quickly jumps up and begins turning chairs back upright, putting papers back together, and ensuring the room is back to the way it should be. The other students help as well. It seems that Rainelle is beginning to be one of the pack at this school. Even though she is different, I think they all realize that we are all different in our own ways. Each student helps without hesitation or instruction. The room is back to normal in a matter of minutes. No more evidence of vandalism can be seen.

"Thank you, Sam. You may go back to class." Sam grabs his bookbag and gives me a smile as if to say, "thank you". The rest of the students follow.

As the paperwork is being completed by the nurse and the police officer, I look up at the doorway and see the probation officer standing there watching. He is quiet, but when Rainelle sees him, her temper quickly surfaces, but it does not blow yet. I motion for the probation officer to sit down with us. I try to keep the room as calm as possible. The probation officer knows what I'm doing, and he quietly complies, sitting next to me.

"So, what do we do from here?" I ask after a big sigh.

"Well, since a formal abuse paper has been filled out by these officers and the nurse collaborates the injuries," the probation officer stops. He doesn't want to finish his sentence.

"Uh huh," I respond.

"We need to find another foster family for her to go to," the probation officer stops again.

Oh, here it comes. If I could stop him, I would. That speeding train whistle is blowing.

"However, we don't have any other foster families that can take her." The probation officer sounds defeated. He begins to rub his head, hoping for a resolution to appear.

It feels like a huge elephant has entered the room. Rainelle begins to cry quietly. The probation officer, who was once watching Rainelle, turns to look at me with a look of utter disgruntlement.

Moments of silence are deafening and lengthy. It is a horrible feeling. The air is so heavy and stagnant you could cut it with a butter knife. I feel like I cannot breathe. I'm sure Rainelle wishes she were invisible.

"So that means no one wants me... right?" Rainelle bursts out. "No... one?"

The probation officer hangs his head. It is very obvious that he has had this situation put in front of him with her several times. This time is different though. Now there really isn't anyone to take her. Juvenile Hall seems to be the only option. This really is the end of the line for her.

Rainelle jumps to her feet. The chains on her clothes rattle quite loudly. "So, I'm being sent away again!"

It feels like the air was sucked out of the room by a huge vacuum. Oh, the pain in my chest almost feels like a heart attack or an anxiety attack.

"Isn't there anything we can do?" I plead with the probation officer. "She did nothing wrong." My voice trails off.

Tears became sobs. Seeing this rough and tough young lady becoming a completely helpless kid is hard to see. Telling this young lady that she is going back to basically kids jail for being hurt just doesn't seem right at all.

The officer turns to Rainelle, "You have no family that I can take you to." He sounds completely defeated. "I have no other alternative."

Between sobs Rainelle pleads, "This isn't fair. I haven't done anything wrong." Her anger and sobs are turning into a final plea for clemency for her life sentence.

The probation officer begins to get up from his chair while gathering the paperwork for the abuse report as well as the file I had on her for the Second Chance Program.

"I'm sorry, but you cannot go back to the foster house. Since you are going to Juvenile Hall, you cannot continue this program." He holds out his hand to Rainelle as if helping an elderly woman to her feet. They both head to the doorway. With each step, her sobs are louder. She is to the point that she doesn't care who sees or hears her cry. I'm sure she wants to run away, but how can she? Her probation officer has her by the arm, and the police officers are close behind. I suddenly find myself back in the park when my mother had me by the arm pulling me away from Mildred while I was crying and screaming "why?"

"Wait!" My voice is so soft I don't think I even hear it in my own mind. The room does not change, so I have to say it again, "Wait a minute." I close my eyes as if begging for an answer from God or even Mildred. I feel like I'm standing on the high dive with my toes dangling over the edge, so high up I can't see the water below. With my eyes closed and my breath held, I take the leap of faith.

"I will take her." It falls out of my mouth as if it's water falling from a glass. A huge sense of relief is met with a tidal wave of fear. I haven't even spoke to Charlie about this.

The fall off the high dive is met with me reaching for the surface of the water to breathe. I try to swim, but the water keeps me down. I can't catch my breath.

"You would be willing to take this young lady into your home so she could continue this program and graduate with a clean slate?" the probation officer asks me in a manner of questioning my decision. I can't blame him. I'm questioning my decision, too.

I look at Rainelle and our eyes met. Her eyes are deep red from crying, and my eyes are probably full of fear.

Coming to the surface from the dive into the unknown, I take a breath to speak. "Yes sir, I would." I smile at Rainelle.

The probation officer looks down at the floor, momentarily lost in thought.

"Is this okay?" There's a lump in my throat as big as a softball.

"Well, you're a part of our community outreach program with the Second Chance Program, and it would be allowed." The probation officer searches his mind for a reason why this cannot work. "Let me make some phone calls."

The probation officer steps out of the office with his phone in hand. I can't quite hear what he is saying.

"Are you sure you want to help me?" Rainelle asks with puppy dog eyes.

"Sure thing, kiddo. You deserve a chance in this world. Besides, it would be nice to have you. But," and I stop, realizing just what I did, "you have rules with me too." I have to instill in Rainelle that this will be no picnic.

"Yes, Ma'am, I understand." Rainelle runs over to me and throws her arms around me. Tears fall once more, but this time, they are tears of gratitude. "I feel safe with you."

The probation officer comes back into the room and says, "Well, the paperwork is started. This arrangement is temporary until I can find another foster family to take her. She can go home with you, but first I need to take her by the hospital for documentation of the shoulder injury with an x-ray." He turns his attention to Rainelle, "Is that okay with both of you?"

"Yes, it is," I say as I look into Rainelle's eyes. "Take good care of her."

I jot the address of the manor down on the piece of paper to give to the probation officer. As the probation officer and the two police officers are leaving to take Rainelle to the hospital, I give the piece of paper to the probation officer.

"Can you please bring her by the manor when you are finished at the hospital?" I ask.

"Sure, I will," the probation officer says.

"What do you mean, manor?" Rainelle asks cautiously.

"Oh, you'll find out soon enough, but first we need to go to the hospital." The probation officer motions for Rainelle to leave the room behind the two police officers.

"We'll see you in a few hours after we leave the hospital and pick up her things," he says as they all exit the room and eventually the school.

The office has an eerie feeling after such an exciting afternoon. The quiet is almost welcomed.

"Mrs. Mary?" the nurse asks.

"Yeah."

"When are you going to tell Charlie?" She giggles.

Oops. "I suppose I better tell him now." I take a deep breath. "I hope he understands."

"You know, I knew Mildred for many years, and you remind me of Mildred more and more each day." The nurse puts her hand on my shoulder.

I feel a huge presence in the room. I hope it is Mildred, but I will never know.

"I hope she is pleased with me." I leave the office to find Charlie.

CHAPTER 16

THE REST OF THE SCHOOL DAY PASSES, and between new paperwork and Charlie's class schedule, 1 run out of time to tell him about Rainelle before the doorbell rings. This may go over like the Titanic, but 1 already have my ticket.

Opening the door, 1 see the officer alone. Rainelle sits in the back of the police car.

"Is everything okay?" 1 ask.

"Sure, 1 just can't have any children in the front while I'm driving," he reassures me.

"Oh okay, is she allowed to come in?" 1 ask in an eager tone. He heads off to retrieve her.

"Who is that?" Charlie asks as he comes to the door.

"Well, 1 was meaning to talk to you about this, but 1 got sidetracked, and we didn't get a chance to talk." Now, this isn't like 1 brought home a pet frog. This is a little bit, well, 1 guess a lot bigger, than everything combined.

Charlie looks beyond me and sees the police car. It's dark outside, making it hard to see who gets out of the car.. 1 reach over to hit the light switch so everyone can see better. As 1 do, the entire exterior of the manor is lit with a blanket of light.

1 watch Rainelle's face change as she takes it all in as she exits the police vehicle. The front porch is absolutely huge compared to what she is used to seeing. The bushes and trees even have their own lights. Rainelle's jaw lingers open in shock. 1 remember that feeling well. 1 felt the same way when 1 first came to the manor with Mildred and Antoinette.

Rainelle grabs her bags, and the officer helps her get to the grand entrance staircase.

"This is the manor?" she whispers to the officer.

"Yep, this is the manor," he says with a grand smile.

"Hey honey, come on up here." My arms are open, welcoming Rainelle into our manor.

Rainelle runs to me and drops everything she has. She almost jumps into my arms. My heart is warm with joy.

"Mar?" Charlie is so lost he doesn't know what to do.

"Let me get her settled, and then we need to talk." I'm almost afraid to talk to Charlie because I did not consult him before this huge decision. It was more of a spur-of-the-moment push from Mildred.

"All set?" the officer asks, getting ready to leave.

"Yes sir. I can't thank you enough for everything you have done for her today," I say with a deep smile of gratitude.

"Ma'am, it's people like you that make me glad I have my job. If everyone was this thoughtful and helpful, this world would be a much better place to live in." He reaches for my hand. "Thank you for caring about these kids."

"Absolutely!" I say while shaking his hand in response.

I turn back to Rainelle. "Well, kiddo, let's go inside. I have some people I would like you to meet."

"People?"

"Oh, you have no idea young lady," the officer says as he shuts his door to leave. His attempt to contain his giggles is hard to handle.

As we make our way up the stairway to the front porch, Rainelle is taking in everything she can. Her head is turning every which way and then back again. I remember that feeling of being completely overwhelmed by the grand entrance. It was a bit embarrassing to feel so excited just to walk into such a beautiful place.

As we reach the top of the stairs, we step onto the porch. Rainelle turns around to look down the steps and out into the front yard where the trees and bushes are lit up. The entrance with the gate is too far to see from the front porch. Even though she tries, she can't see it.

The door swings open, and Charlie is standing there waiting for an explanation of why Rainelle was just brought by a police car. I see the questions on his face. I try to play it off so that Rainelle doesn't feel out of place.

"This is Charlie, my husband." I look at Charlie.

Rainelle holds her hand out, and her chains rattle as she shakes Charlie's hand. Rainelle seems totally oblivious to the noise that her chains are making.

"And if you look over here," and I turn to my right, "Antoinette will help you to your room."

"My room?" Her eyes brighten. "Antoinette?" she questions.

"I will explain everything after you get settled," I assure her.

"Come now, child." Antoinette holds out her hand for Rainelle to follow her.

"Rainelle, I will have a sandwich for you when you come back down. I know you haven't eaten since you were at the hospital," I yell up the grand stairway to the second floor. The stairway is open, so I don't have to yell loudly.

"Yes, Ma'am," she says as she and Antoinette disappear down the hallway to her room.

Finally, I turn to face Charlie, standing next to me in shock. He doesn't look like he knows where to start. Well, I don't really know where to start, either.

"She's part of the Second Chance Program." Maybe that wasn't the best place to begin. His eyes open wide as I finish that.

" Uh-huh," he says with suspicion.

"She was in foster care and her foster dad abused her," I whisper. I don't want Rainelle to know I'm telling him.

"And..." he prods me for more information.

"She was going to be sent back to Juvenile Hall since there were no more foster families to take her," I add.

"Juvenile Hall?" he questions.

"That was the only place they could put her since she had

no other home to go to." My explanation doesn't seem to be working.

"So, why is she here?" He's concerned, and I can't really blame him.

"If they took her back to Juvenile Hall she would be disqualified from the program." My heart begins to melt.

"They would have taken her to Juvenile Hall even though she has done nothing wrong? Didn't you say she was abused?" I can see that Charlie is now understanding why I did what I did.

"Yes, and I just could not allow that to happen." I straighten up in my conviction.

"What about Millie?" He has a right to be worried about our daughter. Rainelle was right. People judge her without knowing her. Charlie is doing it now. Even though they both are in the same building at school, they don't cross paths during the day.

"She will be fine with her." I know I'm talking without really knowing, but if she has been in foster care, then surely, she has been around toddlers.

Charlie knows I'm in way over my head. He sighs and pulls me close, and I feel the warmth of his love.

"I know Mildred would love for you to take in every child you find . I'm glad you found Rainelle, or should I say, she found you."

Antoinette and Rainelle reappear at the top of the steps, announced by the rattling of Rainelle's clothes. With each step, they rattle more and more.

"Honey, your chains—" I begin.

"I know, they're too loud. I'm sorry. I'll take them off tomorrow. I just don't have a lot of clothes."

"Well, we will deal with that later," Antoinette says as she goes down the hall. "Come along child, food is this way." Antoinette sounds just like she did when I came to the manor. Oh, what a welcoming sound.

"After you get your sandwich, you can get settled in. We can talk tomorrow." I smile.

"Yes Ma'am," Rainelle says, trying to be on her best behavior.

I hear a giggle come from Antoinette. "Child, she is Mrs. Mary here. We don't call her ma'am." Antoinette purses her lips as she speaks.

"Oh yeah, I forgot," Rainelle says with a timid tone.

"See you tomorrow," I say to Rainelle.

"You okay?" I ask Antoinette.

"Sure am. Just getting Rainelle settled then I will check in on Millie. I put her down a long time ago, but I want to make sure she's still asleep." She turns in Rainelle's direction. "You know, will all that chain noise and all." Antoinette winks at me and then leaves the room.

"Thank you so much for everything," I say.

I honestly don't know what I would do without Antoinette. I had no idea just how much she really does.

The night comes to a close, and as I lay in bed, I can't stop my mind from going over the events of today. This has been really hard, not only on me, but dang, I don't know how Rainelle made it through the day. Day after day being so guarded and afraid of being hurt by the ones she is entrusted to. I don't understand the foster system. How can it allow this type of abuse? I can't save everyone, but I can help her.

CHAPTER 17

I'M STARTLED AWAKE by the horrible ringing of my phone. Who on earth could be calling me at this hour? As I grab for my phone to get it before Charlie hears, I glance at the alarm clock. 2:30 AM. What? 2:30? Oh, this can't be good.

"Hello?" My voice sounds like I just smoked two packs of cigarettes. I could never imagine smoking to begin with. I anxiously wait for the person on the other end of the phone.

"This is the police, Ma'am. Is this Mrs. Parker for the School of Art?" the man on the other end of phone asks in a stern and gravelly voice.

"Yes, Sir. Can I help you?" My voice sounds a bit more feminine and much more appealing. "Is everything okay?" I'm not sure why I even ask that. If someone is calling me in the middle of the night, something is definitely wrong.

"Ma'am, this is Officer Angelo with the police department. Could you please come down to the school? We have an issue that I need you to see." Seriously? I feel like I just finally got to sleep. My heart sinks. What could be wrong now? What if the school burnt down or was broken into? Surely something is horrible for them to be calling me.

I call Alfred to meet me. I'm not going to the school in the middle of the night by myself, and I don't want to wake Charlie. He gets up much earlier than I do.

As I'm getting dressed, Charlie begins to stir.

"Mar, where ya going?" His voice is faint, and I'm pretty sure he isn't fully awake.

"Honey, I need to go to the school. The police called me. Alfred will meet me there. I've got this. Go back to sleep." I sneak out of the bedroom, ensuring I have the right clothes on and shoes. I feel like a teenager trying to sneak out of my house and getting dressed in the dark. I glance down at my shoes to make sure they match. The last thing I'd want is to show up to talk to the police and have my shoes mismatched.

Most of my path is dark, so I walk carefully. But as I turn the corner the bright reds and blues of police lights illuminate my path for me. What can it be now?

Slowly, I hear yells from the police and ... Oh no. Kids. They better not be kids from my school!

I see not just one police car, but three. Not just one officer, but now four or five more. The scene is becoming a bit blurred from the howling sirens and the strobes of blue pulsing against the buildings. I still don't know what happened. I feel so disoriented, like it's a horrible acid trip.

Looking over at one of the police cars, I see a young man sitting in the back. I get a closer look and relief fills me. He's not one of mine. I feel a sense of relief but only for a moment.

"Mrs. Parker! Mrs. Parker!" I hear a young man yelling my name. Unclear on where the yelling is coming from, I venture closer to the police cars. I have to shield my eyes.

When I get closer to the police cars, I see a young man on the ground with an officer handcuffing him. He is crying profusely. As I get closer, the young man is screaming for me over and over. This forces me to get a closer look.

The young man yelling my name is lifted to an upright position by the chain between his hands around his back. Oh, that had to hurt. Then he is slammed to the ground in order to sit down with his hands cuffed behind him. The young man has his head hung low in shame. He then lifts his head.

"Oh no!" I can't believe my eyes. "Not again!"

The young man begins to plead with me. I have a hard time recognizing him at first, but then it hits me. Avery. I can't believe Avery would do this again! I turn to look at the police car with the young man in it that I saw at first. I notice that it's one of the boys who vandalized my wall before. Wondering where the third boy is, I look around until I see him. He is already handcuffed and standing behind the other police car.

"Mrs. Parker, I didn't do it!" Avery yells.

The police officer does not believe him. He grabs his arm and shakes him while telling him to be quiet. Strange, but it seems to be in their training to shake the kids into submission.

Why would he do such a thing? Why, while being enrolled in the Second Chance Program at this very school? This is the exact thing that he got arrested for to be in this program. I feel heartbroken and sick to my stomach. I'm so disappointed.

"Avery?" I say with a hint of hurt in my voice. "What happened?" I have to know. I want to know why! Where did I fail? What did I do wrong?

"I didn't do it Mrs. Parker!" Tears and snot are rolling down this young man's face as he pleads for someone to listen to him. I get a clear look at Avery's face—he has a black eye and a fattened lip, and his face is covered in dirt from being pushed to the ground.

As I look at the wall where the paint was sprayed once more, I notice that the paint is different. This time it looks more like graffiti than art. Just letters sprayed on the wall. It isn't a picture at all. Something doesn't feel right.

After looking closer, I notice words like punk and a few more that I don't even attempt to say.

"Mrs. Parker, I tried to stop them," Avery yells. "I tried to stop them!"

But if he tried to stop them, why was he here in the middle of the night while they were spraying my wall? He should have been home, at his home. I walk over to where Avery is sitting next to the police car with his hands pulled behind his back in shackles.

"Can I speak to this young man?" I ask the officer.

"Yes, Ma'am." The officer steps back so I can get closer, but he doesn't go so far away as to not have an eye on his prisoner.

I bend down to talk to Avery. Oh, my knees again. I'm still hurt that he did such a stupid thing. I want answers.

Attempting to keep my cool even though it is really hard to do at this hour, I ask "Avery, I'm quite upset this happened again. Now tell me the truth! Why did you do this again?"

"Mrs. Parker, I swear to you. I didn't do this." The tears flow once more. Seeing a rough and tough teenage boy cry isn't something to take lightly. He looks around, embarrassed about crying, but I think at this point, it just doesn't matter. Having me listen to him is much more important than his neighborhood status at this point.

"Really? Why should I believe that?" My voice is high and quite loud.

"I used to run with them. You know, I got in trouble with them last time." His head drops while trying to explain. "We live in the hood together, and I heard that they were mad I was going to school here. They said I didn't deserve to be in the Second Chance thing, and they did it." His voice is trying so hard to keep up with his lungs, but he just can't keep his breath. He's not accustomed to crying so hard. "I think they're jealous."

"Jealous?" I question.

"They have probation officers, and they got time in Juvie. They've been gone for months. They were released today. I didn't go there. I got to come here. They mad, they mad at me so," his street slang is coming back out. Avery stops to gather his emotions, "they said they goin' to show me."

"Show you?' I ask again. "What did that mean?"

"You know, this." He shrugs toward the spray-painted wall. "You know I don't paint like this."

I look the wall over. I do know.

He tries to show me his hands, but they are in handcuffs behind his back. "Look!" He gets up and is quickly pushed back down by the officer. He wiggles around to show me his hands. "Look, I don't even have any paint on my hands."

Avery has a very valid point. He doesn't paint like this. His paintings are artistic and creative. This spray paint is just letters.

It looks like letters marking ownership, like territory ownership. Like gang letters.

"I followed them here, and I tried to stop them," he pleads.

"Wait here," I tell him, as if he could really leave.

I turn to the officer and ask, "Can I see the other young men's hands?"

"Ma'am?" the officer questions.

"Yes sir, I want to see the paint on their hands," I respond.

The officer takes me to both young men, one at a time. Sure enough, both young men have paint on their hands.

"Officer, I think that young man over there," and I point in Avery's direction, "did not have anything to do with this."

"And why would you say that? We caught all three boys here," the officer says with a stern voice. "If anything, he is guilty by association."

"Yes, I understand that, but they have evidence on their hands. Avery does not have any paint on him. He goes to school here." I feel anger building deep within. "He says he was trying to stop the other young men." I plead with the officer.

"And you actually believe him? These kids will say anything to get outta trouble," he says with a chuckle.

Now, that was uncalled for, but I attempt to answer without the same smart-Alec antics. "Yes, officer, I do."

He looks over at Avery, wondering what to do.

"He is in my Second Chance Program. He tried to stop them, not participate with them," I add.

"Second Chance Program?" the officer stops. "What did he do to get into this program?"

Oh no, why did he have to ask me that? I can't lie to him. If I lie, then I'm no better than the boys painting my wall. If I tell him the truth, well then, it will be the nail in the coffin. I can't just stand here. I have to tell him.

"He was caught spray-painting my wall," I say, hopefully low enough to where it is covered up by the roaring sirens.

"This wall?" The officer shakes his head in disbelief. Yeah, if I were in his shoes, I probably would be doing the same thing. Not knowing Avery, he does seem guilty by association.

The officer walks over to Avery and tells him that he still has to take him to the police station. I'm not happy with this. The police cars drive off into the darkness.

I follow them down to the station with Alfred.

"Are you sure you can handle this Mrs. Mary?" Alfred asks.

"Yes, I'm sure." I'm determined to help this young man. I know deep down he did not paint the wall. He was telling me the truth.

Standing at the magistrate's desk, I tell him my findings and that Avery should not be charged. He was just in the wrong place at the wrong time. I notice a lady speaking to Avery while he is sitting on the booking bench. I assume that's his mother. She is yelling at him, angry she's at the police station in the middle of the night for him, again. I feel like I need to go over and help his defense.

"Mrs. Parker, this is my mom." His mother is dressed in pajamas and shivering from the cold air.

I reach out my hand to shake hers. "Hello, I'm Mrs. Parker from the School of Art," I introduce myself.

She looks at me strangely, sizing me up. I'm not sure why she is doing this. It looks like she recognizes me, but she is not sure where from, just like at the courthouse . Cautiously she answers, "Hello, sorry we had to meet at this hour."

She turns to Avery with a look of death. Oh, boy, Avery is in trouble.

"If it is any consolation, I don't think he did anything wrong," I plead with her.

"Mom," Avery tries to talk.

"You be quiet!" she says sternly in his direction. "Why do you think he did nothing wrong?" she asks me. She is judge and jury, and, quite frankly, Avery doesn't have a chance.

"He goes to my school, The Second Chance Program?" I say.

"Oh yeah, he's in that through his probation officer."

"Well, he told me he was trying to stop those kids and 1 believe him."

"Mom," Avery tries to speak again.

His mother just puts her hand up, instructing him to shut his mouth. "You believe him?"

"Yes, 1 do." I feel like I'm his attorney begging for forgiveness. "He is a good kid," 1 have to add. Why am 1 defending him to his own mother? Why am 1 the one telling her of all people that Avery is a good kid?

1 can see the defeat in her now. She seems to be in over her head with him. 1s his father in the picture? 1 do not dare ask.

"And you run the school where he goes now?" she asks.

"Yes, 1 do, and he has turned around so much that quite frankly, he isn't even the same kid that painted the wall the first time." My voice calms. "He's even teaching the Art of Spray-Painting."

"The Art... of Spray-Painting?" she looks at me like I'm nuts. "Teaching?" 1 have her attention. "As if there is such a thing."

"Yes, Avery paints with art, talent. He skillfully paints instead of just spraying graffiti on a wall." 1 look at Avery, and he is attentively listening to me. He looks shocked I'm talking to his mother in his defense.

"Mom," Avery tries to speak again. This time she is calmer and willing to listen. "Mom, I've been doing good at school. Really."

"Good? 1s that how you ended up here?" It is a stark reminder that we're all standing in the police station.

"He was actually trying to stop the other kids, but it didn't quite happen that way," 1 add.

"Stop it? How?" Her questions are harsh and very direct.

"Mom, 1 heard the ga..." and Avery stops dead in his tracks.

"You may as well finish your sentence. I'm not stupid Avery!" His mother is irate and justifiably so.

"1 heard the guys in the gang talkin' bad 'bout me. They mad 'bout me gettin ' off."

"What do you mean?" she asks again with a sharp tongue.

"Goin' to that school instead of Juvie," Avery finishes quite painfully.

Avery takes a deep breath and takes the deep dive.

"They said they goin' to get me kicked out." Avery's voice sounds pitiful.

"How?" I ask.

"Paintin' and that. If the wall got painted again, it had to be me." Now his tone is softer, more subdued.

"This is why you tried to stop them?" I ask.

"Well, yeah." His head is down once more.

Avery's mother sighs and looks at me in dismay.

"Mom, I didn't do it. I promise I didn't." Avery is pleading with his mother, not about the charges, just for her to believe him.

The magistrate has been listening to our conversation.

"You really didn't do this, did you, kid?" he asks from behind the desk.

"No, Sir, I did not. I tried to stop them," Avery says.

The magistrate comes from behind his desk and over to us. He instructs Avery to stand up and turn around, and then he takes the handcuffs off Avery. I feel like crying. I think Avery wants to cry, but you know how that would look, a young man crying in a police station? Oh, not this tough young man.

"Can I take my son home then?" Avery's mother asks.

"Yes, Ma'am, you can," he says while walking back around the desk.

I reach for Avery's mother's hand, "I did not get your name."

"Angelica," she says with a smirk. I think she recalls where she knows me from. I want to ask, but this is not the time or place for that. We all just want to go back home.

We leave the other two boys there to be booked for their vandalism charges. It's late, and I need to go back to bed. Alfred is half asleep in his seat, so I have to wake him to leave.

"See you in school Monday?" I look at Avery. "We can talk when your mom brings you, okay?"

"Yes, Ma'am," he answers.

The way he answers me catches his mother completely off guard.

"Yes, Ma'am?" She looks at Avery. "Since when do you talk like that?"

"Since I began school," Avery says with a smirk.

"It's respect, and I demand respect. He is very polite and respectful." I smile.

His mother purses her lips and rolls her eyes. "Maybe this school program is working." I think I hear hope in her voice.

"I know it is." I'm so proud of Avery and the progress he has made.

"Have a good night," I say, then I wave my hand at the magistrate. "Have a good night, or morning," I add with a chuckle.

"Thank you, Mrs. Parker," he says with a wave.

***

Monday comes quickly, and I don't think I ever really recovered from Friday's police department visit. I almost forget Avery and his mother are coming in this morning. I'll need to go to my office first then.

On the way there, school feels different. I can't put my finger on why, but it does. Oh well, it will come to me.

In my office, the secretary is already behind her desk doing her normal duties, which is ten things at once. I'm careful not to disturb her. I simply put my hand up and wave hello. She waves back with that friendly smile I love to see each day. Then she motions me to my office. Putting her hand over the phone so the other party cannot hear, she says softly, "They're in your office." I quietly go in.

Avery is sitting in one of the chairs, focused on his phone. His bookbag sits by his feet. His mother, Angelica, sits next to him. I politely sit in my chair behind the desk, trying to ignore how much I desperately want to go back to bed.

"Hello, again," I say to both of them.

Avery waves silently, otherwise staying glued to his phone. His mother is quite different than at the police station. I finally take a moment to look at her.

I know that when we were at the police station, she looked at me quite strangely. She knew me, but I cannot recall her. She looks like an average, overworked mother with drab clothes on, nothing corporate or businesslike. Just a pair of jeans and a normal top. She looks a bit unkempt, but it could be remnants of the weekend. Her hair is short and tossed. She's not wearing makeup except, maybe, mascara. No jewelry, no wedding ring. Raising anyone alone can take a toll, but raising someone with Avery's past? I understand her wrinkles and the wisps of gray in her hair. I am a bit taken aback by what her age appears to be. She can't be much older than me, but she looks older. Enough judging. I need to gather my attention. I'm not sitting in Charlie's wonderful café peering out the mirror-like window. I need to focus.

"I'm glad to meet you." I direct my conversation to Avery's mother.

"Please, call me Angelica," she says as she sits up in her chair. It looks like she is desperately trying to make a good impression.

"Well, Friday night sure took a lot out of both of us," I say with a chuckle. It isn't at all funny, but I want to break the ice.

"I keep trying to tell Avery that having friends like that will only get him into trouble." She glances over at Avery, and he is noticeably disturbed by his mother's response.

"I have not had any issues with him here in school," I mention.

"Well, at home, I guess it's different." She looks over at Avery, almost begging him for any response.

Avery is still holding his phone close up to face as if he is trying to slip into the pattern of the chair.

"Avery?" I ask, bidding for his attention.

I get this big, forced sigh that a mother would get. Well, I'm not his mother, and I will not tolerate that here. I decide to let this one slide since she's sitting here.

"They're my friends, Mom," Avery begins right off with an attitude. He sits up in his chair to get a better vantage point for the fight that is about to take place. I, however, need to be the neutral party here and keep the peace.

"Friends? The same friends that vandalized my wall last time? The ones that you were with on Friday night?" I ask.

"No," he pauses, knowing that this is not the real truth. I raise my eyebrow. Lying to me is not good at all. We established that on the first day of school.

"Well, yes." Ah, the truth begins to come out.

"Remember the first day of school here?" I try to jog his memory.

"Yes," he says as he lifts his eyes from his phone but only for an instant.

"I told everyone in the program that people, places, and things need to change in order for you to change into a different person to make this program work. Didn't I?"

"Yes." His face is still buried in that phone.

"I told him to stay away from them." This I-told-you-so attitude from his mother is not helping at all.

Avery breaks. "But you don't un'stand. I just hang with them." His anger is building, bringing the street slang kid to the surface.

Avery's mother looks at me as if to ask for help, defeated.

"I need this school and all but," he stops. "They be my homeboys."

What? They be my what? Oh no, he didn't just become gangster on us. Mother or no mother in the room, I will not tolerate this type of behavior in my school.

"Now you listen young man. Put that phone down and listen to me," I demand.

Avery looks stunned. I haven't talked to him like that before, but you know what? This is how it has to be.

"You, young man, are no gangster, hip, whatever. You will conduct yourself like a young adult and talk respectfully in my school, as well as at home. Your mother does not deserve your attitude and neither do I. After what I did for you on Friday night, you think you can come here and act all entitled and ungrateful? Oh, no. Not here."

Avery's mother's eyes get as wide as a dinner plate. I'm not sure if I should keep going, but I can't find the strength to stop.

"I know you didn't do any of the painting on my wall that night. That is why I stood up for you with your arresting officer. You are a good kid. So why the sudden change? Honestly, the officer was right. You should be charged just for associating with those gangster boys!"

Avery is speechless.

"Well?" Angelica asks.

A defeated sigh comes from him. His phone is now in his lap, turned off, and his attention is finally mine. He looks at his mother and his whole demeanor is shifting back to what I know of him.

"Mom, I'm sorry." He looks up with his black eye and all.

His mom smiles but does not break the momentum he has.

"You know how bad our neighborhood is." He looks at his mom. "Everyone there makes fun of me going to this art school. I know they're doing bad things, you know, like sellin' drugs and all. They say that I can't make money sittin' in this place. They all say that it's the sissy school, the rich kid school." He looks at me, "I'm sorry, Mrs. Parker, but I'm not a sissy." He is pleading for forgiveness. I tried to stop them when I heard what they were gonna do. That's how this happened." He points to his eye. "If I don't run with them, they'll treat me like a sissy. I'll probably get beat up again."

I feel the pain in his voice. He's trying to fit in, but fitting into both worlds isn't going to work.

"Avery," I pause to gather my thoughts. "You are a good kid. I know it. Your mom knows it." I'm sure my confusion shows on my face. "So why are you trying to fit into a crowd that could care less about you? They want you to fail. They want you to get addicted to drugs, run in their gang. They want you to go back to Juvenile Hall, and they will be on the outside laughing at you while you are locked up." I'm trying so hard to show him the big picture.

"And you will go back there, too," his mother adds.

"Why don't you get good grades here, graduate, clean your record up, and go to college?"

"Tsss," Avery lets out a sound that is quite annoying.

"What was that for?" his mother asks, taken aback.

"Me? College?" Avery picks up his phone again. His attention is lost.

I stop him. "Put your phone back down, young man. You have the potential to become anything you want to be. You just need to dream it and become it."

"Yeah, like what?" Here we go again, Mr. Pessimistic Attitude.

"What do you want to be when you grow up?" This is a loaded question. Gang members believe they are already grown up, no matter how old they are.

"I dunno." Avery shrugs his shoulders.

"You have no idea what you want to be?" I ask.

"Nope." He crosses his arms and closes himself off to any ideas.

"You paint so well, why not a painter?"

"Yeah right, with my spray paint?" he adds.

I must admit it seems far-fetched, but here it goes. "What about painting for movie sets?" I throw out there an idea, hoping it will intrigue him.

"Never thought of that." A light comes on in his eyes. He sits up a bit more.

"You know what I see?" I lean over to him. "I see you as a spider."

"A what?" Both he and his mother are confused.

"Yep, a spider." I smile.

"Why? How?" Avery is very confused and intrigued.

"You are going through life in one place, here." He looks around the room. "You are like a spider spinning a web in one place." I wave my hand around to show him the room. "But have you ever seen a spider spin a web to another tree or wall?" I ask.

"Yeah, but I just thought it was another spider."

"Sometimes it is. How do you think that spider gets to the other tree or wall? It is the same web, just bigger, right?"

"Yeah," he says with interest.

"Have you ever walked between trees or something else and gotten caught up on a strand of spiderweb?" I ask, hoping for him to get the point.

"Yeah, I hate that." He rubs his face like it just happened.

"Have you ever thought of how that one tiny spider can do that?" I ask again,

"Never really thought about it."

"That spider has to take the chance." I hold my finger up like an 'ah-ha' moment. "Then, if he spins his web long enough and at the right time, a gust of wind will pick him and his long string of web up so he can, in a sense, fly to the next tree or wall." I move my arms like I'm the spider flying in the air.

"Spiders don't fly." Avery begins to giggle.

"No, but he does this with blind faith. The wind will blow him to another location so he can spin a web bigger than before." I'm hoping that he can visualize this happening. "Then the spider can spin an even larger web so they can either connect or start another one. Have you ever walked through a yard or through a doorway and walked right into a huge spider web? Some webs are beautiful. How about when they have the morning dew or a light rain on them?"

He laughs. "Yeah, it's spooky."

"That spider had to have faith that he could reach the next tree in order to make that spider web for you to walk into. But they need to do this to catch bugs to survive." I smile once more.

"I hate that." Avery begins to rub his face again as if he just walked into a spider web.

"I see you as a spider." I make sure that I have his full attention while I point right at him. "But I think you're afraid to fly out of your comfort zone. The only way you can spin a beautiful web of your own is to have faith that the wind will carry you to another tree." I lean back in my chair.

Avery's face lights up.

"Have faith. Learn how to spin your web and get out of the neighborhood that keeps you tied down. Remember what I talked about at the very beginning of class this year? In order to fly you need to do what?" I ask.

"Change everything. People, places, and things." He reiterates what he has learned.

"Exactly!" I'm so proud of him for allowing me the chance to get through to him.

"Now, spider," I wink and point to the doorway, "go to class."

Avery gets up with a renewed attitude. Next thing I know, his arms are wrapped around my shoulders. He had a hard time reaching me over the desk, but his efforts were well worth it.

"Mrs. Parker?" he says as he releases me and stands back to look at me. "Thank you for believing in me."

"You got it kiddo," I smile like a proud parent. Wait, I still need to talk to Angelica. "Now get to class. I need to talk to your mom for a few minutes, okay?"

"Bye, Mom." Avery steps over to his mom and kisses her on the cheek before heading out. "See you tonight." And he is gone.

Angelica looks at me with a mix of confused wonder and gratitude.

"See, he really isn't a bad kid. He just has bad friends." She adds, "I don't know how you do it with these kids."

"Most of them aren't bad kids. I try to show them that. I think he got the message."

We both sit in a calm that is very much welcome.

I look up at her. "So, have you figured out where you know me from?" I ask.

"Yes, I have." Worry creases her eyes.

"You have ?"

"Yes. I'm ashamed of it." Her face sinks.

"Ashamed? Why?" *How did we meet?*

"You knew me as Angel." She tries to jog my memory.

"Angel?" I look toward the ceiling, as if my memories are stored there.

"We were in English together and," she stops. The blood drains from my face and I feel like I'm going to pass out.

"You're... Angel?" I say in disbelief.

"I'm so sorry for what happened at that Homecoming dance and everything afterward. I really didn't think Jake would go through with it."

Horrific memories flood my mind. I remember believing that I had friends, Angel being one of them. I went to the homecoming dance with them. Jake was my date, my first date. I thought he liked me. I wanted to be in the *in* crowd. I was given something, a drink or a drug, that made me pass out. I woke up naked, and everyone had laughed.

The next morning at school, Angel passed out naked pictures of me at the party doing really bad things. She made fun of me for being a virgin, well before the dance I was. I was so embarrassed, and I hated her. I got into a lot of trouble for pushing her down in the hallway at school, but I had to defend my honor—or what was left of it. She was a popular cheerleader, and I was nothing, a nobody. Invisible. But now, she is here in my office. How the tables have turned.

"When I think of what we did to you, I often wondered where you were and if you would ever forgive me." Angelica's voice trails off.

"I haven't thought of that until now." I'm lying. When the school burnt, I had good memories and bad memories flooding in a flash. How could I ever forget that?! I was absolutely humiliated. I was a virgin until that party, and everyone knew it. Angel made sure of that, and then the pictures ... I had acted like I never minded. I couldn't give her the satisfaction of letting her know it still bothered me, even to this day.

"I was so horrible to you back then."

My mind is reeling, and I start thinking of Avery. He's so much older than my Millie. "But," I stop before I put my foot in my mouth.

"Yeah." Angelica pauses. "Avery is a lot older." She stops again. This is going to hurt.

"Avery was born a year before the Homecoming dance. My mom was taking care of him so I could finish high school." The truth is finally out. Now look who wasn't a virgin. I'm speechless.

"Once everyone found out I had a son at home, I began to lose my friends." She sounds sad, and I fight the victorious feeling within me. She knows how I felt all along.

"I had no idea." Trying to appease her is not easy. I'm still angry with her. That was traumatic, and I hated people for a long time after. I'd thought Jake actually liked me. But, now after hearing her side of the story, she just wanted to belong as well. Kind of like me. That's sad.

Angel looks at me with apologetic eyes. "I'm truly sorry. After all these years."

"You know," *if only Mildred was here,* "I understand what you did and why you did it. You were just trying to fit in like I was. Well, you *were* fitting in, kinda."

"It's okay," she assures me.

We sit in silence for a moment, neither sure how to keep talking. Finally, I ask the burning question in my mind. "Where is Avery's dad?" I'm afraid to ask, but I can't hold it in.

"Oh, he was long gone before Avery was even born." Her face turns to sorrow.

"Did you ever get married?"

"No, I just stayed by myself and made Avery my priority. I got a good job, and we moved out of my mom's. I got a place, not in a good neighborhood obviously, but it's my place. Never married anyone." She has a look of accomplishment about her. Sure, she is worn down, but rightfully so. She is raising Avery on her own. At least they are together and trying to make it.

"What happened to you after school?" she asks.

"I went to college. Studied art and business. My mom died. Then," should I tell her about Mildred? I'm afraid to tell anyone really about Mildred. What if she judges me? But wait, I'm not ashamed of Mildred. She basically raised me after my mom died. Sure, I was already in college, but I was by no means a grown-up yet.

"Mildred," I stop.

"You mean the Bird Lady in the park?" she interrupts me.

"Yeah. Her name was Mildred." People should remember her properly. "We became very close and well," oh here it goes, "I took over her school, the museum, and the manor when she died."

"Wow, I had no idea. Everyone thought she was just a homeless lady feeding the birds in the park." She seems shocked, not used to being wrong.

"I met my wonderful husband at around the same time, and he teaches here as well, now." I feel a great sense of accomplishment. "He owns the Café, Charlie's Café, and now he is teaching here so our students can learn to create masterpieces, serve them, and someday, own and run a restaurant as well. He teaches cooking, and , baking, along with the back side of running a restaurant. Stocking, finances, you know, the stuff no one talks about."

"But you have the same name as when we were in school." She looks confused.

"I do that because of my artwork. I stayed Mary Parker because my own artwork is in the museum."

"I had no idea. You always had that sketchpad thing with you." She seems more normal than I have ever seen her.

"Yep, and now I'm giving back by running the School of Art and museum to keep Mildred's legacy alive." I glance around the room, reassuring myself this is really real and not a dream.

"Do you have children?" she asks.

"Funny you ask. I do. Her name is Mildred." My face is beaming with joy.

"Well, that's fitting."

"I wanted to honor her. Mildred is in my heart every day. Having Millie just makes it that much more special." I show her the pictures on the shelf.

Angelica glanced at her watch. "Hey, I need to head to work."

"It was really nice talking with you," I say.

"Yes, it was. It healed old wounds," she adds.

"Thank you." I feel a great sense of forgiveness.

"Can we stay in contact?"

"I would really like that." I get up and walk around my desk. I felt the need to hug her. I want her to know I mean it. "I need to start my day as well."

We go our separate ways, but our hearts are now together. She doesn't have to walk this life alone anymore. Now she has a friend. We both do.

I need to go talk to Mildred and feed the birds after school today. It has been far too long since I have done so. Thankfully, the day goes quickly and I'm able to go visit the park bench that has Mildred's name on a plaque. I feel guilty for not coming here enough. I know life gets in the way, but that is no excuse. The birds still need me. In some sense, I still need the birds.

With the bag of birdseed in my hand, I reach in to grab a handful and spread it out in the air like a fan. This way, I can feed more birds at one time, and they aren't all fighting over the same pile. Mildred taught me that.

When the food is gone and the last bird flies off, I gaze over the water at the horizon. The sun is at a perfect height to make tiny sparkles on the ripples again.

"Oh Mildred. I'm in so far over my head," I say softly.

I feel a sense of peace come over me like a blanket sheltering me from a storm.

"I'm trying so hard to make you proud of me," I mutter once more, but this time I feel a tiny tear roll down my cheek.

Grasping the empty bag where the birdseed once was, I can almost hear her voice in my ear. "Oh, child." The wind blows a gust, and my hair is blown across my face. I don't know, it could have been the wind, but I could have sworn I heard her. That southern drawl and her elegant disposition trying to console me. Whatever it was, it worked. I feel renewed. I take one final deep breath in and stand. I need to get home before anyone worries. But first, I think I'm going to go to the local pound and see if there is a Shih Tzu there I can take home.

I'm so excited to get home with our new bundle of joy, I call ahead to get Antoinette and Alfred to keep Rainelle busy so she doesn't see me arrive. When I arrive, I head to the sunroom to wait.

"Rainelle, honey, can you come down here?"

Rainelle comes around the corner looking nervous, as if I'm going to scold her. She is not accustomed to being called for anything good. This time is very different. She plops down on the sofa, and I give her a look that Mildred used to give to me when I plopped down like that. I do, however, notice the sound of chains is gone.

"Excuse me." Her voice is apologetic. She adjusts so she can sit like a lady. She tries, at least, even if she doesn't quite get it.

"You've been doing well in your schoolwork and, well," I pause to add suspense.

She looks around the room, first at Antoinette, then at Alfred, looking for answers. Both of them just smile and keep their mouths shut.

"When we spoke in my office, you saw I had my stuffed dog. You know the one, D.O.G. You moved here but never brought him home. I wasn't sure why but then I got to thinking."

I reach behind me and pull out the stuffed dog and hold it up.

"I brought him home to you." I hand the stuffed dog to Rainelle. She still looks confused, but her nerves dissipate.

"Awe, thank you. D.O.G." She wraps her arms around the cute little stuffed dog.

"You know, something just does not feel right," I add. "You need something better."

I cue Antoinette to bring the pet carrier into the room. Rainelle's face lights up like it's Christmas morning. She gasps, and I can tell she wants to pounce on the cage to open it, but she doesn't dare move until she is instructed to.

"Go ahead," I say.

Rainelle gets up from the couch and cautiously walks over to the cage. A little whimper comes from the darkness inside the cage. She looks up, and her eyes are wide saucers. Her mouth is bursting with joy. She opens the cage carefully so she doesn't scare whatever's in there. The door opens. A tiny, grey, curly-haired puppy bounces out and immediately licks Rainelle's face. Rainelle giggles, and I think she starts to cry because she hides her face for a minute.

"Well kid, what are you going to name him?" Alfred asks.

"I know!" She jumps to her feet, scooping the puppy into her arms. "D.O.G.!" she exclaims.

"You're going to name a dog, Dog? Just Dog?" Alfred is unaware of our conversation about the stuffed dog in my office and the name she gave him. Rubbing his head as he always does when things are out of sorts, he thinks harder about the name as if that will make it make sense.

"No, it's Dee Oh Gee," Rainelle says with a big giggle.

"That sounds perfect," I add.

"Aw, he is so precious," Antoinette says as she begins to stroke his head.

"Now, this is not just a dog Rainelle." I get her attention. "He is *your* dog, and since he is yours, you need to feed him, teach him to go potty outside, and take care of him."

Rainelle is hugging her new buddy. She is so lost in the moment.

"Rainelle, did you hear me?" I ask to see if anything I said was heard.

"Yes, Ma'am," she giggles. "I mean, Mrs. Mary."

"He is your responsibility."

Rainelle sets him down. "Come on D.O.G.," she commands.

"Um, wait a minute," I stop her.

"Yeah?" she questions.

"Your little boy has been in that box for quite some time for a little puppy. I think he needs to go outside before you go up to your room with him."

Rainelle giggles, "Oh yeah, right."

Rainelle goes outside along with Alfred.

"Come on, little guy," Alfred says.

They soon disappear out the door, leaving Antoinette with me.

"Oh boy, a puppy?" Antoinette shakes her head.

"Well, not just a puppy. She lost her puppy when she was moved from one of the foster homes. Besides, she has been doing well, so I thought she needed something as a reward."

"Uh-huh." Antoinette nods skeptically.

"Hopefully she'll learn responsibility," I add.

Antoinette gets up from her chair. "Well, let's hope so. She deserves a reward, but I do hope we don't have too many accidents." Antoinette purses her lips together much like Mildred did when she questioned something.

"Let's hope not, but I think she and D.O.G. will be just fine." I smile. "Besides, having a puppy in the manor will add some excitement."

"Excitement?" she asks. "As if we need more of that." She winks and leaves the room.

I take a deep breath and think of Mildred. "Everything will be fine." I pick up the stuffed D.O.G. "As for you, you can come back to school with me. Hopefully, you can help another kid."

I give the stuffed animal a hug, almost like it is a real dog.

"Ha, see, you're already helping me," I whisper.

CHAPTER 18

AH, QUIET...sitting in my office I glance around at my desk. I'm actually ahead of the game today, for once. Who should I check in with today? Rainelle has adjusted well, Avery is back to normal, Sam is still happy as ever ... Joseph.

When I reach the shop class, they're getting ready for a field trip. I like to see the teachers engage with the students outside the classroom. It's not good for them to always be stuck inside.

"Where are y'all going?" I ask, excitement seeping out of me.

"To the woods," the teacher says while gathering paperwork.

Normally this would sound way off for a school, but a shop class needs wood to work on.

"Can I tag along?" I ask.

Joseph notices me and gets excited.

"Hey, Mrs. Parker!" Joseph says with a burst of energy.

"Well, hi there, Joseph." My energy level matches his.

"We're going on a field trip today!" I'm pleased to see him acting like a kid again.

"I heard; I actually just asked if I could tag along with you guys."

"Oh cool!" Joseph turns to the teacher. "Is she coming with us?"

"Well, it looks like she is," he says as he looks my way.

I lean over to the teacher. "I'm not here to watch you. I'm here to observe Joseph." I look over in Joseph's direction. "But, he doesn't need to know that."

"Ah, okay." I can feel the relief in his voice. I'm not sure if my being here is upsetting his class. I don't think so.

"Everybody ready?" The teacher asks as if he is a tour guide. Everyone heads to the door.

"We are going out behind the school." The teacher leads the way confidently.

When we all get out there, I see Alfred driving a tractor pulling a small trailer and a forklift with large wheels, the tractor he uses on the grounds. It's fun to see Alfred so involved with school activities. He seems to be everywhere, doing everything.

I think I'm just as excited as the class is to know what we'll be doing.

"The walk is not far, but I can't see everyone getting in a bus to go less than a half mile to the woods for this trip," the teacher says, trying to get everyone out in the fresh air.

As we begin the walk, I realize I don't have the right shoes on for this journey. My feet are killing me. It's not long before I lag behind, trying not to show my pain.

We walk up on a vacant lot. Most of the trees have been cut down to create a clearing to build yet another brick building to take up our precious resources. We all stop at the edge of the property.

"This property belongs to a family friend of mine. He's clearing the lot so he can build something on it." I can tell he really doesn't want to say what is going to be built on it. After all, we don't have many trees left in Chicago. That's part of why I'm so careful with the trees at the manor.

The students gaze at the property. A few are on their phones, and this upsets the teacher. Rightfully so.

"Now, I need all of you to pay attention here. We are still in class. This is not a leisurely stroll outside to be on your phones."

The students on their phones get the message and scramble to put them away.

"All of this wood is up for grabs for us." He begins to point to the trees on the ground, waiting to be something great.

"I want each of you to look over the wood and pick out something you can work with. I don't care how big or small. If you can make something great with it, then put this tag on it with your name written on it and we will load it up."

Joseph says, "It doesn't matter how big?"

"Well, within reason," the teacher rephrases.

The students linger, unsure if they're allowed to go into the mess or not.

"Get going," the teacher instructs. "Find something you want."

Alfred fires up the tractor and drives right to the middle, so the trailer is in a good position to be loaded.

Some of the kids have already tagged their wood pieces. Joseph is taking a bit longer.

"What's he doing?" I ask the teacher.

"He is very meticulous when he picks out his wood to work with. He takes his time to study the wood. I think he is creating his art in his mind beforehand, a sign of a true artist. I've been watching him closely." The teacher keeps his eyes on him even while he is talking to me. He has a faint smile. He admires Joseph for his ability.

He wasn't very meticulous when he carved my table. Finally, he finds the perfect piece.

"I found mine," Joseph yells out.

Alfred begins loading all the wood the students tagged. The trailer is quite full.

"Okay, let's all go back to the classroom and sort out our wood." The teacher instructs everyone to head back to the school.

Joseph walks beside me. I'm glad he feels comfortable walking beside me.

"I want to thank you again for this." His voice is low but clear.

"This?"

"Well yeah, this program," he explains.

"I just started the program. It is up to you to make it what it needs to be. And it *is* up to you to complete it." My voice is labored due to walking and, oh, my feet are killing me. I need him to understand this is not a get-out-of-jail-free card.

"Yeah, I know, I just get to do all of this. I love this class!" he adds.

"I'm very happy to see you're doing so well." My face is beaming with joy.

As the students all get settled in their classroom, I hear the forklift running down the hall. Hmm, well I have always wondered how he gets all that wood into his shop class. How could I have known that the forklift is driven down the hallways? I'm sure *that* is not a normal occurrence in other schools.

The wood is taken to the side of the classroom with all the tools. This classroom is a bit different from most. It has a large open area with hand tools at the tables. The larger tools, such as huge, stationary sanders and presses, are bolted to the floor for safety. We even went so far as to install a vertical table saw with plexiglass guards so students can cut their plywood upright safely.

The students are sent to their drawing tables and as I watch, each student takes out their drawing board and begins. This is something I didn't think about. Each student needs to draw what they are going to carve before they start . So, the students should learn how to draw first. I'll have to think about this for next year. For the most part, the students are sketching their drawings pretty well for not having training. Imagine what they could accomplish with training. .

Seeing the classroom has settled down, I take a breather and go back to my office to rest my feet.

After a few hours, I go back to the shop class to check in.

When I get there, the students are working with chisels, saws, and even some with a small handheld chainsaw. Of course, the teacher is close at hand watching their every move, and they all have safety measures such as goggles and protective gear. I even see plexiglass walls set up so no dangerous pieces go flying.

The teacher is standing with Joseph at the lathe. He is teaching him how to take the bark off his wood. However, Joseph isn't using the lathe. He has Joseph using a tool that takes the bark off with a big blade. He has this under control, so I'm not worried. At least, not yet.

With each pull toward him, the bark comes off like he's peeling potatoes for Sunday dinner. He has to sit on the wood while he does this because the wood is too big not to, and he has to get the best angle and pressure for the bark to come off. With each stroke, it comes off like butter.

Still watching, I notice Joseph get out a strange pencil that is quite large in diameter. He begins to etch his drawing onto the large piece of wood. This will tell him where to cut. The teacher then gets the handheld chainsaw and turns it on. He shows Joseph how to use it and then hands it to him. The teacher stands back.

Joseph begins gouging into the wood, creating an extremely rough outline of his project. It is still totally unrecognizable. These projects are going to take a lot of time to complete. Pleased with what I'm seeing, I head back to my office. I don't want to disturb a masterpiece. I'm sure I'll see the final project when it's finished.

Having had a busy day in shop class, coming home to the manor and relaxing is at the top of my to-do list. However, when I arrive home, it is anything but relaxing.

I hear that the TV is loud and Rainelle is laughing in the TV room. I go to the doorway and see Rainelle in front of the TV, but she isn't watching it. She has her phone in her hand while laying on her back on the floor.

"Oh Rainelle," I mumble to myself in disappointment.

I do the only thing I can think of at the moment to calm the house down a bit, and turn the TV off.

"Mrs. Mary, I was watching that," she says, even though she doesn't look at me.

"You were on your phone, not even looking at the TV." Rainelle has a little bit of an attitude, but she knows I'm right.

With the TV commotion gone, I notice another noise that has been quite normal lately. I look over at D.O.G.'s cage. I see this poor, helpless puppy scratching at the door to get out.

"Rainelle, please pay attention to your puppy," I demand.

Rainelle goes over to the cage, and when she gets close enough, she exclaims, "Ewe, you stink." She backs up and I think she is going to lay back on the floor and ignore her dog.

"Rainelle, are you not going to pay attention to D.O.G.?" I ask.

"No, he stinks," she reminds me. She has an attitude that is growing with each passing day.

"Rainelle, please put your phone down and come sit by me." I instruct her to sit by me in front of D.O.G. She sits down but reluctantly.

"Can we talk a minute?" I have to remember I'm not her mother and I need to talk softly to her.

Rainelle sits beside me, but she can tell that I'm not pleased at the moment.

"Honey, look at D.O.G.," I request.

"Yeah, I see him," she says with a childish indifference.

"Do you hear him crying?" I am pleading with her to just come down off her high horse for a minute or two.

"Yeah."

"Why is he crying?" I ask.

"He just wants to get out of his cage," she says like I should already know.

"Yes, he does, but that's not all." My tone is serious.

"What do you mean?" Her voice is puzzled.

"Let me show you something different, okay?" I ask.

"Umm, okay." Attitude is back.

"You were in several foster homes, right?" I want to just yell at her to take the dog out of the cage and take better care of it. But she would never hear me that way. I have to get inside her to have her see what I'm talking about.

"Yeah." She suddenly becomes the rough and tough girl once again.

"No, wait a minute." I have to calm her down again. This could go really bad, really fast. "I don't mean anything bad about it."

Rainelle looks at me like she wants to blow up. I'm afraid that she is going to have another temper tantrum and I'm going to have my manor destroyed.

"Honey, you were in foster care because of what?" I ask carefully.

Rainelle is on the verge of crying. "My mom didn't want me. No one wanted me."

"I'm honestly sorry that you had to go through that. When your mom didn't want you, you had to go into foster care." I want her to make the horrible connection, but I'm sure she already has that part.

Rainelle gives a big, forced sigh, and I can see she is getting irritated.

"While you were in foster care," I have to gather my thoughts because the next question is not going to be pretty, "how did you feel about your mom?" I don't want to upset her, but it's inevitable. She has to learn.

Tears form. Her fists are clenched, and I'm waiting for Mount St. Helen to blow, causing catastrophic damage.

"I felt like she didn't love me. She just threw me away." She tries to fight the tears, but they are too hard to fight.

"Do you know why I'm asking all of this?" I ask cautiously.

She tries to talk between the tears, "No."

"Okay. Look at D.O.G.," I instruct once again. "When you first saw D.O.G. you were all happy and hugging him. He was licking your face because *he* was so happy. He was happy he now had a new mom that loved him."

Rainelle looks at D.O.G., and her face lights up with a smile in remembrance.

"Now D.O.G. is crying all the time. He's sitting in his cage wondering why you won't come play with him, right?" I turn to get a better look at her to ensure she is really listening. "He is like... he is now in foster care. He is in his cage wondering if you are going to come back. You left him." I have to keep going. "He probably feels that you just threw him away like you don't love him anymore."

Suddenly Rainelle's face changes. She sees the correlation between her and her mother and D.O.G. and her.

Rainelle looks at me with the saddest eyes I have ever seen. Her heart is broken.

"I did the same thing to D.O.G. that my mom did... to me?" Her face is so hurt. I feel horrible, but I had to make her feel what her poor little dog was feeling.

She goes over to D.O.G.'s cage, opens the door, and pulls out her long-lost friend that she threw away like her mother did to her. She wraps her arms around him. Once again, he begins licking her face.

"I'm so sorry!" she cries. "I'm so sorry. Oh, you do stink."

"See, he just wanted attention from his mommy, you."

Rainelle puts D.O.G. down and runs over to me. Next thing I know, her arms are wrapped around me and the tears are flowing once again.

"I promise I will take better care of him. I promise," she exclaims.

"He loves you." I pull away so I can look into her eyes. "And I love you, too."

She wipes her nose on my shoulder. Ugh, that's gross, but I'm okay with it.

"You do?" she questions in a childlike voice.

"Yes dear, I do."

Rainelle picks D.O.G. back up and heads outside to let him go potty.

Then I hear, "You need a bath." I'm renewed with hope again. Rainelle is going to give her dog the bath he so desperately needs. His cage does stink really bad.

With them gone, I decide to go see what Charlie is doing. I miss him.

After going upstairs to change my clothes from the day in the woods, I find Charlie in his usual element, the kitchen.

"Hey, Babe." His eyes light up when I walk into the room. He reaches over and kisses me gently.

"I had to talk to Rainelle about D.O.G.," I say as I sit next to the island where he's working feverously.

"You did?" he asks while rolling out dough.

"Yeah." I find myself taking a deep breath, then exhaling the day away. "You know, I got D.O.G. for her to learn responsibility and well, the poor boy was in his cage crying to have her take him outside and give him a bath."

Charlie adds flour little by little. "What happened?"

"Well..."

Charlie stops his rolling and begins to clean his hands. Then he sits next to me. When he does this, I know I'm important to him and he actually wants to listen to me, not just hear.

"What happened?" he asks.

"I had to open a door I really didn't want to." I look down at the floor, covered in flour from Charlie's work.

"What door is that?"

"I had to talk about how her mother threw her away into a foster home and that she felt like her mom didn't love her." My eyes lift to meet his. I can see the shock on his face.

"You didn't."

"Yes, I did." I need him to understand the conversation I had with Rainelle was just as hard on me as it was on her.

"And?"

"D.O.G. was in his cage crying, and I had to show her that while she was in foster care she was crying for her mom as well. D.O.G. felt like Rainelle didn't love him anymore, just like her mom." It pains me to say that again.

"Well, I didn't hear any furniture being thrown around," he says with a giggle to lighten the mood.

"Ha, well no." I chuckle as well. "However, she did understand how D.O.G. was feeling and well, now she is giving him a bath because he stinks." I laugh harder.

"Yeah, I was going to mention that to you. I heard Antoinette saying that the cage was well, pretty stinky."

"Rainelle promised that she is going to take better care of him. I know I tested her responsibility, and she pretty much failed. Hopefully she will do better with the responsibility of having him. She has never really been held accountable for anything as far as I can see." I sigh. I hope I'm making progress.

"Everything will be fine." Charlie puts his arms around me once more and kisses my forehead.

"What are you making?" I change the subject.

Charlie hops back up and returns to his dough. "*This* is going to be an apple turnover with cinnamon and nutmeg topped with a sugar glaze."

"Can I have one when you're finished?" His description makes me hungry.

"Sure, but I need to get this together for my class tomorrow. It is very simple, but I must say, very tasty."

"Oh babe, your mom would be so proud of you." My smile radiates from deep within my soul.

"Yeah, I just wish she could be here to see what I'm doing with the kids."

"She is always with you."

I get up to leave Charlie to his work. He knows I'm right. His mother is always with him.

CHAPTER 19

THE NEXT MORNING AT SCHOOL, I force myself to sit in my office and do paperwork. I don't like doing paperwork, but it must be done. Looking at the files for the Second Chance Program, I feel things are going alright. All this focus is beginning to give me a headache, so I cradle my head. A soft scuff of shoes on the carpet draws my attention. Another teacher stands in the doorway. What do you want? Another problem? Oh, why can't anyone deal with problems other than me? I just want a day where things are smooth and all the kids get along.

"May I help you?" I ask, trying not to sound so irritated by his mere presence.

"When we started the Second Chance Program," he starts.

Oh, here we go! Another teacher complaining about something. I catch myself rolling my eyes, so I quickly compose myself. It's unprofessional to roll my eyes when someone is asking for help. I'm just so tired.

"You told all of us that if we ever needed help to come to you." The teacher looks a lot like I feel. This can't be good.

"Sure, please sit down, and let's talk." I try to sound upbeat even though I'm far from it.

"No, I think I need you to come down to my classroom and just watch." He motions me to come, and I do.

My legs feel like lead. With each step, I imagine another horrific sight or some mess in another classroom. I'm trying to keep an open mind, I really am. This school year has been very trying.

As we arrive at the pottery classroom, we peer through the glass at the kids working diligently on their pottery assignments or just making things in general. I'm not sure if there really is an assignment at hand or not. I'm just here to observe, per his request.

The door is closed, and we are watching through the glass. The kids have no idea we are there.

"Take a look at Azza." He points over to the young lady sitting alone with her clay on her wheel.

Oh yeah, I sent Azza to pottery class to learn how to calm herself down. I guess it isn't working.

I watch Azza, and so far, she seems to be concentrating on her wheel with her clay. She molds it and wets it just as instructed, but her hands are not gentle with her clay. She is telling it to do things and it will not listen. She begins to punch the clay into submission. This makes the clay angry. She turns the wheel on, and this is where things go horribly wrong. Water and clay spin out of control and onto her clothes. She gets upset, and now she is spinning out of control. I look at the teacher in despair.

"This happens every day. I just don't know how to calm her anger down for her to manipulate the clay without the anger." The teacher is begging for help. He's at his wit's end, and I can't blame him for it.

I don't know anything about pottery, but I'm sure I can give some help in this matter.

"Can I try to help?"

Without hesitation, "Please."

We enter the classroom, and I calmly walk over to Azza. She looks at me like I'm the reason she is failing. I notice some kids with their phones taking videos of the meltdown. I motion for them to back off, so she does not see them. I'm sure that will only add fuel to the already blazing fire.

"Hi Azza, I just came down to see how you're doing," I say in an upbeat tone, trying to break the anger.

"Look!" She points to her disastrous glob of clay. She scrubs at the clay mixture on her face with a towel.

"Can I try to help you?" I'm in way over my head, but she doesn't know that. For all she knows, I can do pottery and have no problem with the potter's wheel. I put on a smock.

"I guess so. I hate this class!"

I pull up a chair behind her, directly behind her. I sit in the chair and wrap my legs around hers to reach the wheel controls. This puts my arms directly behind her arms so we can work together as one person.

"Can we start over?" I ask in a calm voice.

I get a grunt of anger, but she quickly realizes she is between me and the potter's wheel and cannot get out. I put my hands on top of her hands and then we attempt to connect as one person working together with the clay.

"Grab your clay like this and shape it like this." I have her hands beneath mine, and she is basically doing the work that my hands are instructing her to do.

We are not in sync at all. It seems a big mistake trying to have her follow me, but then she begins to let go of her anger and we become one.

"Push your finger in the middle of the clay at the top to form a hole." She does. It's a small hole, but it's a start.

Suddenly she hits the wheel full blast and we both have clay all over us. This is not quite what I wanted to wear today, but it is okay for now. I hear some of the other students attempt to laugh under their breath. I gave them the stink eye to tell them to calm down because I'm really afraid that she is going to go into a rage again.

"Okay, let's try something else." I get up and sit in front of her. Our knees are touching to form a circle around the potter's wheel. We are face to face, and I think she understands I really am trying to help her.

"Will you try something?" I ask. "Put your hand on the glob of clay. Do not turn on the wheel yet," I instruct. Oh, I don't want to be in the front if she turns on the wheel once more. I probably would have to go home to change.

She puts her hands on the clay as I ask. She is looking for instruction. Her eyes meet mine. Her breathing has slowed down but not enough for this to work.

"Now close your eyes," I instruct in a soft, soothing voice.

She closes her eyes and keeps her hands on the clay.

"Become one with the clay."

She opens her eyes and looks at me like I'm asking her to do something impossible.

"Really?" she asks. "How do I do that?" She is getting frustrated again.

"Just trust me and close your eyes," I instruct her once again.

She grunts but complies.

"Now don't say anything, but talk to the clay with your mind. Open your mind and listen with your heart. What does it want to be? A bowl, a vase? A dish?" My voice is still soothing.

I watch Azza with her eyes still closed, and she looks like she's concentrating hard. She squints her eyes and wrinkles her nose. It is taking a lot of effort for her to get out of her comfort zone.

"What do you see?" I ask. "Don't open your eyes."

"I guess a vase?" She pauses, "I'm not sure, but I think a vase."

"Okay great, so now, with your eyes closed, what do you do to make this glob of clay become a vase?" I ask.

"Um, I need to start putting a hole in the top to form the inside." She feels her way around the mound of clay and finds the top. Carefully she finds the center and pokes her finger deep in the top to form the hole.

"Now keep your eyes closed. What is the clay telling you to do next? It wants to be a vase so how do you do that?"

"The hole needs to be a bit bigger." She puts the next finger, her middle finger, into the middle of the clay along with her first finger. This makes the hole a bit oblong, but it is a great start.

"Now what is next?"

"It needs water to keep it moist." She reaches for the water.

"Okay." She said *it* needs water. It's working!

She gently finds the bowl of water with her eyes closed and scoops up a small amount of water to put on her glob of clay.

After the water hits the clay, she caresses the glob as if to tell it she is there to help it.

"Okay, now what is it saying?" I ask for the next step.

"I need to turn on the wheel to help mold it," she mentions.

She hesitates, reluctant to keep going. She has hit a roadblock.

"What's wrong?" I ask.

"This is stupid!" She opens her eyes and pulls her hands back in anguish. I can see the pain of failure in her eyes. She begins to look around the classroom to see if anyone is watching her. She is taken aback when she sees all the other students working hard on their potter's wheel and not paying any attention to her. Feeling safe again, she looks up at me.

"Honey, close your eyes. I'm right here to help you." I instruct her to get back in the idea of connection with the clay. She does reluctantly.

"What is it asking for next?"

"It needs to have the wheel turned on but," Azza opens her eyes and looks up at me, "I can't."

"Why not dear?"

"This is where I always make a huge mess, and then I get mad," she informs me.

"Well, this time, let's be careful not to get too messy." I want her to smile right along with me. "It's okay to be messy in pottery class."

She gives a deep sigh and tries again. While closing her eyes, she puts her foot on the controls of the wheel and slowly begins to push the controls down. Once again, the wheel spins out of control.

"See I told you!" the outburst of anger flies.

"Honey, stop!" I grab her hands gently. "Don't be afraid of the wheel. Courage is not the absence of fear, it is the ability to do something that frightens you. Now, let's try again but slower, and let's conquer your fear together."

She closes her eyes, takes in a slow breath, and begins to push the controls again. This time she has more control over the speed, and it begins to turn slowly. Her hands caress the clay.

"Okay, now what?" I ask.

"I need to open the hole up in the center."

She finds the center of the clay at the top and gently opens the hole with each turn.

"Careful, not too fast," I mention.

She slows the wheel down.

"Now what?"

"I need more water." Her voice is a bit more confident.

Azza reaches down into the water bowl and scoops up more water. With the wheel turning the clay, she drizzles the water over it. She then feels her way back to the top of the clay.

"Now, feel the clay. Feel the shape, the texture. What is it telling you?" I whisper to her.

She begins to manipulate the clay while it is turning on the wheel. It changes shape, becoming a glob with a bigger hole in it. It isn't pretty, but it is progress.

"Now, I need you to go back to the top. Put your hand in the hole you made and gently pull upward inside the hole."

With the wheel turning, she reaches down inside the hole and pulls upward. The clay wobbles.

"Remember to listen to it. While your hand is going upward on the inside, hold it on the outside and both hands move up slowly together."

Azza does this several times until it feels tall enough.

"Now Azza, stop the wheel and open your eyes," I say.

With the wheel still going around at a slow speed, she opens her eyes. The wheel comes to a rest. She looks at the clay. It looks like a vase. She looks up at me and smiles from ear to ear.

"I did it!" she exclaims.

"Now, you are nowhere near finished. Is this what the clay told you it wanted to look like?" I ask with a giggle.

"No, I guess kinda." She appears puzzled as to where to go next.

"Okay, well since you know how to do this and talk to the clay while you are doing it, I think I can allow you to finish it."

I get up from my chair and grab for a wet towel. I clean my hands off, and then I untie my smock. The wheel has slowed to a stop. She is no longer working on her vase. Her face appears almost sad. Oh no, what did I do? Did I say something wrong? Did I hurt her feelings?

"What's wrong?" I ask.

"Nothing," she says in a calm voice. Then I see her face soften. This young girl full of rage is no longer the same girl before me.

"Are you okay?"

"No one has ever taken the time to work with me like that." She begins to tear up. "You taught me how to do this, you know. Conquer my fear." She smiles and looks down at her creation.

"Honey, I just taught you how to listen to the clay. It can talk to you if you listen to it."

"It's crazy, but you were right." She tries to wipe the clay off her chin, smearing more clay across her face.

"Now keep going. It needs to get done before it hardens," I say.

Azza directs her attention back to her clay and turns her wheel back on. She looks like a pro at this now. She places her hands in the bowl of water and then begins caressing her vase to change its shape with each move.

Before I leave the classroom, I turn to Azza once more. "Honey, let me see it when you are finished."

"Yes ma'am," she says with her back to me. She is really concentrating and is afraid to take her eyes off of it.

Looking over at the teacher, I see he is sitting at his desk with his chin perched up on his hand and his elbow on his desk. My mother hated for me to do that. He is focused on Azza, too. What just happened here?

"Thank you for coming into our classroom Mrs. Parker." He says it like I'm just there for a visit.

"Sure thing," I say with a smile as I head out the door. "My pleasure."

Leaving the classroom, I feel a great sense of peace. I got through to Azza. She did not have a temper tantrum, although it was close by. She did not destroy anything. Not to mention, 1 taught her how to make a vase. And get this, 1 never did pottery in my life. No one has to know it though. Not even the teacher. 1 pulled it off.

Then again, maybe 1 just got lucky.

CHAPTER 20

AFTER SCHOOL, I SETTLE in the sunroom to bask in the solar heat of the day. This room looks just like Mildred left it. All the wonderful pictures on the grand piano of the children are still there, so I get up and take a closer look for old time's sake.

The photos are covered in a thin layer of dust. Antoinette has been very busy with school activities and ensuring everything is being fulfilled to the satisfaction of the judge and probation officers, which is a better use of her attention than taking care of me and this manor. Holding the frame in my hands, I turn it around to look at the back for the name of the child in the picture and the year. Most of the photos are of dancers in their finest attire. Some are of young boys in their tights holding poses of elegance and grace. Most boys would laugh nowadays. Back then, they were the cream of the crop, much like the Russian dancers that are praised when seen or the young lads lifting their female counterparts high into the sky on stage. The spotlight is on the ballerina, but they play just as important a part as she does.

Antoinette walks though the hall and pauses in the doorway. "Oh Mrs. Mary, I meant to dust in here," she says apologetically.

"Antoinette, you work harder than anyone I know," I say with a giggle. "Come sit with me," I request. "You know, this may be a good job for Rainelle to take over. She can do some work around here, too," I add.

Millie wanders in with her usual bounce.

"Mommy." Her voice is so refreshing and young. "Whatcha doin'?"

"You mean, what are you dooo-innnnnng?" I correct as I pull her close. "It's doing, not doin'."

She tries to mimic me, but it gets lost in translation somewhere. At least she is talking in whole sentences even if they are very broken. She sits beside me, wanting to be a part of the gang here with me.

Antoinette sits in one of the oversized chairs that I used to sit in when I came to see Mildred. She lets out a huge sigh, and I can see just how tired she really is.

"You know, I have an idea." I want to bring it up with Antoinette.

"Yes?" She straightens her apron.

"I want all of these photos taken out of here and cleaned up, of course, first. Then I want plaques made, small ones. I want to display these pictures, along with the plaque of their name in the walkway of the museum." I count the pictures. "I want Mildred's painting on display in the museum, also."

Antoinette looks a bit surprised that I want to remove Mildred's painting from its home up above the huge stone fireplace.

"I think I mentioned doing this a while ago, but things got to be so busy here that we just forgot to do it. I want the kids to understand who Mildred was and why this school is operational." My mind is racing with ideas.

When Mildred spoke, her slow southern words were matched by gestures of alluring charm. You could see the ballerina inside her frail body holding poses with grace and elegance as she spoke. Before her death, Mildred had a presence surpassed by none, but I tried to emulate it. She was my idol, my mentor. Her eyes spoke the truth. Her southern drawl captured the attention of everyone near her. Her stance was poetic, resembling the ballerina she was when she was young. Even when she sat at a table, her posture was erect and her legs were always crossed at her ankles, just as she taught me.

The portrait in question is a huge painting of Mildred above the massive fireplace. The portrait artist had her in a dancer's pose while he painted it for her mother. I've stared at it for hours before, feeling her dance in my mind. I feel my muscles tense up as if I'm the one posing and dancing. It is like watching a show on TV and feeling your muscles tense when the actor is doing something strenuous. It's a strange feeling.

The beautiful portrait of Mildred was a gift from her mother. Mildred was in her prime of life, and the pose shows it to perfection. The woman in the portrait is quite young but still grown enough to be able to bestow such grace and elegance. Her arms stretch open, steadying herself on one foot while the other stretches far to the ceiling. Her hands are elegant; each finger has meaning as if floating on thin air. Her chin is stretched to the sky with a sense of grace, confidence, and poise. Her face is painted with blush and pale-colored lips. Her eyes are deeper than the ocean and are captured in time. Even though her eyes when I met her many years prior had lines of wisdom, they still bestowed the very essence of her wit and southern charm. I remember gazing into her eyes when we would sit for hours in the garden, talking about life. She made it look so easy. That was far from the truth. Even with the features of a young woman, her eyes cannot hide the woman I knew.

I still remember seeing this portrait for the first time. She told me of how she won a dance recital that night and that her mother had the portrait painted from a photo taken that evening. Oh, how I longed to see her dance.

"I want the huge oil painting to be made into a tribute for all the kids to see." I walk over to the grand fireplace and gaze up at the painting before me. The sheer size is magnificent.

"What will you put in its place?" she asks.

"Where? Up there?" Millie points high up above her head. I don't think she realized the big portrait of Mildred was up there. Afterall, it is a long way for such a little girl to see.

"That's Mildred honey." I move over so Millie can see.

She giggles. "I'm Mildred, silly." Her laugh is so contagious Antoinette and I both laugh hard at her innocence.

I look over at Antoinette, wondering if now is the perfect time to tell Millie where she got her name. She obviously realizes that her name is Mildred just like the lady in the picture. Antoinette and I smile as she settles deeper into her seat. She wants to see how I'm going to explain this one. Little does she know I've been waiting for this day for a while now.

I pull Millie close and begin, "Mildred, do you see that picture up there?"

"Yup." She looks up and rubs her nose.

"Do you know who she is?" I ask.

"Yup, she's a balbena." She is so proud of her answers.

Antoinette and I cackle like geese but then realize we're laughing at Mildred, so we quickly quiet down.

"Honey, do you mean 'ballerina'?"

"Yep. Balberena." Mildred is so sure she is saying it right. I'm not going to correct her again. We need to talk, not be educated right now on manners and speaking.

"You know her name is Mildred, right?"

"Yep, like me!" She gives a little hop.

"Yes, dear, just like you." I lift my right hand and bop her on the nose with my index finger ever so gently.

"She is a very special lady. Did you know that?" I ask once more.

"Why?"

"Mildred was so special to me that she was like a mother to me. She was so special to me that I named you after her." And I point up to the painting.

"So," she puts her finger up to her nose. It looks like she is trying to think really hard. "Is she my g'andma?"

"Your grandma?" I look at Antoinette, wondering how to answer this question. In an essence she is. But, not really. But, to me she is. Oh boy.

"Well, I guess that is kind of right," I admit.

"Wow, my g'andma is pretty." She looks up and gets a big smile on her face.

"Someday I'll tell you more about her. Is that okay?" I push back the curls from her face. She looks so much like me when I was her age. We both have these unruly curls. Her's are red too, but mine are more of a dark auburn from age.

Millie seems to be satisfied with her information about Mildred, so I return my focus to Antoinette and our conversation about the photos.

"Getting this portrait of her where it belongs is important. Today's kids don't even know who she is, or," I pause, "was."

"Maybe you and Charlie can have your portrait up there," Antoinette suggests, staring up at the painting.

I smile, imagining it with her. "That sounds good, but we don't have one."

"Well, that may have to change." She smirks.

We sit in peaceful silence for a while as Millie plays with her imaginary friend again.

Antoinette's attention shifts to the doorway. I cannot see what caught her eye.

"Mrs. Mary, we have a surprise for you." Antoinette comes to her feet.

"We?" Whom could *we* be? "Now, close your eyes," Antoinette instructs me.

I do so, and then I hear some shuffling in the room. I can hear Millie trying to whisper, but it isn't easy for her age.

"Okay, you can open them now." Antoinette instructs.

When I open my eyes, I'm struck by lightning. I see an angel before me. But wait, this angel has a faint resemblance to someone. Oh, it can't be though. I'm in shock, but it is a pleasant shock. Millie jumps all over the chair, bursting with energy.

The young lady before me twirls round and round like she is a model on a runway. Her long brown curly hair is tame and appealing. I think I may even see some highlights. Her clothing is beautiful. A black dress with black boots leads to a frilly pink top. As the young lady completes her turn, she faces me. Oh my, it is Rainelle!

Stunned by the presence of an angel, I'm at a loss for words. Her hair is beautiful, and it is not draped over her face at all. Her face is done with concealer to hide her birthmark. She is absolutely beautiful! Rainelle has lipstick on, and up against her foundation to conceal her birthmark, her lips are beautifully formed to perfection.

Oh no, I can't. I stop! Not now! I can't stop crying.

"Do you like it?" Rainelle asks. Rainelle is like a shy little girl asking for approval.

"Oh, honey, you look so different!" I wipe my tears away.

"She came to me and asked if I could help her with a change," Antoinette says.

"I helped! I helped!" Millie makes sure that I know that she helped with the big secret.

"Change?" I ask, directing my question to Rainelle.

"Yep, I don't want to hide like I did before. I know I still have black on, but I really am trying to change. Do you like my new boots?" She pulls up the edge of her dress and shows me her new low-rider dress boots. They have a zipper in the back as well as a heel, and she is displaying them like a shoe salesman. I have never seen Rainelle in a dress, ever. Her legs are so muscular and perfect.

"They look perfect," I say with a huge smile.

"Antoinette talked me into this pink top, and you know, I kinda like it." She twirls once more. "I got my ears pierced, too!"

She pushes her hair back to reveal her earrings. What a complete transformation. I'm looking at a young lady now, not a goth girl by any means. Her outfit is very professional and tasteful. It isn't over the top, like a dress with high heels. It is very everyday classy. I love it.

"You remind me of a diamond," I say.

"A diamond?" Rainelle sounds confused.

"Yes."

"Why?"

"When I first saw you, you were hard as a rock from deep within the earth, waiting to be found. Then, you came to this school and the layers began to come off, chipped away little by little. Then pressures of life got you with your foster home. Do you know what happens when you apply heat and pressure to the right kind of rock?" I ask.

"No."

"The heat and pressure transform it into a diamond. But you still need to clean the rock to get the diamond out. With you going through this transformation, you have found your diamond." I gesture to her. It is quite difficult to keep speaking. All I want to do is cry and hold her.

"However, even though you are a diamond now, the work isn't done. You need to keep going to polish and cultivate it. That means you need to keep going the way you're going, and you will turn into the beautiful young lady, I mean diamond, that God intended you to be." I want to make sure she knows that this is not the finish line.

She nods. I think she gets it.

"I wanted to finally change, and I wasn't sure how to do it, but Antoinette helped me. She took me to the hairdresser, and I got my hair done. It's a bit shorter, but it brings out the curls more. And they showed me how to take care of the curls, so they stay nice."

"Yep, they can be a pain. I know." I run my fingers through my own unruly curls.

"And I was able to get some cool clothes for school," she adds.

"When she came to me, I wasn't sure how I was going to do this, but she let me help her," Antoinette says.

"And," Rainelle interrupts Antoinette, "I learned how to do my makeup." She smiles so big all I see are teeth. That will be next on our list.

"Marvelous!"

"You know, being in foster care, no one taught me how to be … what do you call it?" Rainelle turns to Antoinette.

"A lady."

"Oh yeah, a lady. And now I feel like I can become a lady and not be laughed at."

"We would never laugh at you," I remind her.

"I never had anyone care about me."

"Come here, dear." I reach out my arms toward her. She falls into my arms and holds me tight. "You look lovely, but you know you don't need to cover up your birthmark to be beautiful, right?" I ask softly.

"I know. I'm just not ready for that yet."

I smile gently. All in good time.

"I love you," she whispers. She backs up like she accidentally slipped. Did she really just tell me that she loves me?

"Aw, honey, we love you, too!" She leans into me once more, and I hug her close. This young lady just needed someone to open the door for her so she could step out into the world. There is no reason for her to be so angry and fight for her place. She has a place now.

She jumps up and springs into action.

"I'm going to find Alfred and show him!" She bolts out of the room like a newborn colt trying to find its legs and bursts into laughter.

"What's so funny?"

"I have to learn how to walk in these boots with a little heel on them," she explains, still laughing.

"Yeah, it takes time, but you can do it," I call after her. I'm not sure if she heard me, though. She's already off and running.

"I'm so happy with how far this young lady has come in such a short time. When she came to live here, I thought you were nuts." Antoinette bursts into laughter.

"I know, right!"

"But, I knew you had all of this under control. Mildred was absolutely right about you. You find the best in everyone just as she did. She is no longer a street kid. She is a young lady in the making."

After all the fanfare, Charlie decides to celebrate and make this night special. He fixes a beautiful dinner, and we all sit in our own dining room, not the kitchen at the school. We sit together, eating, talking, and laughing. This feels right. Even Millie is behaving in her highchair. She is about ready for a kid's chair, but

I need to find a booster seat for her instead.

The phone rings, and I let Antoinette get it. We're having family time.

"Mrs. Mary?" Antoinette comes into the room hesitantly.

"Yes, Antoinette?" I turn my head toward her.

"You may want to take this call." She holds the phone close to her chest. These phone calls make me feel ill. When I get them, someone dies. First it was my mom, then I got the call about Mildred. I'm just not really sure I want to take the phone from her, but I have to.

Slowly, I hold the phone to my ear and say, "Hello, this is Mrs. Parker."

I feel the hammer drop when I realize that the person on the other end of the phone is a social worker for Rainelle. Maybe it's a check-in kind of phone call? I soon know it isn't. My facial features must have changed because Charlie begins asking questions I can't answer yet.

"Uh, huh," I pause, "Okay, are you sure?" I feel the blood rush out of my body like someone pulled the drain plug out of a boat in anticipation of its final doom on the bottom of the ocean.

I drop my head. "I understand, okay." Then a pause again, "Thank you for calling, goodbye." I pull the phone back to my chest in total disbelief. I turn away from the dinner table in hopes they don't see me push away my feelings, but it's too late.

I give the phone back to Antoinette and slowly go back to my seat.

"Antoinette, I believe Millie is finished with her dinner. Can you get her cleaned up please?"

Antoinette knows what that means. I need Millie out of the room.

"Come on, dear," she says, helping Millie out of her highchair and guiding her out, leaving Charlie and me at the table with Rainelle.

"Rainelle, we need to talk to you," I begin. Oh God, I can't do this!

Charlie looks at me out of the corner of his eye, wondering

just what is going on. Rainelle takes another bite of her dinner and then puts the fork down on her plate.

"Sure, what's up?" Rainelle is still happy with her new transformation.

"Honey, that was your social worker…" My voice is trailing.

"Um, okay." She, too, thinks it was just a welfare call.

"Honey, you have a new foster family." Oh my God! I said it! It just spilled out like word vomit. I couldn't control it. I couldn't stop it. It just happened.

The color drains from Rainelle's face, like she isn't wearing make-up after all. Her face goes flat, closing her off just like when I met her for the first time. Her excited, full-of-life features are overcome by a hollow darkness.

"When?" she asks calmly.

"She said tomorrow morning," I say softly.

Rainelle stands. Her eyes are distant as she pushes herself away from the table. D.O.G. gets up with her, his tail wagging like it's in a race.

Rainelle glances over at the new photo on the hutch, sitting in a pretty glass frame. In it, taken only a few days ago, Charlie, Antoinette, Alfred, D.O.G., Millie, Rainelle, and I are gathered in the garden. We look like a big, happy family. She reaches over and takes it off the table, tracing her finger along the frame. Her hands shake. Next thing I know, the photo slams to the floor, and glass flies everywhere. Rainelle screams.

"I thought you wanted me! No one wants me!"

She storms out of the room and up the stairs in a wailing cry. I reach out after her and stop myself. Her pain is raw, and I feel it raking across me, too.

"What just happened?" Charlie asks, staring down at the glass.

Taking a deep breath, I say, "The social worker is coming to take Rainelle away to a foster home." I look into Charlie's eyes unable to contain my distress.

He reaches over for my hand, trying to console me. But it doesn't work.

"If they take her, she won't be in the Second Chance Program, and she may have to go back to Juvenile Hall for not completing the program."

"Can they do that?"

"I guess they can do anything they want." Anger rises up in me again.

We can hear Rainelle throwing her stuff around the room. I feel like I want to do the same thing. Her sobs can be heard all around the manor. Antoinette comes around the corner with Millie, holding back her own tears. Millie is all around too young to understand what is going on.

"Is there anything we can do?" Antoinette asks.

I look at Charlie, having a conversation with no words. He smiles deep and warm. It's the kind of smile that could melt the world.

"Are you sure about this?" I ask.

"Are you?"

The time passes like a speeding freight train. We both want to speak, but each of us is afraid to say anything.

"She fits here." I take another deep breath. "I can't let her go."

"Let's go up and tell her." Charlie holds out his hand, and we head up the stairs. "Wait, I need to make a phone call first." I stop and make the call to the same social worker who just called me. I tell her what I want to do. She says she will look into it.

Hanging up the phone, I look at Charlie, and I'm not sure if I should be happy or worried. It doesn't matter. We go upstairs anyway.

Rainelle's room, to say the least, looks like a tornado hit it. Her suitcases are on the bed, and she is packing her brand-new clothes that Antoinette just picked out for her. I notice that she has her hoodie back on, and yep, it is up over her head again.

"Honey, can we talk for a minute?" I ask.

Charlie and I sit on her bed. Rainelle sits on the chair beside the bed.

"Honey, we are so sorry," Charlie starts.

"I know." Rainelle speaks to us in a calm tone that is almost scary. It is too cool, too calculated, too rehearsed.

"Honey, Charlie and I talked downstairs." I want to just jump up and hold her, but I can't.

"Rainelle, we don't want you to leave," Charlie bursts out and says it.

"But I have to go." Rainelle begins to cry again. "They said so."

D.O.G. comes up the stairs to her bedroom and put his head on her lap. She begins to pet him.

"Go away!" she yells.

D.O.G. doesn't listen. He just keeps nudging her hand, begging for her love and affection.

"Stop it!" she pushes him away.

"Why are you being like that to him?" I ask.

"I have to!" Rainelle yells. She knows that yelling at me is wrong, but she cannot contain her feelings. "I can't take him with me! It is just like last time. I get a dog and then I have to leave it." She has a hard time speaking. Her tears are taking her breath away. "I hate this!" Rainelle picks up a shoe and throws it.

"Honey, please wait." I try to regain her attention.

Rainelle stops for a moment before the big storm returns.

"Honey, we don't want you to leave. You are a part of our family." I'm holding her hand.

"But I have to." Her words are blubbering.

"I called the social worker back. She is trying to see if we can keep you." I reach up and touch her chin. Gently, I brush her hair away from her face. Her hoodie is in the way so I push it off her head.

"How can I stay here?" she asks.

"Well, how would you like to be a part of our family," I pause to say the word, "forever?"

Rainelle is in shock. No one has ever even considered keeping her forever. She has been like a rag doll being tossed from family to family, or house to house actually. None of the places she was at really had a family.

"Do you mean, adopt me?" her voice is small, not really believing anything.

"Yes," Charlie says while looking at me and then at Rainelle. "What do you think? Would you want us to adopt you?"

Rainelle tries to breathe normally, but she can't. Her lungs are shaking from all the turmoil and trauma. Then she begins to cry again.

"Honey?" I ask.

"Does that mean you actually love me?"

"How could we not love you? You are a part of our family here. Even Millie loves you," Charlie says in an attempt to convince her that this is real.

"Can I stay?" she asks in a sheepish voice.

"Let me handle this tomorrow, and I will make things happen." I can't tell her that it's done, but I'm going to try my best to make it happen. Rainelle would absolutely die if I lied to her. I can't tell her that she can definitely stay. I'm not the judicial system nor the social worker. I can only do what my heart tells me. I can't let her go.

"In the meantime," I glance around the room, "please clean your room back up."

"Yes, Ma'am," she says with a small smile, a welcome change from the storm before.

Charlie and I head back downstairs.

"Coffee?" he asks.

"Sure thing, I'd love some." I plop in a chair.

Antoinette comes in with the coffee from dinner we didn't get to drink. We take our cups and look up at Antoinette.

"Why don't you get yourself a cup of coffee and come sit with us?" I ask.

"Are you sure?"

"Sure," Charlie pipes up. "Come sit with us."

Antoinette gets a cup of coffee and sits with us. Everyone is well aware of the disastrous evening we had.

"We're going to try to adopt Rainelle." I have to put it out on the table.

"I think that would be a wonderful idea," she says as she sips her piping hot coffee. She then puts her cup down to cool on the saucer.

"You think so?" I ask.

"Sure, I do. Since you opened the program for the kids, I've seen you change." Antoinette notices she is speaking very casually. "Is it okay if I say so?"

"Absolutely. I wouldn't have it any other way," I say.

"You've changed into someone that Mildred would be so proud of. I'm sure she's watching from her, well, wherever she is." Antoinette fights back tears. "Since you took in Rainelle, this manor is becoming more and more complete each and every day. Not just with Rainelle but also D.O.G."

"Ugh yes, can't forget D.O.G.," I say with a little snicker.

"I've noticed it, too," Charlie speaks and I turn to look in his direction. "I see you stand up for these kids. You fight for their rights. You care more about them than their own parents do." Charlie sets his coffee cup down. "*That* is just one reason I love you so much."

I feel like crying, but I want to keep my wits about me.

"When you brought Rainelle into our home here," Antoinette pauses, "I wondered if this was going to be a huge mistake, you allowing a teenager that is obviously in trouble with the law and all."

"Yeah, I know."

"Not to mention then you brought the dog too," she adds.

"Yeah, I know. I was just winging it."

"No, I don't think so. I think you had a plan. You just didn't realize it," Charlie adds.

"Well, I don't know about that." I pick up my coffee and take another sip.

"Rainelle is a part of our family now, whether you like it or not. Millie looks to her as a big sister. I can see it in her eyes," Charlie says.

"Yeah, she surely does," Antoinette adds. "I love having her here. Even though we had our rough times with training the dog and all, she is still a breath of fresh air."

I look down at my coffee cup. I guess my facial features change. We can't discount the obvious.

"What if they won't let us adopt her?" Hopelessness creeps in.

"They would be making the worst mistake ever if they didn't allow you two to adopt that poor child. You run the best school in the city, and you can provide for her." Antoinette points out.

"Well, I'm not going to get my hopes up but," I look over at Charlie, "I sure would like it if they would allow it."

We all retire to our beds, and I can't stop dreaming of being a bigger family with Rainelle.

The morning comes too quickly. When I wake, Charlie is already downstairs.

Antoinette comes into the bedroom. "Mrs. Mary, there is someone at the door for you."

Good God, what time is it? Why would someone come here so early?

After getting dressed to go to the door, I walk down the large stairway. I can hear voices. Antoinette must have already allowed whomever it is inside.

As I turn the corner to the entrance in the foyer, I see a young lady standing there with a city badge on. She has it around her neck for identification. I get closer to get a better look. It is a social services badge. Hmm, this is kind of early, but okay.

"Can I help you? I'm Mrs. Parker," I say cautiously. This looks like a business visit.

"Mrs. Parker, I'm here to pick up Rainelle." The young woman doesn't miss a beat. She smiles as if she is picking up her takeout for dinner with her family.

I, on the other hand, become a bit suspicious.

"Pick her up? What do you mean, pick her up?" I sound upset.

"I knew it!" Rainelle yells.

I turn around to see Rainelle standing at the top of the stairs. She storms off down the hall to her room stomping her feet. This just can't be happening.

I glance over to Antoinette, and she has her hand over her mouth in shock. After last night when we told Rainelle just how much we wanted her to stay, we were all worried this was going to happen.

"Yes, I have orders to pick Rainelle up and take her to her new foster home." She begins to dig through her paperwork.

"I'm guessing that you did not get the paperwork yet that we are adopting her, so she can't possibly be leaving with you now." I sound very firm.

"I have not heard of this. I was just told to transport her." She is obviously young and very oblivious to just how devastating her job really is to families.

"Please wait here," I instruct her.

Going into the other room, I need to use the phone so no one can hear me. I call the social worker that I spoke to last night. She gave me her phone number. I tell her what is happening, and that Rainelle is not leaving with the other worker. I get a lot of apologies, and then she says she will take care of it. Next thing I know, the social worker in my home is receiving a call on her work phone. She answers it, and it is the social worker that I just spoke with. I hear a lot of "uh huh" and "okay", and then she hangs up. She looks at me with a strange look on her face.

"I'm sorry for the confusion. Rainelle *is* up for adoption, not transport," she says nonchalantly.

I feel like strangling her. I can see myself running over to her, throwing her to the ground, grabbing her by her neck, and shaking her because of all the stress we went through last night. Instead, I smile and keep my mouth shut.

The social worker leaves, and I head upstairs to Rainelle's room. Rainelle is back to her angry packing again. She is so used to being torn away, foster family to foster family, that packing as fast as you can has become an art. She is stuffing, pushing, and shoving as fast as she can.

I walk into her hurricane. I have to stop her.

"Well, kiddo," I stop, "Looks like you are going to be stuck with us!" I say as I rush over to her bed and give her a big hug. I'm so happy that I end up falling right on top of her.

"Yeah!" Rainelle is screaming with happiness. "Does that mean I can call you 'Mom' now?"

"Well, here, but not in school. Got it?" I say with a tilt of my head.

"Got it!" Rainelle stops and looks at me with a funny look. "Mom?"

Taken aback by my new title coming from her, I ask, "Yeah?"

"Mom, can you get off of me so I can go to the bathroom?" she asks quietly.

"Oh gosh!" I jump off the bed. "Sorry."

She runs to the bathroom, and we both laugh.

CHAPTER 21

LATER THAT WEEK, WHEN I GET TO SCHOOL, I can't help but feel the school needs freshened up for the students before the year ends. We need it to feel like spring. The dark and dingy walls do nothing for spring. I look for Alfred.

"Alfred, are you able to paint the walls in the entrance and the hallways?" I ask.

"Sure thing," he responds without any hesitation. He looks at the walls and then gets a strange look on his face.

"What are you thinking?" I ask.

"Oh, nothing, Mrs. Parker. I'm just thinking about the walls." I can tell when Alfred is up to something, but I don't have time to ask. "I'll need some tarps so I can keep the paint off the floors and away from students. I don't want them to get any paint on their clothing."

"You know you can get anything you need, and I will handle it," I reassure him.

"Yes, Ma'am." Now, this is uncommon, but it is okay. I still think he is up to something.

This week is proving to be much better than most. Even though it started off badly with the social worker, I guess I really have nothing to complain about. Well, Mildred would kill me if I actually thought of complaining at all.

I remember I told Joseph I would check back with him, so I head down the hallway to shop class.

When I get there, I'm pleasantly surprised to see just how much work is being done. Each student is hard at work on their pieces of wood from their field trip the other day. I scan the room until I find where Joseph is working.

He is in the back of the room where the large tools are placed securely on the floor. I'm not sure how he did it, but he got that huge log up on the lathe. I'm really impressed with what he is doing. I have to watch from a distance for safety, but from what I can see, he has come so far.

Joseph stands in front of the lathe wearing a very heavy vinyl-looking smock, not like the one I wore in pottery class. He is wearing all the safety clothing required for shop class. I am happy to see that this teacher is being careful and following regulations.

Joseph holds what looks to be a chisel. He has it carefully placed to gouge out the pattern that he has chosen with each turn of the lathe. To me, it still looks like a log, but I'm sure Joseph sees a specific pattern. I shouldn't stay long enough to become a distraction. In this class, that would create an unsafe work environment, so I leave.

Today, I need to go home early, since I have a very special court date I need to attend.

When I get back to the manor, Rainelle is still upstairs getting ready. Charlie is sitting in the sunroom drinking coffee.

"Rainelle, are you about ready?" I yell upstairs.

I hear a faint response from her room, so I go into the sunroom to speak to Charlie.

"Honey, are you ready for today?" I think I need reassurance that we are making the right decision. I'm so nervous that the judge may decide she needs to be somewhere else. But why would he? We are already perfect parents to Mildred. This will go fine.

Charlie gets up from his chair and puts his loving arms around me. I'm sure he can see just how nervous I am. He doesn't show his emotions all that much, but I know he's nervous, too.

"She'll be fine here with us. We're a family." His words are comforting.

Antoinette and Rainelle come down the stairs and into the doorway to the sunroom. I turn and once again I'm taken aback. Rainelle is wearing a dress with what? High-heeled shoes? She has her hair curled and her make-up is perfect. She looks amazing. Antoinette is also dressed up in nice slacks and a dress top with her usual shoes.

Mildred comes bouncing around the corner as well. Aw, she looks so cute.

"I'm ready!" Mildred announces like she is going to a big show.

I reach out for Rainelle. "Honey, you still feel okay about this?" I want to make sure everything is all set. I don't want Rainelle to have second thoughts. I've grown close to her over the last school year, but I want the feeling to be mutual.

Rainelle looks into my eyes. She is a totally different young lady than when I first laid eyes on her. She is beautiful inside as well as out. She has a special look about her. I can see she finally feels at ease; she finally feels loved.

She takes a deep breath, and her face softens. "I'm so happy I finally belong." Her smile is endearing. I pull her close and hold her.

"Okay. Let's head to the courthouse."

***

The courthouse is scary, but we get through it. Mildred is asked to be on the stand to tell the judge why she wants Rainelle to be her big sister, and she does great. Even though she is a little girl, she speaks eloquently about Rainelle. Rainelle tears up with each person asked why she should be part of our family. It's a very special moment I wish could stand still in time.

When it's all over, it's official. She has a family: our family.

On the drive back to the manor, Rainelle asks, "Can I go to the prom next weekend?"

I never thought she would be caught dead in a dress, let alone at a dance where she has to be with other kids. I look at Charlie, and I'm lost for words. How can I not allow her to go? It's *our* school.

"Who are you going with?" What mother wouldn't ask that question?

She's reluctant to answer.

"I know, I know!" Mildred is bursting at the seams.

"Sh." Rainelle doesn't want Mildred to spill the beans. "No one really."

I know better. If she wants to go to a dance, a prom no less, there has to be a boy involved.

"No one? Really?"

"I know, I know!" Mildred yells once again.

"Antoinette, do you know who the lucky guy is?" I ask.

Antoinette looks at me and pushes her lips together as if they were just glued together with super glue. "Not going to hear it from me."

"Well, Rainelle, who is it?" I beg her to answer.

"It's Sammy!" Mildred can't hold it in any longer.

"Sam?" My face is full of joy, but I don't want to embarrass her.

"Mildred!" she says, already embarrassed.

"Sam, huh. He's a good kid. Sam from the program, right?"

Rainelle looks down into her lap. Now she's really embarrassed. Then she mumbles, "Yes, Ma'am."

"Honey, that's awesome! He really likes you." Oops, I said it.

Her eyes snap up to my face. "How do you know?"

How am I going to get out of this one? "He told me."

"What?"

Now the whole car is laughing.

"Rainelle, he told me a long time ago," I tell her with a matter-of-fact tone.

"Really? He did?"

"Yes! And I'm sure you two will have a great time." I turn back to the front, glad Charlie has been driving. We're almost back to the manor.

***

When Friday arrives, Antoinette is playing the fashionista and helping Rainelle look like a queen for her first date. Oh no, her first date? I remember my first date. I thought I was in love with my date, and I ended up drugged and raped. Should I not allow her to go? But wait, I can't hold her hostage. I'm responsible for her and her safety. What should I do? I'm not prepared for this. I have lots of time to get ready with Millie. But with Rainelle, we jumped straight to the teenager phase, and I have to have *that* talk.

I head up to Rainelle's room, nervous of what could happen.

"Rainelle, can we talk for a minute?" Rainelle is trying to adjust her makeup in the mirror.

"Sure." After touching up her eyeliner, she turns to me. "What's up?"

"Honey, I want you to be very careful tonight." I sit down on the bed. Oh, this is familiar. When my mom tried to talk to me, I did not want to listen. How can I make her listen to me? "Honey, there are several things I want you to know." My face becomes very serious.

"Oh no, is this *the talk*?" she plops down on the bed beside me, a strange look in her evening gown.

"No, Honey, I'm being serious for a minute."

"Okay."

"I know I don't have a lot of time, but I know we haven't talked about the icky stuff." Oh, I feel so stupid.

She laughs. "You mean sex? It's okay, you can say it."

"Well, yes, sex." It's so strange that I can't say the word to her. I was always taught to be a lady and not to speak of things like that. Charlie and I have a special relationship, and I honestly don't even think I've said the word sex to him. Wow, this is strange.

"Um, I haven't really, well, you know." She wrings her hands.

A huge relief washes over me.

"Okay, so now, are you?" I know the horrible life she endured with her foster families before, and this whole conversation becomes even more awkward.

"Thinking about having sex?" She has a surprised look on her face. Am I really asking if she is going to have sex with Sam? "Um, no." She stands up again. "Sam is nice and all but honestly, he is the only one that has ever talked to me like I'm a person. I thought we could go to the prom more as friends."

"Okay, that sounds good." Now onto the next question I'm afraid to ask. "Have you ever done any drugs?" I feel like I should have had this conversation before we adopted her. It's like we're getting to know each other all over again, but this time it's on a much more personal level.

"No drugs. Since I have been going from foster home to foster home, I've seen drugs, and I have seen what they do to people. Honestly?"

I'm afraid of what she is going to say next, but I'm ready for it.

"One of my foster dads actually drugged me and then, well, you know." She suddenly becomes a shy little girl again.

I touch her hand to show her that I'm there for her.

"After knowing what drugs can do and what can happen to me? Drugs are never coming near me ever again." She is very set in her ways.

I nod. "I'm just a phone call away if you need me." I want her to know I'm her safety net.

"Um, Mom?" She looks at me like she wants to burst out laughing. "The prom is literally in our backyard, at the school," she says with a giggle.

"Oh yeah." I feel so stupid. Maybe I'm overreacting. Afterall, it is our school. Our school is safe. I take a deep breath, and sigh. She's right. I'm overreacting. Everything is good. I just have to calm down and allow this young lady to have fun and make her own decisions. I have faith in her. I just wish I had faith in myself not to overreact. I think I'm way past that.

A soft knock sounds at the door and Antoinette opens the door slightly.

"I think Sam is here for you," she announces. She has a huge grin on her face.

"Antoinette, stop! It's just the prom." Rainelle is giddy, an odd sight to say the least.

Rainelle bolts to the top of the stairway, and we follow just to see the sights.

As we get to the top of the stairs, Sam is standing in the front of the manor with flowers in hand. His tux fits him to perfection, and he appears very manly, not childlike by any means.

Rainelle gasps as she sees him. I think she really does like him. She just doesn't want to admit it.

"Can I go?" Millie asks.

"No honey, this is just for Rainelle and Sam." Antoinette picks Millie up.

We head down the stairway and into the foyer to meet with Sam. Rainelle is very cautious navigating the steps with her evening gown and high heels. She must have practiced because she does not miss a step. Her dress flows behind her and her head is held high with dignity. Her hair is up off her neck and a few curls drape over her shoulder. Oh my, she is a picture of beauty. Goth Girl is gone forever.

CHAPTER 22

THE SCHOOL YEAR HAS COME TO AN END. The day before graduation, each class has their own party in celebration. I'm sitting in my office trying not to cry. It's been a really hard year. I can't tell if I'm relieved or sad that this program is over. I have such a horrible whirlwind of emotions. As I attempt to clean my desk, I'm drawn out into the hall by a commotion outside my office, only to be blocked by my secretary.

"Mrs. Parker, I need you to please stay in your office for a little bit. We're doing some work out here."

Work? What kind of work? I want to ask questions, but I really don't want to hear the answers. Instead, I go back to reminiscing about the past year. I open the drawer to my file cabinet and pull out the files for the kids in the Second Chance Program. I check the final grades for each participant, and it looks like all the kids have passed. I know that the judge will be happy.

"Mrs. Parker?" I hear outside my office doorway. "Can you please come in here?"

Oh no, not now! What could go wrong on the last day of school? I'm almost afraid to leave the safety of my office. When I get to the doorway, I notice a few students standing there along with Alfred.

"Alfred, what is going on?" I'm so confused now. Why is he here? Oh yeah, I asked him to paint, but there's no way the painting is finished so soon.

As I go around the corner, I notice a few more students standing in the conference room doorway.

"What on earth is going on?" I ask.

Some of the kids laugh.

"Can you please step inside here?" Alfred asks.

I turn to enter the room and see Joseph standing in the back. I'm puzzled by what is going on. Then I see it, and it takes my breath away.

"My table?" I'm so shocked my voice is raspy.

In place of the old conference room table Joseph had carved on the first day, sits a brand new one. It is absolutely beautiful and fitting for the room despite its massive size. A section down the middle looks like a river that runs through the beautifully grained-wood.

"Did you?" I look at Joseph.

"He sure did." Joseph's teacher is standing in the back, and he walks up to me.

Joseph's face is beaming.

"But how?" I ask as I look at Joseph and his teacher.

"He started with the wood from the field trip. Then, well, why don't you tell her?" The teacher turns to have Joseph explain.

"Well, when I first came to this school, I did something really mean to you and the table that was in here before." His head hangs low just speaking about it. "I carved in your table with my knife. I was angry, and I didn't want to be here."

"Yeah, we got off to a rough start," I admit.

"Well, when you put me into shop class," he looks toward his teacher, "he taught me how to make a table to repay you." His hand caresses the tabletop. "It's the least I can do since I was so angry and hurtful."

"But how did you do this?" I run my fingers over the river.

"That actually wasn't that hard. I had to have help, but I learned how to make it," Joseph says with a smile from ear to ear.

"It's an epoxy, and he did it himself after we researched how," his teacher boasts.

"Yeah, it really wasn't that hard. It was messy but kinda fun to do." He runs his hand over it again. "The top had to be put into a huge frame so nothing can get out. Then I mixed the epoxy, and added some blue. He helped me pour it in and smooth it out. Feel it," he instructs. "It is so smooth that it's like it's not even there." His face beams.

"This," I stop, feeling like I want to cry, "this is so beautiful and," oh here it comes. I can't stop the tears. "You made this for me?" I put my hand over my face to hide the tears. These tears are beginning to look like an ugly cry. I can't stop it.

Joseph comes around the table and puts his arms around me. I wrap my arms around him. He is a bit taller than I am, and it's a bit strange because he's so young, well a young man. Then Joseph bends over and asks me to look under the table. I do.

"Look! Even the center of the bottom was spun on the lathe, and it was very heavy. It is a foot thick!"

"And how many inches is that?" I ask.

"Umm, twelve." He laughs. "But look here." He reveals an etched plaque.

The plaque reads "Mrs. Parker, with love, Joseph" and the year next to his name.

Oh, here come those tears again.

"Thank you so," it's hard to speak, "Thank you so much."

Everyone standing in observance applauds. Joseph blushes. I think he's embarrassed to be in the spotlight. I will be so eternally grateful for this table, and I will make sure I have a lot of meetings in this room.

The rest of the day is more about celebrating and completing any projects that are not completed. Some classes are still taking their final tests, but for the most part, the year is finally over. Graduation is the final stage of the game.

Graduation day finally arrives, I don't know if I'm excited or sad. Maybe a lot of both. I've been waiting for this day for a long time. I enter the front door to the school and walk through the grand entrance with its high ceiling. I look over to the display cases with awards and trophies and get a sense of accomplishment, even though I have not taught in the school. Looking upward, I notice the wall over the hallway is still covered in tarps. "Oh, Alfred, I was hoping the painting would have been finished before graduation," I mumble to myself.

All the kids are running around in organized chaos. Many of the kids bring their parents up to me and introduce me to them. It's hard to be cordial with all the commotion. It is like a turbulent current, a welcomed storm in the midst of a celebration.

I enter the gymnasium and see the room is just as full as the hallways. The students are grouped in the front with their respective teachers in the rows behind them. Beyond the teachers, the parents and relatives sit patiently waiting for the graduation to begin.

On the stage at the end of the gymnasium sit the faculty and staff of the school. My chair is next to a seat with no name on the back of it. These chairs are nothing special, not like a prom or wedding. They are just brown metal chairs.

The chairs for the students are rented, and they are all white. They are perfectly placed in rows with a wide aisle down the middle. The floor is covered with the same protective cover we'd used for prom, to keep the gymnasium floor safe from scratches from chairs or girls in high heels.

Off to the right is the orchestra. All of the music will be live. It's beautiful to see the strings, the violins, the wind instruments, the piano, and the horns. They will all be played with the precision the musicians have learned through the years. The feeling is elated, and everyone seems to be on their best behavior as they listen to the orchestra play some songs they learned throughout the year as opening music.

The time is near. The announcement sounds for everyone to take their seats. The orchestra begins to play once more, an upbeat tune but nothing over the top. The song helps the room come to order.

Everyone is in their places and the music begins, ushering in the pomp and circumstance. From my seat on stage, I can tell whom the parents are of the kids playing in the orchestra as they stretch their necks as far as they can to get a glimpse of their kid. None of the students in the orchestra are graduating this year.

The music stops, and it's my cue to enter the stage.

"Thank you all for coming to the School of Art graduation ceremony," my voice cracks.

The room comes to a roar. As it begins to simmer down, I cue the orchestra to play their graduation waltz. This song seems to go on forever, but it's still the song everyone dreams of hearing when they attend this school.

Each child comes to the stage one by one and is handed their perspective diploma after their name is read. Parents cheer when they hear their child's name. I'm glad to see they are involved with their children's lives. It is far different from the other graduation ceremonies in the city school system.

Nothing is said about the Second Chance Program until all the other students have received their diplomas. The participants are all sectioned off to be at the end of the regular graduation ceremony. It's their time to shine. Not mine, theirs.

I go to the podium again. I'm nervous. I'm not sure why. I've done this several times. Today is different. I not only have the judge here but also their respective probation officers. As I stand, I take a glimpse out into the audience. All eyes are on me in anticipation of my next word. Gathering my cue cards, I carefully place them on the podium. I don't usually use cue cards, but I want to ensure this graduation is special and in order.

Standing behind the podium, I take a quick glance down at my husband. He winks at me, and I know everything is going to be okay. Lilly and her family are sitting with Charlie and Mildred. I take the pen I brought up with me in my hand and roll it around in my fingers to divert my anxiety into the pen and not into my speech.

"I would like to congratulate the graduating class for their excellence this year."

The gymnasium begins to clap, whistle, and roar with excitement. I wait for the crowd to settle down.

"This is all wonderful, but we are far from over." My face beams with joy.

I turn to Alfred and give him a thumbs up. He begins the next phase.

"Now, I'm excited to say we have a special group of young men and women with us tonight."

I check to make sure Alfred is getting their chairs ready. They are placed up on the stage along with all the faculty.

"When I call your name, I would like you to come up and take a seat on the stage here."

People begin to look around to see who the students are. The classmates of the school already know, but the parents from the community may have had no idea, until now.

Alfred isn't quite finished setting up their chairs, so I turn back to the audience.

"While we are still setting up for the next part, let me explain to everyone what the Second Chance Program is." The room quiets.

"If you remember, last year the city school had a horrible fire. They did not have a gymnasium because the fire was focused on that end of the building. I went to that school when I was a child. I saw my old school burn. I couldn't help but see my memories from that time burn to the ground. I felt horrible they didn't have any gymnasium to have their prom in." I smile and look over at the principal of the city school whom I invited to our graduation. He gives me an encouraging nod.

"I wanted to help. We hosted their prom here, in our gymnasium. Our students worked very hard to provide the other school with a prom full of life and splendor . The culinary department learned new foods, new pastries, and everything looked and yes, tasted, extraordinary." The room claps. "That's not all folks. The art department made our gymnasium into the most magical forest one could dream of. Please give them thanks as well." The room roars. "And... the other students worked feverously on lighting, photo booths, and many other sights and sounds. They all earned grades and extra credit for all these projects. However, it did not end well." I pause, careful about my choice of my words. "We had some problems but nothing we couldn't handle. The outside of our gymnasium was spray-painted." I stop and smile. "I didn't see it as vandalized. I saw it as art. I ended up going to court and well," I look at the judge, "what I saw broke my heart.

"I felt compelled to talk to the judge. The judge and I came up with a program to help kids in the judicial system. We created the Second Chance Program to help kids turn their lives around." I look around the audience. "You know, to give them a second chance." I smile. "A second chance at life."

The room starts to stir with approval.

"Mildred founded this school with her husband many years ago. This school is special. This school is the very essence of what our great city needs. Here we can create a program where kids can learn a craft, a skill, or a trade. To help them find a passion to live for. A dream to strive toward. A better life than drugs, jail, or even possible death." I drop my head, thinking about Alice.

I look over the group once more.

"Kids, can you come up here and tell them yourselves?" I step back from the podium.

The kids stand up, and one by one they walk up the steps to come onto the stage. As I turn to greet them, they notice the chairs for them.

They are all acting so grown up. All of them are in their dress clothes, but these are covered by their graduation gown. They each have their graduation caps on with their tassels, all ready to be moved over to the other side to signal a graduate. Each of them radiates pride as they walk to the stage.

Then Antoinette comes to the stage. This is not in the program, so I'm a bit worried. She approaches the podium.

"Hello everyone. I'm Antoinette. Most of you know me and some do not. I handle the back-office stuff, not only with the school here but also with the museum. Anyway, that is not why I'm here tonight. This is not on your program for a reason." She looks at me with a mischievous smile.

She turns back to the microphone. "The kids and I put together something special for all of you tonight." She turns to the kids. "Ready?" she asks.

All of the kids smile and nod. Suddenly, a big white screen

rolls down from the ceiling. We don't use this very often, and quite frankly I forgot we had it. Antoinette turns to Alfred and gives a nod. The lights go dim. Anticipation in the room escalates.

The screen lights up and the show begins.

Music.

The title is scripted on the screen: The Second Chance Program

The first part of the video begins with Avery in handcuffs. The gym is pulsing with blue and white lights from the screen. Avery is being put in a police car.

The audience is gasping because this is not a normal occurrence for our school.

I'm not sure who took a video of this but well, there it is. There is a voice-*over. It is Avery.*

> My name is Avery.
>
> I joined this program after vandalizing the school gym.
>
> I guess you can say I'm the reason this program was started.
>
> This program gave me a new life.
>
> Because of this program, I learned I can use my spray painting for good instead of vandalizing walls like I did to the gym.
>
> I have been teaching other kids how to spray paint art rather than vandalize property.
>
> I'm so grateful Mrs. P. believed in me.
>
> I now believe in myself. My mom is now... well, my best friend.
>
> I used to be in a gang but thanks to this program, I'm no longer in it.
>
> Thank you.

The next scene in the video is of the officers bringing in the participants. This is the first day of school. There is Alice being escorted in the room. Then Sam behind Alice. The video pans over to Rainelle, and wow, she looks so different, in her black goth clothes with black around her eyes.

As each participant enters the room, you can see on their faces that none of them really wanted to be there. It looks like they were sentenced to be there. And then there is me.

The kids all yell, "Mrs. P.!" They all clap in joy.

The next part of the video seems to be broken down into each student.

Alice is first. I have no idea who was getting all of this on video without me knowing it. Alice is being handcuffed and dragged out of the school by an officer. The room gasps. Alice's part of the video ends with her and the police officer walking out the doors.

The next student is Nicholas. He is shown ripping paper off his schoolbooks and eating it. The room comes to a roar with laughter. Then the next part shows Nicholas in the classroom with Charlie in the kitchen. Nicholas is carefully placing flowers on a huge wedding cake for a school project. He stands up and smiles at whomever is videoing him. The crowd claps.

> My name is Nicholas.
>
> When I got arrested, I was told by my probation office about this program.
>
> I honestly didn't want to be in this, but I'm sure glad I tried.
>
> Mrs. P. taught me I could make flowers with sugar instead of spit balls.
>
> Since I started it, I now cook! I bake and make really cool foods.
>
> Chef Charlie gave me a chance in his cooking class.
>
> Who knew?

The room cheers as Nicholas tells his story.

The next student is Azza. There are video segments of her having temper tantrums with clay flying all over the room. The room laughs. Then I'm shown sitting with her. The sound is turned up, and I feel a bit stupid.

> My name is Azza.
>
> I was mad at everyone, I hated everyone.
>
> When I got arrested, I found this program.
>
> Mrs. P taught me to talk to clay, I know, strange.
>
> Now I make beautiful pottery and I can concentrate on everything else.
>
> I no longer have a temper, well, unless my little sister gets to me.

"Now just close your eyes and talk to the clay," I say in the video. Azza hits the wheel too fast, and I'm covered in clay.

The room laughs again. Then it shows Azza as she controls her anger and creates beautiful pottery. Azza is shown standing behind a table with several pieces of pottery she created. Some are vases, bowls, and pitchers, some are painted bright colors, and some are kept white. Again, the room claps and cheers.

I look back at Azza, and we smile at each other. She is bright red from the embarrassment.

Next is Joseph. There is the photo that was taken for evidence showing where Joseph carved into my conference table. The video shows the police putting him on the ground and another officer holding up a knife.

> My name is Joseph.
>
> I was in a gang, dealing drugs.
>
> It was hard to get out, but when I got arrested, I found this program.
>
> I carved my name on the conference table the

first day I got here.

Mrs. P saw I liked working with wood, and I was put into shop class.

I learned how to work with wood, and I made a new conference table for the school.

The clips show Joseph working in shop class concentrating hard on his work. Then, there is a picture of the beautiful new conference table he built for me, and then I'm there crying again, hugging him. Again, cheers and applause resonate through the gym.

Next is Hunter. The video shows Hunter swaying back and forth while he chews his nails. The crowd doesn't quite know how to take it.

Hunter.

I like to draw cities.

Thank you.

Hunter is quiet. Then pictures of his cityscape murals float across the screen. The buildings are each drawn to perfection and the skyscrapers touch the hearts of all who see them. I can hear the "ooohs" and the "aahs" with each passing picture. And then, there it is, Hunter with a big smile on his face, standing in front of one of his city murals. My heart is warm with joy. The room cheers.

The video turns to Rainelle, Goth Girl herself. Every time the video camera is pointed at her, she looks angry. She always has her hoodie pulled up over her head and her hair draped over her face. Pictures of her in her glory of destroying everything in her path are right there for everyone to see. Her eyes are like daggers.

My name is Rain ... Rainelle

I used to be known as Goth Girl because I dressed in all black.

When I found the Second Chance Program I was
lost, angry, and trying to be invisible.

I found that when I gave people a chance, they
actually cared for me.

I was in foster care, but I found a family that
really loves me.

Now I have a permanent family here.

Mrs. Parker is now my mom.

The video shows her complete transformation. The young,
angry girl is now dressed in nice clothes, no longer in all black.
She has her hair and makeup done. She is absolutely beautiful!
She is smiling. Oh! She's kissing Sam! The room laughs and claps.

I glance back at Rainelle, wondering just how long this thing
with Sam has been going on. She shrugs and smiles.

Sam is next. He looks like a normal, everyday kid.

My name is Sam.

I was arrested for hacking into places illegally.

Since coming to this school and seeing how
wrong I was, I decided to give back.

I created a program to keep all schools safe from
people like me.

Oh, wait. Is that a picture of Sam sitting at a computer?
He has a look of horror on his face. Sam wasn't supposed to be
anywhere near a computer. I hope the judge didn't see that.

There is only one more participant left: Avery. The video
opens with Avery getting arrested. I'm sure the only reason this is
on the video is because it happened right here at our school.

The video stops abruptly, and murmurs go through the
crowd. Everyone seems to be wondering what happened. After
a brief moment, the screen goes to a live shot. Alfred? What on
earth is Alfred doing in the front lobby?

The show continues.

"Is this on?" Alfred asks. The camera is bouncing all around as Alfred tries to figure out if it's working or not. "Oh, it is? Okay." The camera steadies.

I look over toward the seats for the kids, but they're gone, off the stage. I worry momentarily, but then I see them on the live feed with Alfred. Avery is on the screen.

"Well, everyone, as you have seen the video isn't competed, well not yet." He waves. "Hello, I'm Avery ... again. We, the Second Chance Program, want to give you, Mrs. Parker, a final gift."

The camera pans to the front lobby. The lobby is not painted yet. I wanted it completed for this graduation. But oh well.

"Mrs. Parker, you have given us the gift of our future. We all were on horrible paths of destruction. You gave us the gift of life, where we were able to alter our dash. Now we have a dash we all can be proud of. This is our gift to you."

As Avery finishes speaking, the camera lifts up to where the white dingy paint cloths are hanging off the wall. Now I'm *really* getting nervous. What on earth have they done?

Slowly the curtain lifts away from the wall, revealing the bottom half of the wall.

The crowd is in complete awe. My jaw drops to the ground. I can't believe what I'm seeing. Each child's face is on a huge mural in the main lobby of our school. Hunter, Rainelle, Sam, Joseph, Azza, Nicholas, Avery, and who is that? Alice. She is up on the mural as well. My heart fills with joy. I look over at Charlie as tears slip down my cheeks.

Words below the participants' pictures read, SECOND CHANCE PROGRAM. Then in smaller letters, IF YOU WANT TO SEE A CHANGE, YOU HAVE TO BE THE CHANGE!

The rest of the curtain falls to the ground, and the entire mural is revealed. My hand covers my face as the tears roll down. I can no longer control my emotions. I open my eyes again to see if it is real. And there she is.

It is a beautiful picture of Mildred at the top with her hands stretched out over the kids. She even has her birds perched on her arms. Her smile is most inviting. It is a masterpiece I could never have imagined.

The gymnasium is boisterous. People are clapping, whistling, cheering. The excitement is uncontainable.

The lights come up, and Antoinette comes back to the podium. The kids come back into the gymnasium and back up on the stage as well.

"I would like to introduce you to the graduated participants of the Second Chance Program!" Antoinette welcomes all the kids to stand and be recognized. The crowd roars with excitement.

"As I call your name," Antoinette tries to talk over the crowd, but it is quite difficult. They all get quiet again. "As I call your name please step forward and receive your diploma.

"Avery... Pollics."

The room roars as he stands and comes forth. As he gets closer to the podium to receive his diploma, he scans the audience. He is so busy looking around that he almost trips. Once he gets up to the podium, he notices his mother, Angelica, standing. He stares at her watching as she holds her face trying to keep back her own tears of approval. I believe Avery is trying to hold back tears as well. He just wanted his mother to know he is really a good kid, just in a bad neighborhood with so-called friends trying to bring him down.

When he reaches for his diploma, the room cheers. With his diploma in hand, he turns to the audience and holds it up high. The tears are no longer at bay. His smile is big enough to tell the world he is worthy. He wipes the tears with the other hand and then waves to the audience as he steps back for the next person to get their diploma.

"Nicholas... Thatcher."

Nicholas jumps to his feet and begins to dance to the podium. His arms are waving up and down trying to get the audience to roar even louder, like he is at a basketball game trying to rile up the crowd as he scores another point or two. He reaches for the diploma, and his excitement is so big that instead of reaching for the diploma, he puts both arms around me and buries his face in my shoulder. Again, the room cheers. He gathers himself enough to put his diploma in his right hand and waves to the crowd.

"I did it!" he yells.

Everyone is still standing, clapping so hard. The mood is electrifying. He steps back.

"Rainelle... Hensley."

Rainelle tries to hide in her seat, but that is impossible. The room claps and yells. She is so used to pulling her hair over her face that when she attempts to do so, it begins to come out of the beautiful hairstyle Antoinette did for her. She takes a deep breath, lowers her hand to her lap again, and stands. The audience claps even harder. She puts her hand over her face from embarrassment. She's not used to this type of attention. She looks back at the other participants, and they all push the air as if they are pushing her to the front podium. She turns back to the podium and notices I'm there standing, waiting for her with the diploma in hand.

"Come on, you can do it!" I cheer her on.

She comes forward with her hand to her face. Slowly, her hand lowers, covering her mouth. Her eyes are full of tears. Sherealizes they are all cheering *for* her. No one is making fun of her. I notice the aura around her is beautiful and accepting. No more running from life. She is the life now.

As she gets to me, I wrap my arms around her. I know she is unaccustomed to me doing this in public, but I can't help it. My eyes are burning from the tears pulling my makeup into them. She is no longer Goth Girl. She is now a woman getting ready to take on the world. She takes her diploma and raises it up to the sky. It is subtle, but a celebration in her world. She steps aside for the next person.

"Sam... Beckett."

Sam is so focused on Rainelle that he almost doesn't hear his name called. He looks like he is in shock and then jumps to his feet and almost skips to the podium. His bright eyes are full of joy and his blond curls bounce with each skip.

Reaching for his diploma, he glances back at the kids and gives them a funny look. His face scrunches up like his nose itches. He is trying not to open his mouth as he smiles. His neck shrinks down, then he bounces back up. It looks comical. What a character. He heads back to make room for the next person.

"Joseph... Ogden."

Joseph is quite the opposite of all the kids that came forward. He stands up and looks ten feet tall. His back is elongated, and he holds his head high. He looks like a senator taking the stand to accept his office. He walks very smoothly with almost a gangster swagger to his gait. He is proud. He is accomplished. He made it.

"Hunter... Ashford."

Hunter, being the youngest of the bunch, isn't sure what to do when he comes forward for his diploma. He is shy. All of a sudden, I notice a hop, and he stops with both feet before regaining his stride again.

When Hunter makes it to the podium, he sways back and forth from the excitement, and he does his best to contain his stims. He is so excited that it's hard, and it makes his movements jerky but full of joy. He reaches for his diploma and almost drops it. His face lights up as he opens his mouth wide with elation. He looks at me with adoration. I take a few moments to look at him. I do not dare reach out to hug him. His autism would not allow it. I know he needs affection and touch, but I have to keep my distance and allow him to bask in his fame.

He goes back to the seat just as quickly as he came forward.

"Azza... Syed."

Azza waits for Hunter to get back to his chair before she stands up. She adjusts her gown, pushes her hair into submission, and walks forward. Here is this young lady, so angry in the beginning, standing before me in a dress and high heels under her gown. Her tassel is wrapped up in her hair, so I pull it back where it belongs. She smiles sheepishly. She's crying, as well. She looks out into the audience to find her parents, and they are glowing with approval. To see the change in their little girl must have been too much to bear. She glows as she raises her diploma up to show her parents. The room continues to cheer.

"And last but not least," Antoinette pauses.

I look back at Antoinette, wondering who she is going to announce. All of the kids are accounted for.

Antoinette looks at the audience, attempting to keep her composure.

"This young lady was taken out of the program the very first day. However, she completed her sentence, completed detox, and then completed her final year of studies in the distance learning part of the school."

The students gasp as they anticipate her arrival.

"Alice... Gardner."

The audience remembers seeing Alice in the video being taken off in handcuffs. How is she here?

Alice walks down the side of the gymnasium with her probation officer. Something is a bit off. She is in handcuffs. She's wearing a pair of jeans and a t-shirt. We are all quite confused. She comes up on stage. Her probation officer instructs her to turn around. This allows the audience to see her handcuffed arms. The handcuffs are a bright, shining silver that seems to reflect the lights. He pulls out a key and removes the handcuffs. The room is quiet, but then someone begins to clap in the back. It starts with her mother. One person clapping turns into two and then a hundred. The room begins to realize just what is happening.

Alice comes forward. Antoinette has her cap and gown in hand. She hands them to her and instructs her to put them on. Alice looks back at her probation officer, standing behind the other kids on the podium. He gives a smile, allowing her to proceed.

Antoinette holds up her diploma, and Alice reaches for it with tears in her eyes. She looks back at her probation officer. He gives her a proud nod, silently instructing her to get up and speak. Antoinette steps back to let her get closer to the microphone.

Standing at the podium with her diploma in hand, Alice gathers herself so she can speak. She clears her throat.

"Hello," she starts. Her voice is raspy. She takes a step back from the microphone and clears her throat again, takes a deep breath, and begins again.

"Hello. I'm Alice. Yes, I had a rough first day. I'm not sure if you all know, but I actually got kicked out. I was sent to Juvenile Hall and then to rehab.

"My conditions for graduation were to help others struggling with addiction and to complete my program on the computer through distance learning. I'm alive to talk to you today. Thank you for kicking me out of the program. You—" She backs away from the microphone to get herself together again and then continues, "You, Mrs. P., saved my life by holding me accountable. I wish to thank you from the bottom of my heart."

The room cheers as Alice leaves the podium. It's as if she never left the program. She is still one of the team.

The kids all come forward and wrap their arms around Alice to welcome her back into the pack. Side by side, the participants stand while the room cheers. Then the judge comes up to the podium. The students are still standing as he speaks.

"Hello, I'm the judge that helped get this pilot program off the ground with the great help from Mrs. Parker and her team." The room cheers. The judge turns around and looks at each student with admiration instead of judgement.

"In order for these students to graduate, they needed to come to school every day, study and get good grades, and stay out of trouble." He waits for the room to calm down again, much like a politician making his acceptance speech.

"I'm happy to say that all of them did this except for one student." He then turns to the students. They all of a sudden became very nervous. Who failed?

The room gasps all at once.

"Now don't worry," he attempts to console everyone in the room. "I would like to inform you that," and he turns around to look at Hunter, "Hunter Ashford did not do this."

The room is in shock. Most of all me. How could Hunter not make it?

"Hunter, could you please come up here son?"

Hunter is very scared to go to the front, but he does as instructed. The room is deafeningly quiet.

"Hunter not only graduated from the School of Art in the Second Chance Program, but he also graduated from the local college with an associate degree in Art!"

The room can hardly be contained. My breath is taken away, and I think my heart skips a beat.

"So, Hunter?" He opens up an envelope. "Here is the graduation certificate for your degree. Your *associates* degree." He hands it to Hunter.

Hunter is so excited that he rocks so hard it looks like he is dancing on the stage. The judge then tells Hunter to go back with the other students.

"Now there is something else I would like to add to this." Everyone is waiting with bated breath. "I want all of you to know," he pauses, "as of today, your records will be sealed. You are all free to go!"

The room roars with cheers, clapping, and yelling.

The kids rush over to me and pull me to the front. Everyone is dancing, laughing and some are crying.

"We can't thank this lady enough for believing in us!" Avery yells into the microphone.

Just then the whole gang comes up to the microphone and says all at once,

"We aren't just the Second Chance Program... WE ARE THE SECOND CHANCE KIDS!"

The orchestra starts to play, and the gymnasium is in full swing. Graduation is over, and the program is a success.

I look at each one of my kids in this program. They feel like they all are my kids now. Well, especially Rainelle. She is here to stay. She is no longer in the foster care system. She is my own daughter now. She runs over to me and holds me tight.

"Thank you," she cries, "thank you, Mom."

Rainelle leaves with some of the other kids. Charlie is holding Millie. Lilly and her family are close behind Aunt Jackie. Oh, wait.

Who is tagging along with Aunt Jackie? Is he really with her or is he just walking behind her? Aunt Jackie stops and stands with us. This man stops as well. He is obviously with her. Do I ask? Hmm, he is kind of cute. Aunt Jackie deserves to be happy. I guess it's okay.

Lilly gets closer to me and gives me a big hug. "I knew you could do it." She smiles as she adjusts one of the children beside her. She is such a goofy mother.

Angel steps around the mass of people. She has a look on her face like she wants me to speak to her in private.

"Can I speak to her for a moment?" I ask for my family to step aside so she has some privacy. Her head is lowered. I'm unsure why.

"I," Angel begins to tear up, "I'm so happy that you took the time to believe in my son." She lifts her eyes up to meet mine.

"It wasn't me." I put my hand on her elbow, holding her tenderly. "He had to believe in himself first."

Angel puts her arms around me, holding me close. I feel she is truly sorry for everything. Not just for the homecoming party so many years ago, but for everything. Her face is warm. She begins to turn to leave.

"Hey!" I stop her.

She turns to me.

"Let's get together and catch up when all of this blows over."

"Sounds great." She smiles and once again turns to meet Avery.

When all of the pomp and circumstance has quieted down, we're able to return to normal for the rest of the summer.

***

The first day of summer after graduation is warm, and I think it's time to take Millie to the park.

"Are you ready?" I ask up the stairs, waiting for Millie to come down.

"Yes, Mommy." Millie bounces around the corner with Rainelle in tow. Millie's red curly hair is completely out of control, and her ringlets mirror the bounce in her step.

"Wait!" Millie stops. "I need my ball."

When we finally get to the park, we look for Aunt Jackie. She is much older now. Rainelle, Millie, and I find a nice patch of green grass to set up our picnic while we wait.

Eventually, Aunt Jackie arrives with her new boyfriend. He looks nice and is holding her hand. He is a gentleman.

"Let's go to this bench near the birds." I take Millie's hand to ensure her safety near the water. The birds fly all around, as if to welcome us, well, me, back. I have missed them so.

"So, these are your birds?" Rainelle watches them flitter around.

I smile. "They were Mildred's. Now they're mine. Want to help me feed them?"

They both nod, so we settle on the bench, and I put the bag of food between them.

"Take a handful like this." I put a few seeds in Millie's hand since her hand is so small. Rainelle scoops some up tenderly.

Millie looks at her hand and begins to throw the seeds directly at the birds.

"No, Honey. Throw it up in the air. Like this." I take another handful in my hand and show them just how to feed the birds. With the seed flying up in the air, each bird is able to get a piece; some even get two. Rainelle catches on quickly, but something's still not quite right. Some of the birds seem more skittish than they should be. I look over at Millie and chuckle as I notice her feet, swinging joyfully over the edge of the bench.

"Your feet dear, stop swinging your feet." I gently put my hand on her knee. "It scares the birds."

Millie stops swinging her feet as instructed, and I feel Deja vu. This is just like when I sat here with Mildred, and she taught *me* how to feed the birds. I had to learn not to swing my feet as well. A breeze swirls around us. Millie looks up at me, her hair flying in the wind.

"Mommy, look." Her hair is all over her face.

I take a moment to breathe in the essence of success. Reaching inside my blouse, I pull out the locket Mildred gave me, holding it first in my hand and then to my mouth. I glance over at Aunt Jackie. She is far too preoccupied to know what I'm doing. I give it a gentle kiss and tuck the locket back into the safest place I have, next to my heart. I close my eyes and whisper, "We did it, Mildred."

"Who are you talking to, Mommy?"

"Oh, I'm just talking to Mildred." She won't understand.

"You mean the balbena?"

"Yes, Baby, she is the ballerina."

"You mean that lady there?" She points over to the end of the bench.

"What lady?" I ask. Rainelle follows my gaze and shrugs.

"The balbena lady." She is very insistent this time.

"What do you mean?" I ask with a quiet whisper.

"The Balbena, you know gran'ma, balbena." She is getting upset.

A few seconds go by, and Rainelle returns her focus to the birds.

"Balbena is with me all the time," Millie says in a very matter-of-fact tone.

"Do you mean Mildred?" I ask with a wavering voice.

She nods her head yes. "Mildred."

Did she just say that? Did she just say Mildred is always watching us?

Aunt Jackie has joined us, and her mouth is wide open, "Did she?"

"Come on, let's play." Millie reaches out for Rainelle and her imaginary friend at the end of the bench. They all run off toward the nearby grass.

I feel a warmth radiate from deep within. Mildred, my dearest Mildred, is always near to me. A warm breeze blows against my skin. I close my eyes and take in the moment. "I love you. Thank you for watching over us." I open my eyes and gaze over the water. The sunlight dances on the ripples. I reach into my shirt and pull out my locket once more. Holding it close to my face, I kiss it again. I can't help it. Mildred has been with Millie this whole time. I just didn't realize it until now.

EPILOGUE

SECOND CHANCE KIDS

Joseph went on to be a furniture designer. All of his creations are hand carved with great detail. His company employs inmates from the local prison who work at his company to get reduced sentences. His program has been successful so far. Ironically, his son was just busted for vandalism to school property, carving his name in his desk.

After Sam graduated from the Second Chance Program, he was discovered to have been secretly designing a program while in school. This was in direct violation of his probation, but since he designed it to stop kids like him from hacking into the school's database the judge dismissed the charges. Sam gave that program to the local school systems to safeguard their records. The school system found the program he designed was so safe that they now use it in all school systems. He later went into the armed forces and now creates technology for cybercrimes police use and national security. His work is highly classified. He still keeps in contact with Rainelle. They have become life-long friends.

Azza became very successful with her pottery to the point that she now has her own pottery magazine. I read an article in her magazine where she talks about becoming one with the clay and listening to it speak to her. She is featured in shows all over the United States. Her pottery has been showcased also in Home and Garden stores. Her photo is her logo. Truly stunning.

After graduation, Rainelle opened up an animal sanctuary shelter. She ironically calls it Second Chance Pets. Her trusty sidekick D.O.G. is right by her side caring for the animals. Her sanctuary is not just for dogs and cats, but also for horses and other small farm animals who need refuge. They usually come from kill auctions. They are nursed back to health and sent to stables, farms, and petting zoos to be used as rehabilitation animals for people with disabilities. The judge came and picked out a puppy for his granddaughter. I visit her often. Rainelle sings while cleaning the cages and her voice is still angelic.

Avery was a great surprise. After graduation, a talent scout found his work and recruited him for set design. His work can be seen in a few top-ten movies. His company can be found working not only in the United States, but also in foreign countries in foreign films. He fulfilled the dream he said would never happen and was able to make enough money that he could afford to move his mother out of the horrible neighborhood. They now live near Hollywood. What a change. I still talk to Angel from time to time.

Nicholas graduated with his flower creations that turn any plain cake into an edible masterpiece. He was working under Charlie, learning everything he could before venturing out into the world. I had no idea how trained Charlie really was. He found his passion in his own way, teaching what he learned from his mother before she passed. I still laugh about how chewing on paper to turn it into paper mâché turned into such a beautiful craft from sugar and fondant. Nicholas' creations have been featured in wedding magazines. I even heard a rumor that one of his cakes was in a superstar's secret wedding, but it has not been confirmed.

Alice was a surprise in this program. Although she was kicked out after violating her probation with the program, she was able to get cleaned up while serving her time in Juvenile Hall. She completed her necessary classes and was able to graduate along with her classmates in the program. I heard she may be working in a treatment center trying to help people recover from drugs and alcohol. However, you know HIPPA; we can neither confirm nor deny she is there.

Hunter's work was discovered from one of the many

photographs taken in school. There was an architect at the graduation who noticed his work and hired him on at his firm in architectural design. He draws huge murals of cityscapes on the entrances to office buildings in several countries. Hunter later got married and settled down. He now teaches others with autism that dreams are possible, if you want them badly enough.

The judge that set up the Second Chance Program with me retired. His program was rated one of the highest programs in the state. His recidivism for teen offenders returning to Juvenile Hall was so successful that the program was adopted by other government agencies. Before he retired, he revised the foster care program to better screen the housing criteria. No other instances of abuse have been reported since the new laws were implemented.

As for me, I'm still here at the manor. Mildred would be proud to hear the sound of kids filling the halls. Each year, a new batch of kids are in the Second Chance Kids Program. They come in with new problems and new dreams waiting to be discovered. Each year has its own issues. In the beginning it is tough, but when graduation comes each year, the hardships seem to disappear. It has become quite rewarding to help each student realize their dreams and passions in life. Seeing the change happen is truly breathtaking.

My life-long friend Alfred passed away, but his son took his place. I see Alfred in almost everything his son does. I feel his protection as I walk through the manor. I'm sure he's keeping watch with Mildred. Antoinette and I often sit out in the garden, renamed Alfred's Garden in his honor. The birdhouses are full of song and the loud cheeps of babies.

Millie has decided she wants to be called Mildred. She is proud of her name and isn't afraid of being made fun of, and she is now studying ballet. She is growing like a weed. Her legs are so long that when she stands on her toes in pointe, she appears to touch the moon. I'm so proud of her. She also helps out with the school, and I think she may become Antoinette's right-hand.

I've never stopped hearing Ms. Mildred in my ear. "To see a

change, you must be the change." Even though Mildred has been gone for many years, her legacy—her dash—still lives strong behind these iron gates and touches kids' lives, one at a time. I honestly believe we are, indeed, changing the world. It all started with Ms. Mildred: her dreams, her passions, her drive to make a difference. Her vision of change emulates today in all who dare to dream.

Remember, to see a change, you must be the change. Are you up for the challenge?

ACKNOWLEDGMENTS

FIRST AND FOREMOST, SEBY, my loving husband, has stood by me in all my endless nights of typing away on my computer. With each passing day, you would encourage me to keep going. Some days you needed to stop me because of exhaustion or feeling lost. While working together in this world of uncertainty, we have witnessed some horrific events and some triumphant victories in recovery. If I can reach just one person and change their life of addiction and despair into a life of gratitude and healthy decisions, I feel I have accomplished what we strive for together. At some points I just wanted to give up. You kept me grounded. You are my rock.

My mother, Lanny Hill. Mom, you kept asking me daily how I was coming along with my book. It forced me to keep going. I had some rough patches, but you still insisted that I keep going.

And lastly, I heard someone say something that resonated with me and probably will forever:

"It isn't over until you quit."

Rainelle, you have given me the will to keep moving forward. I was so close to giving in when you told me that. It made so much sense. I was given a second breath of fresh air. It isn't over when you think it is over. It isn't over when you are down and out. It isn't over until you quit trying. Then it is over. I did not quit! Special thanks.

I would like to thank the district court judge for the 5th Judicial District, Judge James H. Faison III. This book was inspired by his proceedings in Treatment Court in North Carolina. He takes the time to listen to the defendants before him. He searches beyond the crimes to see if something could change or alter the person's behavior. His court room is run quite different than most. People who stand before him admire his attempts to reinforce positive changes. Thank you, Judge Faison, for being such an inspiration to many. I pray your works continue to be heard through my writings of changes to come.

ABOUT THE AUTHOR

ROSE JONES, was raised in snowy northern Ohio; however, she found her passion in the coastal living of Wilmington, North Carolina. Married to husband Seby (Chip) Jones, together they help people in recovery from addiction. Rose serves as a mentor to teens and preteens regarding addiction and living with addicted parents.

Rose enjoys riding motorcycles, theater productions, and home improvement. Rose is very supportive of our veterans through the American Honor Guards of NC. She is a graduate of Cape Fear Community College with an Associate in Arts as well as a BA in Sociology from the University of North Carolina of Pembroke. It was in college that she found her passion for writing.

Rose also enjoys rescue animals, and she has four cats: Kelly, Sadie, Loki, and Luna. She has two Chinese Crested Powderpuff dogs, Molly and Maddie, and – yes, they have hair.

Rose is currently working on her next book about enduring love on a 19th-century plantation.

Connect with Rose:
rosejones.author@gmail.com
Facebook: Author Rose Marie Jones
Instagram: Rosejones8681
Twitter: @authorRMJones1

MILDRED THE BIRD LADY

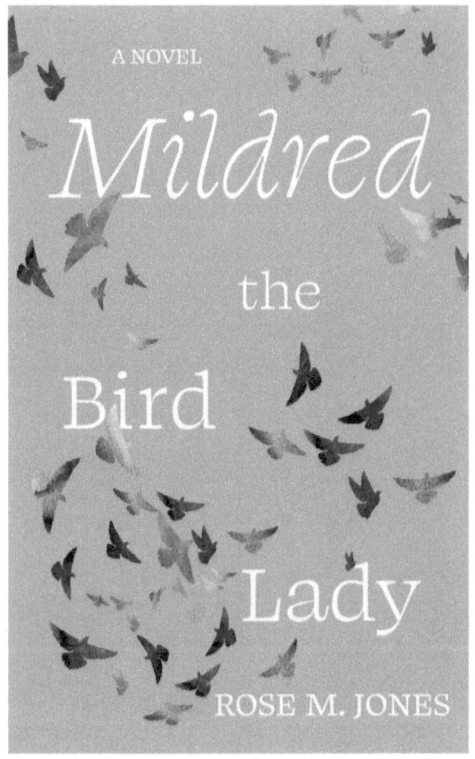

A CHANCE ENCOUNTER in a Chicago park between inquisitive 4-year-old Mary and the eccentric Mildred begins a lifelong, unconventional friendship. Despite her mother's admonishment not to engage with Mildred, Mary finds herself drawn to the kind "Bird Lady."

Impressed by Mary's independence and creativity, Mildred shares the lessons of her gilded life and becomes a mentor for Mary. In their moments together, Mildred teaches Mary about courtship, manners, ethics, art, culture, and life's little luxuries. Through the twists and turns of Mary's life, Mildred's influence is felt time and again, like a gentle beacon guiding Mary toward her true passion.